THE BLUE MANOR

THE BLUE MANOR

Jenny Jones

VICTOR GOLLANCZ

LONDON

First published in Great Britain
by Victor Gollancz
An imprint of the Cassell Group
Wellington House, 125 Strand, London WC2N 0BB

A catalogue record for this book is
available from the British Library.

ISBN 0 575 05818 8

Typeset by CentraCet Limited, Cambridge
Printed in Great Britain by
St Edmundsbury Press Ltd, Bury St Edmunds, Suffolk

For my mother Mary Church,
gardener and musician,
with love.

Acknowledgements

This book owes its genesis to Robert Graves, master magician of words and ideas, and his extraordinary *White Goddess*.

The quotations from the poems set by Duparc are to be found in *Twelve Songs*, ed. Sergius Kagen, published by International Music Company, New York.

My fascination with Epping Forest comes from my mother's family, especially from my great-uncle, James Brimble, whose book on London's *Epping Forest* contains some of the most beautiful photographs ever taken of the forest.

Fortunately, there is no third motorway cutting through Epping Forest, and I trust there never will be. Only dense trees lie between Amersbury Banks and Jack's Hill: there is no lane leading to the Blue Manor.

Despite generous help from Brian Hibbins and Owen Staley in matters astronomical, I have taken some liberties with the timing of the cataclysmic variable of the Corona Borealis.

My gratitude yet again to Tim Crawley for his invaluable criticism and encouragement.

And to Edward, Rosie and Henry, my love.

J.J.

Prelude

The headlights caught him for only an instant. The man standing at the side of the road, his hair slicked down by rain, his hands covering his face, was hiding his eyes.

He looked as if he was about to step out into the road, into the stream of fast-moving traffic.

She nearly stopped. No, it wasn't even nearly. Women travelling on their own, late at night, do not stop for strange men standing half-hidden by the roadside.

Anyway, he wasn't alone. In that brief glimpse, Ruth had seen two shadowy figures sitting on the bank behind him. There were no details to be seen, it was too dark, she was driving too fast.

She thought little of it. He wasn't alone, the others with him would prevent any kind of accident. She drove home fast, crossing the motorway into the forest, turning quickly into Coppice Row. The trees were thicker here, almost hiding the entrance to the lane.

She stopped with familiar impatience to open the gate, then drove too fast through the tree-lined avenue. It didn't matter, there would be no other visitors that night.

It was just the three of them.

Ruth left the car in the drive, barely registering that there were no lights on in the house. The white roses were the only relief, a pale gleam around the edge of the terrace. She went up the few steps to the front door and opened it.

It was like stepping into an oven. Airless, suffocating. The curtains had probably been drawn all day, she thought. Heavy velvet, blocking out the sun, blocking out the air. For all its size, the house was oppressive. She left the door open and cool, rain-damped air flooded through the porch into the hall.

'Shut the door.'

'Fresh air,' she said mildly, turning on the lamp which stood beside the door.

Simon was sitting at the long table, blinking in the sudden brightness.

'What are you doing in the dark?' She didn't expect him to answer and, indeed, it was a superfluous question. It was perfectly obvious what he was doing. The bottle of whisky was half-empty.

She sat opposite him, the door still open, the insects beginning to blunder around the hall.

She poured herself a drink. Well, why not?

'How was it tonight? Any nutters?'

'Not really.'

'You wouldn't tell me anyway, I know.' He paused, turning his glass in thin fingers. 'So, was the kick good and strong? Many souls pulled back from the brink? Gratitude, a feeling of a job well done, a small light to shine in the darkness of a sad and evil world?'

He was standing now, moving across the room to the lamp switch.

Darkness. She put the glass down. 'Where's Kate?'

'In bed, where do you think? It's *late*, Ruth!' He was standing quite still and she could hear his breathing, hard and stressed.

'Any calls? Anyone come?'

'No, were you expecting someone?' His voice had lost its edge, was merely tired. She went to him, carefully circum-navigating the table and chairs.

'Bed?' She took his arm.

The shudder was not quite concealed. Unhurriedly, to show him that she had not noticed, Ruth disengaged her hand and moved back to the door. She pulled it shut.

'Come on, you need to sleep . . .'

'You're telling me!' Sudden violence, the words sharp and hard.

Excuses, the usual honest, harmless, explanations? Or not? Ruth looked at her hands.

'Well, I'm going to bed. Do you want anything, some herb tea, cocoa . . .?'

Silence. She had not expected a reply. She made him a drink anyway and went to bed.

That night, she dreamed that the man was standing there again. His hands covered his eyes, his hair pressed flat and dark by rain, standing there beside her bed about to step forward.

Ruth shifted, turning away, and jolted against Simon's body. They both shrivelled apart, salt on a slug, cellophane near fire.

The dream was over and she lay awake, and it was only the shapes of curtains which made her think of two figures, further back, watching him.

Chapter 1

Flaring light dazzled him. Instinctively he raised his hands to cover his eyes and as he did so a hawk lifted away into the night sky.

A roaring sound, the light glaring and he stepped back out of the road.

Not a moment too soon. A spray of leaping mud; red lights vanished into the distance and already another car was crashing through the night towards him.

Byrne stepped back again, hands dropping, his eyes watchful now, frowning. Slowly he turned round. Behind him the trees were dark, rain-drenched and drab. Scrubby undergrowth of brambles and ferns.

The air smelled of petrol, of machinery and oil and pollution. There was a mess of litter by his feet, soggy paper, shiny cans, orange peel . . .

It was late, long after midnight. His last lift had driven nervously, shying away from the lorries like a scared rabbit.

He was tired of hitching, small talk with strangers; he'd had enough for one night. He needed to find shelter, somewhere out of the rain. It was too late to look for a hotel or guesthouse; a shed or garage would do. It was midsummer, he wasn't going to freeze.

He'd come too far, too quickly.

The road was violent and noisy, the grass beneath his feet slick with grease. He began to walk along the edge of the forest, parallel with the road. He was looking for a path, anything to get away from the traffic.

It was raining and the road was hideous. Perhaps he shouldn't have left, perhaps it would have been better to face it . . .

There was no path. After a while he realized that he should have gone back towards Epping. There was no break in the dense woodland, and he could see nothing on the other side of the road either. But the rain was letting up and he saw the moon, fleetingly visible between the thinning clouds. He could sleep rough under the trees.

The road was quieter now, a brief pause in its activity as it ran towards the city. And in that unusual hiatus, he heard a twig breaking, a rustle of leaves on his left. He stopped, watchful. There was someone there, no bird or fox would make such a disturbance. As if in confirmation, in the deep darkness between the trees he saw a small, unsteady flame.

A tramp, probably. He was about to move on when someone shouted to him, 'Hey, could you come here for a minute?' A woman's voice, nasal, cockney.

He hesitated, standing by the road.

'Please?' A softening of the tone, something vulnerable and fearful. A hitch-hiker, like himself, who'd found herself in trouble? Perhaps he ought to investigate. Reluctantly, he pushed through the undergrowth towards her. Holly caught at his jacket, brambles snagged around his feet.

And then he saw them, at the side of a small clearing, their faces underlit by a candle. Three of them. They sat cross-legged on the ground, beneath the shelter of a tarpaulin slung between trees. A man and two women.

The women had to be twins, or sisters at least. He couldn't tell which of them had spoken. Their eyes were outlined in identical black, the lashes sticking together in spikes. Dark hair fell in rats' tails about their shoulders. They seemed to have been dressed from jumble sales, in layers of lace and satin and torn velvet. Silver chains hung round their necks.

Like them, the man was very pale, with short dark hair and a waxy skin split by an ancient scar from forehead to mouth. He was wearing an antique DJ, a paisley scarf knotted round the neck. His eyes were unfocused, staring at the candle, like the two women.

Druggies, Byrne thought resignedly. He didn't need this. But he remembered the fear in the woman's voice and took a couple of steps nearer. 'What do you want?' he said.

For a moment no one moved, no one said anything. Then the man looked up, straight at Byrne, and smiled. The scar pulled his mouth sideways. He raised his hands, palms upwards, as if to say, well, here we are. Now what?

He looked like David. Not the scar, not the tatty clothes, but the action. That helpless smile, those open hands . . . Now what are you going to do? And he, Byrne, had run out, run away.

It was then that the two women stood up and moved towards

14

Byrne. He was still assaulted by memory, captured by the mental image of David standing there, that sick smile and those empty hands. He merely noticed that the women were both thin, almost emaciated. Only afterwards did he remember how they moved exactly together, precisely mimicking each other, step for step. They crossed the clearing and positioned themselves on either side of Byrne and he could smell sour sweat, a heavy musky scent.

But it was the man who spoke. 'Travelling, are you? Going far?' This was a cultured voice, an old-fashioned BBC voice. It went strangely with his ragged appearance, with these two shabby women. He was still smiling, but there was no friendliness in it.

Before Byrne could answer, one of the women had moved her hand under his jacket, feeling for the inner pocket. He moved quickly, blocking the action, but somehow he was too late.

'What are you doing?' His Swiss army knife lay in her hands. 'Give me that!'

'In a moment. Look,' she said softly to her companion, snapping it open. A glance between the pair of them, complicit, secretive. Then, together, they turned to the man seated on the ground.

Only one of them moved. The woman with the knife crossed the grass, and no twigs snapped, no brambles snared her skirt. She squatted down under the tarpaulin next to the seated man.

It was dangerous. He knew it was dangerous. He should get out, quickly. He said again, 'What are you doing?' but his voice seemed thin and irrelevant. He lunged forward, but the other woman was hanging on his arm, holding him back.

'Watch,' she hissed in his ear. 'This is for you.'

Her weight on his arm was out of all proportion to her size. He tried to shake her off and abruptly there was an extraordinary sensation, as if his strength was draining away, leeched by this touch on his sleeve.

He shouted, 'Look, what is this? Who are you?'

The moon had disappeared behind a cloud and he couldn't see her face. He stumbled, his knees suddenly weak and useless and her grip on his arm tightened, keeping him upright.

'Wait . . .' she said. 'And remember.'

And then the woman holding his knife offered it to the man sitting on the ground. He ran his finger along the blade, testing its sharpness. He said, 'Go on, then. What are you waiting for?'

And then he moved the candle to one side and she knelt in front of him. His hands were spread wide, lying loose and relaxed on the grass. He raised his head as if to look up at the stars, and with precise and delicate care the woman drew the knife, backhanded, hard across his throat.

It happened in dead silence. A thin dark line appeared on the white skin and instantly founted blood. The man's eyes were closed, hidden, his mouth calm, unmoving. And then he was toppling sideways, the front of his jacket wet and shiny with the pumping scarlet.

Byrne made an indistinct noise of shock. A protest, a rejection. There was something surreal, horrible, about the way the man had offered no resistance, had just let it happen, the way David had opened his hands to him and he had run away . . .

He wanted to run now, to get out of here and away from this – rite of sacrifice. That was what it was, there were no other words. But still the enormous weight of the other woman bore down on his arm and he could not move. Her other hand snaked up his back, under his jacket, round to his neck. He felt her cold fingers there, sharp as bone, and the pressure began to build.

'No – !' But she was immovable, like rock or the earth itself, clinging to his limbs, pulling at him.

There was singing in his ears and stars before his eyes. And then only blackness, weighting him down to the ground.

Byrne hauled himself into a sitting position and put his hands to his temples. They came away sticky with blood and then he remembered, sickeningly, that other gushing blood, the man toppling sideways on to the grass.

He remembered David again, that face repeating through his mind, and those words. *Go on, then. What are you waiting for?*

No. Enough. He looked up sharply into bright sunlight and a flare of pain ran through his head. Those others were gone. This was daylight, the morning after . . . He was quite alone in the clearing and there was no sign that anyone else had ever been there. No hunched shape dressed in black. The tarpaulin, the two women, even the candle were gone. The smell of his own blood was sickly, reeking in the still air, but the other blood had dried. Just a few stains, a few rusty drops, splattered on the ground. Flies were already gathering. Byrne stood up, a sour taste in his mouth.

He leaned his hand against a tree and looked around. The grass at his feet was bright, touched with dew. It was uncrushed.

Had he been dreaming?

And then he realized that his rucksack had been searched. His clothes were spilled on the grass, but his wallet with his cash, his cards and driving licence was gone. The photograph of Kristen was missing, too. And stuck in his belt, crusty with blood, the open knife winked in the early sunlight. He drew it out and turned it over in his hands.

Through the trees he heard the traffic roar.

What had happened? His memory of that strange death was oddly unclear. Who were those people? He couldn't understand why they had waited for him before killing the man. What kind of murderers were they, to search out witnesses?

This is for you, she'd said.

He didn't need this. And where was the body? He looked around: no signs of disturbed earth, no recent grave. Had they carried that man away, had they transport somewhere? He could see no footprints on the wet grass, no tracks in the muddy patches other than his own. There was nothing to prove what had happened, except his memory.

Why had they left him living, a witness to their crime?

More than that. A participant, in all but deed. A black pit there, waiting, beckoning. No, not in the sunlight, not in the morning sun.

They'd even taken his wallet. They'd stolen his identity. Well, they were welcome to it.

And that led to another line of thought. Perhaps they wanted to implicate him in the murder, if that was what it was. Murder was surely the wrong word. Last night he had seen it as some blood ceremony and certainly there had been no kind of struggle. The scarred man had tested the knife, had smiled, like David. But there was no body and Byrne wasn't sure that he could trust what he remembered. It was too much like a hallucination, too confused in his mind. He hated the way he kept mixing it up with what had happened in Yorkshire.

He felt ill. There was a painful bruise on his temple, the skin

17

split and sluggishly bleeding, but he didn't know how it had happened. Perhaps they'd kicked him, but he didn't know for sure.

It was all so bizarre, so unlikely. He ought to tell the police, report what had happened, that strange, acquiescent death.

And then he stopped. He couldn't possibly go to the police. Where's the body? they'd say. And what were you doing, walking through Epping Forest late at night? They'd need to know who he was, all the background. Where do you live, who can vouch for you?

Nothing, nowhere, no one. God, what a mess! He subsided on to the grass again, his head in his hands. They'd have his details by now, the military police would have circulated them. They'd know who he was right away. And then it would start again, the psychiatrists and counsellors, the questions.

He couldn't bear it. It was part of why he'd bolted, why he was here now. All that fuss. He'd come south in order to get away from it. He had no intention of being catapulted into the public eye as the witness in a murder investigation.

But, but, but. He had no money, no driving licence, no means of identification. No identity. Those women had stripped him of everything important, leaving him with only a blood-stained knife and a headache.

He was thirsty and his head hurt, and from the cloudless sky it looked like the day was going to be stinking hot.

He needed a drink. A stream or a pond: water would do. It was a matter of some urgency.

He turned his back on the road and set off into the forest.

He found a stream before too long, a muddy trickle that did little to help. Before moving on, he buried the knife in the soft leaf mould by the bank and then washed his hands free of the rich, deep-coloured loam.

He wasn't going to the police. He knew that as soon as he'd buried the knife. If he hadn't gone to the police in Middleham, why should he be so scrupulous here? Perhaps he was getting a taste for non-involvement. He sat down for a while, his back against an oak tree, his knees drawn up. There was a wafting, pungent smell he identified as wild garlic. A thrush preened itself on a nearby log. It paid him no attention. Sunlight dappled the ground.

For a while, for a very few moments, the deadly flood of memory stopped. The forest was full of sounds, faint rustling noises, birdsong, the trickle of water. The road seemed very far away although the low roaring of traffic underlay all the other sounds. This was seductive, lingering here under the trees. A man could forget things here. And London would be hot, smelly, crowded . . .

There was nowhere else to go. He could lose himself in London, no one would know or care who he was.

He got to his feet once more. Leaves rustled. Between the beech trees at the top of the bank, he saw something glint in the sunlight, a small sparkle of silver.

He knew what it was. He abruptly remembered the silver chains around the women's necks. He ran to the top of the bank, slipping on the leaf mould, and found only an empty beer can, catching the sunlight.

His heart was pounding, his breath uneven. He was more disturbed than he'd thought. What if they were still nearby? What if this was some elaborate game of cat and mouse? Perhaps they were watching.

He scanned the forest, but the trees stood quietly, their leaves barely shifting. No sign of anyone, anything. He was about to turn back to the road, then he saw it.

A hint of blue through the leaves, a lake perhaps, something cool and welcoming. He was already walking towards it, that faint gleam of shining water through the trees.

It took much longer than he thought. He knew that Epping Forest was not large, that it was bisected by roads and tracks, and yet he seemed to be walking beneath trees for miles before getting there. He was being pulled further in, away from ordinary life, away from his purpose. A new life, that was what he'd wanted. A new start in the smoke, where no one would know or care.

The sun was at its height when at last he saw it clearly. He was walking along the crest of a rise. To the south, in a dip in the forest, a blue house waited. Not water at all. It was built of blue-grey stone the colour of water and in the sunlight seemed to sparkle at him. It rose high into the branches of the surrounding trees, three or four storeys of it. A gothic fantasy of some sort, he thought, his attention caught.

It reminded him of somewhere. He couldn't think where, the

memory just teased at the back of his mind. He knew it, somewhere beyond memory.

Behind it he caught a glimpse of water, half hidden in a grove of trees. There were trees everywhere, coppices, woods, as if the forest had rolled back like a tide, leaving the house beached there in the valley amidst pools of green. It was framed in trees, its blue stone and tiles gleaming through the leaves.

The road sounded only faintly where Byrne stood; at the house, he thought, you probably wouldn't hear anything at all. He was drawn by its sheltered aspect, the way the trees curved around it, softening the harsh perspectives.

Who would live there, he wondered, in such isolation? Some flash business man, an aging pop star . . . ? Perhaps not. It could well be empty, there was such a feeling of silence about it. He found himself walking through the forest.

The house waited, open and welcoming.

Chapter 2

The gate was made of wrought iron, its paintwork cracking. Patches of rust showed through. It was set in a vast, straggly hedge over three metres tall. The gate opened at his touch, creakingly.

He was in. Behind him the forest was dense and solid. In front of him lay more trees, set on gentle slopes, as if the hedge had let them through. The hedge was beech, like so much of the forest. It was surely part of the forest, dividing like from like. Beeches, birches, oak and hornbeams stood on either side of it. Ancient trees, full of deep shadows even in the bright sunlight. He heard the cawing of rooks high in their branches.

He walked a few steps through brambles and bracken. When he looked back he could no longer see the gate. It was lost in the undergrowth, hidden in the shadows beneath the trees.

The wood gave way to spreading parkland, dotted with Spanish chestnuts and yews. There were thistles and nettles everywhere. To his right he saw a driveway, straight ahead lay an orchard. He walked towards the drive, wanting to do the right thing. He'd sneaked in the back way, and this was private property. He looked down the drive towards the main gate. A cottage stood there, a run-down, dilapidated place, its thatch scrappy and untidy. It was clearly unoccupied.

The house was probably deserted too, no more than a ruin. He just wanted a quick look at it, to see if he could remember where he'd seen it before. Perhaps in a painting or something.

He dumped his rucksack behind a clump of brambles. The drive was cracked and split by weeds. Its edges frayed into the greenery which ran beneath the trees.

The house was largely hidden by trees, although he was still aware of its cold, blue-grey stone. As he approached he saw that some effort had been made here and there. A rosebed, remarkably clear of weeds, the Iceberg roses dead-headed, neat and orderly. An attempt at a herbaceous border where delphiniums had been tied to stakes. The wall around the terrace overflowing with pansies and geraniums. But the rest was a wilderness, unkempt and dishevelled. Whoever lived here needed a serious gardener, someone not afraid of hard work.

The trees parted and he saw the house. Why did it look so familiar? Had he dreamed its existence? It seemed to belong to some vivid, unconscious night journey. He'd been there before, in dreams.

The house matched the state of the garden. Leaded windows reflected the sun back at him crookedly, several panes on the upper floors being cracked or broken. The deep-vaulted roof was covered with blue-grey slates, but many were missing or misaligned. The roof itself appeared too steep, too precipitous, and light slid from it like oil. The paintwork was dull and flaking. He knew that there would be rot everywhere, damp and dry.

And something else, something more unsettling. It seemed fragile, unstable. The proportions were too tall, overweighted. The pointed towers rose from sharp, impossible conjunctions in the roof, the perspectives out of true. He stood still for a while, trying to work it out, trying to decide whether he had found it unsafe in his dream too.

Something moved at the door to the house and he changed focus. There was a woman standing there, watching him.

She was at one side of the front door, a small trowel shiny in her gloved hands. For a moment he received a disconcerting image, that this woman was part of a cameo growing in finely etched relief from the fabric of cold stone.

She put down the trowel and came forward to the top of the steps as he walked towards her. Her face was fine-boned, her eyes deepset, warm and brown. She looked weary, a smudge of dirt on her cheek, light brown hair flopping untidily over her eyes. She was a little overweight, her figure pleasantly curvy. Her skin was lined, darkened by sun and wind.

He saw that she had been clearing the stone troughs that stood on either side of the front door. A mess of leaves and roots was spread over the splintering lintel.

She sighed as she looked at him. She appeared to be rather tired. 'It's not open to the public,' she said flatly. 'Nor likely to be.' Her voice was a warm alto.

'I'm not a tourist,' he said. He could not explain why he had been drawn to the blue-grey house, hidden by trees.

At the same time he noticed her sagging shoulders, the

22

depressed edge to that beautiful voice. This was someone who worked too hard, worried and fretted. The house would be too much for her, the garden overwhelming.

'Are you lost? Selling something?' She sounded suspicious, as if he might suddenly produce a suitcase full of dusters and tea-towels. He held out his hands, showing that they were empty. He had the beginnings of an idea, a wild idea, and needed a little time.

'I've had nothing to eat for two days,' he said, 'and I'm far from home.' He wondered if she were maternal, the kind of woman who wouldn't turn someone away hungry.

She sighed again and took off her right glove, fishing in the pocket of her jeans. She seemed faintly irritated. 'Here you are,' she said, holding out a couple of coins to him. 'There's a bus to the village at the lane end in half an hour. You can get something there.'

'Thank you, but no. I'd rather work for any money you give me.' What was he doing, what was he *saying*? The house towered over them, blocking out the sunlight. She was watching him speculatively. He'd got her attention. For a moment their eyes met. He saw her considering him, weighing him up.

'We're in no position to employ anyone.'

He held his breath, and then she put the money away.

He exhaled. A crazy, unwanted sense of relief. She would take him on, he would be the gardener. He was going to stay here for a while, and—

What? What was he *doing* here, this wasn't part of the plan.

(The dead man. Those two women.) And all at once, like the trailer to a film, he saw it. He'd work in the garden, he'd weed the beds and plant out, clear the borders and the drive and make some attempt at the grass. Keeping the lawns and borders straight would be a full-time job, by itself. He need never go back, he could try to forget . . .

He knew she was still watching him. 'Food, a roof? I don't need a wage. There's that cottage at the end of the drive. I know about gardening, I used to have a landscaping business.' It was true, he had no need to lie here.

She was unconvinced. 'Have you references? Where do you come from?'

'I was robbed,' he said. 'Hitch-hiking south. They took everything, my wallet, my luggage.'

23

'Have you reported it to the police?'

'Not yet.' He saw that she was frowning, undecided. 'That's an alchemilla you're holding there,' he said helpfully. 'It'll do well at the front of the house.' He remembered something he'd read once: alchemilla for protection. Plant it at the gate or boundary. Its leaves, cupping dew and rainwater, hold safety in their grasp.

Her gaze did not shift. Her eyes were wary. Faint lines creased her forehead. She was younger than he, but not by much. Late thirties, he reckoned.

'And will you mow grass? Fix fences, decorate, reglaze, cut hedges and weed the vegetables? There's enough work here for a small army.'

'Anything. Whatever you want.' Anything to stay. He'd even work in the house, if that was what she wanted.

She smiled suddenly and came down the steps to meet him. The sunlight touched golden lights in her hair. 'I'm Ruth Banniere,' she said. 'And your name—?'

Without thinking he said, 'Phizackerley. Phizackerley Byrne.'

'*What?*' Her entire face changed, lightened, enlivened. She looked twenty years younger. 'How amazing! What a wonderful name!'

He almost found himself smiling in response, but he shouldn't have used it, not now, not to just anyone. What was happening to him? 'My parents had a sense of humour,' he explained.

'Well, either that or a passion for the eccentric. Look, are you serious? Is this a genuine offer? Help in house and garden in return for board and lodging?'

He nodded, his eyes running past her to the house waiting beyond. The blue stone seemed even colder close up.

'The cottage at the gates would be ideal,' he said. 'Then I needn't put you out.'

'No, you couldn't stay in the house anyway. We're full. But come and have a cup of tea, come and meet the family. Let's see what we can find in the way of bedding for the cottage.' She peered more closely at him. 'On second thoughts, let's leave the family till later. You look ready to drop. Wait here and I'll bring tea and sandwiches.'

He smiled gratefully, and sat on the steps to wait for her. It was done. He was in.

He wondered if he'd lost his mind.

*

'Are you *mad*?' Simon Lightowler put down his book. 'A complete stranger, a half-starved tramp with no belongings, no references—'

'He was robbed,' Ruth began.

'He *says* he was robbed. I don't believe a word of it. He's probably on the run. Why come here, what brought him to this God-forsaken dump? Does he think the manor's stuffed with antiques or something? Big mistake number one. Not too bright, this chap. Either he's a crook or a fool, or both. He's probably on drugs. This is lunacy, Ruth.'

'I could do with some help round the place. He knows about plants—'

'Good God!' Simon stared at her. 'Is that all it takes? And where is this paragon now?'

'I gave him a sleeping bag to take to the cottage.'

'We're so rich you can afford to give away sleeping bags? You know we'll never see it again, or him.'

'Simon.' She stood up and started clearing away the mugs and plates. 'I need the help. For right or wrong, I think he's trustworthy. I am *not* naive about these things and there's certainly no other way I'm going to get any help with the heavy work.'

'Now that I've dropped out? Is that what you mean?' He sneered at her. 'It's your bloody house, I suppose. What's he called, anyway?'

'Phizackerley. Phizackerley Byrne.'

'And I'm Benjamin Disraeli. Damn it, Ruth, you do make me wonder sometimes just who it is who needs the psychiatrist round here.' He was standing too now, tall and thin, stoop-shouldered, sallow-faced. 'At least there's nothing here worth stealing. I suppose we need merely worry about being murdered in our beds.' A crack of laughter as he left the kitchen. 'What does Kate think about it?'

'She's not back yet.' Ruth followed him into the hall. 'He's coming here for supper tonight. I said he could take his meals with us, until the cottage is sorted. Don't look at me like that!'

'We've got to sit round a table with this . . . this vagrant?'

'Why ever not? He's clean, says please and thank you in the right places. He had his own business, he says. Anyway, it'll give you a chance to get to know him.'

'I don't need anyone else in my life!'

25

'How do you know? And anyway, this is *my* house and *my* money that keeps it going.'

'So you keep telling me.' Simon slammed the door and she was left staring through the dusty windows to the overgrown wilderness beyond.

'I don't care,' she muttered. 'I don't, I really don't.'

He'd left his book behind. *Futility*, by Gerhardie. She let it lie and went out into the garden.

Chapter 3

Phizackerley Byrne unlocked the door to the cottage and pushed it open. The smell hit him first, the musty old smell of mouse droppings. The room before him was uncarpeted, sparsely furnished and thickly coated in dust. The windows were filthy and only a dim light filtered through the room. It was dingy, indistinct with dirt. Balls of fluff clung to the skirting boards, grime lay in the cracks on every surface.

He put the sleeping bag down with his rucksack on the stairs and crossed the room to the sink beneath the window. The tap was stiff at first, and then there was a splutter, a clanging of pipes somewhere and finally a gush of brown-stained water. There was a dried-up sponge on the window sill which he dabbed in the water, then drew across the window at eye level. In the distance he could see the house, a quarter of a mile away, its brittle form almost concealed by trees.

He stood there, regarding it. What was its strange appeal? He could no more leave now than fly through the air. This was why he had come, why he was staying. The house was a magnet, a fascination, a dream or a memory – he didn't know which. It worked on so many levels.

The most obvious thing was that the house was almost falling down. It called for work and money and effort. It should never have been neglected, let fall to ruin like this. And because he was a practical man, a precise and careful worker, he could see what needed to be done.

But there was something else. He wanted to understand its secrets, its history, its past. Why should such a great house be hidden away like this? A similar house anywhere else would be set among wide vistas, ordered gardens. This was concealed by the trees, almost as if it were a place of shame. And although the sun was shining and the sky was cloudless, the blue stone still appeared cold.

He turned back to the room. A utility table, two kitchen chairs, one of which had fallen over. He picked it up. The table was scratched and pitted, bleached with sun and scrubbing.

There was a cupboard under the sink, some shelves on the wall where he found pots and pans, chipped china and cutlery. A small sofa covered in a blanket of knitted squares stood in front of the hearth, the only colour.

There was an ancient trunk under the stairs, its lid open. It was full of books, old, faded and dusty. He lifted one out and blew away the dust. *Freckles*, by Gene Stratton Porter. Nothing of interest, just old-fashioned romances and adventures. At least fifty years out of date, he estimated.

Upstairs was more of the same, but the mattress seemed in reasonable condition and again water gushed from the taps in the bathroom.

He shrugged. It would do. He was only going to be here for a while. This was a temporary sanctuary, a small diversion. This was how he presented it to himself. A few days' relief while he worked out what to do. A bit of a holiday. He kicked off his boots and spread himself on the bed. He hoped to fall asleep quickly but it took ages, as usual. He watched a spider spinning webs across the window, slowly binding together the corners with an intricate filigree.

It hit him then, as it hadn't all day. A whole day without remembering, not really facing it, although of course it was always there, a not-so-distant ache.

Kristen. What was he doing here?

He awoke some hours later to the sound of hammering on the door. A young female voice called, 'Hello? Hello? Are you there?'

He lay for a moment, trying to remember who he was and why he was there. The familiar depression, the familiar dread made him slow to move, memory pounding through his mind with the subtlety of a sledgehammer.

The girl shouted again. 'Hey! Come on!'

He went to the window and pushed it open. She stepped away from the door, looking up at him. 'Oh, hello. Mum says dinner's ready, if you're hungry.'

'I'll be right down.' He pulled on his boots and splashed water on his face. He found his way downstairs.

As he opened the door, the girl said, 'My name's Kate Banniere.' Her head was tilted to one side and he saw that she was very pretty, with wide dark eyes and a delicate, heart-shaped face.

'Phizackerley Byrne.' He held out a hand to her.

She grinned. 'I almost didn't believe Mum when she told me. What do your friends call you, Phiz?'

'Sometimes. Or just Byrne.'

She had come on a bicycle and went ahead, back to the house. He took his time following her, enjoying the warmth of the evening. It was very quiet. He heard only the rooks and the faintest rumble of traffic from far away. As he walked down the drive he wondered what he was doing there. He would have to go into the house. He would have to meet the rest of the family, whoever they were.

And he absolutely didn't want to. They'll ask questions, he thought. This running away would only work as long as he made no friends, no connections. They would need some kind of story, some background, like everyone else, and he really didn't want to – couldn't bear to – go over the whole saga again. Irritated, he swung a stick at the heads of cow parsley. A scattering of flowers, pungent, sharp-scented. Why hadn't he seen this coming?

It might not be so dreadful. He was just the gardener, the hired help. Why should they be interested? He'd keep quiet as far as possible and let them invent their own version . . .

The house loomed over him. The girl was waiting for him on the steps to the terrace. Instead of going in through the front door, she took him to the left, following the terrace round the side of the house through a gate in a high wall.

He could see lines of vegetables in the walled garden, lettuce, leeks, beans, bordered by trim hedges of box. Someone had been at work here, someone cared enough to keep a fair-sized kitchen garden in spanking order. Ruth, he supposed. He couldn't imagine Kate spending much time on her hands and knees in the dirt.

And then he was crossing the threshold into the house and it was all right. The coldness of its stonework was lost in a blaze of colour. The kitchen was painted mustard yellow, but the china was blue and white and a green glazed jug full of marigolds and cornflowers stood on the side.

It was immediately welcoming. Unlike the inhabitants.

Kate was introducing him to a thin, middle-aged man at the

table. 'This is Simon Lightowler, he's a sort of cousin. He lives here too.'

Byrne held out his hand but the man ignored it.

'Come far, have you?' Simon said.

Ruth was handing Byrne a drink, something fruity with bits of orange in it. She was wearing jeans with a brilliant emerald T-shirt, a tiny gold chain around her neck. She was bronzed with sun, relaxed with her hair flowing loosely over her shoulders, but he noticed the tense set to her shoulders.

He said, 'Yes. I was away for a while. I needed to find work, and there's not much doing back home.'

'And where is home?' The man rushed on before Byrne could reply, 'No, don't tell me, let me guess. You had your own business up north, landscape gardening Ruth tells me, but the recession hit, the bank foreclosed. You lost your house, lost your car, your friends don't want to know and your wife ran out. You're on the road, honestly on your bike following dear Lord Tebbit's kind recommendation, and as chance would have it the Blue Manor was the first stop. Dear me, aren't we fortunate?'

Thank you, friend, thought Phizackerley Byrne. He said, 'My wife died. She didn't run out. But otherwise you're not far wrong.'

A silence, an embarrassment, just as he expected. What small victory was this, to cause such discomfort and unease? What had he become? He sipped his drink. Non-alcoholic but perhaps it was as well. He waited for the next attack.

'Yes, but why? Why *here*?' Simon's eyes were deep-shadowed, his face drawn. But Byrne saw that he had been good looking once beneath the sallow skin and bagged eyes.

He shrugged. 'Chance, as you said. Serendipity.'

'I love that word,' Ruth said. 'Leave him alone, Simon, it's not fair . . . You're not vegetarian, are you?' She turned to Byrne.

He shook his head. He hadn't been asked that for years. He noticed Kate watching him across the table, weighing him up.

She was so young, not much more than nineteen or twenty he reckoned. A wide grin and a slightly crooked nose. Her hair was cut very short in a shining bob.

Ruth Banniere shared her daughter's wide smile but not much

else. She seemed worried and tired again, that strain round the eyes, a downward turn to the mouth.

'Is this all the family?' he found himself asking. He remembered her saying that the house was full. It didn't make sense.

'All who live here at the moment,' said Ruth. 'Very little of the manor is habitable. I'll show you round later, if you like.'

'There's the Dogfrog,' said Simon, 'but it keeps out of the way.'

'A dog?' Byrne was surprised. Dogs usually investigated strangers in his experience.

'It's just a stray,' said Ruth. 'Comes and goes.' She was putting a large casserole down on the table, baked potatoes in a dish. It smelled heavenly.

They began to eat.

Later it struck him how incurious they had been. Ruth had talked about her plans for the garden, Kate about her college course. Simon had kept silent, but whenever Byrne looked up he noticed Simon watching him. He found the whole situation awkward and difficult. It was unclear whether he was being treated as a guest or merely tolerated as hired help. Certainly Simon made not the least attempt to be friendly. Byrne didn't linger after the meal, gladly putting off the tour of the house till some later date. 'I'd like to get the cottage straight,' he said. 'If you don't mind.'

Ruth gave him cleaning things and put them in a box together with some tea bags, milk and cereal. 'It's so you don't have to tackle us over breakfast,' she said kindly. 'We don't want to frighten you off.'

He liked the way her face lightened with the mild humour, he liked the way she had fended off Simon's more barbed comments. But he knew, as he walked through the tree-lined avenue in the twilight, that he wouldn't be staying for long.

Chapter 4

He turned on the light and put down the box on the draining board, unpacking the food stuffs, the Ajax, Flash, rags and dusters.

The room was squalid in the electric glare. Every scratch, every chip and broken thing was exposed. It was filthy but he wasn't in the mood for housework.

He could go to bed, but it was still early and anyway he'd spent all afternoon asleep.

It was a warm night. He opened the door and pulled one of the chairs across the floor, scraping it on the wooden boards.

Cawing, the rooks suddenly took off from the trees around the cottage. He was momentarily startled by the noise. He'd forgotten the trees, forgotten that they were full of life. There were hundreds of birds circling the high branches.

He sat for a while in silence after the birds had settled. Somewhere an owl hooted, distant and mournful. It was peaceful, balmy. A glass of beer would go down well, he thought, but there was no chance of that. There was a yellowish glow to the sky in the south, from the city. But in the north the sky was dark blue, pinpointed with stars. He knew their names, he checked their familiar outlines.

When the memories started up, as he knew they would, he decided to try reading. There was enough light from the room. He went inside to fetch a selection of books from the trunk.

In the glaring light, he flicked through various volumes. There was little to catch his attention. Most of the novels he'd never heard of, but some he vaguely remembered seeing by his mother's bedside. *Return to Jalna* by Mazo de la Roche. Anne Hepple, Georgette Heyer, Dornford Yates.

He sighed. Another, larger book contained pretty photographs of Epping Forest accompanied by a dated text extolling its beauties.

He sat down with it. It made gentle reading. He skipped the chapter on history, and came to a photograph of twisted trunks and a surprisingly vivid quote from Milton's *Comus*:

The nodding horror of whose shady brows
Threats the forlorn and wand'ring passenger . . .

A scrap of paper fell into his hands, a brief note. *See you tonight*, it read. *The usual. All my love, E.*

He turned it over. Just an initial, *J.* It was very old, dry and yellow. Handwritten in ink, a glowing, careless script.

The door behind him banged, flapping shut in a gust of wind. In the sudden dark, the piece of paper frisked out of his hand, up into the branches over his head.

He stood up, but the message had gone.

It wasn't for him, anyway.

They stood by the hedge. They watched Byrne enter the cottage, watched the door close behind him.

They moved along the hedge until the house came into view, golden light shining from a couple of windows on the ground floor.

The man stood very still. His hands reached out and touched the leaves of the beech hedge. They shivered beneath his touch, or it might have been that he was trembling.

The two women standing at his shoulders leaned against him, pushing him towards the hedge. His eyes were weary, unsurprised, as twigs entangled themselves in his clothes and jabbed into his flesh, digging deep furrows into veins and arteries.

Blood was beginning to flow now, dripping through the leaves. He made no sound, no effort to get free. They were still pushing and he was held there, pinned like a black carapaced beetle against the pin.

After a while the body stopped twitching, although the blood continued to flow for some time.

They stood back, leaning against the trees that stood nearby. Bark encrusted their flesh, twigs twined with their hair.

Leaves wound themselves round the body hanging in the hedge. They pressed into crevices and cracks, found their way through the labyrinth of clothes. They grew through the orifices, into the pores of the skin.

And in the morning, when Byrne awoke, there was no sign of the man or his two companions. Even the blood had gone.

✳

In the house next morning, the phone rang. Simon picked it up and said, 'Hello? Hello? Anyone there?'

Nothing. He shrugged and put it down. Ruth had just come in, so he said, 'One of your little lambs, I expect. Why on earth do you let them know your home number?'

'I don't. There must be a fault on the line. Kate keeps getting it too and there's never anyone there. It hasn't happened to me yet.'

He saw that she was ready for school, sensible skirt and blouse, unexciting shoes.

She said, 'I've asked Byrne to start on the hedge. It's a massive job, but it has to be done.'

'I thought the chainsaw was broken.'

'It is. He says he prefers to work manually.' She sounded neutral.

Simon frowned. 'It'll take for ever. It's a waste of his time.'

'I'm taking the saw in to get repaired this afternoon. He can use it tomorrow. He's going to check the boundaries today, to see what's involved.'

'You know, Ruth, I very much doubt that Byrne's going to be the answer you're looking for. You'll be lucky if you can get him to stay. That's a man with a past, if ever I've seen one. A stubborn and independent man.'

'Do you think so? I find him very easy.'

'That's because he's out to impress. He's on probation. You just wait.'

She was putting on her jacket, checking her bag for keys. She gave him a peck on the cheek. 'Well, we'll see. All right, love? I'll be a little late, as I said. Kate's around, if you need anything.'

He watched her go, watched the Escort wind slowly down the long drive to the trees. Then he picked up a book and tried to read.

Byrne lowered the clippers with relief and climbed down from the stepladder. Lunchtime, he reckoned, from the position of the sun high overhead. He stood for a moment surveying the results of the morning's work.

The beech hedge stretched away before and behind him and only a tiny proportion was now neat and tidy. It was over three metres high, with vigorous branches and shoots pushing it well out of arm's reach. The whole thing was over a mile long. If

Ruth Banniere's chainsaw was worth repairing, he would certainly be ready to give it a go.

He turned back to the house, mopping his face.

The high sunlight reflected off the slate roof, sparkling, lively as light on seawater. The manor looked ancient, although Ruth had told him it was Edwardian, less than a hundred years old. A century is enough for people to leave their trace on a building, he thought. In that space of time generations could grow, procreate, mature and die. People had loved each other there, written love letters, made assignations. People had laughed and cried . . .

And he wondered how much love there was in the manor now, how much laughter. Simon Lightowler was near the edge of a fully fledged breakdown, he reckoned. There was a vicious, destructive edge to the things he said. Self-destructive. And Ruth run off her feet, Kate too young to be much help. It was people that gave the place the air of heaviness, of brooding weight, there was nothing intrinsically wrong with it. The proportions were slightly out, although he'd seen worse.

But as he crossed the west lawn towards the kitchen garden, he felt disinclined to enter the house. There was nothing he could rationalize. Just a gut reaction that the house was waiting to overbalance, to fall, to crush its inhabitants. He wanted to stay outside, amongst the green and living things.

He opened the back door. Simon Lightowler was sitting at one end of the long pine table. There were two glasses in front of him and a large square-shouldered green bottle, rather less than half full.

'Ah, there you are,' he said, reaching for the bottle. 'I was waiting, you see.' His eyes were vivid as jewels in the yellowing skin. 'A little gin, an apéritif, a sweetener to the spirit?'

'Thanks, but what I really need is water.' Byrne went to the sink and poured himself a glass. 'It's hot work out there.'

'You won't mind if I drink alone?' Simon was already finishing a glass, ignoring Byrne's words.

Byrne found bread and cheese. He'd brought in some tomatoes from the greenhouse. He put out plates for himself and Simon but the other man pushed his away.

'A liquid lunch, you see.' He seemed already well away and continued to drink steadily, refilling glass after glass with meticulous care while Byrne assembled a sandwich for himself.

'I think I'll take this outside,' said Byrne mildly. 'There's a breeze there.'

'Don't fancy the company, eh? Well, I'd like to show you something.' Simon lurched to his feet. 'I'd really like to show you something. I'd like to introduce you to the manor. Phizackerley Byrne' – he threw open the door to the hall – 'meet the Blue Manor. Manor, meet Phizackerley Byrne.' For a moment he stopped, frowning. 'It's a damn silly name,' he said. 'What are you really called?'

Byrne said nothing. He was looking at the house.

The kitchen passage led straight into a large panelled hall. The room seemed full of books. Bookshelves lined the walls, books spilled over the oblong table which stood in the centre of the hall. It was surrounded by a mixed collection of chairs. There were various items of heavy mahogany furniture, desks, sideboards, whatnots.

A stairway reached up through two storeys in a complicated series of half-landings and balconies. It was supported on every level by a number of carved wooden pillars. These ornate obelisks formed an arcade on the ground floor, and several other book-lined corridors grew out of this shadowy walkway and disappeared into other wings of the house.

The hall was sweltering with heat. The sunlight came from a deep window, a third of the way up the stairwell. In dusty rays, the sun fell on clutter and mess. Magazines and newspapers lay among the books on every surface. Coffee mugs and glasses left rings on the long table and sideboards. There was a cricket bat in the umbrella stand, and a battered straw hat was half-cocked over the Wedgwood bowl on the desk.

A stone fireplace took up most of the wall opposite the front door. In the corner beside the stairs, he saw the elaborate cage of a lift, the tarnished bars twisted into art nouveau floral patterns. And although sun was flooding in through the stair window, Byrne felt no desire whatever to enter the heart of the manor.

Nothing moved there, no shift of air or whisper of sound. No presence from the past wafted beneath the level of his senses, no presage of fear touched his spirit.

The manor was waiting, that was all; he felt it again. The corridors running from its centre were empty, free from furniture, open and ready for – something. He didn't know what, and he very strongly didn't want to find out.

It was too blank. There was no character in the house, no atmosphere. For all the clutter there was no sense of family life, that people moved through it on their daily business. It was like a stage set, something false. He stepped back, almost knocking into the man who stood behind him.

'Fun, isn't it?' Simon said. 'It always makes me feel like that, too.' He walked past Byrne into the hall and picked up a book from the table. 'Do you like reading? There are more books through there.' He gestured to a door on the east side of the house. 'That's the official library, although the whole house is running with books.'

'I don't read much,' Byrne said. 'There's never been the time.'

'Why do people always sound so virtuous when they say they never have time for reading? I would have thought it a rather shameful thing to admit . . . or are you a man of action, someone who makes an impact on our multicoloured, media-inspired world? The telly's in there . . .' He nodded to another door opposite the kitchen. 'But Ruth doesn't approve. And you'll be far too busy, of course, to waste your life away in front of the box.' The words rattled on as he wandered around the hall, putting down one book and picking up another, arranging the piles of magazines, opening one here and there until the hall was filled with brightly coloured pictures of gardens and clothes and people and houses and food. Byrne watched the way Simon's path wavered and wandered quite aimlessly between the table and mantelpiece, between the sideboard and cushioned chair. It was as if he was trying to give the house some character, some semblance of liveliness. It made no difference.

He saw, over the front door, some writing enclosed in a rosewood frame.

'What's that?' he asked.

Simon glanced up. 'No French either? Dear me.' And then he quoted it from memory, his voice suddenly deep and rich and eloquent, caressing the words as if they were made of silk.

> De sa dent soudaine et vorace,
> Comme un chien l'amour m'a mordu . . .
> En suivant mon sang repandu,
> Va, tu pourras suivre ma trace . . .

Prends un cheval de bonne race,
Pars, et suis mon chemin ardu,
Fondrière ou sentier perdu,
Si la course ne te harasse!

En passant par où j'ai passé,
Tu verras que seul et blessé
J'ai parcouru ce triste monde.

Et qu'ainsi je m'en fus mourir
Bien loin, bien loin, sans découvrir
Le bleu manoir de Rosamonde.

He smiled a little and without looking at Byrne translated the last verse.

> . . . And thus I wrought my own death
> Far, far away, without discovering
> The blue manor of Rosamund.

'Welcome to the Blue Manor, Mr Byrne,' he said. 'Our great-grandma Rosamund built it, she used to sing the song that goes with these words. We didn't know her, she died before the war.'

'Who's "we"?'

'Ruth and I, of course.' Simon raised an eyebrow. 'Did no one tell you? We're cousins, we two. We share the same bed and the same ancestry and the same genes.'

'And the same house?'

He put the book down. 'No,' he said quietly. 'We don't share the house, and we never will. It's all hers.' His voice was self-mocking. 'Although *I* am the prisoner here.' His eyes glinted wickedly at Byrne, fully relishing the melodrama.

'Hello, are you having the tour?' A light cool voice from one of the landings above them. Kate was standing there. She came down towards them.

'You've been drinking,' she said resignedly to Simon. 'Wherever do you get it from?'

'How clever of you, dear little niece, to notice. See, I'm even holding a glass, so you can be quite sure that your inspired diagnosis is accurate.'

She glanced at Byrne. 'Did you bring it with you? Didn't Mum tell you Simon's not allowed . . . ?' She stopped.

'No, to both questions.'

'What's it got to do with *him*?' Simon was shouting now. 'He's not my keeper, no more than you are, little miss goody fucking two-shoes.'

'I had a letter from Tom this morning,' Kate said coldly. 'He'll be arriving on Saturday.'

Simon turned to Byrne. 'Hah! There you are, you don't have to stay here after all! Your cue to leave has materialized. You can get away from here with honour, if you're quick, because the handyman's coming to stay.'

'He's not coming to work in the house, he's got to work on his book.'

'Oh, his *book*!' Simon's voice was high and excited. 'This great masterpiece, this amazing literary landmark – as if there aren't enough in the world already. What's it about?'

'It's a novel. Spanning the century, but from a post-post-modernist approach.' Kate regarded him with dislike. 'Go on, let's have it. Do-re-me constructionalist, the author, who he? Form and text and all the bright array of gaudy ideas.'

'Come again? Do I hear the words "author", "form"? Is the citadel crumbling?'

'See you later,' said Byrne. He went back into the kitchen, leaving the hall suddenly silent, waiting again, predatory for action and emotion.

It was a relief to get back to the interminable hedge. He turned away from the house and started to clip.

There was a rhythm to his actions, something regular and satisfying. Leaves and twigs fell beneath the stepladder in spiky drifts. Overhead, clouds ran over the sun and he thought that there might soon be rain . . .

He wasn't going to stay here. There was no need to put up with scenes like that. Too difficult, too heated and distressed. He'd rather take his chance with the world he saw over the hedge.

Not far away, just beyond the trees, the road waited. He thought, I'll walk down the drive, along the lane, hitch a ride and get on with it. As soon as Ruth gets back I'll explain. Tomorrow I'll go. Tomorrow.

He saw her car drive through the gate late that afternoon, but instead of going on to the manor the car stopped and Ruth got out. From the back she took a heavy piece of machinery. He walked towards her, meaning to take the weight of it.

'Oh, hi, Byrne,' she said. 'Look, it should work now. They fitted a new chain and there's some petrol in the garage. You can use it right away, unless you've had enough today . . . ?'

'Ruth, I'll do a bit more this evening, but I think I'll be moving on tomorrow.'

'Leaving us? Already?' Her face and voice were cool, but he knew she was disappointed.

'Kate's friend Tom is arriving at the weekend. She had a letter this morning. Perhaps he'll be able to help you out.'

'Tom? The new boyfriend? Oh no, I don't think he's that type. I expect Tom Crabtree to spend his time in the library, his mind on various exalted levels. No, he'll be no help at all.'

'Still, I think it's time I went. I'm sorry, Ruth. It's been more than kind of you to take on a stranger in this way, don't think I don't appreciate it, but—'

'Has Simon been drinking again? No, don't answer that.' She paused, looking at him. Her hair was coming down again, softening her face. 'Where will you go, Byrne?' Gently. 'What will you do?'

He said, 'The city calls, I think. I'll find something there.'

'With no money, no papers, no *name*? It's not your real name, is it? Where do you come from, who *are* you?'

Her warm brown eyes were demanding too much.

'It's no great mystery,' he said, shrugging. 'Just a boring old mid-life crisis. I wanted a change, I wanted to try something else.'

'And your wife died.'

'A very long time ago. It's nothing to do with anything.' He could not afford her sympathy. He wanted her to stop asking questions. 'It's all right, Ruth, really it is. I'm not suppressing or hiding anything.'

He was lying, of course. Why did her concern draw only lies from him? Kristen's death was as vivid to him as if it had happened yesterday. It wasn't long ago, not at all.

And he was hiding much more than that. Those two women. The dead man looking at him with David's face, his hands empty. *What are you waiting for?*

Why did he keep pretending that it hadn't happened? He had seen a murder take place.

Two murders. 'Ruth, do you get a local newspaper? Have there been any reports of missing people?'

She shook her head. 'We don't take it. Why, have you lost someone?'

He wondered whether to tell her. But she looked tired and this was becoming dangerous and he couldn't handle telling her. 'No, I came across some people in the forest. On the way here. They were rather . . . strange.'

'Drunk, probably. Or drugged. The forest's the nearest dumping ground for the East End. You get lots of disreputable types wandering around. It's not really very safe.'

'Do you get much trouble here?'

'No. We're a bit out of the way. Most of the bodies get dumped closer to the High Road. You need persistence to find the manor.' She gazed at him speculatively. 'Stay with us for a bit longer. Get your bearings, find out what you want from life—'

'And in the meantime, cut the hedge?' A day or two, he was thinking. Perhaps. Until the hedge is finished.

Ruth was smiling at him. 'Early supper tonight. I've got to go out later. You'll stay, won't you?'

He liked her, he liked the way she flicked her hair back. He was aware of the warmth of her generous body, standing so close to him. She was getting too near, in every way. This was madness, all of it. He nodded. 'For a bit. Now, any special wrinkles to this thing?'

They bent together over the saw.

Next day he was out at the hedge again. He was working hard, determined to get it done as quickly as possible because he had promised Ruth he would. But then he was going to leave. Dinner had been another ordeal, Simon monosyllabic, Ruth determinedly and, it seemed to him, artificially cheerful. Even Kate had been subdued. This eating with the family was definitely more pain than pleasure.

The chainsaw made the job much faster, although he hated its noise. He watched the twigs and branches fall to the grass like litter and thought about making a bonfire.

As the machine sliced round one of the bends in the hedge he saw someone approaching through the forest. He turned the saw off and the sudden silence was a relief. The figure through the trees was moving slowly, as if disabled or very old.

The man had to be over eighty. He held a silver-topped cane in one gloved hand. There was an immaculate panama hat on his ancient head. He was wearing a cream linen suit of excellent cut, stagy, glamorous clothes quite unsuited to a walk through the brambles and leaf mould.

The man stopped some way from Byrne and took a handkerchief from his pocket, dabbing his forehead. And then the silk dropped and the man looked straight up at him.

His eyes were a golden-brown, an unusually pale colour. His hair was bleached white, his skin grey and unhealthy. It was as if age had drained all vitality from him, leaving a face wizened and lined like a walnut. A faint hairline scar slightly puckered the side of his mouth.

Byrne said, 'Hello, do you want someone?'

The man stood there for a minute, leaning on the stick. Then he began to come closer. He was getting nearer and the only thing keeping him out of the manor was this frail barrier of leaf and twig.

'Can I do something for you?' Byrne said.

'So you're the new gardener,' the man said, his voice as dry as dead wood. 'I have some advice. Unsolicited, and possibly unwelcome, but that cannot be helped. I advise you to get out. Get away from here, while you can.' He was coming closer as he spoke, treading calmly on nettles and thorns as if they were no more than grass. 'This warning is purely for your benefit. As a token of my good will, I have here a present for you.' He threw to Byrne a brown leather wallet across the line of beech.

For a moment it fell open in Byrne's hands. It was instantly recognizable: his own. He saw familiar plastic cards, driving licence. And a full sheaf of bank notes. Fifties. More cash than he had ever seen before in one place.

And when he looked up the old man was walking away, his tall, thin figure disappearing between the shady trees.

Two people stepped out of the trees to accompany him, two women dressed in black. They stood at either side of him and one of them looked back at Byrne.

Her eyes were black with kohl, her face whiter than bone. She smiled at him and drew her forefinger across her throat, a potent reminder.

He dropped the wallet on the grass, his hands shaking. He couldn't move, couldn't think what to do. And then they were gone, and again he thought of dreaming, of visions and hallucinations.

But they were real, and wanted something of him.

Chapter 5

'Simon's an alcoholic, you see. It's best if we don't keep any booze in the place, it's just not fair on him.'

Kate was waiting for him at the cottage. He didn't want to talk to her, he didn't want her there at all. He wanted a stiff whisky and time on his own and most of all he wanted out.

She was carrying a plate of sandwiches and a flask. He stared at her blankly until she put them in his hands. He waited for her to go but she led the way into the cottage. God, this was *not* what he needed.

He put the plate and flask down on the table, the wallet on the sideboard. Her eyes flickered round the room.

'It's a bit bare, isn't it? You know there are stacks of furniture and pictures and things in the attic at the house. You could make this really nice.'

'It doesn't matter. I'm leaving.'

Leave *now*! his instincts screamed. Get out of here right now, don't bother with this.

'That's why I've come. This is not purely a social call. Do you really have to go so soon? Can't you stay?' She was looking directly at him and he thought, distractedly, how attractive she was, how potent with youth and energy and sensuality.

She was young enough to be his daughter.

He turned his back to her, washing his hands at the sink. 'I'm flattered, of course. But this is putting things off. I need a proper job, somewhere to live.'

'What's the rush?'

He turned round. She was holding the wallet which he'd put on the sideboard. 'There's over two thousand pounds in here. Posh credit cards. The driving licence is in your name, so perhaps it's genuine after all. Who are you kidding, Mr Byrne? You don't need a job, not for a while at least.'

He was annoyed with himself for leaving the wallet out. And why was she poking round, what was she up to? 'The money's not mine,' he said. 'Some madman gave it to me an hour ago.

He just stepped out of the forest. He had two women with him. They were dressed in black. Do you know who they are?'

She avoided his glance, looking beyond him towards the manor. 'No . . . how peculiar. But this *is* your wallet, isn't it? You must have dropped it somewhere.'

She was lying. She knew who they were. He could hear it in the neutrality of her tone, see it in the studied coolness of her gaze. It was a trick Ruth used more subtly.

'Stay with us. Please.' She put her hand on his arm.

'No, why should I?' He felt very angry. 'Give me one good reason for staying.'

'We need you,' she said softly.

'All this place needs is a great pile of money. There's nothing I can do to make any real difference.'

'No. It's not like that. Mum . . . wants you to stay.' And before he could protest that it was nothing to do with him, she went on, 'She gets so tired, you see. And Simon's no help. Then there's this charity work, it really gets to her.'

'Well, why does she do it? Doesn't she have enough on?'

'Poor old Mum . . . She's caught up in guilt. Haven't you noticed? She feels guilty that she owns the manor, that it's all hers and that Simon feels it so badly. She thinks it's her fault that he's so loony, and then of course there's the state of the house and the garden running wild, there's my lack of a father and the dreadful state of the world, from politics to global warming.' She smiled charmingly. For a moment he really disliked her. 'You name it and my mother worries about it. So it seems logical for her to spend what little free time she does have on the end of a telephone listening to all the poor despairing sods in Essex.'

'She listens?'

'She's a Samaritan. You know, those people who listen to the suicidal, the druggies, the bankrupts and victims.'

'Quite a responsibility.'

'Yes, but there's a let-out. You're not allowed to do anything, you only give comfort, not advice. You have to sit and listen while they cut their wrists and turn on the gas and take the pills.'

He was silent for a while, remembering times not far distant when the knife had beckoned. 'It must be hard,' he said.

Kate sighed. 'It's ridiculous. No wonder she gets so depressed.'

'And you think my help in the garden might lighten the load?' he prompted.

'I *know* so. She wants to feel that something in her life is coming right, getting better . . . I wish you would stay.'

He stared at her in frustration. 'This is nothing to do with me.'

She took no notice. She went on as if he hadn't spoken. 'I'm so worried about her. She needs someone else around.'

'Not me!'

'But you're the gardener.' The bright sunlight suddenly caught at her face, stripping it of prettiness. She seemed older, the shape of her bones sharp and angular beneath the skin. It was unnerving.

'There's always been a gardener living in the cottage,' she said.

'No one's lived here for years!'

'And that's what's so wrong. That's why—' She stopped abruptly. 'You should stay, Mr Byrne. You're needed here. Why don't you regard this' – she pointed to the wallet – 'as payment? A couple of months' wages. That's what it is, of course.'

'On the contrary, it gives me the freedom to leave.'

'Running out, Mr Byrne? Again?'

He went to the door and held it open for her.

'Goodbye,' he said. 'I can't say it's been fun. Tell your mother—'

'You tell her. You owe her that.' She raised her chin and he wanted to pick her up and physically put her outside the door.

Anything to get rid of her.

'All right,' he said. 'I'll tell her myself.'

She marched past him and out into the sunlight.

He waited at the side of the drive at four that afternoon and waved Ruth's car to a halt. She rolled down the window and smiled at him.

He saw at once that she'd been crying. 'What's wrong?'

'Oh, nothing . . . It's – ' She made a visible effort. 'You've been getting on so well! I can't tell you how grateful I am. It makes such a difference to the whole place to get the hedge in order and once that's finished we could—'

How could he say it? She was so vulnerable, and he'd promised to stay. He said, 'The chainsaw makes a difference. It shouldn't take too long. But, Ruth, I'm so sorry, but I think you'll have to find someone else to take it over. I can't stay here any longer.'

'Don't say that!' A naked edge to her voice, something rather desperate. Then, more composed, as if a rigid clamp had come down over her words and her feelings, she said, 'What's made you change your mind?'

She opened the door and got out. She stood there leaning against the car as if she'd no energy to stand upright and he wanted to hold her, to take some of the weight of it.

'I've got my wallet back,' he said. 'An old man came out of the forest and gave it to me. He had two women with him, two women dressed in black. Do you know who I mean?'

She didn't answer his question. Her face was turned to him, studying him as if she was going to want to draw him from memory. 'I don't know what to do,' she murmured. 'Someone else might try bribery, or flattery, to hold you here . . . Would feminine wiles work?' She half smiled, to show it was a joke. 'What would you recommend? Of course, you're perfectly free to leave whenever you want. You've been marvellous. It's just that – that I'd hoped. I thought you said yesterday you'd stay for a bit . . .' She trailed off.

'What's upset you, Ruth?'

'Oh, never mind. It's not your problem, like the manor is not your problem.' She turned her back on him, opening the car door once more.

'I'll finish the hedge. All right?' He never knew what made him say it. Was it because she turned away from him, as if he was just one more disappointment? Or a consciousness that he had run out too often? You can overplay that card, he told himself. It doesn't solve anything.

And then she suddenly kissed him, a quick peck on the cheek, and he saw genuine happiness in her eyes, a smoothing of the skin on her forehead.

The power he had over her was terrifying.

He returned to the hedge thoughtfully and entirely missed the glint of binoculars from the house.

Chapter 6

'*Flat fields,*' he wrote. '*Treeless and empty under a wide and dull sky . . .*' Tom Crabtree stared through the grimy window with dissatisfaction. They were running alongside a road, a monster road, six lanes crammed with cars and lorries.

The train was more crowded than Tom expected. He stood part of the way from Cambridge, the carpet-bag on the floor between his legs, notebook in hand. It was hot, but he was wearing jeans and a white T-shirt. Uncluttered, cool. He rarely made mistakes about clothes.

He was impatient with the slow movement of the train. He wanted to be *there*, to end this brief journey, to see Kate again, to get settled into The Book.

Kate came first, of course, gorgeous, wonderful Kate with her infectious smile and heart-shaped face. He amused himself for a moment remembering her physical presence, the long, smooth brown legs, the high, rounded breasts. He told himself that the fact that she came with a stately home attached was just icing on the cake. In that hot and crowded train, approaching Harlow, he remembered only one detail about the place, the odd fact that the Blue Manor could only be inherited through the female line.

'Then it'll be yours one day,' he'd said casually.

'What's it to you?' Her head was on one side, her eyes considering him, suspicious.

'Nothing. Nothing at all.' He had shrugged.

'It's *not* a stately home, anyway. It's far too small, less than a hundred years old and needs a largish fortune spending on it. If you're after me for my money, prepare for disappointment.'

'Money? Me? Kate, really!' Injured pride of ludicrous proportions and she'd laughed and thrown a cushion at him. But still, it had been enough.

'Come and see for yourself,' she'd said later. 'You could work in the library. It's quiet, and full of the kind of stuff you might find useful. There are books everywhere.'

This was an invitation he had no intention of refusing. It was almost too good to be true. A summer in the country with Kate, somewhere quiet to work that would cost him nothing, some space in which to gather his thoughts about Kate, about his book, about how he was going to live while he put it together . . .

He watched the buildings thin out, saw the patches of green increasing, the wispy willows, the slow winding of a stream. Two girls across the carriage had lit cigarettes, despite the ban. A rustle of disapproval from the thin-lipped man next to him, but nobody said anything. Apathy rules, he thought. Grey smoke drifted towards him.

He leant his head against the window and wondered if the train would be on time. He hoped Kate would be there to meet him, that he wouldn't have to hang around too long.

'Kate, it feels like years!'

'A fortnight, that's all.' She was laughing too.

Tom placed his bag in the boot and slid into the front seat of the Escort. He kissed her again, ruffling her hair until she looked like some punk urchin.

He regretted it immediately. Kate should be exquisite, perfect, immaculate. He took a comb from his pocket and ran it through her hair, straightening the mess.

She grinned at him, touching the freckles on his nose. 'Got your sun oil?' she asked. 'It's going to be a hot summer.'

'It'll be worth it. A month in the country with you and no hassles with the landlady . . .'

'Just a small novel to write, a brief account of a rather dull period in humanity's history. The twentieth century, according to Tom Crabtree. A couple of afternoons should see it off. A real rest cure.'

' "With you there, my love, summer's lease hath all too short a date." ' He was teasing her, frivolous and exhilarated for once, and she was loving it. She had been there, waiting for him on the platform and he wanted to give her presents, dance with her and swing her round. He started rooting through the cassettes in the glove compartment and found what he wanted. The familiar songs of Steely Dan filled the car.

'That's better.' She frowned, mock-serious. 'Let's have a pact. Outside the library, no poetry, no Eng. Lit., no academic one-upmanship or capping of quotations. We have a higher purpose here.'

'Good Lord, a sacred mission? I thought I was going to laze around, acquire a tan and join the leisured classes.'

'Leisured? At the Blue Manor? You wait. Now,' she said as they pulled out of the station car park, 'are you prepared for the family?'

'Your mother Ruth and cousin Simon, all right and tight,' he said promptly.

'Tight's just about the word for it, where Simon's concerned . . . And agoraphobic, and paranoid, although there's no harm in him. He's no trouble once you get past the words.'

'Fairly damning, that. Are you as objective about me, too?' He looked at Kate sideways.

'Only to friends.' Something hidden in that triangular smile, something that put him at a distance. 'And then there's the mystery man.'

'Who?'

'He's called Phizackerley Byrne. Don't laugh. He turned up at the manor out of nowhere looking for work. Mum nabbed him before you could say guardian angel and set him to work in the garden. He's living in the cottage, so he's not really at the manor much. He comes in for meals.'

'Does that mean I may be excused garden duty?'

'While Byrne's around, you might be in luck. He's always talking about moving on, though.'

'Do you see much of him, then?'

'He must be forty if he's a day. And definitely, but definitely, not interested.'

'Gay, is he?'

'No, I don't think so. He says he was married but his wife died.'

They were passing through the outskirts of Harlow.

'Do you have many other friends, kindred spirits, round here?' He watched the blocks of offices and warehouses with resignation.

'Not here. In Epping or Theydon Bois, nearer the manor.'

'The Blue Manor . . . Kate's enchanted palace, her castle home.'

She shook her head. 'No, it's great-great-grandmother Rosamund's house, really. It always will be. She chose the name, she organized the architect . . .'

'But now only three of you live there.'

'It's enough.'

Enough for what? he wondered. 'And me,' he said. 'Four people, this summer.'

'Bliss,' she said. 'It's going to be bliss.'

They drove out of the town past the industrial estate and superstores, the factories and dry ski slope. He smelt melting tarmac and exhaust fumes and rolled up the window. He could see very few people. Everyone would be closeted away in their flats with their televisions and videos, or off down the precinct. He knew how places like this worked for he had grown up in just such a new town. He would probably still be there now, he reflected, if twelve years ago his mother hadn't made friends with Alicia Lightowler at a local CND meeting. Kate's Aunty Alicia.

She called her aunty although Alicia was really a cousin, and that by marriage. Kate had explained it to him once but he couldn't remember the details.

Alicia was like a godmother to him.

She sent him books for his birthday, books for Christmas. Every year she met him and his mother in town and took them to dinner at the Ivy and to the RSC. And when Tom made it to Cambridge, where Alicia was teaching, she'd made a point of introducing him to her other students. It was at one of these lunch parties that Tom met, for the first time, a second year undergraduate called Kate Banniere.

Tom never questioned Alicia Lightowler's interest in his education. It had seemed only natural that an elderly woman should want to encourage a bright, hard-working young man. Right and proper. And when he confessed to Alicia that he wanted to be a writer, she had encouraged him all the way. Indeed, it had been Alicia who suggested that he try a novel.

You have an eye for connections, she'd said. It lends itself to fiction, on a large scale. Why not give it a go?

And so here he was, being driven through the Essex landscape by Alicia's cousin once removed, some pads of A4 and six sharp 2B pencils in his bag, ready and raring to go.

Gradually Harlow gave way to open fields. They drove round the vast roundabout at the junction with the M11, the Escort taking them into a different countryside, one shadowed by dusty trees. The remnants of Epping Forest, he supposed, having bothered to look at a map before leaving Cambridge. It took ten minutes to get through Epping itself, what with the pedestrian crossings and cars trying to park or turn. He found himself increasingly impatient with the delay.

And then yet another motorway, and there again was the forest, tired with traffic fumes, littered with drinks cans and torn paper and plastic cups. They turned off the main road. There were some big houses backing on to the trees, several cars gleaming in each drive. Roses tumbled carefully over old grey stone and whitewashed walls. He rolled down the window and saw that opposite them a car park was crammed. The golf club was doing a roaring trade.

'This really is the sticks, isn't it?' He knew his prejudices were showing. Essex man, the East End gone rural. Wide boys and fading pop stars and scrap-metal dealers and cars, cars, cars.

'Depends what you mean by the sticks,' she said cheerfully. 'There's civilization within easy reach.' She pointed and through a haze of heat he saw a signpost to the city. 'Fifteen miles to central London.'

'Do you go there much?' He was drumming his fingers against the side of the car with impatience.

'Not often.' The Escort had turned away from Theydon Bois and was cutting down a small lane on the edge of the forest. 'There's so much to do at the manor. You'll see.'

'How does your mother manage?'

'She's into the Puritan work ethic,' Kate said briefly. She glanced at him. 'It's a complicated burden, maintaining the Blue Manor. Ask Mum tonight. It's her story.'

Tom leant back in his seat, squinting against the sunlight. She was looking good, he thought, a bit tanned, dark hair slightly sweaty, curling at the temples. This was exactly what he needed. The open-necked shirt and full cotton shorts seemed nothing less than an invitation. He reached out a hand and touched her thigh, stroking the smooth, warm skin.

He saw the dimple at the side of her mouth deepen.

'We're nearly there,' she said. 'Got your social smile ready?'

'I need a little encouragement,' he said. 'A little moral support . . .' He leant over and kissed the nape of her neck. His hand had slipped under the material of her shorts. 'Shall we pull over?'

The lane they were in was darkened by birch and beech trees.

There was more forest ahead, thick and shady. He saw a dirt track running away into the trees. Kate pulled down on the wheel, and the dry earth turned to dust as the car left the road and halted.

Tom kissed her, reaching over. It was long and slow, and he knew that she would be soft and moist, ready for him. A fortnight. It felt much longer. He opened the door and walked round the car to her side.

He saw, beside the track, out of sight from the car, three people.

He stopped dead, his hand on the door handle. They were sitting cross-legged on the ground, a man and two women in conventional black rags. Leather jackets, dusty fringed skirts, layers of skimpy cardigans and scarves. They looked very hot, although heavy kohl eye make-up was the only depth in deadly pale faces. Their eyes were downcast, as if meditating.

The man looked up at Tom. The two women sat slightly behind him, one to each shoulder like wings. His hair was dark and cut very short, his skin and eyes entirely colourless. A deep scar ran down the side of his face from the corner of his eye to the mouth. His black clothes were torn and greasy and there was something about him of decay, of disease and rottenness. Tom took a step backwards.

He turned to Kate, who was staring out of the car window at him.

'Let's move on,' he said, surprised to find that his voice was so even. 'Somewhere else.'

'What's wrong . . . ?' But she had seen something in his expression, although he had tried not to frighten her. She had started the engine before he sat down. She said, 'What did you see?'

He said, 'Nothing. A mess. Nothing.'

Chapter 7

A mile further on, Kate turned into a driveway. There was no house name, nothing to mark where they were going. Inside the gates stood a dilapidated cottage with mullioned windows and a thatched roof.

'That's where Phizackerley Byrne is staying,' Kate said. 'It's a bit of a mess, but he doesn't seem to mind.'

'Is this all your mother's?' Tom asked.

'Yes.' She looked faintly embarrassed. 'There's no money, though, as I said. It's virtually a ruin.'

'Couldn't she sell some of this land? The price of property round here must be extortionate, even now.' He thought for a moment, answering his own question. 'And even if she doesn't want to sell, what about leasing? Market gardeners, farmers . . . surely your mother could make something of it?'

'The terms of Rosamund's will don't allow it. There's a trust fund which gives her enough money to keep it going until the first of January two thousand.'

'Then what?'

She shrugged. 'Whatever she likes, I suppose.'

At that moment the car swung round a bend and Tom had his first sight of the Blue Manor.

He'd seen photographs and Kate had told him a little of its history, but he was still surprised. He saw it as an Edwardian mansion composed of a cold blue stone, partially softened by ivy and climbing roses. He felt immediately drawn to it, by the graceful way it soared among the trees, its towers and gabled roof reaching into their branches. Not conventional proportions, but imaginative, organic almost, complementing the trees. There was that Spanish architect, what was his name? Gaudi, that was it. Stricter than Gaudi, less elaborate, but something of that quality. He understood completely why Kate's mother had not sold the Blue Manor. Neither would he, if it were his.

He had never seen anywhere more beautiful. Until that moment, he had thought that architecture would never move him. He knew about it, he'd made an effort to know something of all the fine arts; he had visited St Mark's in Venice, the cathedral at Rheims, stately homes and castles and country houses throughout Europe. He lived in Cambridge, surrounded by architectural gems. But he had always thought that he was missing something. That there was an area of appreciation he simply did not share.

The manor was different. It fitted him. It was entirely unlike anywhere else he had ever lived, but he knew it was home. Not the council flat where he had grown up, not his bedsit in Cambridge, but like some Platonic ideal of home. Somewhere the spirit could soar, expand to fill those aspiring, yearning towers. It would fold itself around its inhabitants, he thought, shield them from the trivialities of the outside world . . .

It was his for the summer. And for longer than that? his mind suggested. He pushed the thought aside.

For the first time, he began to realize that staying at the manor might be more complicated than he had anticipated.

'Hello, you must be Tom. I'm so glad you could come.' The woman with Kate's eyes moved forward as the Escort swirled to a halt in front of the steps. They shook hands while Kate made the introductions. Ruth Banniere was wearing jeans and a shirt, an ancient straw hat covering soft brown hair. She spends her spare time in the garden, Kate had said once. She prefers plants to people, and music to either.

Twigs and branches were caught together in difficult angles around her feet. She kicked some of it aside. 'Sorry about all this,' she said, flustered. 'There's so much to do everywhere and it's difficult to know where to begin. I thought I'd tidy up the entrance to welcome you.'

'Or to fire me with enthusiasm?' He smiled at her, taking his carpet-bag from the car. Her unnecessary apology implied a kind of awkwardness he did not normally associate with Kate. 'This is a marvellous place,' he said. 'It must be marvellous to live here.'

And you writing a book, he thought. A firm grip of vocabulary, a mastery of the language. What would Alicia say? But then awkwardness is catching. Ruth Banniere's unease was communicating itself rather too clearly.

Ruth was frowning. She had seen something. 'Kate, you

mustn't leave books out. I know it's hot, but there's quite a heavy dew in the mornings.'

She was looking beyond them to the ramp which ran down the side of the steps leading to the front door. Halfway down the ramp a book lay, its spine broken, splayed wide, open to the sky. Ruth bent to pick it up.

'Poetry, too. Where's your respect, girl?' She was only half ironic.

'Waiting for next term. I didn't leave it there, anyway. Must be Simon.' Kate showed no interest. She went to the front door and pushed it open.

The house was stifling after the brightness outside. Tom saw only dark shadows and hidden corners while his eyes adjusted. He stood there, blinking.

'Come in, do. Kate can show you round. There's a room for you next to hers,' said Ruth, leading the way into the hall.

Gradually his eyes adapted. He saw a beautiful but ancient rug on the floor, worn thin in places, its deep vermilion and gold glowing softly. Books everywhere, lining the walls, scattered over every horizontal surface. The long table with its graceful but not matching chairs, the strange arcade supported by pillars of carved wood . . . Odd splashes of colour, from the roses in a jug on the table, from the open pages of magazines, to the glinting metal of the lift in the corner. But even Tom recognized that it somehow missed being comfortable. By a long way.

'Well, where's this poem you told me about, then?'

'Over there.' Kate pointed to the wall over the door. It was written in an italic script, flowing and elaborate. Tom could not make out the text, but she'd told him what it said:

> Far, far away, without discovering
> The blue manor of Rosamund.

Hopelessly romantic, he thought. And yet he was moved by this arrival at the manor, impressed and intrigued. He couldn't wait to get to know it.

'Would you like some tea? Or something cooler? There's homemade lemonade in the fridge.'

'Lemonade sounds lovely,' Tom said.

Ruth Banniere nodded, as if he'd given the correct answer.

'Kate will show you the ropes. I'll take the lemonade out to the terrace.' She disappeared down a passage leading off the hall.

As they went upstairs, Tom said to Kate, 'Is she always like that?'

'Like what?'

'Ill at ease, nervous. Jumpy.'

'Well, she gets tired,' Kate said reasonably. 'She's a good sort, my mum.'

'The clarity of the young.' A dry voice from the first landing. A man was standing there, tall, thin, black hair untidy. He was cradling a square-shouldered bottle to his chest, the familiar green of Gordon's gin. Simon Lightowler, thought Tom. Ruth's cousin and lover, Alicia's son. Right and tight.

'Welcome,' Simon said. 'Leave your cares behind, leave your troubles at the door. There's no need to worry, no need to fret. Only perfect people are allowed in here anyway.' He stood aside to let them pass, his eyes glittering.

'What happens to the others?' asked Tom.

'They get drunk,' he said equably. Tom looked away, embarrassed. He saw something furry frisking round Simon's ankles, a snap of teeth and pointed ears.

'I didn't know you had a dog,' Tom said as a diversion, squatting down and holding his hand out. Immediately the creature bolted off down a corridor to their right. Tom stood up again, feeling a little foolish.

'Badly brought up,' said Kate, and it was not clear to whom she was referring. 'No social graces at all.' She smiled brightly, and Tom knew she was annoyed.

'That way,' said Simon, pointing where the animal had gone. 'The guest wing.' His grip on the gin seemed less urgent. He smiled suddenly, disarmingly. 'I'm glad you're here. Kate gets rather bored sometimes.' His glance passed over her, indecipherably. 'It's too remote.'

'Fifteen miles from London?' Tom raised an eyebrow. 'I've known places more isolated.'

'Of course.' Simon shrugged. 'But you need a car to get anywhere. And then you have to ask yourself whether it's worth the effort. Hours on the tube, or nonstop traffic jams.'

'Do you get away much?'

The smile became rigid. 'No, not much. It's quiet. I like it here.'

Tom remembered Kate had said that Simon was agoraphobic. He felt embarrassed again, stupidly maladroit.

'Come on,' said Kate. 'This way.'

Simon watched Kate and Tom go, and leant back against the wall. He was breathing rather fast, his hands sweaty. Too much gin. He should stick to whisky, gin never agreed with him. That stupid row with Kate and the man Byrne the other day . . . His head was swimming, his words were getting too detached, too precise. He felt an increasing disorientation, reality taking its usual short walk off the end of the pier.

The boy had been allowed in. No tree had fallen in front of the car, no animal had leapt at his throat either. The guardians of the house were keeping out of the way. He didn't understand it. Why had there been no barriers to stop these strangers? Was this some kind of game?

He heard their voices from along the corridor with foreboding. Tom so elegant with his nicely cut blond hair, smooth with energy and confidence; Kate, the golden girl, the innocent . . . He shook his head, trying to clear it. This was a dream, a gin-sodden fantasy.

The Dogfrog was back, twining round his feet, more like a cat than anything else. Why did they pretend it was a dog? He slid his back down against the wall and put his hand on its head. He'd been practising, it wasn't hard any more. He felt that if he had the nerve to touch it of his own will, then he might have enough courage to face everything else. It was a start, anyway. A small territory he had made his own.

He looked down and for a moment saw the blank, fishy eyes, the pointed red teeth and flickering forked tongue. His eyes refocused. Just an animal, tongue lolling, furry paws, waving tail.

'Why didn't you go for him?' Simon said under his breath. 'What has he done to earn his free passage?' The red eyes were unblinking, ageless, inimical. He gazed into them, fascinated as ever. 'And what do you know, my little aberration? Where will you be at the end?'

He became aware of footsteps on the stairs below. Ruth, coming to check on him. He watched her head and shoulders come level with his own, watched the way her eyes slid over the

Dogfrog as if it didn't matter and then she was standing on the landing.

'Come on,' she said gently, taking his shoulder, pulling him upright. 'You don't need that.' She extracted the bottle from his grip.

'Oh, yes I do . . . Ruth, what's he doing here? Why on earth did Kate invite him?'

'I wanted him here too. It's not much fun for Kate here all summer. And she loves him.' She raised her voice. 'Kate! Tom! Lemonade's ready!'

'Ruth, why did the Leafer let him in?'

'The Leafer?' Her mouth tightened, the lines deepening. 'Not that again. Come on, Simon, give it a rest. The Leafer doesn't exist, it's only a hallucination, a dream. I don't know why you have to go on about it.' A small pause. 'Anyway, I don't suppose Tom will be outside much.'

'The great author . . .'

'There are worse professions.'

'Come on, think of those trees giving their life blood, sacrificing their all for the sake of silly words, silly people's thoughts, cluttering, chattering, going on and on.'

'You're a fine one to talk. How many books have you read this week? Six? Ten? You fill your whole life with words written by other people.'

'And you fill your house with stories and novels and poems. Look around you. And now you've even imported your own tame spinner of tales to add to it.'

She ignored the bitterness in his tone. 'I'm sure Tom will help out in more solid ways than that. You know what the house and garden require. Many hands . . .'

'For God's sake, Ruth, not everyone shares your obsession with the house.'

'But he does,' she said softly. 'Didn't you notice? He's half in love already.'

'And what about Kate? What does she think about her lovely new boyfriend falling under the enchantment like this? Is he going to be yet another sacrifice in the cause of the house's survival? Is he going to end up drunk or mad too?'

She didn't say anything. She turned and went downstairs and he realized that his hands were still shaking. I wish this were over, he thought. I wish Ruth could face it. We're getting too close this time.

In the house he was watched by the Dogfrog. Outside, the Leafer took over. Ruth said it was agoraphobia mixed with alcohol that did it, and sometimes he knew she was right. They were not really there waiting for him. He'd read the books about it by the psychiatrists and mystics and wise men. These were projections of his subconscious, delusions which made him think he had no control. Externalizations of his fear of outside.

But still he could not bear to go out, although the Leafer had never hurt him and the Dogfrog was at best an unnerving companion. Indoors he found it easiest to keep moving. He knew what the women thought, but it wasn't the alcohol. He had found every drop in the house long ago, and it wasn't what he wanted, not really.

In truth, he didn't know what propelled him, wandering restlessly from room to room. Perhaps at some level, unarticulated, instinctive, he was aware that the answer, if there was one, lay within the manor. Sometimes he looked at the books that lay open on most surfaces as if they might offer consolation. But their dry texts were only reminders of other lives, other more vivid worlds.

What was he trying to evade?

It's getting worse, he almost said to Ruth. The corridors wind too much, the ceilings are too high, none of the doors shut properly and the shadows are deep where they have no right to be. The books are no real defence, their words contain only lies. The Dogfrog never leaves me alone now, it's getting nearer all the time, and whenever I wake in the night the Dogfrog is closer on the bed, closer to my face. He imagined those sharp teeth raking through his skin, tearing at his eyes, chewing on his lips and tongue. It's not like that, he told himself. It's just an animal, a household pet with red eyes. Ruth, can't you get me out of here?

But it was too late for that. She should have sold the manor immediately, as soon as she reached her majority. She had known its history, and she had once made an attempt to escape the place. She'd even got as far as university and what a disaster that had been. But she was anchored, embedded in the house's past, and there was no way of separating her from it or him.

He couldn't leave anyway. There were a thousand reasons, more . . . The library, the books. All he had ever wanted, all he thought he needed. Thirty thousand of them, history, philosophy, poetry, drama and fiction. Memoirs, letters, biographies, pensées, essays . . . firmly inclined towards the arts, scattered with texts he knew from university and afterwards. The collection proper stopped in 1954, when Ruth's mother had died. A few popular novels had been added since then, some volumes of poetry. Most of the newer additions belonged to Ruth. Music, scores and songs. Lieder and French melodies, complete editions of Ravel and Brahms, Beethoven and Schubert. All of Chopin in the pale pink Polish edition that she loved so much.

He saw her shoulders sagging, the weariness, the passivity. She rarely played the piano these days, and never sang. She had no energy left for anything extra. None left to contemplate the trauma it would take to get him out. She was exhausted.

That charity work does you no good, he said once, skating round the subject. It's too much, loading that on one person. You've got a full-time career, and that's more than enough.

You're jealous, she said. You could make more of an effort to get over it. Agoraphobia is not uncommon, they can treat it these days.

And in such terms did they always evade the truth of the Blue Manor. They never spoke plainly, never touched the terror of his captivity. Putting words round what was happening would give it too much validity. It would only make things worse. This way they could pretend to themselves that the Dogfrog and the Leafer and the terrible past were mere dreams, temporary delusions.

After all, no one else was ever affected by them.

Irritated, he closed the book that was lying open on the sideboard and put it back on the shelf.

He thought, I'm losing it. It's almost gone. The possibility of escape, of redemption. It was a feeling at the end of his fingertips, reaching out to touch his hands, to hold his hands and pull him free of the place. It's failing, he thought. There's not long to go.

Chapter 8

Kate and Ruth were preparing dinner. 'Have a shower, unpack, relax, put your feet up,' Kate had said when Tom offered to help. 'You can start work tomorrow, but tonight you're on holiday. Enjoy it while you can.'

The shower was a good idea, taken in the white-tiled room the size of the average living room. The bath was mounted on lion's feet and someone had hung bunches of purple plastic grapes around the copper taps. He almost laughed aloud. Kate, he thought. Exactly her kind of thing. The shower was wonderful, refreshing and oddly efficient, given the general decrepitude of the place. He washed away the dust and grime of travel, feeling an unusual impulse to sing.

Crossing the landing to his room, he heard them moving around downstairs, chattering and giggling. For a moment he stood at the banisters looking down into the empty hallway. A number of passages led from it, but he couldn't for the life of him work out where the kitchen was in relation to the bathroom. The upper floor did not correspond to the lower, there was no pattern, no long, winding passages here. All the main rooms upstairs seemed to radiate from the central stairway, divided from each other by bathrooms and dressing rooms. There was only one long corridor running along the length of the house, and that appeared disused.

He was intrigued by the shape of the manor, and wondered if the architect's plans still existed. Had it been designed like this, or had there been alterations and extensions? He didn't understand how the house connected up.

From below came the chink of glasses, the pop of a cork. Festive, jolly sounds. He'd join them. Go down as soon as he was dressed. No point in hanging about up here on his own.

And then he heard a man's voice. Not the actual words, just the timbre of it, light and amusing. Simon, drawn by the sound of women's voices. Or perhaps it was the sound of wine being opened. Kate and her mother were laughing, and then Simon joined in and he felt suddenly left out, a stranger, visitor, outsider.

A shaft of light opened briefly on to the darkened hall from the passage on the left. He heard a snatch of conversation, something about young Lochinvar, love's young dream.

Himself. His sense of humour abruptly evaporated. Was Kate laughing, too? At him? Had she sent him up here, out of the way, trying to get rid of him?

He returned to his room and sat on the bed, shivering slightly, although it was warm.

What was he doing here? A sudden conviction hit him that the presence of Tom Crabtree was emphatically not required at the Blue Manor. Kate and Ruth and Simon were a family, they were complete, the three of them. Mother, father and child. Except Simon Lightowler wasn't Kate's father, and she didn't know who her real father was. But Simon had always been there, Simon fitted the bill.

He envied Kate her family, envied her this extraordinary, disintegrating, wonderful house. Tom had no family, no home. His mother had died when he was eighteen and he had never known who his father was. He had grown up on a council estate, and the only enduring legacy from his mother Laura was a passionate love for books. *Some people say that life's the thing, but I prefer reading.* Laura had written the quotation in a flowery copperplate on sugar paper and hung it in the narrow hallway of their flat, over the front door.

They went to the library twice, sometimes three times a week, using their full quota of books. It was their chief recreation. A single parent working part-time in the local day nursery could afford little else. Alicia brought them books, of course, whenever she came to stay, armfuls of books, the latest paperbacks, secondhand hardbacks, anything she thought they might like.

Laura liked historical novels and poetry and American private eye stories. He was addicted to fantasy and science fiction, but by the time he reached adolescence their tastes overlapped. And when he was studying for A levels and started to read the classics and more literary works, Laura kept pace all the way, right up to the time of her stupid, unnecessary death.

He was still angry about it. Even now, six years later, sitting on a sagging double bed in a room where the windows didn't fit their frames, putting off joining Kate and her family, he was still angry. A hit and run driver, leaving her sprawled in the slush only yards from where he moved through the library, choosing his books.

Ruth reminded him of Laura, although they were not alike physically. His mother had been too thin, pale-skinned, pale-haired. She had been fastidious, ethereal, finicky about food. Her wispy hair fell forward over narrow, delicate features. She looked comfortable only when she was reading, curled up in an armchair, herb tea cooling.

When he was very young he had thought of her as a princess or a naiad, some exotic creature doomed to a mundane, earth-bound life.

There was that same faint air of otherworldliness about Ruth too, lines of disappointment round the eyes. And more than that. As he dressed he fretted on what made him remember his mother so vividly whenever he looked at Ruth.

She was not a happy woman. Life was hard for Ruth although he didn't know why it should be so. She had a job, she had a daughter and a lover. The house was wonderful, the garden a dream.

He pulled himself up short. No, it wasn't. The garden was a mess, and so was the house. Simon was a drunk. Who was he kidding? For a moment he frowned, resisting the grudging paths his own mind was suggesting. Middle class, went the litany, secure, professional, private, leisured, spoilt.

He half smiled. There would be little enough leisure here. The book was going to take up all his time. He was really going to get on top of it this summer. And, starkly, the thought struck him again. What was he doing here?

There was Kate, of course. But their love affair was only a term old, and who knew which way it would go? He had come because of Kate, but now it seemed reckless and unwise. He had never before spent an entire summer with a girlfriend. He had always been independent: some people called it selfish. He'd wanted to travel, to move round and see the world, without ties or responsibilities or companions, *on his own*. That was the crucial bit. That was how you made your way in life. You could rely on no one else. He had no intention of relying on Kate, either.

Why on earth had he promised to spend three months here in *Essex*, of all places? What had possessed him? And although big roads thundered around Epping and Theydon Bois, although you could see the glow of London in the dark, this place, the manor, was remote and isolated. No buses came down the forest lane, the nearest station was miles away. He would be shut up here with the three of them for the entire summer, no film or theatre, no art galleries, no proper library.

What on earth had got into Alicia? Why had she sent him here? What kind of a story could he possibly make out of this . . . wreck?

Chapter 9

'Well, *we* booked late and the only venue left anywhere in Edinburgh was the bus station.' Ruth ladled out fruit salad with abandon.

'Useful for those with a hazy sense of direction.' Kate was grinning at Ruth. 'Follow that bus, you could say, and there you'd be, in the end.'

'It was worth it. The programme was a mite ambitious, I seem to remember. *Pericles*, *Ubu Roi*, a mime version of *The Marriage of Heaven and Hell*.' She was enjoying this, Simon thought, presiding over a full table, remembering other, more optimistic times.

Phizackerley Byrne was saying even less than usual. He'd shaken hands civilly enough with Tom but now seemed preoccupied. He sat at the end of the table, toying with food as if his mind were on something quite different. He had nothing whatever to contribute to this conversation about university life. He'd volunteered that he'd gone into the army after school and that was that. Not enlightening.

Simon noticed that Tom was looking at him again. If he were American, Simon noted abstractedly, he'd probably call me 'sir'.

'Were you at Edinburgh too?' Tom asked.

'Yes, but I wasn't part of the drama society. I'd graduated a couple of years earlier. Ruth invited me along for the ride.'

'What did you do?'

Simon frowned, pretending to think hard. 'This and that,' he said. 'As I wasn't part of the show, I got landed with all the odd jobs. I mainly remember being sent out for fish and chips. Edinburgh's a *nice* city, full of people who never drop a consonant.' His voice took on a precise Scottish lilt. 'But the Fringe does let the place down so, those untidy students. Who knows what they get up to?' His voice returned to normal. 'Happy days. It was always windy, and the rain never stopped.'

'Nothing's changed, although we did do better than the bus station.' Kate was animated. 'A church just outside the city centre. Never less than a dozen punters. It was fine.'

'I bet you never had Esther Rantzen, either.' Simon gazed sourly into his glass of fizzy water. 'She did a programme on unsuccessful Fringe shows. In '74 Ruth and co. were the stars.'

'Enough to put you off for life, I would have thought,' Tom said.

'It didn't.' Ruth was looking at Simon. 'It gave him a real taste for it. RADA, local rep, the odd advert.'

' "And where is Simon now?" ' Simon finished for her. 'Not sweating my guts out at the local comprehensive, that's for sure. You know that's the choice, don't you, Tom? Those of us with arts degrees, either teaching or nothing much . . .'

'Or everything, the whole world open, anything we want.' Tom shrugged. 'It's non-specific, unconfined, that's all. You're thinking of it as a narrowing down, a kind of incarceration, and you're wrong.'

Images of imprisonment, enclosure. He's already affected, already under the spell, thought Simon detachedly. He should get out, now. What is Kate up to? There's no harm in the boy, he doesn't deserve this.

And then Byrne stood up, thanked Ruth for the meal and left, all in the space of less than a minute . . . And that's another one, Simon thought, another one under the spell. I hoped Phizackerley Byrne at least was going to get away, I wish he had. Ruth's starting to lean on him, I can see it happening . . .

Ruth was talking to him. 'And what would you recommend? Give us the benefit of this worldly wise experience.'

He could not bear mockery from her, not from Ruth. 'I wouldn't be filling my spare time listening to neurotics, for one thing.'

'Is this so much better? Where are you now, Simon?'

All at once, he swept his hand over the table and knocked his glass flying. Clear liquid ran over the tablecloth. 'At home,' he answered softly. 'At home, where we all belong.'

'This isn't my home.' Kate, leaning forward across the table, forced him to meet her eyes. 'I'm getting out of here one day. I'm going to have my own house. I shan't stay *here*!'

He stared at her for a moment. He felt old, worn-out, tired, and she was fresh and pretty as cherry blossom, and yet at that moment their eyes were like mirror images of each other.

'Go to bed, dear,' he said gently. 'Sweet dreams.'

'Don't patronize me!'

'Sorry. Sorry . . .'

'Did you have to do that?'

'Embarrass the young swain?'

'Embarrass Kate. On Monday I'm going to make an appointment with Dr Reynolds.'

'It'll cost you. He charges when no one shows up.'

'I've talked to him already. He's prepared to come out here, so you won't even have to leave the house.'

'Oh, whoopee, that's exactly what I wanted to hear.' Simon began to stack the plates. 'Reynolds doesn't matter, I'll see him if you want, if you think it'll do any good.' He ran water into the sink, noticing a new crack in the porcelain under the tap. 'But I like Tom. He's a nice lad, he doesn't deserve this. You should get rid of him, Ruth.'

'Simon, I've had enough of this! There's nothing wrong with the house, nothing we can't sort out together.'

'That's what terrifies me. It's not only Tom who should get out of here. Why don't you take Kate, why don't you all pack your bags and go?'

'Will you come too?'

'I can't!'

'But Reynolds might have some suggestions, something to offer.'

He stared at her helplessly. So many times, so many useless attempts at explanation . . . 'This is not a mind diseased, Ruth, however it may appear. There is an external reality in this house, something horrible and wrong. You're so close to it you can't see it any more. How do you get round the Leafer, what else can explain the Dogfrog?'

She began to speak slowly and clearly as if to a difficult child, typical teacher-speak. 'The Dogfrog is merely a stray, something that chooses to live with us. It's nothing special, nothing weird. Just an animal, a small, rather stupid animal. And the Leafer doesn't exist. It is not real. You know this to be true. You have acknowledged it many times.'

'Yes, but I was lying. You can make me say anything you like, I only want to please you.' He wondered if it were true. 'But leaving them aside, think what's going on here. None of us can get away. We're all trapped. Why do you think that man's

68

still here? What's-his-name Byrne? He *said* he was leaving at the end of the week. It's Saturday now and there's no sign of him going.'

'And I for one am extremely glad of it. He's a good worker.'

'And that's another thing. Does he have to join the family every evening? I know food and accommodation were part of the deal, but can't he cater for himself? Or is he some macho meathead?'

'Of course he's not! Byrne knows more about plants and gardens than I do, and he's always courteous, always even-tempered.'

'So what? He's got nothing to say for himself.'

'Well, you certainly more than make up for it. You really are extremely objectionable at times.'

'Thank you for that kind vote of confidence!' The anger was flaring again and he thought, I'm going to hit her one day, I'm going to do something dreadful . . .

He said, 'I make mistakes. I get drunk and then I don't know. But Tom and Byrne are here for a reason, Ruth, really and truly, just like the Leafer and the Dogfrog.'

'I know what's wrong here,' she said quietly. 'There's no order, nothing is fruitful, only weeds grow. It's degenerated too far. It's like chaos. Nothing works, nothing is in its place. It's falling apart, perhaps entropy is a better word. Simon, if we can just get the garden sorted, I'm sure that what you see as the Leafer will disappear. And when the house is straight, these dreams about the Dogfrog will cease.'

'Dreams, Ruth. Is that what you think? Pipe dreams fading into smoke, fading into air?' He tried to believe her, he wanted to believe in dreams. Most of the time he believed they were dreams.

He started muttering, silly words, meaningless words. Nothing else would encompass what he thought. 'I'm going to bed. Tell Byrne to move on. Do Tom and Kate a favour and send them off somewhere too. They don't need us, two worn-out old crocks.'

'Speak for yourself. I don't think of myself with quite that degree of self-pity.'

'You go too.'

'Is that what you *want*?'

'No. No. Oh God, Ruth, don't go – ' He was reaching for

her, holding on fast like a man drowning. 'Don't leave me, don't go.'

He saw, over her head, the Dogfrog squatting in the corner of the room. He saw its sleek head and bulbous eyes watching him. He saw approval in the slant of its head, satisfaction in the long, slow blinking of its eyes.

'Get me out of here, Ruth, get me away,' he said, but his words were lost, muffled by her hair, by the sweet, warm, generous flesh of her shoulders.

'Come on, old boy, come on. Bedtime.' Her arm was round his shoulder, guiding, guarding. 'Reynolds will call on Monday. Just two more nights, two days.'

'It takes three,' he said, but she didn't hear that either.

Words are like breath, he thought. Scattered wantonly into the air, and like viruses, like disease, others sometimes catch them and absorb them into their own souls. Ruth helped him upstairs as if he were ill, and he saw on every surface books and magazines and newspapers lying open, shouting their words into the air.

Chapter 10

Phizackerley Byrne walked slowly down the drive towards the cottage. He was angry with himself for not speaking, for not asking them about that old man who'd had his wallet.

For two days he'd said nothing. He'd felt blocked at every turn, usually by Kate. She must have known what she was doing. She'd been vivacious and chatty and he'd not felt free to say anything. That evening he'd noticed that she was avoiding his eyes again. Of course, she was focused on Tom: Tom was the centre of attention, the handsome young lover with his shining blond hair and soft white hands. His brand new, gleaming white T-shirts and loose linen jacket. He was presenting himself with an appealing mixture of intelligence and deference that didn't deceive Byrne for a moment.

Tom was out for what he could get, and who could blame him? The young are always predatory. Tom had found a nice little number for himself. Free board and lodging, Kate as romantic and sexual interest, a long hot summer to pursue whatever dream was currently obsessing him. He didn't dislike the boy: Tom just seemed very young, naive and absurdly ambitious about his novel.

And Kate could handle it. He had decided she was not naive, quite the opposite. The way she had rifled through his wallet, the way she quite candidly asked him to stay for her own reasons, the way she handled Simon. It added up to someone confident and in control.

Unlike Ruth. This was really why he was staying at the manor, why he entangled himself with this difficult group of people. Never mind about the old man, never mind about the strange death – had he dreamt it? Had it really happened? He wanted to help Ruth: it was quite simple. Something in him responded to her warmth, her absurd willingness to take on the troubles of the world. It made her vulnerable, but it also revealed her strength. Anyone else would have gone under years ago. And yet Ruth had taken on the extra work for the Samaritans, was out in the garden each day, ridiculous straw hat jammed over that lovely hair. He was still thinking of Ruth as he opened the door to the cottage.

Someone had been there. Open on the table, under the electric light, newspaper headlines leaped at him.

ARMY WIFE DIES IN BOMB BLAST

Twenty-eight-year-old Kristen Byrne was killed instantly yesterday by a car bomb. It happened in the secluded Dales village of Middleham, near the army camp at Catterick. The device was placed beneath a Saab belonging to Mrs Byrne's husband Major Phizackerley Byrne. Major Byrne, who has recently returned from duty in Northern Ireland, was unavailable for comment. Mrs Byrne was six months pregnant . . .

He stared at it blankly, for a moment shocked into a familiar state of refusal and grief.

He didn't recognize the newspaper report, although there had been enough of them at the time. He was appalled by its continuing power to move him. He screwed the page into a tight ball before throwing it in the wastepaper bin.

There was another page beneath it and a picture of himself, quite recognizably himself, despite the uniform, the cropped hair and unlined skin, the unshadowed eyes.

ARMY OFFICER GOES MISSING

Major Phizackerley Byrne, 40, was reported missing after an exercise on the North York Moors over the weekend. Major Byrne, whose wife was tragically killed in a terrorist bomb attack earlier in the month . . .

This one came from the *Gazette*, one of the local rags. He hadn't known it would make the press, but of course the loss of a cat would make news in Middleham.

He was shaking. What on earth had possessed him to give his real name here? He'd let it slip, he'd been seduced by Ruth and the house, he hadn't been thinking.

But who had rooted out the cuttings, who had put them on the table for him to find, and why? Would he be reported to the police? The military police were looking for him too. There was a whole network of people up in Yorkshire wondering what had happened to Phizackerley Byrne. But who had made the connections here?

And at once his mind turned to the two women who had stolen his wallet and knife, to that strange death. The old man who had returned the wallet to him must have seen all his ID.

He didn't want this. He didn't want to be reminded like this, unsubtly, crudely. It was too close anyway. He had trained himself to put away thoughts of Kristen and David. He had no desire to face that abyss again.

There was nothing to be gained from dragging it up again, from dwelling on it. He'd run, he'd left Yorkshire and the army in order to get away from it.

He'd rather cut the hedge. And if someone round here wanted him gone, wanted him away from the manor for whatever reason, he didn't see that he was under any obligation to stay. He'd simply walk out.

He went up the narrow stairs to the bedroom, resolved to leave the manor in the morning.

There was something on his bed. For a moment he thought the shadow across the pillow was human, someone's head, the hair spread wide over the cotton. But then he saw what it really was, and drew in his breath.

Over his pillow, skewered by his own knife, the knife he had buried in the forest, lay the body of a barn owl, its wings opened wide and bloody where he laid his own head.

He stood, revolted, furious. This was a desecration, something cruel and implacable. Its message was plain.

Get out.

He moved forward. Gently he pulled the knife free and carried the pillow downstairs with the bird. He left it on the draining board while he went outside and dug a large hole by the gate. He buried both pillow and bird. An act of expediency, not sentimentality.

By the time he had cleaned his hands and tidied away the mess, he had changed his mind. He'd always been stubborn. Contrary, Kristen called it.

He was going to sit it out. Let the army come and get him. He was not going to run any more.

Chapter 11

Tom lay on one elbow on the bed in Kate's room, looking down at her. There were already small lines at the corners of her eyes, crinkles in the golden skin. He could see what she would be like in ten, twenty years . . . one of those mobile, humorous faces, sharp with intelligence.

'Tell me about this place,' he said. 'Your mum wasn't really in the mood for stories tonight, was she?'

'No.' A small pause. 'Don't let Simon throw you. It was a bad day. He's always nervous when someone comes to stay. He'll settle down, tomorrow will be better.'

'Sure . . .' He didn't want to talk about Kate's uncle, cousin, whatever he was; Tom wanted to know about the manor, now, urgently. 'So, who was the architect, when was it built?'

'Nineteen-o-five is the date given. The architect's name was lost – I think he was very young, it was his first commission or something. He was killed in the First World War, and never completed another house, as far as we know. He worked from ideas given to him by Rosamund. She was the designer, the originator. Great-great-grandma was a singer, an operatic soprano who was rather in vogue for a time. She travelled all over Europe and the States . . . She paused long enough to marry and to give birth to two children, Roderick and Elizabeth, but the marriage collapsed and the husband disappeared shortly after Elizabeth was born. Yet more fatherless children,' she said softly. 'They crop up everywhere, don't they? Anyway, Rosamund built the Blue Manor as a home for the children while she pursued her career. She left her sister Margaret in charge back here. The general opinion is that Rosamund was pretty neurotic, a thorough-going man-hater. Unusual for the time, but not unknown. The only evidence for it is the entail on the manor. It bars any male issue from inheriting.'

'And how did the son – what was his name? Roderick? – how did he take that?'

'He was part of the reason why, I think. He had quite a reputation locally. Something of a rake . . . No one was safe,

74

apparently. All the girls in the village kept their heads down when Roderick Banniere was home. Rather a nasty piece of work, I believe.'

He was interested in this, imagining the two children growing up here together in the enchanted world of the manor. And that one of them should go wrong, do something dreadful . . .

He saw Kate looking at him, saw the faint curving smile and laughing eyes.

' "Let him kiss me with the kisses of his mouth for thy love is better than wine," ' she said.

Tom laid his finger across her lips. 'Enough of that. Remember the rules.' He was faintly shocked by the quotation and for the moment the past receded. There was only the present, only the beautiful present with Kate in his arms and the quiet sounds of the night. He smiled at her in the gloaming. 'Now, Kate. Beautiful Kate . . .'

It was so sweet, that moment of entry. She marked it with a small gasp, as she always did, for although it was no longer a surprise, she had the need to acknowledge the invasion.

The completion. Tom was motionless for a moment and she felt her flesh holding him, enclosing him. His hands framed her face, his eyes searched hers with intensity. And then the shift, the movement, slow and gentle at first while they stared at each other as if they were strangers, discovering souls . . . His eyes dropped as the movement became more insistent, more demanding.

He arched his back, finding her breast with his tongue, the nipple between his teeth. She loved this. In her mind she imagined three men, holding, caressing, entering, stroking. She thought of them, one on either side of him, concentrating on her.

And then she forgot the others and thought only of Tom, of his fine, elegant body, his intelligence, his . . . innocence. His mouth was now on hers and his tongue invaded her too. His fingers, on her shoulders, were digging in and it would be painful at any other time. But she loved it when he forgot to consider her. When his need took over so that she wanted to fight him, to bite and scratch and wound, to make sure that he knew the reality of her, who she really was.

'Jesus!'

75

She screamed too, a sharp pain across her shoulder, burning her skin.

Tom sprang away from her, and cold air rushed in between them. He stumbled against the bedside table and it toppled, spilling the books and the lamp over on to the floor. The noise and the sudden cold and the pain assaulted her.

She was gasping, her hand pressed to her shoulder. She saw Tom turn abruptly away and in the late evening light she saw something crawling across his back, some dark creature creeping between his shoulder blades.

He slammed the switch by the door and she saw only dark weals of blood streaking over his white back.

Blood on his back, as if it had been whipped or lashed by something. Not my nails, she thought stupidly. She was shivering. My nails are not sharp like that. She saw more blood well up from the thin red streaks and begin to dribble over his skin as he threw open the door and stood there for a moment, looking out on to the landing. She heard him take a few steps, but nothing else.

Nothing. No sound, no figure running, no distant door slamming, nothing. The house was quiet, waiting, quiescent. He came back into the room, his face almost unrecognizable with strain.

'Tom!' Her fingers, touching her own shoulder, were wet with blood. She stared at them, and then looked up at him. 'Tom, what—'

He was white and furious in the bright light. He cursed suddenly and crossed the room to the open window, dragging the curtains across.

'Are you all right?'

'No, I'm not fucking all right! Who was it, did you see?'

She shook her head. 'I had my eyes closed. Tom, your *back*!' He was twisting round, looking in the dressing table mirror. 'What happened?'

'God knows!' He was searching the room, as if he might find something broken, fallen, some explanation. He went to the door again, went further down the corridor. She waited, staring after him, not wanting to leave the bed.

He came back and sat down beside her, cautiously feeling over his shoulder. 'Who else is staying here, in the house? What's going on?'

'Tom, I . . .' Kate sat up, pulling the sheet with her, suddenly chilled. 'There was no one there. There's no one else in the house apart from the four of us.'

'You think I *imagined* this?' He stared at the blood on his hand. 'Your shoulder, too.' He touched the slashed skin. The shaking was worse.

'Who was it? Who could it have been?'

'Loopy cousin Simon perhaps? Mystery man Byrne?' He raised an eyebrow, and there was nothing humorous in his expression.

'*Simon?*' It was ludicrous. 'He's not like that! And Byrne . . . no, no, I can't believe it!'

He was pulling on pants and jeans. The wounds to his back were high across his shoulders. Again he went to the door and opened it, looking up and down the corridor. 'I didn't hear anything,' he said. 'No footsteps, nothing. I didn't even hear the door open!'

'Shock,' she said through numb lips. 'We couldn't hear anything because of the shock.'

'There's a reason for this, an explanation.' He seemed to be talking to himself. 'There's a reason, there has to be. What's going on here?'

She stood up, reaching for her night shirt. She put it on, avoiding his eyes. 'It must have been the Dogfrog, that's all. Tom, I need something warm, something comforting. A hot drink, chocolate, tea. Let's go downstairs.'

He was hanging back. 'The *Dogfrog*? Surely not!'

'Are you nervous? It'll have run off somewhere. It's very rare for it to behave like this. Come with me, Tom.'

But he stood there watching her until she'd left the room, half running down the stairs as if she wanted to get away from him. He heard her footsteps retreating, becoming lost in the greater silence of the house.

He went out on to the landing and looked down into the hall. The books and magazines gleamed palely up at him. He could smell the bowl of honeysuckle Ruth had put on the hall table that evening. He was about to follow Kate down when he heard it.

A soft, whispering sound, like the turning of well-oiled wheels. It came from the long corridor behind him. He turned and leaned against the banister, staring down the corridor at that row of shut doors, the fading wallpaper and uncarpeted planks.

This is where the hero, in films and books, always investigates, he thought. He goes to seek out the monster or the vampire or whatever it is, and tackles it.

But the cuts on his back were painful and should probably be washed. He was no hero anyway. He was a chronicler of events, not a participant. Tomorrow, when it was light and sunny once more, then he might investigate the long corridor. Not now.

But as he walked towards the stairs, as he slowly went down to the half-landing, he felt that going to find Kate was no soft option. He didn't know Kate at all.

She belongs to the house, he thought, and to no one and nothing else.

Chapter 12

'This Dogfrog thing,' Tom asked Simon at breakfast. 'Where has it gone?'

There was no shadow in the corner, no presence lurking around Simon's ankles.

Kate's cousin looked crumpled as an unmade bed, unwashed, exhausted and unloved. He reached across the table for the coffee. 'I don't know,' he said wearily. 'Why?'

'We were attacked in the night.' Tom was too furious to care how it would look. Deliberately, wanting to shock, he stripped off his T-shirt and twisted round in his chair. He heard with satisfaction a small gasp from Kate's mother. 'Why do you put up with it?'

Simon stood up. 'Ruth knows,' he said. 'I expect Kate does, too. Why don't you get her to explain?'

'You don't have to be so mysterious about it, Simon.' Kate was looking only at Tom. 'You see, it's not really a pet,' she said. She was speaking rather fast, trying to get it out before her nerve failed. 'It's a kind of stray, it doesn't belong to us. It came out of the forest years ago. It's quite tame. It seems to want to stay with us. There's not usually any trouble, it's more or less house-trained, but Simon says that sometimes it goes a bit mad, although apart from last night I've never seen it happen.'

There was a twist of amusement about Simon's mouth which Tom did not miss. 'There you are, then,' Simon said. 'There's your explanation.'

'There's nothing tame about this one,' said Tom. 'It needs taking in hand, some proper training.'

'It's just a bit shy,' said Kate.

'*Shy?* The bloody thing needs to be shot! And anyway, why on earth do you call it the Dogfrog?'

'Tradition,' Kate said. 'All the pets that have ever lived in the house are called that, aren't they, Mum?'

Ruth sighed. 'It's not very sensible, but then such traditions rarely are.' She was serenely unaware of the inadequacy of the platitude. She turned to Tom. 'I'm really sorry it hurt you.

Perhaps the heat set it off. It was almost tropical last night. We'll shut it out this evening, we can't have it doing this to our guests . . . Now, let me see that back. Has Kate given you some antiseptic?' Her voice was very mild, and he thought, this is how she speaks to those people on the phone, those suicidal fools who can't cope. Ruth was still talking. 'Are you going to start work today or would you like to get acquainted with the garden? I'd love to show you round.'

'And what if this "pet" decides to attack again?' He couldn't leave it alone. There was something about this that went beyond mere eccentricity.

'There's no need to worry, Tom,' Ruth said. 'It often sleeps during the day, and anyway if you're in the library you can shut the door.'

'It doesn't like the sun,' confirmed Kate. 'Its natural habitat is deep forest.'

He stared from mother to daughter. Both faces were smiling at him, friendly and undisturbed. He thought, am I imagining this, why do I find this story so unacceptable, so bizarre? I need to look at this creature, observe it closely. It'll be quite clear once I've actually seen it . . .

'Look, there it is!' Kate pointed to the door.

A long snout peered round the jamb, orangey-red eyes gleaming. He saw patchy fur running down its lean, wiry back, off-white, grubby-looking fur in terrible condition. Grey skin showed through here and there. Its front legs were much higher than its haunches, so that its head seemed to jut forwards awkwardly. It slunk into the kitchen, hugging close to the wall. Its claws clattered against the tiled floor. Tom stood up and crossed the room towards it. He squatted down, not too close, and examined it.

It looked more like a hyena than anything else. Tom's knowledge of the natural world belonged to childhood days and David Attenborough and he couldn't remember much about hyenas, except that they scavenged. But why would a hyena be roaming the British countryside? It was too unlikely. Perhaps it was some kind of hybrid, or a throwback.

He stared into its eyes. He saw nothing there but inimical hatred. For two pins, he thought, it would rip my throat out. Its lip curled slightly, revealing yellowing teeth. A waft of foul-smelling breath struck him.

80

He stood up hastily, turning back to the table where three pairs of eyes watched him. 'What is it?' he said. 'A hyena? One of those Australian wild dogs?'

'Nonsense,' said Ruth briskly. 'A cross collie, I think.'

And when he looked again at it, the front legs seemed more in proportion and the fur glossy. It had been in the shadow of the wall, of course. He must have been mistaken. 'OK,' he said. 'But shouldn't it be on a lead or in a cage or something? It's not safe as it is.'

'A lead! What a good idea.' Ruth went to the cupboard beneath the sink and brought out a ball of string.

'You'll need a collar. I'll get one in the village later,' said Kate. Tom glanced sharply at her. There was something surreal about this conversation, something quite lunatic.

It was a relief when there was a tap on the back door and Byrne came in, dressed in jeans and an open-necked shirt, already slightly sweaty from walking in the sun.

'Morning,' he said in that slow, soft voice. 'The kitchen garden today?'

'You've finished the hedge?' Ruth suddenly flushed with pleasure. 'Oh, wonderful. This is really splendid. I must come and see right away ... Why not take a day off, Byrne, treat yourself?'

'I'd rather keep going.'

'On a Sunday? Oh, no!' But as she spoke she took down a floppy straw hat that hung by the door.

'Well, you're going to be out there,' Byrne said reasonably. 'I'm happy to take a turn.'

'Fresh air. Now that's the thing.' Simon was watching them. 'Honest labour, "sheer plod makes plough down sillion shine" and all that. The night's dreams will recede.' He was pouring coffee, his words skittering wildly, frivolously.

'Are you going to give them a hand then?' Kate said.

'Not today, dear. Some other time, perhaps.'

The phone rang.

Simon picked it up. 'Hello?'

Nothing, dead silence. He put the receiver down, frowning. This was getting beyond a joke. Through the window he could see Ruth at work in the kitchen garden. Byrne was there too, working alongside. They were deep in conversation. For a while he watched them, the way they moved together along the narrow paths to the greenhouse. They were framed by the window like a Dutch painting. It seemed tranquil, peaceful.

He wished he could join them, but it was far too hot anyway. Instead he pottered around the kitchen for a while, desultorily tidying and straightening. For a while he arranged the cookery books on the window sill. Vegetarian and Indian cookery together, low-fat and Japanese separately.

Then he sat at the hall table thumbing through a magazine. Before long he was up again, off to the library, searching for a book which contained a half-remembered line of verse: *The late year lies down the north*, but he couldn't find it anywhere. Perhaps it was a song, something Ruth used to sing.

He left the books of poems on the table and went upstairs. He stood for a while at the landing window, watching a flight of swallows high in the sky above the lake.

In the bathroom he filled the tooth mug with water and began to drink, swallowing pint after pint. And as the water ran, as it dripped over his mouth and chin, he began to cry.

It was a relief to get out of the house. The fine gravel paths dividing the kitchen garden were hazed over with dandelions and couch grass. Ruth was on her knees, fork in hand, struggling with a thistle.

'It'd be much easier to spray weedkiller on this lot. It's not as if you want anything else to grow there,' Byrne said.

'I know, but I can't feel it's right. I don't trust chemicals. Upsetting the natural balance, as they say.'

'So you're going organic?' He surveyed the web of intricate paths, the maze of box hedging.

She sat back on her heels. 'One day it's going to be a market garden, or a nursery. I have this dream. I'm going to give up teaching, take early retirement or something. There's no satisfaction in education nowadays. Too much paperwork, too many cuts, too much competitiveness . . . I'd really like to spend my time out here, getting it right, making it fruitful and productive.'

Byrne knelt down beside her and started to pull at weeds. 'Have you always lived here?' he asked.

'All my life.' She sighed. 'I grew up here with Simon. It's why he loves it so much. It's home to both of us. Alicia, Simon's mother, looked after me as if I were her own child.'

'What happened to your mother?'

'I never knew her.' She sounded sad. 'She died when I was born.'

'Your father?'

'Listen, why don't you take over here and I'll sort out those lettuce seedlings?' Ruth had stood up, turning away from Byrne, but not before he had seen the pallor in her face, the panic in her eyes. There were so many areas out of bounds. His past, her father . . . Byrne wondered, yet again, why he had not asked her about the old man.

He got to his feet and followed her over to the greenhouses.

'Ruth, there's something else. Something I've been meaning to ask you ever since I arrived.'

'Go on.' She sounded encouraging but there was tension, wariness, in the way she bent over the trays of seedlings on the ground.

'I never told you what happened before I arrived here, did I? You see, I'd been hitching and these three . . . vagrants took my wallet.'

'Hitch-hiking is always so risky, isn't it?'

'I can usually take care of myself. But this was different.' He paused, wondering how to present it to her. 'I'm not even sure I'm remembering something that actually happened, or whether it was some kind of dream, a hallucination.'

She glanced at him. 'You don't look like someone who has trouble telling what's real.'

'There were two women,' he went on. 'And a man. And one of the women used my pocket knife to kill the man—'

'That trick!' She was almost laughing at him. 'Oh, poor Byrne, a stranger in the area and not knowing about our local celebrities.'

'What?' He stared at her.

'Performance artists, I think they call themselves. They delight in upsetting the unwary. How horrible for you to come across them like that! And you say they're the ones who took your wallet! Well, I think it's time someone put a stop to their tricks, it's not fair.'

'Ruth, this was for real!'

'Why didn't you report it to the police, then?' she asked, rather sharply.

'There was no body,' he said. 'I must have fainted or

something because when I awoke they were gone. But my knife was stained with blood and there was blood on the grass.'

'They've been known to use unusual props,' said Ruth, wrinkling her nose with distaste. She pulled off her gardening gloves. 'Some people find them offensive. They love to shock. But taking your wallet! Now, that you must do something about. In our blessedly material society, theft of property has always been rated more highly than damage to the sensibilities, hasn't it?' She was twinkling at him, as if it was some kind of joke. 'You really ought to have gone to the police.'

He drew out the wallet from the back pocket of his jeans and showed it to her.

'Oh, you said you'd got it back, I remember.' She was frowning.

He nodded. 'That old man. He had it. The two women, those performance artists, were with him this time. They seemed to have transferred their allegiance. Do you know who he is?'

'Was everything there? Your money?' She was ignoring what he'd said.

'Yes, and more. But who is this man? Why does he hang out with those two hags?'

'I've no idea.' She shrugged. And all the signals were: don't ask any more, change the subject, I don't want to talk about this.

He put his hands on her shoulders, forcing her to look at him. 'Ruth, come on. What's the big secret? Why did he do this?'

'I don't know! Why should you think I know? It's nothing to do with me. Perhaps you should go and find him so you can ask him yourself. If you can't bear to leave it alone!' She pulled herself away from him, searching in her pocket for a handkerchief. She was near to crying.

He was appalled. 'Ruth, I'm sorry. I didn't mean to upset you.'

'I'm not upset! But you've got your wallet back. I don't know what the fuss is about, I don't know why you want to keep *on*!'

And she whisked away from him, half running down the paths towards the orchard, scattering the seedlings as she went.

Tom and Kate stood together in the library. He was carrying his folder with his pads of paper and 2B pencils. He could find nothing to say. The library was like Paradise to him.

84

The room was lined with books, like so much of the manor, but the shelves and the floor were of a pale, clear wood and the effect was the opposite of dark and gloomy. Faded Persian rugs of soft blues and greens were scattered here and there. There was a baby grand piano standing by the door, its top propped open. Stacks of music were balanced on the stool.

The room was built into a bay, and tall, wide windows and glass doors looked out on to the meadow which had once been a lawn. It was stiflingly hot, the morning sun streaming across the dusty spines.

Kate went to the bay and opened the French windows. Fresh but not noticeably cooler air flooded through the room. 'There,' she said, sparkling. 'What could be better?'

'Hm?' He had taken a book from the shelves, a history of Epping Forest.

'English history over there, literature and criticism here, poetry and drama . . .' She pointed out to him the various categories and he listened with half an ear. He was looking at the desk. It stood in the bay, mahogany, he thought, wide and elegant, with two rows of drawers on either side and an ink stand. There was a chair he'd sell his soul for, light and graceful and upright. 'Rennie Mackintosh?' he hazarded.

Kate nodded. 'There used to be four of them, but they're rather fragile. The others didn't survive.'

'I'll take care, don't you worry.' He looked round at the shelves again. 'Lord, who on earth put all these in order?'

'Rosamund started the collection, I think. But it was John Downie, her son-in-law, who put it in order and used it most. He was a fanatic reader. He'd been gassed in the First World War and was confined to a wheelchair. That's why there's a lift in the hall, why there are no steps inside the house, only ramps.'

He had opened his folder and started to lay out the paper and pencils in the straight lines he always found so harmonious.

He heard her say softly, 'I'll come and get you when lunch is ready . . .' and then there was the sound of the door closing.

He was alone in the library. For a while he roamed the room, checking that the Dogfrog was nowhere about, working out the categories. Then he sat on the Mackintosh chair and stared out of the window at the bright meadow of grass, dappled by the leafy shade from the surrounding trees.

The sky was cloudlessly clear. Somewhere he could hear a

lark sing dizzy, elaborate trills. The house itself was quiet around him. It sounded as if everyone else had gone out.

This was it. This was what he had always dreamed of, time and space and freedom to write. This was his great chance to find out whether he had it in him to be a writer.

The house waited, its blank and empty rooms inviting invention. He remembered what Alicia had told him. She'd said that he would find a story here, held within the bricks and mortar of the house's structure. 'It's full of stories,' she'd said. 'Not just books. Everyone who stays there finds it. Stories seem to proliferate in the manor. Rumours, gossip, history . . . it's almost a kind of Babel. If you want to write, your story will find expression at the manor.'

But now he knew something else. The house itself would be the centre of his book. With this first thrill of excitement he let his mind wander around the idea.

The manor's existence spanned the century, its inhabitants had lived through all the great upheavals. He thought of John Downie, anchored to a wheelchair, wrecked by that vicious, wasteful war, ordering the room where he now sat. He thought of Rosamund, the singer who had hung that strange poem over the front door, who had rejected men, including her own husband.

The poem. There was no author's name on it, he didn't know who'd written it. He stood up again, went to the shelves and found the section for poetry.

A volume of Baudelaire, another of Verlaine. But nothing else, not even an anthology. It was a song, he remembered, and went over to the piano. The pile on the seat consisted of Schubert, Schumann, Wolf, Fauré. He stopped there and scanned through the three books of Fauré melodies. All very charming, very exquisite, but nothing under the right title.

He turned back to the piano. A volume of songs was open on the stand. He picked it up. The songs were by Henri Duparc, a name he didn't recognize. A slim volume, just a dozen songs.

And there he found it, 'Le Manoir de Rosemonde'.

It was strangely apropos. *Like a dog love has bitten me . . .* The wounds on his back were still painful.

The first song in the book caught his imagination, too. *My child, my sister . . . to live together.* He sat back in the Mackintosh chair and thought.

There would be years of research, letters, diaries, newspapers, records to be looked up, if he decided to take the family's history literally. This could be an enormous project, something which would take more than one summer.

And he had an idea. The French poems had set it off. His pencil was already in his hand, the lined page open before him. He would do the research, of course he would. He would be conscientious, a real scholar . . . But he could start now, just start and fill in the details later. He wrote:

There is a child in one of the upper rooms. She is arranging her toys in a line on the bed, humming quietly to herself. The two dolls are separated by a bear, but she is not looking at them. She starts to talk to the furry creature on the floor.

'Now, you sit there like a good baby and don't fuss. I want none of your nonsense today. There's too much to do.'

Her pictures are stacked against the wall, their faces turned away from her. There is a rug by the bed, a chair and dresser over by the window, but nothing else in the room. The trunks and packing cases are still downstairs.

She hears the men moving about, clattering over the bare boards. The house smells of fresh paint and new woodwork, bracing, uncomfortable smells.

Elizabeth sighs. She looks round. The Dogfrog is waiting so she makes him jump up beside Letitia. She is glad he's come with them, although Roddy always teases her about him. He's jealous, Mummy says, because he doesn't have a private friend too.

She can hear Roddy stamping along the corridor downstairs, whistling shrilly. A door bangs, and she hears him outside. She crosses the room to the window and looks down.

He is there, kicking at a pile of bricks left by the builders. He looks up and sees her.

'Well, Lizard, how do you like it?'

'It's all right,' she says cautiously.

'It's better than that, shrimp. This is really something special!'

He takes off then, running across the terrace and jumping down the steps to the newly seeded lawn. She watches him tear across the bright grass towards the trees. Soon he is lost in the great shadows.

She looks down at the wall beneath her window. Bare grey stone, harsh-coloured, harsh-textured. It will look better with

climbing plants on it, she thinks. Mummy will plant them, or
Auntie Margaret. Ivies are pretty all the year round and grow
quickly. They have leaves like hands, with fingers to wave and
cling. Elizabeth knows that once there is an ivy around her
window, waving its friendly hands at her, she will be quite safe,
the new house won't feel nearly so strange.

She's glad that all her friends are here, the dolls and the bear
and the Dogfrog. And when she helps her mother plant the ivy
under the window then the garden too will begin to feel like
home.

Tom shifted uneasily against the chair. It felt as if his T-shirt
was sticking to the scratches on his back.

Not bad, he thought, the Dogfrog fits in rather well. The girl
is Elizabeth, Rosamund's daughter. The house has recently been
finished, it's 1905, they've just moved in . . .

And the brother, Roderick. Where was he off to while the
house was being arranged? Running like a mad thing through
the trees . . . Roderick would be off down the village, of course,
leaving the domestic stuff to the women . . .

He stood up, his eyes scanning the shelves. How old were
they, and why had he assumed that Roderick was the elder?
Kate would probably know, or Ruth. This was a family which
kept records, family trees, diaries, that kind of thing. Alicia had
said as much.

He gazed out of the window at that great meadow of grass
rippling in the slight breeze, the clear sky stretching far and
wide. Did he really want to clutter his story with facts? Couldn't
he just write the tale, set here, using names from the past? After
all, everyone concerned would surely be dead by now . . .

It was such a very long time ago.

Chapter 13

Phizackerley Byrne decided to skip lunch at the manor. He took bread and cheese from the kitchen and ate it in the cottage. He needed to think. Why had Ruth become so upset again? He wished he hadn't pushed it, and yet he couldn't see what he'd done wrong. There were so many no-go areas, so many things she didn't want to face.

He wondered what the block was. Why she wouldn't talk about her father, about that old man or the Dogfrog or any of these mysteries? She lived in the manor, she owned it, but she seemed to have no curiosity about it. It held her like some enchantment, draining will and energy . . . He stopped. This was getting absurdly fanciful.

Beer, that was what he needed. A long cool pint or three in an ordinary English pub on the green. And perhaps one or two enquiries to make, if the opportunity arose. He set off down the long lane and the tarmac bounced the heat back at him.

He wasn't going to take the money to the police. Why speed up the process of discovery? He knew that someone was on to him, that it was only a matter of time before his recent past was common knowledge, but he felt no urge to hurry things along.

He was going to find out who that old man was, and why he wanted Byrne out. And those two women. He had no doubt that they had been behind the mutilated owl and the newspaper cuttings. Whoever they were, whatever they wanted, these were the techniques of terrorism.

Performance artists! It seemed ludicrous. He didn't believe it. They were thieves and worse. Had the hags given the wallet to the old man, had he asked for it? What relationship were they to each other?

At the road he turned left, away from the forest and the Epping High Road. The first pub he came to was the Sixteen-String Jack. He opened the door but the place was crammed to overflowing with youngish men in open-necked shirts. The scent of aftershave and clean sweat was too much, the monotonous throb of music overpowering.

He walked on, down the hill into the centre of the village.

There were two other pubs, each similarly crowded. People spilled out on to the pavements, clustered around the doorways. In the end he pushed his way to the bar of the Bull and drained one pint standing there. He decided to take the next outside, but the benches were all occupied.

He crossed the road to the green. He passed a crowd of children and adults gathered around a Punch and Judy stand and paused to watch for a while. It was quite funny, a rather adult show, sending up politicians and the media. The Judy doll looked remarkably like the current minister for health . . .

He smiled and turned away, searching for some shade. A long avenue of mature oak trees bisected the green. He settled against one of them, and sipped his pint. He could hear laughter from the Punch and Judy, the shrieks of children.

He was wondering where to start. There were a number of elegant houses round the green, Edwardian or earlier. He considered asking at the pub, but somehow he didn't think that an elderly man in such a beautifully cut suit would spend much time in the local boozer. Tomorrow, he'd try at the post office. They'd probably know anyone of pensionable age, anyone with such remarkable style . . . Theydon was a small place to tackle.

A fair proportion of the population was sitting in front of him, sniggering at the show. It didn't lend itself to full-throated laughter. And then the sniggering changed to something else, an uneasy murmuring. Abruptly, the gathering broke up. Several of the adults pulled their children away, rushing them across the grass out of sight and sound of the show, their faces affronted and angry.

Byrne didn't understand at first. He finished his pint and stood up, wandering closer. Only a handful of children remained, and one little girl was crying.

The top of the stand was splattered with red paint. The Judy doll was splayed across the canvas, the top of its head sliced open. A shiny mess of red and white dribbled from the plastic skull to run over the front of the kiosk.

Clever, he thought, if somewhat ill-judged . . . As he watched, a woman came round the side of the stand and picked up the cap on the grass. Only a few coppers . . .

'Not much of a take,' he said, and then he recognized who

she was. Her black hair hung straight in greasy rat-tails, her white skin was like the underside of a fish.

'Killed anyone else recently?' he said.

A sort of laugh, a twist to the side of her mouth. And then, lightning quick, her hand darted out and scooped at the red and white mess on the stand.

She flung it in his face before he realized what she was doing. Slimy offal ran over his skin, not paint, not plastic. Gagging, he reached out, grabbing for her wrist.

But she was already away, streaking across the grass towards one of the big houses. In a fury, he pulled back the curtain of the stand, expecting to find the other two there, the man with the short hair and the other woman.

It was quite empty. He stood there, trying to clear the stuff from his eyes and mouth, watching her disappear into the large, red-brick Georgian house at the end of the green.

There was no answer at the front door. He leant on the bell and hammered with his fists. In frustration, he stood back and looked up at the blank windows. No curtains, no sound. If he hadn't seen her enter the house, he would have sworn that it was empty.

Cursing under his breath, he walked to the side of the house to see if there was a back entrance.

'Byrne? What are you doing here?' Kate was standing at the gate. 'Whatever happened to you?'

Tom Crabtree was with her, his mouth prim with disapproval. 'Been in a fight, have you?'

'No! Some damn female threw this muck at me!' He was too furious to wonder why they were there. 'She came in here. I recognized her at the puppet show, she was the one who stole my wallet.'

'She came *here*?' Kate sounded incredulous. 'She can't have! This is where Uncle Peter lives.'

He stared at them. She mistook it for incomprehension.

'Great-uncle Peter. He was married to Aunty Alicia. He's Simon's father.'

And then, as if on cue, the door opened.

The old man stood there, the pale linen uncreased and immaculate as ever.

'Ah, there you are, all of you. Do come in.'

Kate went up to him and stood on tiptoe to kiss the man's cheek. Crabtree held out his hand. The man looked over their heads to Byrne. 'I think you need to get cleaned up,' he said. 'Do come in.' It sounded the most gracious of invitations.

'There's a woman here,' Byrne said. 'I want to speak to her.'

'Of course you do,' said Simon's father. 'But I'd like to have a word first.'

'She's the daughter of my cook,' he said. 'Jan's not been well, but there have been signs of an improvement lately. She's – rather depressed, has been getting into bad company.' Peter Lightowler was standing at the door of the downstairs wash-room while Byrne dabbed ineffectually at his shirt with a sponge.

Kate and Tom were making tea in the kitchen. There was no sign of the woman with black hair.

'She's damned dangerous. I met her once before—' Byrne stopped. Should he mention that bizarre event, or not? There had been two of them. What about the other?

'Where is she now?' he said.

'Upstairs, resting. Jan's on medication.' Byrne could see Lightowler in the mirror, could see that the lines on his face were deep and harsh. 'But she sometimes forgets to take it and then we get these extraordinary outbursts. I'm so sorry you've been inconvenienced. You must allow me to make reparation.' He took from his breast pocket a bill-fold and peeled off a twenty-pound note.

This was absurd, ridiculous. Byrne dried his hands and turned to face the man in the door. 'I've not quite got through the money you've already given me.'

'But you're still at the manor, I see.' Lightowler's voice was unstressed, amused. He was relaxed, leaning elegantly against the door.

A pause. Byrne said, 'I don't like having my hand forced. You can have it back, now I know who you are.'

'Keep it.' The man spoke abruptly. 'It doesn't matter.'

'I don't understand this. *Why* do you want me to leave?'

'Ah, that's easy.' Lightowler shrugged. 'I very much want to reopen communication with my son. I'm afraid it's one of these complicated things that always seem so ludicrous to outsiders. We have been – somewhat estranged. And as you see, I am no longer young and it seems . . . inadequate to approach the end of life with the closest of family relationships under stress. A private matter, you understand, between father and son. I felt, rightly or wrongly, that a stranger on the premises was an unnecessary pressure in a delicate situation. Nothing personal, I do assure you. But since young Tom Crabtree's arrival, I shall clearly have to think again.' He came towards Byrne. 'My apologies, Mr Byrne, for any embarrassment I may have caused you.' He was holding out his hand, and Byrne took it.

It was an explanation of sorts. Lightowler could be telling the truth. It just seemed rather unlikely. There was too much money involved, too much coercion.

'And now I hear the sound of tea being poured. You will join us, won't you? To show that there's no hard feelings?'

Byrne followed him along the hall to the drawing room. In the doorway he paused, staring.

The room was lined with shelves. It was full of books, ancient books with leathery spines and indecipherable titles. Many of them were in French or Italian, Byrne saw. They looked valuable, but he was no expert. The room reminded him unavoidably of the library in the manor.

Kate was sitting on a leather chesterfield, pouring tea. Tom was examining a volume of poetry, his mouth soundlessly shaping the words.

The words Byrne wanted to say to Peter Lightowler seemed wildly inappropriate, brutish and vulgar.

He said, 'But what were you doing with my wallet?'

At the same time Kate spoke, and her high, light voice dominated. 'What's this about, Uncle Peter? Who is this woman?'

The old man settled himself next to her, ignoring Byrne. 'Jan. She's poor Louise's daughter, you remember.'

'I thought she'd gone to college.'

Lightowler shook his head. 'It didn't work out. She's been seduced by the world of entertainment . . . or, rather, by a certain person with a liking for melodrama. He's the puppet master. You know, the show on the green. The puppet show.' He looked at Byrne, standing rigidly by the door. 'Do come and sit down, Mr Byrne. Let me tell you about our strange puppeteers . . . I believe the fashionable term nowadays is performance artists.'

Almost against his will, Byrne found himself sitting on a chair with his back to the window, taking tea from Kate, behaving as if this were a perfectly ordinary tea party.

Lightowler settled himself more comfortably against the sofa, and the light caught sideways across his lined face. There was a sensual curl to his thin mouth, an ironic droop to his eyes. He was wearing a paisley bow tie, and his cufflinks were studs of emerald. It was not hard to see where Simon's theatrical inclinations had come from.

Lightowler was revelling in the attention, enjoying the performance. 'You have to see them in context. The puppet show is a rather unusual slant on an ancient tradition,' he said. 'It's very much a local variation on the original theme. Blood has always been spilt in the forest, after all. Some say it was the site of Boudicca's defeat by the Romans and that over eighty thousand Britons died at Amersbury Banks, those great earthworks between the manor and the High Road. There's no proof, but the legend persists . . . And of course, it's the first dumping spot out of London. It's not unusual to find some section of the forest cordoned off while a search is being made. Murder, drugs, violence, rape . . . the forest has seen the lot.

'Not all of it has been so black, however. I can remember when they used to run special trains from the East End. Charabancs, coaches, everyone came to the forest on bank holidays. It was quite the thing, a very jolly kind of place. People came courting, came with their families . . . works outings, youth clubs. At Rigg's Retreat there was a helter-skelter, and a fair on Chingford Plain. I think there's still a fair there at Easter and Whitsun, even now.' He sighed. 'So long since I've been to a fair. But somehow blood will out, as the master said. Our black puppeteers are a fair synthesis of the forest's past, don't you think? Well in accord with contemporary life. Think of those films and video things. I don't know why people should pretend to be squeamish, when you've only to turn on a TV . . .

'But enough of this. I do apologize, a favourite hobby horse of mine . . . Now, Tom. Do tell me about this exciting project of yours. It sounds most intriguing.' He conferred the honour of his attention on Tom as he spoke and it was as if Byrne had never been in the room.

Tom, most unusually, was caught off guard. 'Well, it's very

94

good of you to give your time and I'm immensely grateful, but I don't know how far this is going to be an accurate record.'

'Tom's going to write about the family!' said Kate.

'I thought I would fictionalize the whole thing. I don't want details,' he protested.

'About the house, and what happened there.' Kate was really taking off on this, Byrne could see, playing up to Lightowler all the time. He wondered what the attraction was.

'And you've come to me for information?' Lightowler's voice was smoothly urbane. 'I shall naturally be delighted to help.'

'Have you got lots of diaries and letters and books and things hidden away?' Kate was looking round the room. 'I've never really explored this house.'

'You must come and spend the day here soon, Kate. Explore to your heart's content.' The old man looked at her fondly, and Byrne saw something more than affection in his gaze.

Something avid, something predatory.

Tom said quickly, 'But we wouldn't want to put you out. You mustn't feel obliged . . .'

Lightowler said, 'Just one question, Tom. I think you'll have to make up your mind whether you're going to be writing fiction or history. It would be too easy to offend. For example, what does Ruth feel about this?'

Kate frowned. 'She doesn't want to know. We asked her at lunch. Mum never talks about the past, she finds it depressing. She says she doesn't mind what Tom writes, so long as he changes the names.'

'It's *not* going to be an accurate history, it's going to be a novel. Even the geography of the place will be different. But I'd like to know your side of the story as a background for it . . . if you don't mind, Mr Lightowler?'

There was a faint smile on the cracked face. 'I'm not really the best person for the job, you must understand. It's a shame that Ruth refuses to help, because, properly, the story of the house belongs to her, to the female side of the family.' His hand momentarily brushed Kate's knee as he reached forward to take his tea. Byrne saw, with surprise, that his nails were filthy, lined with dirt. The old man was looking at Tom. 'Kate knows all this, it's ancient history.'

'I had to ask your permission,' she said. 'It's not for me to speak—'

'Ill of the dead?' He completed it for her and she blushed. 'Never mind, my dear,' he said. 'It was so long ago.' He settled back against the sofa, stirring the tea thoughtfully. The performance resumed.

'I never knew Rosamund. I was Roderick's child, born on the wrong side of the blanket, fathered on a village wench, one Jessie Lightowler. My advent caused some distress, contributed to my father's downfall.' He stared, unseeing, into his cup. 'That righteous trio of women, the matriarch Rosamund, her sister Margaret (a bitter, dried-up spinster of no account) and the beautiful young Elizabeth conspired together. Roderick, the only son, the only male, was out. Banished for the not unusual mistake of begetting a child out of wedlock . . .

'Are we boring you?' A sudden sharpness in the dry voice as he looked at Byrne.

'Not at all,' he said courteously. 'But if you don't mind, I think I should be getting back to the manor. I need to change this shirt.' He stood up. 'Thank you for the tea. Goodbye, Kate, Tom . . . Mr Lightowler.'

He found his way out and closed the front door behind him. He wanted to get out into the air, where the remains of the puppet show still stood on the green.

He wanted to get away from Peter Lightowler. It was a reaction he didn't wish to examine, but it was overpoweringly strong. He disliked the man, he disliked his drawling voice, the ancient, filthy hand on Kate's knee, the cool explanation of his bizarre and extraordinary actions.

He didn't trust the way Lightowler had told him to keep the money. It was as if Lightowler was trying to buy him.

He resolved to give it back.

Chapter 14

It was very hot that afternoon. Even the cow parsley was wilting at the roadside, its scent masked by the smell of melting tar. As Tom and Kate walked back to the manor from Theydon, Tom thought of something that had been nagging at the back of his mind. He said, 'Your Uncle Peter never mentioned Simon, never even asked how he was. Don't they get on?'

Kate sighed. 'It's really Mum's fault. She can't stand Uncle Peter, won't even have him in the house. And Tom, do you mind not telling her where we went this afternoon? She hates the idea of me having anything to do with Uncle Peter.'

He frowned. 'You want me to lie? Byrne was there too, remember?'

'I know. Perhaps I'd better have a word with him as well.'

He was puzzled. 'This seems rather excessive, Kate.'

'It probably won't come up. Leave me to do the talking, if you'd rather. Mum's very protective of Alicia, you see. There was a messy divorce between Alicia and Peter, and Alicia was the one who kept the children, the one who brought up Simon and Mum. It's not surprising their loyalties are with her.'

'Why did Lightowler come back to Theydon, then? What's in it for him?'

'He grew up here, but I think it's more than that. He told me he wants to resolve things before he dies. He's almost eighty-five, you know.'

'He had Simon rather late in life, then.'

'Not really.' She shrugged. 'Simon's in his mid-forties.'

'He looks older.' Tom squinted up at the cloudless sky. Burning, blazing blue. 'I'd give anything for a swim,' he said, changing the subject. He'd had enough of Kate's complicated family relationships.

'What a good idea!' Kate ran her hand down his bare arm, her fingers light and cool. 'As soon as we're home.'

'You've got a pool?'

'Nothing so obvious. But there is the lake.'

'Sounds wonderful.'

He hadn't explored the grounds yet, not beyond the terrace and kitchen garden. He wanted to see more of the manor's surrounds, to get the feel of this strange place isolated within a triangle of woods, within a triangle of motorways. It had always been isolated, he thought. When Rosamund built it, when Elizabeth and Roderick lived there, it would have felt remote because of the woods, the forest all around. London would have been quite a journey away. Some of the people living in the village would never have been there . . .

And now the manor was remote again, because of the roads. Not far off he heard traffic thundering. To Stansted, to Cambridge, to Birmingham . . . A noose of bright, fast moving machinery surrounded them like a necklace of fine jewels.

They approached the lake through the wood beyond the kitchen garden. A wide expanse of water lay open to view, cool and calm as glass, beneath tall trees. It was hidden from the house by a hedge, by shrubberies and orchards.

It lay in deep shade. The water was quite black, fathomless. There was vivid green weed covering one part of it. A small island choked by rushes and weeds stood in the centre. There were no ducks, no water birds, no ripples from fish.

There were rocks around the perimeter of the lake, vast slabs of granite and sandstone, deliberately placed there in Rosamund's time, said Kate. She had planted the rhododendrons and azaleas, the magnolias and flowering cherries. 'It's a real wonderland,' Kate said. 'The garden of Eden . . .'

'Complete with weeds.' Tom was becoming faintly depressed by the scale of it. 'This is going to take infinite resources, infinite time,' he said. 'I can't imagine how your mother can contemplate it.'

'We can't do anything else.' Kate met his eyes. 'Mum's not unrealistic. There's a long-term plan for all of this. The kitchen garden first, and then everywhere else. We've tried other things over the years. At one time we thought the flower garden would be the thing, but economics took over. We need to grow saleable produce. The rest will have to run wild for quite some time yet.'

'It'll be that much more difficult to sort out then.'

'Have you any other suggestions?' Kate stopped and faced him with imperfectly suppressed anger. Behind her the lake was undisturbed, an impassive black mirror for their actions.

'Do you think she hasn't *tried*? The National Trust won't look at the Blue Manor unless we can endow it. We can't sell it, can't even lease it out. It belongs to us, whether we like it or not.'

'Simon doesn't seem overmuch concerned.'

'He has his own problems,' she said.

'*What* problems? What is it with cousin Simon? Why is he so difficult?'

'He's a drunk.' She shrugged dismissively. 'All sorts of hang-ups and neuroses. Mum thinks he just needs reassurance, an extended period of rest and recuperation (he is an actor, after all. Resting carries no stigma), but I don't know. I think she'd be better out of it.'

'Leaving the manor?'

She seemed shocked by the idea, as if it had never occurred to her before. 'Leaving? Oh no. No, no one ever leaves the manor before the time is right.'

He stared at her with frustration. 'Kate, I just *don't* understand.'

'It's all right for you, it's all material for your book, it doesn't really matter.' She swung away from him, gazing out over the lake. He could see that she was breathing hard. He took half a step towards her and then stopped.

She turned towards him. She said slowly, 'You'd better go, Tom. Get away from here.'

'What do you mean?' It was like walking on quicksands, this shifting ground of incomprehension between them. He desperately wanted to clarify, to understand what she meant but he found himself saying weakly, 'What are you playing at?'

She looked at him, and it was just Kate, dear, familiar, pretty Kate with her short dark hair and pointy chin. Then he saw a glint in her eye, and suddenly understood. This was a joke, a small farce.

'Leave the manor, Tom. You don't belong. This won't make a book for you.' And the kindness, the tolerance in her voice was the most artificial thing of all.

He looked at the glassy surface of the lake, at the graceful birches and beeches overshadowing it, and knew he didn't want to swim there. It was stagnant, clogged with leaves and weed.

'Let's get back to the house,' he said. 'Whatever you think, I know I can write this thing. I want to get down to work.'

She did not argue, but as they walked towards the house across the grass meadow, Kate said, 'I mean it, though. This is nothing to do with you. You should get out.'

He saw, beyond the kitchen garden at the end of the long drive, the neat outline of the thatched cottage by the gate. 'I'll stay there,' he said, not really meaning it. 'If it becomes a problem, I'll move in with old Phizackerley Byrne.'

Chapter 15

In the sky that night, the brightening star was seen for the first time by people living in and around London. It had been heralded in the papers and media for quite some time and it was almost an anticlimax to see it there.

Twinkling quietly, a pinpoint of light flared amber and gold over the northern horizon, within a half-circlet of other, more subtle stars. Its impact would have been limited to technical journals and enthusiastic amateurs were it not for the approach of the year two thousand.

The point that there were still five years to go to the millennium made little difference. People had always argued about the exact dating of Christ's birth. The significance of this new star was exalted and exaggerated, particularly by the religious. The more optimistic Christian sects talked of a second coming, of a new beginning for the world. Others saw it as a reminder of judgement, the last trump, the promise of hell-fire. They looked at the destruction of the environment, the spiralling wars and increasing levels of famine.

People found chaos beckoning at the end of the century. The millennium was catching up on those parts of the world following the Gregorian calendar, and it brought with it a sense of crisis.

Add to this a new star, flaring in the north, unstable and unpredictable.

It wasn't really new, of course. It had always been there, for as long as people had gazed at the heavens. But occasionally it brightened, and was classified by astronomers as a cataclysmic variable.

There was something about the word cataclysmic that caught the popular imagination. The media were not slow to respond. The combination of cataclysm in the stars and the millennium on earth was potent in the minds of the unstable. The Samaritans were under pressure, the crime rate enjoyed a sudden upswing, and Jehovah's Witnesses were on overdrive.

It was Sunday, but at the Blue Manor no one had gone to

church, no one had listened to the morning service. They moved through the house, through the gardens and grounds, into the village and through the forest, and if their thoughts ran on the millennium, on the divine, on guilt or morality, then they kept those thoughts private. The house waited in sunlight that day, squatting at the centre of its web of roads, poised and ready.

As some houses seem to, it held its breath.

There was fruit punch that night, but no one was very sociable. Phizackerley Byrne had opted out, withdrawn into solitude at the cottage.

There was a wind blowing up outside, a threat of storm. It would be a relief, Tom thought. The day had been too hot. It had drained energy from them all.

They were sitting round the kitchen table, Kate cutting up tomatoes for a salad at one end. Tom watched the light swing of hair over her face, the delicate line of her jaw. Her eyes were downcast, and he wondered what she was thinking. He stood up and moved round the table towards her.

'Want a hand?' He was given a knife and a board, and herbs from the garden. 'Ah, fine work,' he said. 'Is that all you think I'm good for after all this book learning?'

'Oh, no. We're saving the real excitement for later.' That sideways look again. 'Washing up,' she said happily. 'In case you're feeling unappreciated.'

'So kind.' He glanced at Ruth but her back was towards them, washing potatoes under the tap. There was a mirror over the sink and he could see that she was frowning.

'Can I pour another drink, Ruth?' he asked.

'What? Oh, sorry.' She turned. 'I was miles away.'

'Planning what to do with the barbarians at school tomorrow?' Simon looked up from the Sunday papers. 'It says here that teachers are the forgotten profession. No prestige, no money.'

'So tell me something new. It's almost as if no one really believes the future will happen. As if it's got nothing to do with us how our children grow up, what our culture does to them.'

She's really upset about this, thought Tom. She really cares. 'Do you see much of it when you're being a Samaritan?' he asked.

'Who told you?' Ruth sounded cross.

'I did,' said Kate. 'If Tom's going to be here for three months, he ought to know.'

Ruth sighed. 'Well, OK. We're not supposed to spread it around, you see,' she said to Tom. 'The idea is to prevent us getting bothered at home, because then there would never be any way of putting it aside. You need to remain objective. It would be really difficult.'

'As opposed to the light and subtle way the Samaritans leech off your life as it is?' Simon pushed his glass of punch away, untouched.

'Not that again. I don't know why you're always so horrible about it.'

'Don't you? It's simple enough. Jealousy, my dear, what else? You said so yourself. Why should you go off and give your sympathy and compassion to perfect strangers when here I am, abandoned and alone.'

'Such stupid games you play, Simon. As if you're ever alone! There's always Kate here, or your mother or someone else. Why must you keep on about this?'

'I don't see why you need it, Ruth. All these stories about other people. You spend every day teaching literature to children and then whole evenings go by with you listening to yet more accounts about people's lives. Haven't you got enough on? Or does it block out your own story?' Simon was standing now, leaning across the table towards her. She seemed to take no notice of him. 'What do all these words do for you?'

'It's valuable work,' said Tom hurriedly. 'It really can pull people back from the edge, I read an article the other day about it—'

'The edge? What do you know about the edge? Bright, wholesome little 'varsity boy, what do you know? Your life stretched out between brain and prick, what do you *know*?'

Sudden, harsh and shocking, Ruth slapped him. He stepped back, the mark of her hand red against his cheek. His lips were drawn, his teeth bared like an animal.

A silence, broken only by the scrabbling of twigs against the kitchen window in the wind.

A deep breath, like a sigh. 'You shouldn't have done that,' Simon said quietly, and Tom heard nothing but sadness in his voice. Simon backed away from the table towards the hallway.

The Dogfrog was rubbing against his knees, and for a moment Tom thought he saw its tongue flicker, divided like a snake's.

At the door Simon halted. The twilight caught his face strangely and it looked as if his cheeks were running with shadows, lined with darkness. There was no light in his eyes. He said to Tom, 'My apologies, for what it's worth . . .'

The door closed behind him. Kate put her arm round her mother's shoulders but Ruth shrugged her off. 'Another tantrum,' she said. 'So what? He's hogged the limelight yet again. It's getting to be a habit these days.' Her voice was cold.

'Hadn't you better go to him?' Tom found himself saying. He meant it for Ruth, but it was Kate who nodded.

'Come on, Mum,' she said. 'He's not well, you know.'

'Yes, I know!' She moved across the room to the door. 'But I'm so *tired* of these games. So bloody tired of it.' She held the door wide, waiting for her daughter.

As Kate passed Tom, she squeezed his hand, a quick, confidential gesture: don't worry, I'll be back soon . . .

But she wasn't.

He fidgeted in the kitchen for a bit, not wanting to follow them. The meal seemed to have been forgotten. Almost automatically, he cut himself bread and made sandwiches with lettuce and herbs. He found himself sharply in need of alcohol, resentful . . .

He washed the glasses, throwing the contents down the sink. He put the food in the fridge and swept the floor, listening all the time for Kate's return. Instead, he heard only the scraping of twigs on the window and the hushed breathing of the wind running through the house, through the ill-fitting doors and still-open windows. Reluctantly, he locked the back door and left the kitchen. There was no sound except the wind, no indication where the others might be. He went round shutting the windows, wondering when the storm would strike.

The door to the library was open. He noticed that several books had been taken down from the shelves and were stacked in chairs and on the floor. Some had fallen open, their pages twitching in the breeze. He moved across the room, preparing to shut the French windows. Outside the meadow of grass rippled and swayed in the light breeze. The ivy on the wall waved at the edges of the door.

On the table he found part of the Sunday papers, opened at the article on the variable star of Corona Borealis. He scanned it briefly, noting that the last time it had happened was 1905.

He tossed the newspaper aside. Beneath it lay that first snatch of writing, the brief scene with Elizabeth arranging her toys in the new house, pinned under a paperweight.

He sat down, reading it through, and at the back of his mind he remembered the words of Peter Lightowler, the bitterness and anger. A conspiracy of women, he had called it after Byrne had gone. A systematic campaign to disinherit, to destroy the men in the family . . . Unfashionable thoughts for a man at the end of the twentieth century. Certain feminists Tom knew would have plenty to say about Peter Lightowler, given the chance. What could have happened, what had so infuriated Simon's father?

The volume of Duparc songs was open at the piano again, its pages riffling in the breeze. He wished he could read music, that he could play it himself.

> The grass is soft for slumbering
> Under the cool poplar trees.

He picked up his pencil and changed a word here, a sentence there. And before he really knew what was happening, the next scene began to take shape:

Elizabeth can't sleep. It's too hot and she hasn't done her homework. Restlessly she stands up, walking across to the window where dark leaves wave beckoning fingers at her.

Over the years since they have moved into the Blue Manor, the ivy over the east wing has flourished. She sees branches almost thick as her wrist winding down to the ground. Quickly, without thinking, she sits on the window sill and hoists her legs over. A brief tug on the ivy, to see if it holds, and then she's climbing steadily down, bare feet searching for safety between ivy and brick.

In minutes she's standing on the terrace. The stone is delightfully warm beneath her toes. Carefully, she tiptoes across to the steps leading to the lawn.

She can see quite clearly although the sun has now set. The dusk is like a filter for distant light, and she sees the white roses shining. Overhead the stars are beginning to prick through the dark. One in particular, to the north, flares brightly, throbbing with fiery power.

But the fragrant grass is cool to her feet, delightfully tinged with damp. She remembers that Shadwell has cut it that very day. While she was at her lessons, he was out here, under the sun, cutting the grass . . . She begins to run, putting distance between herself and the memory of the morning's work. The ground seems springy like a mattress, giving energy to her steps. She wants to whoop like an owl, suddenly possessed by wild mischief.

Jumping and leaping, her arms held out, her nightie a-swirl, she dances silently across the lawns towards the lake. There are heaps of grass there, under the hedge, and she's planning to fall into the cuttings and roll around and fling grass into the air and not care any more about her tables or the dates of kings and queens . . .

A black shape suddenly lifts away from the lake, a rook or crow, she doesn't know which, its wide wings beating through the air making straight for her head. She drops down to avoid it and her hand falls on something hard and smooth, something moving . . .

It's a beetle, one of the biggest she's ever seen. A glossy black carapace, weird-shaped horns over its head. It waves its horns at her and scuttles off into the reeds. She jerks back from it. She's nervy and jumpy now, unsettled by these night-time creatures.

And then she hears it. Someone cries out. A woman's voice, miserably frightened, a touch of real despair. Elizabeth stops abruptly, her hand raised to her mouth.

It's coming from the island. Across the narrow silvery sheet of water, she sees a strong, violent movement in the rushes, and the sound of a slap, loud and harsh. Then fumbling, and the woman crying again, and someone's breath, panting.

She takes a step nearer, her feet in the water, wanting to help the poor crying woman. She is not frightened herself, because this is her house, her own garden and lake and nothing awful can happen here.

She says, 'What's the matter? Are you hurt?'

The tumble of moving shapes in the reeds is abruptly stilled, and a face turns towards her, pale and strange.

Roddy, her brother Roddy, spitting words at her she doesn't understand, horrible words, get out of here, little bitch, fuck off . . .

'Roddy, it's me. What are you doing?'

'Get back to bed. Now!' His words are hissed, quietly vicious.

She takes a step closer. The water is up to her knees, and cold enough to make her shiver. And then there is a movement beside her brother, the woman leaping like a wounded bird away from him.

Immediately his hand shoots out and catches her ankle, and at the same time he twists over so that she falls again across him. In that desperate surge, Elizabeth sees that the woman's shift is torn, dirty with mud and water, hanging loose around her.

She turns away, blundering back through the water to the bank, running across the grass to the house, tears splashing on her cheeks. Somehow she manages to stumble back up the steps to the terrace, wanting just to get inside, out of the garden, away from what is happening . . .

She falls to her knees beneath the window, her hands reaching up into the ivy. It drapes itself around her, becoming steps for her feet and handholds for her fingers. It clasps itself there, guiding and guarding. She is distrait, too confused and upset to worry about the climb, but somehow she moves up the outside of the manor, somehow she passes in through the window with no idea of how it is accomplished.

She lies in bed, shivering, her mind glancing away.

At midnight Roddy comes to her. He kneels beside her bed, his face on a level with hers.

'Listen to me, little sister. You've seen nothing tonight, you were dreaming, fast asleep. Nothing happened, only a dream, only a dream . . .'

He repeats it over and over again, his words monotonously worming their way into her mind. At some stage she falls asleep, a deep and heavy stupor, hot and clammy as the night itself.

In the morning she is unrefreshed and out of sorts. She remembers nothing at all until she goes to brush her hair. Wreathing her head like a crown, ivy is caught in her hair, trailing down over the shoulder of her nightgown.

She stares at herself in the dressing table mirror and sees a stranger, someone whose eyes are haunted by more than dreams.

A scratching, scrabbling sound from the window. Tom looked up. He saw the ivy twitch and scrape against the glass of the French windows, five-fingered like a hand. He stood up and crossed the floor to the darkened, blank, shining panes of glass. He moved his hand, matching it to the touch of the ivy on the other side. Had Elizabeth made a friend of the green growing things consciously, or was it intuitive? Was the Dogfrog a real pet, a dog they had bought and trained and fed, or was it some stray from the forest, something attracted by the warmth and shelter of the house, by the easy pickings?

Or was it something else altogether?

All was quiet upstairs. He stood on the landing, listening for voices. He heard nothing. 'Kate?' he called quietly, but there was no reply. Irritated, he walked down the corridor to her room, knocking sharply on the door.

There was no reply. 'Kate?' he said again, and opened the door.

He saw the heaped blankets and heard breathing. She was asleep. For a moment he wondered whether to climb in beside her, but it seemed a shame to disturb her. Gently he shut the door and went to his own room.

He slept, tired by both tension and the heat. At some stage, unsurprisingly, he found the one blanket too heavy and threw it off. In the hot darkness, even the sheet became an irritation, a weight. He turned against it, trying to find somewhere cool on the cotton. His mouth was dry, the air in the room thick and gritty.

He stood up, dazed from sleep, and crossed the room to the window. It was wide open and yet no breath of air moved through the curtains. Outside was as stifled and silent as the room. A mantle of heat lay over the house and countryside. He was sweating freely, and yawned.

Why was it so airless, even with the window open? What had happened to the storm that had seemed so imminent? The trees outside were motionless in the starlight, the waters of the lake unruffled, perfect as a mirror. And yet he had a sense of motion in the air behind him, a stirring from the centre of the house. He stood quite still, listening. Kate, perhaps, coming to join him . . . ?

He went to the door and out on to the landing. The concertina bars of the lift shone in the moonlight. For a moment he thought he saw a shadow behind them, something moving within the lift.

At once he stepped back into the room. The hall and landing were *empty*, there was no one there. He knew no one ever used the lift.

Besides, it was private. Out of bounds, forbidden to him. It was unreasoning and illogical but he knew this to be so. The hall and landing, the corridor running from it, all of these were no-man's-land to him that night.

He shut the door and yawned again, not with sleepiness but from lack of air. The window again, the field of grass and trees caught in the frame, distant and unmoving as a photograph. Still no air, nothing fresh in his lungs. He was aware of more than unease now. Fear was beginning to run through him, the panicky release of adrenalin making his heart race.

He didn't know what to do, he didn't know why it was impossible to leave the room. Was this how Simon felt, unable to leave the house? But this was different, something physical, something badly wrong. His breath was coming in great laboured gasps, he couldn't get enough oxygen . . .

He was trying to calm himself, to think, but there was no air to refresh his thoughts. There was a shifting against his skin, as if a faint breeze was running through the house again. It carried with it a strange, pungent smell, like ammonia. *Ammonia* was seeping into the room. How could it? Where was it from?

His throat was as dry as sandpaper, gulping at the burning gas. Water. He needed a drink. He had to get out of the room. He turned towards the door, and it was like moving against treacle. His limbs were weighted with iron, his eyes fogged and blurring. His eyelids were inexorably closing. He couldn't breathe! Full-blown panic now as he tried to shout for help, to scream, but the noise was stifled by the malodour of the air, clogging in his throat. He began to thresh around, flailing his arms, blundering against the furniture, and abruptly his knees gave way. He fell to the floor, coughing and choking, and poisoned gas flooded his lungs.

In extremis, he heard the clashing of the lift door and the soft whirring of wheels around the landing. They were swishing through the night, coming towards him.

The whirling wheels turned in his head, spinning thought and consciousness into nothing.

Chapter 16

A thumping pain in his head, sickness in his mouth. Something resting on his face, heavy, floppy, smelling strongly of animal . . .

Tom opened his eyes. Thick coarse fabric lay over his mouth. Gagging, he knocked it aside and rolled over, almost retching. Bright sunlight was immediately dazzling, falling from the open window across the room directly into his sweating face.

He was leaning against the bed, the rug there rucked up and disordered around him. The room looked as if a fight had taken place. Chairs were tumbled, a china vase smashed. The pictures on the wall were askew, the bedclothes flung all anyhow over the floor and furniture. The books by the bedside had fallen to the floor, splayed open, some pages torn and crumpled.

He closed his eyes. He felt seriously unwell, unequal to further thought or movement. His chest hurt, the pain in his head was nauseating.

He thought, I have to get out of here. I have to leave this house. Kate was right, I can't stay here, I can't write anything about what happened here, it's all too strong . . .

Somehow he got into a standing position, and made it over to the basin before he threw up, hanging there after the burning yellow bile had stopped. He ran the tap, splashed water over his face and neck and felt only a little better.

He stared at himself in the mirror. He looked bad, his eyes bloodshot, the lids swollen, his flesh pale and puffy.

In the early morning quiet he heard a door open further down the corridor and footsteps, light and springy. Kate. He turned against the basin, holding a towel to his face, partly to hide the wreck.

'Ready for breakfast?' Her heart-shaped face grinning in the doorway. 'Or something else first?' She came into the room, wearing only an outsize T-shirt.

He let the towel fall, knowing she would be shocked, not caring when it came to it.

'Tom! Are you ill?' All playfulness gone, she was at his side, guiding him back towards the bedroom. 'What's the matter, what is it?' She had glanced over the devastation, returning to stare at him. 'Tom, what's happened here?'

'I don't know . . .' The words came thickly, dully. 'I couldn't breathe last night, couldn't get out of here—'

'Couldn't *breathe*? Asthma . . . ? Or were you dreaming?'

'Some dream.' He tried to laugh, but it didn't work. 'I heard wheels . . . There was gas or something. Like ammonia. Didn't you smell it?'

He looked at her, neat and pretty, eyes sparkling, and knew that it had gone nowhere near her. She was refreshed, her hair curling at the back, damp from the shower. She was warm with vitality.

He lay on the bed and closed his eyes, shutting her out. She was still talking, saying that there was no gas at the house, it was all electric now. Gas wasn't possible.

'I smelt it. I couldn't breathe.' He had no energy for anything else.

'I'll phone the doctor.' He heard her move towards the door, open it, talk to someone outside. Ruth, he thought. Ruth Banniere's there too.

'What's wrong? Tom, whatever is it?' That other voice, alto, gentle. The motherly one.

'I'm going to get a doctor,' said Kate.

'No. Don't.' He paused. He wanted them out, wanted to think. Something to get rid of them both. 'Perhaps it was asthma. I had an attack once, years ago. It's OK now, I just want to sleep . . .'

For a while he was aware of them standing there, watching him. Then the door closed quietly.

It was after eleven before he went downstairs, moving cautiously through the house as if it were an enemy. Nothing had changed, it was exactly the same, the mess of magazines and papers cluttering the contours of tables and chairs.

Somehow he expected something to have altered, something to have acknowledged that wheels had run in the night. He expected to see the rugs rucked up because of their passing. He thought the bowl of roses would have wilted under the creeping poison.

There was no sign of anyone else. He knew Ruth would have

gone to work, that probably Kate was outside. Simon would be on the wander, as usual.

He put the kettle on and cut some bread. There were flowers on the table, a generous bunch of purple and white stocks, their scent deep and rich. In the mid-morning calm, the sun-filled room appeared at rest, friendly . . .

The scent of flowers made him feel ill again. Perhaps food would make it better. With shaking hands he put a mug on the table, a plate . . . Ordinary, domestic actions. But in his mind the memory of terror and suffocation remained and he felt sick to the core. He sat down opposite the window. He saw Kate crossing the terrace to a gate in the kitchen garden wall. She did not look towards the house.

There was a telephone by the door to the hall. He could ring for a taxi, get away . . .

'Are you all right?' Phizackerley Byrne was standing at the kitchen door.

'No. Not really.' Tom leant forward, his head on his hands.

'Kate told me you'd had some kind of an attack in the night. Asthma, she said.' Byrne was making coffee, efficiently moving round the kitchen as if it were his own. He helped himself to milk and biscuits. 'Was it asthma?' he asked.

'No. I don't know what it was. The whole room was filled with gas. They say there's no gas in the house, but somehow . . . a cylinder or something. It was ammonia. I couldn't breathe.'

'Frightening. Do you want coffee?'

Tom shook his head. There was a pause while Byrne poured water from the kettle into his mug. He didn't look at Tom.

'The house doesn't want you here.'

'*What?*' Tom stared at him.

'You must have noticed. I felt it straight away.' Byrne sat at the table opposite him. He spoke slowly, staring into his mug. 'It sounds mad, but the house is complete with Ruth, Kate and Simon in it. It doesn't want anyone else. We're superfluous, an irritant to it. It's why I was put in the cottage.'

'Oh, come off it! It's just a collection of bricks and mortar and tiles and wood, it has no character, no personality. I was probably dreaming, or something.'

'Really?' Byrne had lifted his gaze, was meeting Tom's eyes. 'Is that what you think, that you were deprived of breath, made sick and ill by a dream?' A pause. Tom felt cornered by the steady words. He'd said much the same to Kate himself.

Byrne drank some of his coffee. There was something about the deliberate nature of his movements that infuriated Tom.

'Come on, Tom, use your mind. There's something wrong here, something slippery, hidden.'

'What do you know about it? You've never stayed overnight here! I don't suppose you've even been upstairs, have you?' This was getting petty, absurd. 'I don't want to listen to this,' Tom said, more mildly. 'I've got work to do.' He stood up and moved to the door.

Byrne was still watching him. 'Take care, won't you?'

Tom sighed. 'What do you think's going to happen?'

Byrne shrugged. 'Oh, I don't know. Writers' cramp, I suppose.'

An unwilling half-smile, a lightening of the atmosphere. Tom was beginning to feel better. 'That all depends on a good flow of words,' he said.

'Is it difficult?'

'Not here,' Tom said. 'It almost writes itself.'

After Tom had left the kitchen, Byrne stood for a while at the kitchen door looking along the passageway to the hall. Shafts of sunlight gleamed on the glossy covers of magazines.

Tom was right, what did he know? It was true that he hadn't been upstairs. Ruth had promised him a tour, but it hadn't happened yet. Perhaps that evening . . .

He was almost amused at himself. Still here. He'd finished the hedge on Saturday, but somehow it now seemed urgent to get the kitchen garden into some kind of order. He was planning to thin seedlings that afternoon.

He didn't want to leave. He was beginning to be infected by Ruth's enthusiasm for the garden. He wondered if she would join him out there that evening.

Working along the rows together the day before, he had seen a different side to her, confident, calm. He kept clear of questions about the family, and it wasn't difficult to find things in common. He told her that he'd run the landscaping business before going into the army.

'Why the army, for goodness' sake?' she asked.

He sighed. 'I wonder myself, sometimes. Family tradition, I

suppose. My father had always gone on about the variety, the travel, the security. It seemed faintly glamorous.'

'"See new places, meet exciting people and kill them"?' she quoted.

'Ah, but you've got the wrong jargon. It's presented more in terms of peace-keeping nowadays. I was in Germany for a while – that was where I met Kristen – and rather enjoyed the life. Then Northern Ireland, and that was a different thing entirely, much tougher. There was a war going on there.'

'How did your wife die?'

'A bomb. Beneath my car.'

'Meant for you?'

'Yes. Meant for me.' He turned away then, wheeling the barrow of weeds over to the dump. He was aware of her eyes following him. When he returned she was sitting back on her heels, regarding him. She shaded her eyes against the evening sun and said, 'Where were you going to, before you arrived here?'

'London. Regimental headquarters, actually. I went AWOL, after Kristen died. I thought it was time to get it cleared up.'

'What will happen to you?'

'I don't know. It won't be too dreadful. I'll probably claim stress, a breakdown of some kind and it wouldn't be inaccurate.'

'But if you were significant enough for a bomb attack, won't the terrorists be looking for you?'

'It doesn't work like that. You don't have to be significant to be a terrorist target.' He didn't tell her that it hadn't been terrorists who had planted the bomb.

It was why he was putting off giving himself up. He would have to tell them about David. And he didn't want to.

Tom sat in the Rennie Mackintosh chair and read through the last scene he had written, the rape of Jessie Lightowler. He hadn't given the woman a name, but that was who she was. Elizabeth's big brother Roderick having his way with one of the village girls, and incidentally fathering the man Tom had met the day before, Peter Lightowler.

He was excited by the audacity of what he was attempting. This blending of fact with imagination. He was going to write about someone real today, someone he'd met, the young Peter Lightowler. He would be creating fictions from real lives.

It was a form of lying, of course. He comforted himself with the knowledge that if he ever managed to get it into a publishable state, he'd change all the names, all the details which would give it away. But Kate would know how it had been written. She would understand the genesis of the story.

She would approve. He sensed that she liked Lightowler, that she sympathized with the old man's desire to patch over the past. Perhaps Tom's book might help, might do something to heal the acrimony . . .

He would start with an account of Peter Lightowler's childhood. It would have been tough, although there were few signs of it in the man now. But to have been born a bastard eighty-five years ago couldn't have been easy. It would have meant scraping an existence in the village, illegitimate, impoverished . . . He'd have been teased, made miserable and ashamed by that narrow, inter-war society.

This deprived, difficult childhood might do much to explain whatever mistakes Peter Lightowler had committed in later life: he hoped so, anyway.

And at the same time Elizabeth would be changing from child to woman at the manor. Very different circumstances, luxurious, sheltered, protected . . . It would be a magical transformation, that blossoming of sensuality hidden away behind the beech hedge like some latterday Sleeping Beauty.

Roderick was at least ten years older, Tom estimated. He'd be away for much of the time. Oxford, perhaps, and then the continent. The twentieth-century version of the Grand Tour. Tom imagined a clever young man, influenced perhaps by the Bloomsbury crowd, or the Cubists. He'd come home in the holidays and find Elizabeth changed, her figure rounding, curving softly . . .

And although Tom had decided to write about Peter first, it was Elizabeth's face which kept appearing in his imagination. Perhaps there were photographs or a picture of her somewhere. He remembered seeing some heavy albums on one of the bottom shelves near the music.

Photograph albums. Several of a pretty woman wearing that tortured S-shaped corset of the Edwardians, flowers frothing at the bosom. Rosamund Banniere, said the printed words on the back, as Desdemona, as Manon, as Lucia . . .

There were many gaps in the album, as if some photos had

been torn out. No sign of Rosamund's husband or son. No men at all. A small girl, indistinct in broderie anglaise, frilled and flounced, perched on the knee of a sour-faced woman. Again, a little older, in a sailor suit, holding a toy dog.

And then another picture, a young girl out on the terrace of the manor, the ivy forming a dark background. Her legs in black stockings were almost lost against the foliage. Her pinafore dress hung loose over her thin figure.

This was Elizabeth Banniere. Full lips and dark eyes, looking square at the camera. Her hair was brushed into soft waves over her shoulders. Her eyes were gentler than Kate's, but still that heart-shaped bone structure, that triangular smile.

Your treacherous eyes. He remembered the phrase from that first poem in the Duparc book. Baudelaire, 'L'Invitation au Voyage'.

Treachery. A potent word, a potent idea.

As he started to write a fleeting thought whisked through the upper reaches of his mind. How much freedom did he have in this project? Was he capable of making any decisions about this story? He remembered his words to Phizackerley Byrne: it wrote itself.

It is a still, bright day, the sky cloudlessly clear, the shadows of morning deeply colouring the hedgerows. Elizabeth is happy cycling down the drive, enjoying the wind in her hair, the speed. It is almost like flying, she thinks, this silent skimming over the ground.

At the beginning of summer, on her fourteenth birthday, Rosamund has given Elizabeth a bicycle. She has spent the day with Elizabeth at the manor before leaving in the evening for Paris.

Tom stopped. Yes, Elizabeth might have had a luxurious childhood, but it had not been graced by overmuch in the way of maternal affection. Rosamund Banniere would have been at the height of her career before the war, travelling everywhere between La Scala and the Paris Opéra, recitals at the Wigmore Hall . . . Duparc songs. She probably sang them, too. There would have been little time to spare for her children.

So, who would have been in charge at the manor? For a moment he gnawed at his pencil, his eyes abstractedly fastened by the pinpoint hovering of a lark high over the grass meadow. The answer was not hard to find: Peter Lightowler had mentioned Rosamund's sister, Margaret, the 'dried-up spinster of no account': the sour-faced woman in the baby picture of Elizabeth. She'd fit, it would work.

Elizabeth practises up and down the drive for several weeks, and then, one August morning, decides to venture out on to the road. She has in her basket a shopping list from her Aunt Margaret and some money. This is to be her first solo jaunt into Epping. At the gate she sees Shadwell hanging out washing on the line strung between the apple trees. She waves to him, although he rarely acknowledges her existence.

Yes, Margaret would certainly have needed a man's help in the grounds, just as Ruth does. A gardener would always have been part of the fixtures and fittings at the manor. The cottage had been built for him, after all.

This time Shadwell nods, touching his cap to her. Well! A salute from old Shadwell! Perhaps Elizabeth really is growing up, getting truly independent.
　　Out on the road her feeling of exhilaration begins to fade. Elements of doubt arise. What if she falls off? What if anyone sees her? She pedals more slowly, suddenly self-conscious. There is no one near the manor, she'll only meet other people once she gets out on to the main road into Epping. There will be carriages and cars there, of course people will see her. It's market day and the town centre will be full. Will they stop what they're doing, will they turn and stare?
　　The root of this reticence lies in a not unreasonable dread that her skirt is going to catch in the spokes, that she'll fall off, that her clothes will be all over the place or tear or get covered in oil. There are any number of things which can go wrong.
　　Her cheeks are hot with exertion and irritation. Why was Aunt Margaret so unreasonable? She had forbidden Elizabeth to wear bloomers in public. It had caused endless arguments. They had been battling over it all week, ever since Elizabeth had sent away for a pair from a catalogue. The bloomers arrived two days ago, scratchy olive green tweed.
　　Over breakfast, Margaret refused to discuss it further. 'They

are not lady-like, no matter if Mrs Padfield does wear them. What she chooses to do is her own affair. Your demeanour, however, is my affair, and I will not have you looking ridiculous. I don't want to hear another word about it.' She swept from the room.

Roddy raised a sardonic eyebrow at Elizabeth. 'I'll drive you in, if you want.'

'No, it's all right.' She sighed. 'I'll make do with a skirt today.'

'As you please.' He stood up. 'Not long, Lizard. You'll soon be grown up, and then you can do as you like.'

She laughed. 'Is that what you learnt at Oxford? Of course you can't do what you like, grown up or not. The idea! Whatever would Aunt Margaret say?'

'Never mind about Aunt Margaret. Look, if this weather keeps up, shall we go swimming in the lake later today? Shadwell says it's clear of weed at last.'

'Oh yes, that would be lovely!'

She cheered up immediately. And her good mood lasts until she cycles out of the gate and finds herself spinning down the empty lanes towards Epping.

She doesn't fall off, and neither does her skirt tear or get soiled. She cycles into Epping with her head held high and negotiates the traffic with a certain degree of panache. Margaret's shopping list is detailed and complicated, and it takes her over an hour to collect everything. What on earth does Aunt Meg want rosewater for? Elizabeth pushes her bike contentedly between chemist and baker, feeling responsible and adult.

She is dawdling back through the market when some velvet ribbons on one of the stalls catch her eye. She pauses, examining the colours for a moment. She has no money of her own, but Margaret won't mind her borrowing from the housekeeping. She stands there for a while, debating between emerald green and a deep cherry pink.

Through the bustle and noise of the market, the jostling crowd, the cries of the hawkers, she becomes gradually aware of being watched.

It is an uncomfortable tingling between the shoulder blades, the sharp pressure of someone else's attention. She turns slowly, unwillingly. Standing in the door of the butcher's shop a small child gazes at her unblinkingly. He is poorly dressed, in ill-fitting, patched clothes. He is unwashed, his hair greasy with dirt, his boots gaping.

He still stares at her, hardly more than a toddler, hardly out of leading reins, and she smiles brightly at him. She fishes in Margaret's purse and brings out a penny. 'Here you are,' she says, holding it out to him.

He reaches forward to take it, but a rough hand knocks his arm away.

'We don't need charity, miss.' The woman's face is thin and intense. A fine bone structure is overlaid by her expression of strain. Pale, strawlike hair is roughly clasped back in a hasty bun.

'I'm sorry, I just thought . . . some sweets for the little boy.' Elizabeth is flushing, hotly conscious of people's attention.

The woman stares at her, her ice-blue eyes disconcertingly like those of the child. 'You're from the manor, aren't you?' she says at last.

'Yes.' Elizabeth doesn't know what else to say.

'Well, I've got a message. You can tell Roddy Banniere that Peter needs new shoes. Understand? I don't ask for myself, but Peter's growing fast, and—' She stops abruptly. Her eyes look Elizabeth over, from the top of her straw hat down to her patent leather shoes. 'Oh, what's the use?' Her voice is very bitter. 'What's it to you? Buy your ribbons, girlie. Make yourself pretty.'

She turns away, pulling the boy behind her and is quickly lost in the crowd.

He wasn't sure about this. Were the bloomers right, would it have been an issue in 1914? And then Jessie Lightowler's voice: did it ring true? Was he falling into cliché, the worn, proud mother, the silent, watchful child?

The child was right. He knew that, at least. Peter Lightowler's eyes missed nothing, not now, not then. Self-possessed, cool . . . that brief portrait would stand.

Elizabeth is thoughtful on the way home, unusually silent through lunch. Roddy is reading, his book propped up against the water jug. Aunt Margaret is preoccupied with the cook's imminent departure, the possibility of staff shortages due to the recent declaration of war.

'Really, I can't think why we never manage to keep staff. The terms are generous, and no one can say we're a fussy family!' She peers crossly over the table to Roderick. 'I suppose she might be offended by your lack of elementary courtesy, Roddy. I do think you might put your book away at mealtimes.'

'You think this kind of food deserves my undivided attention?' Disdainfully, he pushes at the fish with his fork. 'I don't understand why we can't have proper live-in staff. There wouldn't be all this trouble with them forming relationships in the village then.'

'There's no room,' says Margaret. 'This is not a large house.'

He shrugs. 'The rooms over the stables could be easily converted. It's stupid to live like this. We're not paupers!'

'Neither are we made of money. And really, Roddy, I do think it's time you considered what you're going to do with your life – ' Margaret's broadsides are famous.

He laughs. 'Well done, Aunt. A quick change of the subject, an adroit diversion from the central issue.'

'I want to talk to you about this after lunch, Roderick. Come to the library, please, when you're ready.'

'We're going swimming,' he says, looking at Elizabeth.

'Not straight after lunch you're not. Very unhealthy. And anyway, I'm not sure that the lake is clear yet.'

'Shadwell finished it yesterday. He's given us the go-ahead.'

'Well, there will be plenty of time for that after we've had our little talk. I shall expect you at two.' She frowns at Roddy shortsightedly.

'Very well.' He turns to Elizabeth. 'At four o'clock then? At the lake?'

She nods. Perhaps she'll ask him then about Peter's new shoes. Perhaps.

By the time she reaches the lake, Elizabeth has made up her mind to say nothing. How is she to know that that woman isn't mistaken? She looked desperate, distraught enough. Elizabeth can't imagine her immaculate brother having anything to do with someone like that.

She knows nothing of his friends, he never brings anyone home. But she's seen women who look like exotic birds at Covent Garden, when her mother sang Susanna in The Marriage of Figaro. She is sure that Roddy's friends look like that, elegant, sophisticated, witty. They would make clever jokes, they would be learned and talented at all sorts of things . . . She wonders if she will ever know people like them, if she will ever call them her friends.

She waits for Roddy in the shadow of beech trees, watching the shining light bouncing off the water. The lake is on the border of the manor's grounds, and the beech hedge runs on either side of it.

Elizabeth is a little early, and it is still very hot. Thoughtfully, she takes off her dress and petticoats. She is wearing her bathing costume beneath these, an elaborate affair of frills and stripes.

She hears Roddy whistling through the trees as he approaches, something he only does after he's helped himself to the brandy in the decanter on the sideboard. She sighs resignedly. At least it generally puts him in a good mood. His white shirt is open at the throat, his hair slightly disordered. He laughs when he sees her.

'It's a disgrace, Lizzie, you look like a fairground. This is the way.' He puts down the towel he has been carrying on one of the raised roots. And then, before her horrified and embarrassed gaze, he strips off all his clothes.

As soon as she realizes what he is doing she turns her back on him. An impression of hairiness, of muscles flexing, shining with sweat . . . It makes her uncomfortable.

'Roddy, you mustn't!'

'Don't be prudish. What harm could there be? This is our own lake, our own private property.' He comes up behind her, putting his hands on her shoulders, gently nudging at the material. 'Come on, don't be silly. You're young, you're a child of the twentieth century, born in 1900, even. Lizzie, you don't have to cling to antiquated, provincial ideas.'

She says nothing. He moves away. What harm can there be? And yet . . .

She hears a splash as he dives cleanly into the water. She watches his white body streaking across the lake towards the island in the centre. Sinewy arms cut through the dark, tree-shadowed water.

'Come on,' he shouts. 'It's wonderfully cool.'

She stands on the edge, hesitating. She walks slowly out into the water, just a little way, her toes sinking in the soft mud.

'Take that ridiculous costume off, for goodness' sake, girl!' His voice is alight with mockery.

It is ridiculous, he is quite right. Her hands are a little clumsier than usual as she wriggles out of the garment, letting it fall on the bank. Gasping with the cold of it, she dives forward into the water.

He is waiting for her in the reeds by the island, floating lazily on his back.

She does not want to look, but she is curious. She has never seen him completely naked before. As if conscious of her thoughts he suddenly turns over, sinking down so that all she can see is his head, tight dark curly hair, dark blue eyes . . .

'What did Aunt Margaret want?' she asks. 'Have you told her what you're going to do?'

His mouth tenses. 'She's a stupid woman. It's none of her business anyway. The last thing I need is a lecture from a tired old spinster.'

'I wish you wouldn't talk like that.' She is bobbing like a cork now, watching the jerky movement of a dragonfly.

'Oh grow up, Lizzie!' He is impatient. 'Look at you. You're a woman, and you don't have to behave like a child any more.'

She doesn't like this conversation, she doesn't like the reckless edge to his words. She brings her arms up to hide her chest and tries to change the subject. 'Do you remember when we were little and you said that you were going to cut down all the trees?'

He looks at her sharply. 'When the manor's mine, that's exactly what I shall do. You wait and see.'

'But don't you like them?' She starts swimming a lady-like breaststroke, her head held high out of the water. The water feels delightful, cool and soothing, gently flowing around her.

'You know why we can't often swim in this lake, don't you? Not just because of weed, but also because of all the damn leaves that fall into it every autumn. Shadwell spends most of his time clearing them up. He could be more usefully employed.'

'But the trees are beautiful . . .' She has turned on to her back, as Roddy had done, looking out through the canopy of leaves to the hot blue sky beyond. The leaves are moving, lightly swaying in a distant breeze. She feels that this is a magical, significant place.

For the second time that day she feels the pressure of someone's gaze. She turns her head sideways. He is looking at her, his face expressionless.

She says, 'I met someone in Epping today who said she knows

you. Scrawny, blonde. She said to tell you that Peter needs new shoes.'

He speaks softly. 'Why is there that tone in your voice, Lizzie? Why so critical?'

'Do you know who I mean, then? Peter's the little boy, isn't he? What is he to you?' She turns over so that she is standing on the soft lake bottom, the water up to her shoulders. Her hands drift in circles in the dark water.

'So many questions. None of your business, Lizard.'

'She looked poor. The boy was dirty. Who are they, Roddy?' Something makes her persist.

'Leave it. Stop it.'

'She seemed familiar to me . . .' She pauses, trying to place the memory. The leaves overhead shift, creating patterns on the water. 'I saw her once before,' she says slowly. She can't quite see his face. The sun is dazzling on the water, bouncing off it. She raises her hand to shield her eyes.

'At night-time. Here. You were here too,' she says.

'Shut up!'

'He's your son, isn't he?' She has no idea what she is doing. 'You . . .' She remembers a phrase, an ugly phrase. 'You forced that woman.'

He says nothing, wading through the water towards her. She still can't see his face.

'Roddy, how could you, how could you do that and then not help them? She looked so poor, so tired.'

'Take their part, would you? It's called treachery, you know. Anyway, she was a slut, a stupid cheap slut.'

'But you forced her!'

The blow knocks her head sideways, knocks her off balance. She's falling but there is only water in her mouth and nose. She begins to struggle and his hands catch her and pull her over to the island. Birds take off from the rushes as they get closer, one large black bird in particular. She sees its wings blotting out the sun, even as she's gasping for breath.

But he is careless and rough and she cannot get her breath even then, even though they are now out of the water, lying on the bank, and small insects scatter into the warm mud beneath them. His hand is over her mouth and she tries to shake him off. But he hits her again and she is too confused to scream, too shocked by what he is doing. She does not truly understand, even *when his hands begin to move, grasping at her breasts. Pushing her legs apart.*

There is no safe haven there.

Not now, not ever.

Chapter 17

The pencil dropped from his fingers. He was beginning to shake again. Dear Lord, what was he writing, what was this?

Tom pushed the chair back and it scraped against the parquet floor. He stood up, backing away from the desk. He wanted to get out of the room, away from these words which were falling from his hand to crowd over the white paper. Pages of it, densely written in his small, crabbed, clever handwriting.

'Lunch?' Kate was peering round the door at him, bright-eyed, friendly. He stared at her blankly.

'What? No. I don't want anything.'

'Are you still feeling ill? Are you sure you don't want a doctor?' She was coming towards him, her hand rising to feel his forehead.

He moved away from her towards the window. 'I'm all right, I just need some fresh air – some exercise.'

He was struggling with the catch to the French doors. He could smell her scent, sandalwood or something. He couldn't meet her eyes. He wanted her to go away, to leave him alone to work out what was happening to his thoughts, to his writing.

His fingers winced away from her hands as she coolly took the key from him and opened the door.

'You *are* in a state, aren't you? What about a swim, something to cool you down?' Her voice was kind but her words were unthinkable, nearly as unthinkable as what he had just written.

'No! I don't want a swim.' I don't want to go near that lake ever again, he thought. Not ever.

'Tom, what is it, what's wrong?' He'd hurt her, he could see it in her eyes, the way her hand kept reaching for him as if physical touch could bring him back to normality.

'Look, there's Byrne over there,' he said hurriedly. 'There's something I want to ask him.' And before she could say anything else he had started to walk across the grass field to the orchard.

Halfway there he remembered that he'd left his writing

uncovered on the desk. She could be reading it. In a panic, he hurried back to the house.

The desk with its sheaf of papers stood in the centre of the French doors and there was no one else there at all.

Byrne saw Tom come out of the house, almost running. There was something frantic in his movements, not like his usual, self-contained composure. But then he stopped suddenly and turned back to the house, and the impression of confusion deepened.

Byrne sat up against the apple tree and waited. And sure enough, a little later Tom emerged from the French windows and came towards him once more, walking more slowly.

'There's something I need to ask you. As an impartial observer,' he said, as soon as he was in earshot. He squatted down on the grass beside Byrne, in the shade of the old apple tree.

Byrne was watching him, saying nothing.

Tom had the words ready. He'd probably been preparing them all the way from the house, Byrne thought.

He began: 'I think . . . this thing I'm writing is taking off in a rather strange direction. It's not factual, of course, but it does touch on the history of this family, it concerns people who really lived. Are living . . . And I'm worried that I'll be stirring up something that's best left alone. I mean, what good does raking up the past do? In your opinion? Should one search out the root of any trouble, should one look backwards to find it?'

Byrne took a deep breath. In his experience, what you did was to run as far as possible, as fast as you could, away from the past. But somehow he didn't think Tom was going to be interested in Byrne's past. He had obsessions of his own.

Tom was young and arrogant and predatory. He knew nothing.

'If you're writing fiction, there's no problem. All you need do is to make sure the names don't match. I think your trouble is that you don't believe it *is* fiction, do you? You think you're uncovering what really happened.' He paused, studying Tom's face. This seemed to be the kind of thing Tom wanted. He was even nodding, as if it made sense.

A long exhalation of breath. 'You're probably wrong, you know.'

'It doesn't feel like that.'

'Writer's intuition?' This was a joke, but Tom was in no mood for teasing.

'Perhaps . . . but you must have seen it. This is not a happy family. There is something wrong. Do I continue with this "fiction" and dig deeper? What might I find?'

Byrne looked at the house. Strangely balanced amongst the trees, elongated proportions and all, it seemed to be on edge, more precarious than usual, waiting for his answer.

He said, 'My own experience is that evil or sin, if you can accept such terms, do not just go away. That they will surface, somehow, sometime, and that if they are suppressed the worse the trauma will be.' The house was making him speak the truth. It would not allow him to prevaricate about this. It was drawing honesty from him.

'But what if the innocent are caught up in it? What if people suffer when it's not their fault?'

Byrne was very still. He could no longer bear to watch the house. Instead he was following the pattern of leaves shimmering above them, frail against the hot blue sky. 'No one ever said life was fair. But I do know one thing: evil cannot be concealed. It may go underground, it may appear to lie dormant, but it must feed. It will re-emerge, and may whatever god you follow comfort you then.' He was aware that his voice was bleak. Tom was looking at him as if he'd never seen him before.

'I don't know if it's true,' Tom said. 'I don't know if what I'm writing has any basis in reality, or whether it's a distortion, something horrible emerging from my own psyche.'

'Write it,' Byrne said suddenly. 'Exorcise the ghosts, if they exist. It doesn't matter whether they're your ghosts or the family's. If they're taking over they need expression. Get on with your book, Tom Crabtree. Find out where the evil lies.' He grinned. 'You can always burn it later,' he said. 'It's only words.'

Shadwell is working in the orchard when he hears Elizabeth's scream. Without a moment's hesitation, without thought, he drops the scythe and runs.

He knows who it is, although he has never heard such a tone in Elizabeth's voice before. Filled with dread he stumbles over the low wall to the rose garden. Complicated paths, dense bushes of thorns. Through the gate to the back lawn, across the grass to the lake.

Still crossing those yards of grass he can see what's happening. He sees the movement of white flesh, he sees Roddy's wild face upturned to the trees, sees the girl's arms raised over her head, pinned by his hands.

'Elizabeth!' he yells.

It's enough to stop it, to fracture the mood. He sees Roddy leap away and make for the trees, vanishing into the thicket. Let him. Let him run, the coward. Time for him later.

Shadwell is there now, wading through the water to the island. She's lying amongst the crushed reeds and he falls to his knees beside her, his hands spread widely. Elizabeth, little Elizabeth, curled up like a baby in the mud, moaning, blood on her face, blood on her thighs. He's swearing, words unaccustomed, unheard.

She flinches as he touches her, and he wills the bad words to stop and makes instead gentle, soft noises, the noises he uses to quieten animals. She is quivering, her hands over her face as if to disguise herself, to conceal herself from view. It's her face she wants to hide, not that cruelly exposed body, her face which will reveal what has happened, more than the blood, more than the bruises.

There's a towel on the bank and he goes to fetch it. 'Elizabeth, I'm going to take you home, I'll take you to your aunt.' She lets him wrap her in it then, lets him gather her up. Her arms fall loose.

Carrying her he walks slowly back across the lawn, up the steps to the terrace. He calls, 'Miss Banniere! Miss Banniere!'

Looking down from the gallery, Margaret clutches her hands together. Then she too begins to run.

The doctor has gone. Elizabeth is heavily sedated, sleeping. There are no other serious injuries, although it is too early to say what might result from such a trauma. Elizabeth has said not one word, given no evidence to corroborate Shadwell's story. Margaret sits in the gallery outside Elizabeth's room as the dusk deepens. Her hands are twining together ceaselessly.

She has sent a wire to Rosamund, she has concocted a story for the doctor. An unknown assailant, someone coming out of the forest . . . Doctor Shaw has accepted this lie without question.

The version given by Shadwell has to be suppressed. It is unthinkable.

And yet where is Roddy? Where has he gone?

It is Roddy's continued absence which gives Shadwell's story its terrible credibility: she almost believes what he says. She almost believes that Roderick has indeed raped his sister.

All the time she is listening for the door, for the tread of Roddy's footsteps. Shadwell has gathered up his clothes, has brought them into the house. They hang over the back of a chair in the kitchen and Margaret cannot bring herself to touch them.

Is he roaming the countryside, naked? Has he utterly lost his mind? As the hours wear on, phantasms of anxiety and memory keep her company. She remembers rumours in the village, she remembers kitchen maids who have walked out without notice. She remembers the wild accusation in one girl's face who'd come to the door, heavily pregnant. Roddy had dealt with it, he always dealt with it. Her tired mind frets further. He always seems to have money these days: where does he get it from? She finds it hard to believe that his allowance from Rosamund, although generous, goes so far. So many questions, so many inexplicable problems . . .

She cannot possibly sleep. She has to wait until Roddy comes home, she has to see his face, listen to his excuses.

It cannot be true, what Shadwell has seen. It cannot –

The front door rattles and slams. Footsteps cross the hall. She stands up, her heart beating painfully.

A light comes on downstairs. She stands by the banisters, looking down at him.

At first she thinks that there's been some mistake, that this is some illicit intruder, a wild man from the forest.

The figure in the hall is bare-headed, dressed in a heavy black overcoat. His hair is unkempt, his face streaked with blood.

'Roddy?' Surprisingly, her voice is quite steady.

'Is Elizabeth all right?' He's striding up the stairs towards her. He takes hold of her hands, speaking passionately. 'I couldn't catch him, he was going too fast . . . Tell me about Elizabeth, Aunt Margaret, what has she said? Did Shadwell tell you what happened?'

She pulls her hands away. 'What did happen? Your face . . . Tell me yourself.'

'Elizabeth?' Urgent anxiety in his voice.

'Sleeping. The doctor's been, she'll be all right.'

He's still waiting. She gives him what he wants. 'She's said nothing.'

He sighs, smiling quickly, charmingly. 'Some bastard – sorry, Aunt – came out of the forest while we were swimming. I was over the other side of the lake, and had no idea what was happening at first. It was just chance that I saw what he was doing. I shouted and made after him but he ran off into the forest. I followed—'

'Your clothes are downstairs,' she interrupts, her voice coming from a great distance. 'Shadwell saw what happened, did he?'

'He was coming towards the lake. I shouted for him to see to Elizabeth and took off.'

'Why didn't you send Shadwell? He was dressed, and you must have been worried about Elizabeth.' She feels she's begging him, asking him to make up a better story than this.

He pauses. 'I didn't think,' he says at last. 'It seemed natural to go after the blackguard.' He touches his face, and she sees that the blood is coming from a deep gash streaking from eye to chin. 'I blundered into a tree. That's where I got this. It happened as I was coming back.' His voice is suddenly less sure, less confident.

'You'd better put some iodine on it.' Strange how the habits of nurture endure. 'Go to bed now, Roddy. We'll talk again in the morning.' She is so tired that she can hardly think. He leans over her, kissing her forehead.

'Sleep well, Aunt Meg. Elizabeth will be all right and we're bound to catch whoever it was.'

'Yes, I suppose so.' She turns and walks back down the gallery. She hears Roddy's tread on the stairs, and knows he's going downstairs to get some brandy.

She hesitates at her own door.

There is a rustle of warm air around her ankles, a shifting movement of something passing by her. She looks down, confused.

It pads across the gallery to Elizabeth's room, and scratches at the door. Her numb mind does not register the white fur, reddish ears, reddish eyes, although her own eyes follow it automatically. The creature is an impossibility and her consciousness shifts away from it to something more acceptable. She thinks, yes, I must stay with Elizabeth, she may wake. She needs guarding.

So Margaret follows the creature and goes into her niece's room and sits there, all night, by the bed.

The footsteps that come across the gallery in the small hours
warn her, that and the warm stirring air round her ankles. The
door opens slowly. She sits there, pretending to sleep, her jaw
dropping.

He halts there on the threshold for a minute, watching. And
then he goes away, and the door closes.

She's downstairs before him in the morning. She has washed,
changed her dress, straightened her hair. She's calm and
unhesitating.

She waits for him outside the dining room. Shadwell, at her
request, stands by the door. Roderick Banniere looks quickly
from one to the other. He says nothing, suddenly white. The red
wound in his face gapes.

'I think you should join up, Roddy. Go today, go now, and
sign on. Now that war's been declared, strong young men are
needed. I don't ever want to see you in this house again.' She
can hardly bear to look at him.

'What nonsense has Shadwell been telling you?' He's bright-
eyed, his lips thin. She shakes her head. 'Oh, was it Elizabeth,
then? Dear little sis?'

'Get out, Roddy. Get out now before I call the police.'

Shadwell moves a step closer.

'I'll have to pack.'

'Your things are waiting for you in the car. Shadwell will
drive you to the station.'

Again his eyes dart beween them.

'You're making a mistake, you know. You'll regret this.'

She says nothing, letting him brush past her, watching him
leave the manor, slamming the door.

She hears a movement upstairs.

'Lizzie darling? I'm coming, just a moment . . .'

Without a backward glance she runs upstairs to her niece. She
doesn't even hear the car start up.

Roderick Banniere has left the Blue Manor.

Tom put the pencil down. He thought, and under what circumstances will I leave the manor? No convenient wars these days,
no easy excuse to explain a sudden absence . . .

But I've done nothing wrong, his mind protested. Nothing's
happened to make me run, to dishonour this house or Kate.

There was only this story, touching on areas that were perhaps best left concealed. He wondered if he'd ever let anyone else read it, whether these revelations about the family were too distressing to be disclosed, even now.

He had no doubt that it was true. He knew his own talents well enough to recognize that he had not invented this tale. It already existed. It breathed from the walls of the house, it echoed down the corridors, basked in the dappled sunlight from the windows.

The books that fell open under his fingers. The words from songs that caught in his mind: all these things ensured that the story would be written, and that it was true.

He was mature enough to recognize the existence of two levels of truths: the objective and the poetic or intuitive. What he was writing was true in the latter sense.

It might even be true in both senses. Why else had the customary laws of inheritance been changed? Even if Rosamund had hated men, why had she so debarred her own son from even the slightest share in the legacy? The sin (Tom's mind tested the word) of incestuous rape was surely enough to account for the ban on male inheritance.

Roderick and Elizabeth's lives had been driven apart by that very moment of union. He wondered if they had ever met again. He would have to write more, to find out . . .

He caught himself short here. What was he assuming, why was he taking this *possession* for granted? He acknowledged it at last. The story was possessing him, diverting his creativity for its own purposes . . . And yet, wasn't that how it always felt? Wasn't that what all writing was? The cliché he had always dismissed he now faced honestly. Stories existed in their own dimension, and forced the writer to discover them. The writer's own skill lay in communicating something that already existed . . . God, what would Alicia say? He imagined her mockery, her cynicism. Simon's mother, lecturer in English at Cambridge, would have no trouble in putting down such fanciful ideas as indulgent twaddle.

He went to dinner and it was a relief to laugh with Kate, to tease Ruth. But underneath, he was bemused and disturbed. He talked to Simon about politics and economics and it felt as distant and as irrelevant as a fairy tale.

He wondered what else the manor had to tell him.

Chapter 18

'Let me stay with you tonight.' Kate's hand on his shoulder was warm and friendly.

'With the greatest pleasure.' Tom wound his arm around her waist and drew her close. They were standing on the landing after dinner. The hall beneath them was lost in gloom, the mess of books and magazines hidden from sight.

Ruth and Byrne had gone to look at the evening primroses on the terrace. The tall window on the landing was open at the top and he could just hear their voices murmuring. Simon was watching television in the small room opposite the kitchen, the room they called the dossery, and that door was open too. Tinny laughter, taped applause, a flickering greyish light filtered into the hall.

But upstairs it was quiet.

'Come with me,' she said, and he saw her eyes gleaming in the dusk. 'I've got something to show you, a secret . . .'

She took him by the hand and led him along past the bathroom into the long corridor. All the doors were closed, and their footsteps echoed on the uncarpeted boards. There were no pictures on the walls here, and the faded blue wallpaper was bulging in places, hanging loose in others. There was a musty smell about the corridor, as if it very rarely knew fresh air. Dust, damp, rot.

He was glad they were holding hands; her warmth flowed into him. Towards the end of the corridor Kate stopped and opened a door. Beyond it a narrow flight of stairs led upwards.

There was a light switch on the wall, but she ignored it. She took a box of matches from her pocket and lit the first of a series of candles which stood in wrought-iron sconces. The walls had been painted dark blue, and gilt stars and moons shone there, catching the light from the candles as they went up.

The attic smelt of dust, of mothballs and lavender bags, but there was nothing drab about its contents.

At one end a curtain of shot silk, blue and green, blocked off the rest of the attic. The rest of it was a dream land, a fantasy world of strange juxtapositions and unlikely contrasts.

A rocking horse launched itself over a rug made of crêpe grass, a paper rose between its teeth, a figure made of wire coat-hangers crouched over its back.

At one corner someone had hung hundreds of rows of beads from a ceiling beam. They fell like coloured rain, their gold clasps turning calmly in the warm air.

Kate was moving round the attic, lighting more candles.

A family of ancient dolls sat in ordered rows before a velvet squirrel. They formed the congregation at a marriage, and a bear and a rabbit exchanged curtain rings. A papier-mâché dolphin leapt over the back of a chaise-longue, a volcano covered in sweet paper spewed forth jelly babies on springs.

Tom moved from one tableau to another, touching drifts of lace, bolsters of fur, carved ivory miniatures. On a bamboo whatnot, a circular bowl held the broken heads of dolls, their eyes as wide and unblinking as any goldfish's.

And of course, books. In stacks on the floor, in cardboard boxes and rickety bookcases: Angela Brazil, Frances Hodgson Burnett, Lorna Hill.

A chime of music, Brahms' 'Lullaby', and he turned to see Kate putting down a silvery casket with a tiny ballerina turning on top of it. 'Do you like it?' she asked softly.

'Did *you* do this? Was this your playground?'

She laughed, half embarrassed. 'Oh, this was Grandma Ella's creation. But we all came here, we've all added things to it . . . this was me.' She held out to him a small sculpted model of a woman playing a piano. It was made of some kind of modelling clay, he realized, turning it over, roughly coloured in browns and ochre and tawny red and gold.

'It's Ruth,' he said, delighted. 'It's so *clever*! I never knew you could do things like this.'

She shrugged, but he could tell she was pleased. 'We were always lonely, you see,' she said. 'All the women who grew up here were lonely, really.'

'I thought Simon and Ruth were here together.'

'He went to boarding school from the age of eight. He only lived here in the holidays. And Grandma Ella was an only child.'

'What about you?'

'Mum wasn't in the right financial league to send me away to school. She doesn't approve of private education, anyway. She blames a lot of Simon's neuroses on his school, but I'm more inclined to put it down to his parents' divorce.'

Tom had met both of Simon's parents now: Alicia, his tutor and friend, and Peter Lightowler. They seemed to him curiously well matched, both articulate, elegant, controlled. 'Why did they split up?' he asked.

Her nose wrinkled. 'Two strong-willed people, I suppose. I think there were probably constant fireworks, constant clashes. And I think Uncle Peter had a somewhat roving eye in his youth.'

And has still, thought Tom, remembering that ancient hand on Kate's knee, the look in those pale eyes as the old man regarded his niece.

He put away thoughts of Peter Lightowler and pulled her close. 'I like it here,' he said. 'I love being in this house, I love being with you . . .' It was true. When he was alone with Kate everything fitted into place. 'This present time is all I want.' Her breath was sweet, her body soft and supple against him.

They made love beneath the leaping dolphin on the chaise-longue covered in blue velvet, and it was a dreamy rite of companionship, of tenderness.

It was quite dark by the time they stirred. He disentangled himself slowly and stood up, pulling on his jeans. In the flickering candlelight Kate looked like a child again, her skin close-textured, lightly touched by rose.

'Have you ever spent the night here?' he asked as they dressed.

'No. I was never allowed to because Mum didn't trust me with the candles. I always regretted it.'

'Isn't there a light switch on the stairs?'

'Yes, but it doesn't feel the same with the light on.' To prove the point, she flicked the switch and the attic was flooded with light.

It looked tawdry then, full of rags and tatters and junk. 'See what I mean?' He noticed for the first time that there was an empty lift cage in the far corner, to one side of the blue-green curtain. The criss-cross metal joints gleamed redly with rust. Kate turned the light off and the gentle dimness was restored.

'What's behind here?' He crossed the attic and pulled at the curtain beside the lift.

'Just rubbish,' she said, not looking. 'Stuff nobody wants. It needs clearing, really.'

Tom said nothing. The curtain concealed a carefully constructed wall of furniture, tables piled on wardrobes, stacked with chairs and chests of drawers and trunks. But jutting from an arch formed between a tallboy and an upturned sofa was a wheelchair. On its leather seat sat another of the hollow figures made of wire, a gas mask hooked over its head. Tilted at just the angle to meet his eyes. Blank holes gaped at him.

He stepped back. A taint of ammonia hung in the air about the wire figure and he remembered the sound of wheels running down the corridor to his room.

Kate was at his shoulder. 'The chair belonged to John Downie,' she said. Her voice was calm, and he realized that she couldn't see his face in that shadowy corner.

'Who?' he asked, his voice suddenly harsh.

'John Downie who married Elizabeth, my great-grandma. The one who was gassed in the trenches, a hopeless cripple. People wondered why Elizabeth married a man who was so crippled, and everyone thought she'd never have children.'

He tried to concentrate on what she was saying. He let the curtain drop, concealing that worrying figure in its ancient gas mask.

'But Elizabeth did have a child.'

'Yes, Grandma Ella. Ella who made this attic, who strung those beads up and started weaving the figures.'

'Spooky . . .'

'Do you think so?' She was frowning. 'Don't you like it?'

He saw her disappointment and regretted it. He was stupidly overreacting. 'I think the wheelchair's a bit macabre, I suppose,' he said, 'but the rest of it's wonderful.'

She seemed reassured. They drew the curtain and left the attic, blowing out the candles as they went.

'Stay with me tonight?' she asked.

'I'll join you later,' he said, still holding her hand. 'There's a bit I want to get down.'

'Ah, the family history. Did I set you off again?' She sighed comically. 'My own worst enemy . . . I'm not going to see much of you, am I? What about the here and now, Tom? What about me?'

He saw the dimples and the triangular grin and was sure she

was joking. He touched his hand to her cheek. 'I won't be long. Promise.'

But as he went down into the untidy hall, he thought that the here and now is never enough. The present rests on the past, it is formed by the past. And a figure in a wheelchair still sits in the attic, wearing its gas mask.

Her fingers are very slightly unreliable. Elizabeth is still trying to pin the orange blossom into place when her aunt comes in.

'Oh my dear, let me . . .' In silence Margaret's fingers work deftly and soon the flowers are securely, professionally, in place.

Margaret's face in the mirror is preoccupied, frowning. Don't say anything, Mags, Elizabeth thinks, it's too late to say anything now. But the house is calm around them, giving generous space to their thoughts. Her aunt's voice is cool and dispassionate, the force of her character well under control.

'Think again, Elizabeth. It's not too late. Say the word and we'll call it off. There's no disgrace, no one could possibly blame you.'

'I know.' She stands up and turns to face the older woman. 'Don't worry, Mags, I know what I'm doing.' She has never been more certain.

'It will be a half-life, you know. Not the whole experience.'

Elizabeth is hardly paying attention. She is listening for the quiet swish of wheels beneath them that will tell her Johnny is on his way.

'What if you want children?'

And there it is, the sound of wheels on wood, a murmur of voices, the front door opening and closing again.

'I'm ready now,' she says. 'Give me good luck, Maggie. Wish me well.'

For a moment the two women cling together, and the house is soft with them, gentle as a dove.

'May we hope to see you around in the town a little more now, Mrs Downie?'

Delicately put, my old friend . . . Elizabeth smiles at Dr Shaw. 'Oh, I shall be popping in and out for all sorts of things. You'll probably get tired of the sight of me.'

'That I doubt.' He twinkles at her over the champagne.

'There's one thing you must remember, however.'

'Ah, the great mystery. You really are keeping your maiden name? I did hear rumours.'

She nods. 'Johnny's quite happy about it.' They both look at the man in the wheelchair. He's listening to the Suttons but at that moment glances across at Elizabeth and the doctor. He raises his glass to them, his deep brown eyes, that ironic, sideways smile.

She grins back at him. 'So long as Johnny doesn't have to change his name . . . You realize that's why we had such a big do, so that everyone would know the knot's been well and truly tied, even if the names are different. Do you think it'll work?'

'You're an enchantress, my dear. Anything you want will work.'

'If only that were true . . .' She sighs, not entirely joking. 'We – didn't want the name to die out, not yet. It's what Mother would have wanted. I am the last Banniere who can inherit.'

A small silence, unspoken memories, inappropriate to this day. Dr Shaw hesitates. 'There's been no news of your brother?'

'No, not recently.' She's prepared for this.

Jim Shaw's eyes are kind and understanding. 'It must have been a great shock to him, your mother tying up her property like that.'

'Roddy doesn't need it. He's well provided for.'

'And the manor is a considerable responsibility.'

The doctor is an old friend, entitled to persist. She smiles at him. 'I shall have John to help me now.'

Shaw presses her hand. 'I hope you'll be very happy together, my dear. John Downie is an extraordinary man, a hero, and you are fortunate to have found each other.'

'Not everyone sees it like that, Jim, but you and I know the truth of it.' For a moment their eyes meet, and then Elizabeth's attention is caught by someone else.

'Oh, Erica, what a wonderful hat! I noticed it straight away.'

'Even as you came down the aisle! Yes, I'm sure . . .'

Elizabeth smiles at the doctor and moves on. Jim Shaw knows at least part of it, knows why this marriage is the best she can ever hope for. She has no regrets, not one.

'Tired, lovely?' A faint whisper at her side. Johnny cradles her hand against his cheek as they watch the last of the guests leave.

138

She crouches down, her arms round his chest and shoulders. She feels obscurely like crying. Reaction, after a long, long day.

And yet the sun is only just setting.

'Let's go and look at the garden,' she says.

'What about the clearing up?' He appears desperately tired himself. She feels the familiar surge of warmth for him that she chooses to call love. She's going to take care of him, of this frail and broken body, and if she never has a child of her own it will not matter. Johnny will be comfortable with her, for whatever length of time is left to him.

'Sarah's coming in tomorrow. And if you think I'm going to start washing up on my wedding day – '

'We've got no staff, Lizzie. It'll all be up to you.' He's watching her, the exhausted, wheezing voice deeply serious.

'If I can't manage, then of course we'll get someone in. But I'd like the chance to try. And there's always Mags.'

'She's staying with the Richmonds tonight?'

Elizabeth reassures him. He knows perfectly well that her aunt is staying with friends in the village, that for this, their first night together, they are going to be alone in the Blue Manor.

They have altered several of the rooms on the ground floor, converting the library and study for John, the morning room as a bedroom for herself. These are light, airy rooms. John has the larger area, his own bathroom, dressing room, sitting room. He won't have to wrestle with stairs, not here in the Blue Manor. And Elizabeth will always be there to look after him, well within easy reach. He will not have to do anything for himself, although she's prepared to encourage him to make an effort.

She pushes his chair out on to the terrace and they stay there for a while, the spring evening sweet with the scent of hyacinths. The garden is full of deep shadows, the air very still. There is no sound from the trees, no rustle of leaves or bird calls.

His hand is on hers. It is a moment of deep peace. At last Johnny sighs. Slowly he turns the chair round, so he's looking at the house. The last rays of sun are reflected off the upper floor windows.

The front door is open, and they can see the faint gleam of white from the narcissi on the table.

He says, 'I know why you love this place. It is at peace, isn't it? In harmony with the world. Thank you, Lizzie. Thank you for letting me live with you here.'

'We'll be happy here. This was always meant to be a happy house.' But then she feels his hand shiver and realizes that he is getting cold. 'Come on, let's see if there's any champagne left.'

'Tea.' The faint voice contradicts her. 'A nice cuppa cha, that's what you need, lovely.'

'To bring me down to earth?'

'To warm your heart.'

'And yours.'

The man standing at the attic window hears the woman's laugh, but not her words. He watches her wheel the chair across the terrace back into the house. Below him, he hears the door close and her voice again, now within the house.

Carefully, silently, he shuts the window. He doesn't want any kind of draught bringing her upstairs. He's wearing tennis shoes and moves silently across the dusty boards to the door.

He's not alone in the attic. At his feet a large stag-beetle scuttles, narrowly avoiding the tread of the soft-soled shoes. On the window sill, by the window he has just shut, a black crow cocks its head, watching his movements.

He's taking a chance, but he wants to see what the stakes are. The wedding has been a gift, so many people in and out all day, caterers, waiters and waitresses, guests . . . No one noticed the young man slip upstairs during the reception.

He had wandered from room to room, his trained eye noting the strange obsessive carvings in the rooms, the mantelpieces wreathed with ivy, the polished doors and window sills set with acorns and holly leaves. It was rather too Pre-Raphaelite for his taste, romantic and vague. It disguised the clean lines of the rooms, blurred their proportions.

His hearing has always been acute. He listens at the door for a bit, tracking the movements beneath, the pad of Elizabeth's footsteps, the quiet whisper of Downie's chair as they get ready for bed. It's still early. He hears her help him undress, hears his few faltering footsteps. Downie can walk a bit, he remembers. But his lungs were all to pieces, he has no breath for anything else. Even walking was a bit of a risk. The man smiles. He squats down, and runs his hand over the back of the beetle. It raises its antlers to him, and he puts his finger to his mouth. 'Shhh,' he tells it.

Elizabeth stays in Downie's room for a while. A nice, chaste cuddle, he reckons. He sits in the attic drinking the champagne he'd stolen earlier, chain-smoking. He'll open the windows later, no one will know they've been there.

He waits until midnight before he starts moving again. Quietly, he pads down the small attic staircase to the corridor. Slowly and methodically he goes from room to room, running his hands over the window frames, over the walls and furniture. He touches everything. Every object on the upper floors is marked by him, every acorn carving, every curl of vine.

The stairs creak, so he has come prepared. He takes from his bag a length of rope which he ties to the balustrade. In less than a minute he's on the ground floor. The crow skims over his head, settling on the grandfather clock by the door. He smiles at it.

He follows the same sequence, the same routine on the ground floor. Every object, every wall, every window and door. He wanders from room to room, touching and stroking. He identifies the house as his own.

He leaves the two ground-floor bedrooms to the end. He can hear that Downie is asleep, he can hear every struggling breath he takes. His door is ajar. Probably Elizabeth wants to hear if her husband calls in the night. If he needs her.

He slips inside the room, carefully brushing the wall with his fingertips, picking over the pile of garments on the chair, running his palm over the window panes.

He looks at the thin figure on the bed before leaving the room with something close to pity.

The window is open in Elizabeth's room, the curtains shifting slightly. Quickly he moves round the room, his hands working, spreading, marking. His creatures do not accompany him here.

She stirs, murmuring something indistinct. He stands very still, waiting for her to settle again. A half-irritable moan, a little disturbance; the covers are pushed aside, and she turns over on to her back. She's naked, one hand resting on her hip, her head tilted slightly to one side. Dark hair falls half across her face, half across the pillow. Her breasts are larger than he'd expected, soft and heavy. The deep hollows of her body are lost in shadow.

Silently he moves closer to the bed. He touches it almost automatically, and then, as if of its own will, his hand reaches towards her face. He strokes it downwards over her eyes and mouth.

A tenth of an inch separates his flesh from hers.

His hands frame her face, circle her head. His palms curve round the nipples, curve again to follow the line of her waist, the slight swelling of the hips. His fingers, extended, mark the darkness between her legs. He matches her hands to his, matches his hands to her feet.

He stands in silence at the end of her bed, watching, for a very long time. At length she turns again, pulling the sheet and blankets up to her face.

He still stands there.

He's there when the first light of morning shows through the waving curtain. As if awakening from a dream, he shakes his head, glancing at his watch.

An hour, and then the gates will be open. He has to clear his stuff away. He's busy now, climbing the rope, packing away the remains of the champagne, opening the windows to let the bird out and to clear the smell of cigarettes. He swings himself down into the hall once more, pulling the rope after him, slinging it over one shoulder.

He almost leaves the house then, but it comes to him to do one thing more.

Outside Elizabeth's room, he puts the rope down. He touches his index finger to the four corners of the door and to the four corners of the frame.

Then he leaves the house.

Chapter 19

Reading it, Tom thought that perhaps he ought to go back through it again, this strange, midnight episode and give the man his name. He picked up his pencil and scored through the first 'he' as the man waited in the attic, smoking and drinking champagne.

He wrote 'Peter Lightowler' without thinking and then stopped. Surely, *surely* this interloper had to be Roderick, Elizabeth's banished, sinful, brother?

But the face in his inner mind's eye had light brown eyes and straight blond hair, fine long fingers and a thin mouth, an avid mouth . . .

Disgusted, Tom pushed his chair away from the desk and stood up. Why Peter Lightowler, why should he be there, with his animal companions, acting in this weird fashion?

Why not?

Peter was Roderick's illegitimate son. He had been conceived in the grounds of the manor, on the island in the lake. Elizabeth had been frightened by a beetle and crow then. They had accompanied Lightowler's conception: they were still part of his life in this story.

That had been rape, too. More ordinary, more acceptable, as far as such things can ever be considered acceptable, but Peter Lightowler's conception had been rape nonetheless. What if Roderick had returned to Theydon after the war, what if he had sought out this child born of rape?

What if he had taken his son Peter, adopted him, educated him in more than academic paths? *This is my inheritance*, Roderick could have said to the boy. *Rightfully, the manor is mine. It could also be yours, one day. And there are arts, methods to bring about such things. Listen carefully*, he would say and then instruction would begin, serious teachings of occult and extraordinary import . . .

How could Roderick Banniere have known such things? Tom was himself uninterested in the fashionable areas of mysticism which had, he thought, polluted the twentieth century. He had read Jung, he had even played with the Tarot and the I Ching, and was willing to accord them some use in exploring neglected areas of thought and emotion. But at heart he considered them inessential tricks, props for the weak-willed, for the muddy-minded.

What would Roderick Banniere have encountered in the twenties? There was the Golden Dawn movement. Tom had read a book about that once. Old Aleister Crowley was getting well into his stride about then. No doubt Roderick could have picked up all sorts of odd things . . .

And he would not have dared return to the manor himself. Tom knew the truth of that. Elizabeth and Margaret would never have countenanced his presence, not for one moment.

But Peter, Roderick's son, could arrive there years later, and no one would recognize him. Think about it, Tom told himself. Peter was born in 1910. He'd have been eight at the end of the war, and eighteen at the time of Elizabeth and John Downie's marriage.

He could see it all, he could see how it would go. Peter Lightowler, the boy/man, personable, presentable, charming . . . never less than charming. He would become friends with the Downies, a protégé of sorts. He would worm his way into their affections, and even Margaret would be entranced, enchanted by his intelligence, his culture and wit . . . he would appear young and innocent, and they were so vulnerable.

Margaret, the aging spinster. John, the crippled, wounded hero. And Elizabeth, all her trust, all her joy spoilt in those few dreadful minutes at the lake . . .

They would be wide open to Peter Lightowler.

To Roderick Banniere, his father.

Tom was standing at the French windows, staring out at the grass meadow. There was a half-moon flickering between clouds, and the grass rippled in silver and black waves.

He needed a break. He found the grip of this story, the way it took over his mind and ran beyond his control, deeply threatening. He had written thousands of words that day, more than he had ever written before in such a short space of time. He didn't understand what was happening to him, and while he had been prepared to go along with it while no one living was involved, it now seemed very different.

He had met Peter Lightowler. That very old man, Simon's father, had shaken his hand, had given him tea, had been courteous and, yes, charming.

How could he do this, make up these *lies*? He wanted fresh air, to get out of this place where words came tumbling from his pencil to sour the clear paper.

He pushed open the French windows and walked out on to the grass. It was still warm, although there was a breeze. He could hear an owl hooting over in the forest.

Without knowing why he took his shoes off. The grass was damp beneath his feet, dew settling. He had no idea of the time. He began to walk, aimlessly, over the grassy meadow, around its perimeter and then further, along the beech hedge as it surrounded the manor. He was going in circles, and gradually his worries calmed.

He remembered a documentary he'd seen once about a Buddhist monk walking round and round a sacred mountain until he'd gained enlightenment. It had been hard, it had taken years and years, but in the end he had been venerated as a Buddha.

The soft swish of feet accompanied these more gentle thoughts. It was soothing, balmy, to walk over the cool grass, to let his mind empty of the story he was writing, to clear of his fears and doubts, even of his love for Kate. Thinking of nothing in particular he walked across the meadow to the orchard, and then solemnly round each and every one of the apple, plum, cherry and pear trees.

Hypnotic motion calmed him further.

He felt as if he was walking in his sleep. His limbs were heavy as water. A great physical weariness made his steps slow, almost to ceasing.

Tranquilly, he turned back to the manor.

It was gone.

In its place stood a great forest of rustling trees. They filled the horizon; he could not encompass their presence with his senses or his mind. Massive trunks, quivering leaves, blotted out the rest of the world, overwhelmed his consciousness. The foliage of trees reached to the moon, their roots ran under the earth where he stood. He could feel the earth shifting beneath his feet, shivering to accommodate this new life.

For it was alive, more alive than any usual green, growing

thing. He hardly dared breathe as the trembling, shivering forest filled the world.

It drew him in. He fell to his knees, his hands widespread on the ground, hoping for solidity, for something familiar, but the grass turned traitor. It moved, wrapping itself round his fingers, chaining them to earth.

He pulled back, trying to rip his hands away, but they were held fast. He was sweating with the effort, struggling frantically. This was terror beyond anything he'd ever known. He thought that the blades of grass, knife-sharp, might cut his skin, might start growing into his flesh, might feed from him in some horrible symbiosis. He would be a creature of grass, a host to a visitant more powerful, more varied, more distinct than any mere parasite.

Swearing, he tried again to pull his hands free. The grass held him like wire. He lifted his head to the trees, wondering if anyone would hear if he cried out. He could just see the house now, cradled between the boughs of the forest, hidden and forbidden to him.

Amongst the leaves he could see people, three people. Kate, curled softly sleeping between the forking branches of a willow; Ruth and Simon on either side of a vast oak, their eyes open and staring at him.

In terror, he saw that Simon's hands were outstretched, and that blood dripped from their palms. Blood fell from his feet too; there was a gaping wound in his ankle, and scarlet ran down the knobbly bark of the oak. Simon was whiter than death, his eyes burning at Tom. And then he heard a voice, Ruth's, speaking to him:

You must never stay in the manor again. Never.

And Simon's voice echoed and repeated the words: never stay in the manor . . . Never.

He saw Kate stir, turn over and sit up. She was undisturbed by her position, caught up in the branches of a willow. But something else was wrong, something else made her lean towards him, her eyes wide and beseeching.

She bent forwards and he heard her voice, faint and fading fast:

Help me. Help me.

Her hands were outstretched and no blood stained their palms. Their message needed no such emphasis: Help me. Please. Help me.

He cried, 'Kate! Kate!'

But her name was lost in the rustling of leaves, in the slow movement of sap.

'Tom?' Someone was shaking his shoulder, pulling him round. But his hands were chained by grass . . . No they weren't. He lifted them to shade his opened eyes against the sunlit sky and recognized, slowly and painfully, the familiar silhouette of Phizackerley Byrne.

'Tom, what are you doing here?' A firm hand under his armpit, half dragging him to his feet. 'Are these yours?'

He stared blankly at the trainers Byrne was holding out to him.

And then he remembered and spun round to look at the manor.

It sat in its plain of grass, calm and familiar, bathed in sunlight as if it had always existed, always sheltered between those ordinary, shallow hills.

The only trees were the ones he was used to, the forest in the distance, the beeches by the lake, the fruit trees in the orchard.

The morning was calm and easy about him, and he felt on the verge of madness.

'Another bad night?' Byrne was saying. 'What about some coffee?'

'Coffee . . . ? What? – Kate!' He struggled free of Byrne's support. 'Is she all right, where is she?'

He would have started running, but Byrne's hand caught him, held him steady.

'She's fine. Look there.'

And he saw Kate, dark hair shining in the morning sun, emerge from the kitchen door and empty a teapot on to the soil.

'Jesus!' Abruptly, his knees gave way, and he was on the ground again, his hands over his face.

'Nightmares, Tom, or something else?'

'I can't go back there, I can't go into that house again. I have to get away from here.'

'Come on.' He was unceremoniously hauled to his feet once more and taken, stumbling like a child, away from the house to the gardener's cottage.

*

'I don't understand this! *Why* won't you come back?'

'I told you, I had a dream.' He said it sullenly, knowing she wouldn't believe. Kate had found him in the cottage an hour later, and was now pacing the width of the downstairs room haranguing him.

At least, that was how he saw it. He had said it was a dream. It was the only explanation he could make, it was what he had told Byrne. He said it was a warning, a premonition that he couldn't afford to ignore. He was a writer, an artist, and had to trust to intuition. He knew it sounded ridiculous, pompous, even as he said it. But he couldn't go back to the house in defiance of the vision of the night before.

Sensing her contempt, he tried to put it more positively. 'I want you to come away with me, Kate. Let's go somewhere . . . Paris, Venice . . . London, for God's sake. Let's travel, we've got the whole summer. We don't have to stay here, cooped up in Essex.'

'What about your book? What about this great history?'

He could see that she was hurt, that he had offended her. He didn't care though. He was frightened.

'I'm not the man to write it. It's not working, it's rubbish. It's a waste of time.'

'No, it's not!' Kate bent over the carrier bag she had brought with her and threw on to the table in front of him a sheaf of paper. 'I read it,' she said. 'I sat up for hours waiting for you last night, and when you didn't come I went down to the library and started reading. I know why you're running out. You're scared, aren't you?'

'Too damn right,' he said feelingly. 'How can you want me to go on with this, if you've read it? This is your *family* I'm pulling to bits!'

'For goodness' sake! It's not true, is it? This stuff about beetles and crows and ivy.' She glared at him. 'It's a story, you're just making it up. All you need do is change the names.'

She made it sound so simple.

'But it happened to real people,' he said flatly. 'You showed me the wheelchair in the attic, I've met your Uncle Peter—'

'Make up your mind. It's either rubbish, a waste of time, in which case it doesn't matter, or it's partly invented and you're putting real people into a fictional setting. In which case it doesn't matter either, because you change the names. Listen to me, Tom. You can't run out on this, on *me*, now.'

'I can't live in the manor again.'

'Well, stay here! I don't suppose Byrne will mind humouring your neuroses for a while.'

'I always said I'd come here if it got difficult, didn't I?' He tried to smile at her but it didn't work.

'I'll tell you something,' she said. 'It's a superstition, really, and I didn't think it would happen, not to you. I don't know why, because it's never been known to fail.' She stopped behind his chair and put her hands on his shoulders so he couldn't see her face.

'The manor must always have three inhabitants, not more, not less. I don't know why, but it is always so. Somehow things always work out like that. When I go to college, Ruth lets out my room to one of the students at Harlow Tech. Of course, sometimes more people stay here, or fewer, one or two, but it's only ever for three nights at a time. Three nights, maximum. And there's always some good reason why it never lasts longer than that. Someone comes, or someone has a nightmare or is called away . . . There's always any number of good reasons for people to leave the manor.'

'This is ridiculous!'

'It even works in what you've written, if you think about it. First Rosamund and her two children. Then it's Margaret, Elizabeth and Roddy. Then there's Elizabeth, John Downie and Peter Lightowler—'

'He was only there overnight,' said Tom sharply.

'But Elizabeth's aunt was returning the next day, wasn't she? It's absolutely consistent. The house is haunted, that's what Simon says. But we've never seen anything, Mum and I . . . we've never felt any of this. And Simon's neurotic verging on the psychotic and the drinking makes it worse. I've never believed what he says, and Mum says he only wants attention or something . . .'

She moved round, crouching down so she was looking up into his face. 'But you're not like that, are you, Tom? Are you putting on airs to be interesting too, or do I have to start taking this seriously?'

He sighed. 'I . . . think I should talk to Simon.'

'You'll have to come back to the house, then.'

'What do you mean?'

'Simon hasn't left the manor for over a year. It's called agoraphobia. I told you about it.'

And was there triumph in her voice, an element of *I told you so*? 'Let's leave, Kate. Go somewhere else. This isn't your problem and it's certainly not mine.'

She stared at him. 'Don't be silly, Tom. I can't leave. Don't you understand anything?'

This was hopeless, absurd.

'Finish your book, Tom,' she said softly as she went to the door. 'I'm sure things will feel different then.'

Chapter 20

It was becoming a pattern. Byrne stood by the side of the drive, waiting for Ruth to arrive. He had something to say to her, a question about the layout in the kitchen garden, but that wasn't why he was there.

He hardly admitted it to himself. It was only when she rolled down the window and he saw she was happy that his relief told him the reason. He said suddenly, impulsively, 'How about some tea? Come and see what I've done to the cottage.'

'OK.' She stopped the engine and got out of the car then and there. They walked together back to the cottage at the gate.

He'd not done much, just arranged the books on a shelf and cleaned a bit. He'd put a jug of wild flowers on the table, more on the window sill over the sink, wanting colour, something bright against the drab walls.

'This is better,' she said, touching a hand to the petals. 'Of course, there's plenty of furniture in the attics in the manor if you want anything else.'

'Yes, I know. Kate said so. It's probably not worth it, not if I'm going to be moving on soon.'

'Still playing with that one, Byrne?' She was speculative. 'I think you'll have to make up your mind. I'm not going to nag again. This is up to you, you're all grown up.'

He smiled. 'Maddening, isn't it? This agonizing, this indecision . . . The trouble is, I really do have to move on, sooner or later. There are various things, boring, important things, that I have to sort out.'

'Well, do so. Then come back.'

It was so simple. He wondered why he'd never seen it. Straighten it out with the army, and then come back . . .

'I might at that,' he said slowly.

'We could make the manor so beautiful!' she said. 'When I was little, when we lived here with Alicia, you could see the shapes of the old flowerbeds, the old garden plan. Most of it had been ploughed up in the war and turned over to vegetables so there wasn't much to go on, but there was a white garden,

Alicia said, like at Sissinghurst. And beds of iris along a walk leading to the library. Such extravagance, to have whole beds of a flower that blooms for only a couple of weeks!'

'You could open it to the public with one or two features like that.'

'I know. But it needs *time*. And because there's no money I have to work, and then I'm too tired—'

'Ruth, why do this charity work?'

'Oh, it's little enough! Once a fortnight, that's all.'

'Don't you find it depressing?'

'Sometimes. You're so helpless, you see. You can't do anything.' She paused. 'And yet in some ways that's what makes it possible.'

'You know you're not making a mistake, making things worse . . . ?'

'Sort of. Of course, words are powerful too. You can't be too careful. But there's quite a strict training, and a lot of support. The others help you not to be crass.'

He was waiting for the kettle to boil and he saw her glance at her watch. 'Byrne, I think perhaps I'll put off tea till another day. I'd better get back. Simon will be waiting, and I've got a whole heap of marking to get through tonight.'

She went to the door and he watched her return to the car. Perhaps he would come back afterwards. Help Ruth to realize her dream, make the cottage some kind of home . . . His eyes fell on the bulging wallet on top of the books. Return it now, he thought. Get rid of Peter Lightowler's money.

He put it in his jacket pocket and left the cottage.

He got lost. He decided to cut through the forest, thinking to save time. But that narrow strip of woodland, threaded through with roads and tracks as it was, seemed to wind itself round him so that he failed utterly to find his way to Theydon Bois.

It was so stupid he couldn't believe it. He looked at the position of the sun: Theydon was south-east of the manor, it should have been easy. In the deep shade under the big trees the sun was almost powerless, but it shouldn't have made much difference. He followed track after track for miles, knowing that he must sooner or later come to a road, but instead each track petered out among the brambles and ferns.

He couldn't understand how he'd become so confused. It

wasn't that he was only used to following compasses and maps, he trusted his own judgement. He even used to tease Kristen about her sense of direction.

Kristen. He hadn't thought of her that day, or the day before. For the first time in three months, he had lived through two whole days without remembering her, remembering what had happened. He sat down on the soft leaf mould with his back against a fallen log and shut his eyes against the lancing sunlight.

Part of him knew that forgetting was wholesome, that it was a necessary process of recovery, that it was right and proper that she should begin to fade into memory.

But it was no good. There was anger and guilt and bitterness there, nagging away. It was wrong. None of it was finished in his mind, it was as vivid and terrible as it ever had been.

His mind went over it again, leaving the house that morning, walking in the winter sunlight to the shop up the hill, the shop that sold papers and milk and cigarettes.

Meeting David there.

He was tall, taller by a couple of inches than Byrne. His hair was straight, straw-coloured, always cut to scientific precision, his eyes tawny. He had a trick of rubbing his nose when embarrassed or thoughtful.

It was easy to embarrass David. There was something essentially insecure about him. It sometimes made him stammer. Byrne had pointed out once that he never stammered when he was in uniform. David had laughed, but had returned to it later. 'I think it's like a disguise,' he'd said. 'It's liberating, in a way. You become someone else.'

There was something so honest about him, the way he confided in Byrne and Kristen. He came for supper once, twice a week. He and Byrne played squash at weekends.

Sometimes he kept Kristen company when Byrne was on duty.

He put those thoughts aside. No future there, nothing to be gained from going over it again and again. Had Kristen been unfaithful? Was she in love with David?

He would never know. He fell back into a habit he'd deliberately acquired, that of blanking over the inner chatter. A kind of meditation, only sometimes he fell asleep and he'd never heard that that was the aim of meditation. He was tired and slept then, quietly dozing beneath the ancient trees.

The cawing of a crow made him look up.

He saw, standing at the top of a ridge just ahead of him, a tall, thin silhouette against the rays of the sinking sun. It was impossible to make out details, and Byrne was at first confused.

David Crompton stood tall like that, blond hair blowing in the breeze at the top of the hill at Middleham. But this was Essex, and David – well, David could not possibly be there.

And then his attention readjusted and he realized that this was Peter Lightowler, his pale hair wispy, his pale clothes shining in the borrowed light. He was turned away from Byrne, looking further along the ridge, and there was someone coming to meet him.

Not someone. Three of them, the man and the two women. They moved together and the sun glared round them so that Byrne found himself squinting. He lifted his hand to shade his eyes.

No. He'd been mistaken. Only the two men stood there. Confronting each other, one dressed in black, one in creamy linen.

But the sun was washing around them, blurring the edges. Byrne almost got to his feet, but there was a rustle in the silver birch sapling to his right.

A huge crow perched there, the narrow branch dipping under its ungainly weight. Deep yellow eyes stared at him, unblinking. There was something curiously compelling about its gaze. He put his hand down on the leaf mould ready to get up, and it hunched its shoulders so that the dusty black wings fanned out behind it, half lifting it from the branch. It was about to launch itself at him and its beak was open in a grimace of soundless aggression.

He knew without doubt that it would attack if he moved any further. He subsided back against the log, wondering whether to shout out, scare it off with noise.

But something was happening out on the ridge, something significant, and he most desperately did not want to attract the attention of the figures there.

He saw the man in black move towards Lightowler and then there was something dazzling, something too bright for Byrne to see clearly. He blinked. And when he looked again, there was only one man standing there, one very old man dressed in bleached colours, and if the light glinted on him it was only the late afternoon sun . . .

Peter Lightowler turned towards Byrne and raised his hand. A brief salute, an acknowledgement of the observer's presence, and Byrne found himself shivering.

Then the old man walked swiftly down the other side of the ridge and disappeared into the forest. The crow in the tree suddenly took off, the massive wings flapping noisily, and skimmed over the ridge to join Lightowler.

And then there was no one there. And Byrne, leaning against the log in the forest with the dying sun flickering through the leaves around him, had no idea whether he'd been dreaming or not.

Chapter 21

Simon was waiting in the kitchen when Ruth returned that afternoon. His eyes were clear, his hand steady. He said, as soon as she came in the door,

'Three again. There's three of us again, now that we've had three nights – '

'What do you mean? Where is everybody?' She was putting on the kettle, unloading her schoolbag.

'Tom's left. A dream, a prophetic nightmare, Kate says, has thoroughly upset our little Lochinvar. He's got the wind up, and Phizackerley Byrne is picking up the pieces . . . Not for the first time, I would bet.'

She got down mugs and poured milk as if nothing had happened.

'I didn't think it would last long, this Kate/Tom thing,' she said. 'He's too obsessed with his book to give her the right kind of attention. Sex goes a longish way when you're that age, but it's not enough on its own.'

'Have you heard what I've been saying? Ruth, listen! Tom was here for three nights, and now he's out. Just like everyone else. Don't you understand? Why are you so *blind*?'

'They've had a tiff, it's nothing to get upset about. This three-night thing is a coincidence. They'll probably make it up, he's a good lad. He'll be back soon enough, you wait and see.' She put a mug of tea down on the table, and sat opposite him. 'Anyway, there's something I want to discuss with you. There was a meeting this afternoon after work, fund-raising for the Samaritans. They need new premises, and something that gave publicity as well would be a good idea . . . And I wondered what you thought about opening up the garden for a fête or something? Bring-and-buy, homemade waffles, strawberry teas, that sort of thing. What do you think?'

'God, Ruth, haven't you got enough on your plate?'

'We wouldn't have to do it alone, they'd all help out. This would give me real pleasure, Simon. Try to understand. We live here in this beautiful, amazing place, and why should we keep it to ourselves?'

'It's a dump, Ruth! The manor's a wreck!'

'But we could make a real impact on it, with a little extra help and something to work for. We'll paint the front door and Byrne can cut the grass, we could put pots of begonias around the terrace. I've got lots of seedlings coming on . . . We could cheer it up so easily, and having an event here would make us do it instead of fiddling round with bits and pieces. It would make a huge difference and we could raise money at the same time.'

He saw she was inspired, thrilled by the prospect. He thought, why should I stop her, if it makes her so happy? Byrne's on hand . . . She needs him. Someone steady and reliable, someone to take on the hard physical work. Byrne gives her what I can't . . .

'Don't try getting me to do anything, that's all I ask.' It sounded ungracious, so he tried again. 'You must do whatever you like, Ruth. I suppose it might work.'

'We could have a tombola, and perhaps a fancy-dress competition for the under tens.'

And she was off, planning and making lists and checking her diary, and he wondered whether she really understood what had made Tom leave the manor. He wondered whether she had any idea what was happening at all.

He found the whisky under his bed as usual. Another full bottle, and the empty one taken away. It was like the fairies, he thought with more than a touch of hysteria. But he didn't need to leave out little dishes of milk, he just put the empties there and lo and behold, by bedtime there was another full bottle of Johnnie Walker's best.

He almost caught them once. He'd come to the bedroom early, to change his shirt or something, and the curtains had lifted the *wrong way* as he opened the door. They had billowed towards him, and he saw fleeting shadows trailing black cloth – or was it feathers? – disappearing through the window.

He told Ruth but she'd ignored it. She thought someone in the village was sending the stuff in, and she wasn't far wrong.

He was sitting on the window seat drinking steadily. He had opened the drawer in his bedside table and took from it a Gideon Bible, the one book in the house he knew Ruth would never consult.

It fell open, as usual, at Paul's first letter to the Corinthians. The familiar diatribe against sexuality, the grudging admission that it was better to marry than burn ... His father's handwriting on the bookmark, those other familiar words:

A little consolation, to sweeten your time in waiting ... Marriage will make everything right for you, Simon. Believe me, there is no greater peace on earth ...

Tears in his eyes again, as he read the grubby piece of card with its gilt cross. His father had given it to him when he was eighteen. He had been about to set off for university and he'd known, he'd known even then that he might lose her.

Away from him, who knew what she might do? That had been the first time he asked her to marry him.

He still asked her, fairly regularly, more as a matter of form than anything else and even now he didn't understand why she refused him when it was clear that she loved him.

Why wouldn't Ruth marry him, when she was prepared to share her bed with him? What had he done wrong?

At first she'd said they were too young, and that was fair enough. He'd not thought so at the time. He'd got involved with Laura and what a disaster that had turned out to be. But no one could say they were too young now. And it wasn't his drinking, he knew her too well for that. If anything, it drew her closer to him. She fretted and worried about him, and the great maternal strength in her nature wrapped itself around him ... at least, that was how he liked to see it.

It was a risk, he knew that. Sometimes he thought his drinking might almost drive her away, but he was banking on her sense of duty, her all-pervasive guilt. His father, sending his servants with the full bottles, was taking the same risk.

But it wasn't working. She wouldn't do it, wouldn't marry him and share her worldly possessions with him. The manor and its grounds were never going to be his.

He drank a stiff tot direct from the bottle and placed it carefully back beneath the bed. The Dogfrog was waiting by the door, its reddish eyes watching him closely.

'Come on then,' he said, snapping his fingers at it. 'Walkies.'

It growled at him, a low, throaty rumble. He laughed at it as he went to the door and out on to the landing.

He had a small private challenge on. He was determined to

walk to the end of the long corridor, even though the Dogfrog
was equally determined that he should not.

He didn't know when the corridor had become forbidden
territory. He'd never liked it as a child, it had always felt cold
and damp and he remembered his mother complaining that the
wallpaper would never stay up. It bulged and tore and hung in
trailing, rotting ribbons. He used to dream about those ribbons
of paper, like fingers, wafting through the air towards them.
Alicia had scraped most of them off years ago.

But the corridor was still undecorated, uncarpeted.

He got as far as the first door this time, the first of the unused
guest bedrooms, before the Dogfrog began its surging, horrible
transformation. He tried not to look directly at what was
happening. He turned his face away from the open maw and
mad eyes, knowing that once he looked he would not be able to
stand it. He got as far as the door to the bedroom and pushed it
open and then the breath was knocked out of him as the creature
pounced on to his shoulders. Its claws were tearing at his back,
digging deep into the cloth of his jacket. He knew his flesh
would go next.

'All right!' he screamed. 'OK, you win!'

He fell back towards the landing, but not before he had seen
what was in the room.

Crawling black damp and ribbons of paper. And a mirror,
reflecting his own white and terrified face. He looked like a
mask, or a puppet. He looked unreal.

But the Dogfrog, grinning over his shoulder, was alive with
malice and energy.

Back in his bedroom, he fished out the bottle again. A serious
drink this time, more than usual at one go. He felt the smooth,
smoky fumes twining through his thoughts, smoothing over the
terror, blanking out the fear.

He drank most nights and some days, and Ruth accused him
of bribing someone from the village to bring it in. That was
what she *said*, but he knew what she thought. They both knew
Peter Lightowler was responsible. Simon couldn't discuss it with
her. His father was well out of bounds as a topic of conversation.

He always attributed it to his mother Alicia's influence.
Bitterness, fury . . . it had overshadowed their childhood in the
manor. Really, looking back, he was surprised that Ruth had

ever managed any kind of relationship with the male sex at all. Alicia had presented men either as vaguely feeble-minded, useless, like children, to be petted and looked after and cared for because they were assuredly incapable of running their own lives, or as brutal potential rapists, without honour, loyalty, love or kindness. There was no halfway house for Alicia Lightowler. Not that she had been unkind to him, Simon. Her son was thankfully exempt from this blanket condemnation of the male sex.

But Ruth had taken it on board, with special reference to Peter Lightowler, the hated, the untrustworthy, the great villain, Peter Lightowler. Simon's father.

He was mature enough now to recognize that his mother's hatred grew from some deep emotional wound. Undoubtedly, his father had behaved abominably, had had affairs, had scarcely troubled even to lie. Such arrogance, to hold another's feelings at so little value! He had been much older than Alicia, of course. She would have been dazzled by his style, his poise, wealth, knowledge . . . Until the first betrayal, or perhaps the next . . .

And the other things. The way he always seemed to know what you were thinking, the way he anticipated what you might say or do. He *was* disturbing, there was no doubt about it. And those servants . . .

Three of them. A man and two women who accompanied Peter Lightowler everywhere. At least Simon assumed that that was what they did. He hadn't actually left the manor for months, but he knew his father was never alone. He'd heard from Kate about the sick puppet show on the green and recognized it as their work. In times of febrile intuition, in those weird moments before the alcohol swamped all intellect, he knew that the women were also black creatures, winged, feathered, scaled. Unobserved, unnoticed, they crept into his room with the saving golden liquid, they swarmed over the manor, flowing out into the grass, soaring over the trees and the forest. They could avoid the Leafer like that, escape its boundaries. They were neither human nor animal, but something between. Something abnormal.

The man was different. There was never any suggestion that he was anything other than human. He was physically repellent, with his pale slug's skin, his sly eyes and cropped hair. There was a scar down one side of his face, a scar exactly like Lightowler's own.

Sometimes Simon wondered if the man was an aspect of his father. If the evil, potent side to Peter Lightowler's character evinced itself in this silent creature who stood watchfully beside the two women things. He thought he saw some resemblance between the two of them, between Peter Lightowler and the man in the trio.

Alcohol brings strange intuitions, as the intellect and will relax. Simon acknowledged this connection without rationalizing further. He was content to leave it there. For a time.

Chapter 22

Byrne cut round the kitchen garden towards the back of the manor. He'd found his way there with no trouble, having discovered a path he recognized within minutes of standing up. The wallet was still in his jacket pocket.

He told himself that he'd been dreaming. That the vision of Peter Lightowler and the trio melding into one was a hallucination, nothing solid or substantial. He'd dozed off, that was all. It was a dream.

Through the open French windows, he could see Tom hunched at the desk, scribbling furiously. There was something about the way he sat there, shoulders bent, head lowered, that caught Byrne's attention. For a moment, he stood there, watching.

The words seemed to fall from Tom's pencil without ceasing. No pauses for thought, no chewing at the pencil or scoring through unsatisfactory phrases. Tom was gripped, possessed by what he was writing.

Byrne crossed the lintel into the library. He spoke loudly, deliberately breaking the spell.

'So you came back. The house let you in. Will you stay here, tonight?'

Tom's hand continued to move across the paper, the words tumbling to fill the page. He did not pause. Byrne took one step closer, so that he was standing at the other side of the desk. 'Tom,' he said more softly. 'Tom, what are you doing?'

At last the young man looked up. His face was drawn, deep shadows beneath the eyes, unaccustomed lines of frowning round the mouth. 'I'm going to finish it,' he said. 'There's an answer here, and Kate . . . I need to find out, I need to know what happened!'

'What's the rush?'

'Kate won't leave. She told me this morning. She says she might not even come back to Cambridge. It's Ruth's fault. She makes Kate feel guilty or something. And Simon's out of his head half the time . . . God, what parents do to their children!'

'Simon's not Kate's father,' said Byrne mildly.

'As good as. He's always been here, she says. But anyway, she won't run out on Ruth, not now there's going to be a bloody garden party here.'

It made sense. Byrne perfectly understood the mixture of pressures that would keep Kate there. He was staying himself in order to help Ruth. She compelled those around her to involvement.

Like the manor. You could not leave it alone, you could not walk out and leave it to fall down. Its dilapidated charms – the doors which didn't fit, the dusty windows, the wormy skirting boards – called for repair. For succour. And against the odds, Ruth was determined to rescue the manor, to rescue Simon, and those around her felt imperceptibly drawn into the struggle.

Byrne sat on the edge of the desk, close to the growing pile of manuscript. 'Where is Ruth?'

'In the kitchen, I suppose, if she's not in the garden. I don't know. Look, I really must get on.' Already Tom's hand was fiddling with the pencil, turning it between tense fingers.

'Can I read this?' Byrne didn't know what he expected to find in it, but Tom and Kate evidently discovered significance in the story.

Tom's hand slammed down on the heap of papers. 'No! No, it's private. It belongs to the family!' He was outraged.

'All right, all right.' Byrne moved away. '*Are* you staying here, then?'

'Not overnight.' But already Tom's attention was on the wodge of paper in front of him and his hand was crawling across the blank white sheet.

Peter Lightowler was young enough to appear innocent. Peter Lightowler would make friends with Elizabeth and John Downie, after their wedding. He'd find a way into their confidence, use the charm of youth to beguile their reservations. He could . . . play tennis with Elizabeth. They'd meet at the tennis club, and have tea together. Lightowler would be invited to the manor, he'd make it his business to be pleasant to Downie, Elizabeth's crippled husband. They'd discuss politics, economics. Lightowler would amuse Downie, flatter him, ask his opinion on matters of foreign policy, defer to his maturity. Margaret, Elizabeth's aunt, would be living there too (because three people always lived in the manor). They'd play bridge together, but sometimes Downie would grow depressed, seeing Elizabeth laugh at Lightowler's jokes.

But Downie would always welcome Lightowler, knowing that Elizabeth needed the company. Downie would be frightened of losing her, if he kept her chained too close . . .

Lightowler would worm his way in, a maggot in an apple.

The bridge has gone on for longer than usual, the rubber proving elusive. Lightowler is staying for dinner, as he often does these days.

Towards the end of the meal, John Downie spills his wine.

It spurts across the table, staining the damask crimson, splashing over Elizabeth's blond lace dress and Lightowler's evening shirt.

'There now, look what I've done!' Downie stares at the mess, his lower lip trembling.

'It doesn't matter, John, it doesn't matter at all.'

Elizabeth's on her feet, mopping ineffectually at the table. 'Oh, what a shame, Peter! Your shirt!'

'Sorry, Lightowler. Clumsy of me.' There are tears streaking down Downie's face. 'Sorry, Lizzie.'

'You're tired, dear. Forgive us.' She looks at Lightowler.

'Of course.' He stands up. 'Allow me.' He moves behind Downie's chair and begins to wheel it towards the door. 'Come on, old man. Bedtime, don't you think?' Lightowler speaks gently, unembarrassed. Over Downie's head, his eyes meet Elizabeth's.

She nods briefly.

Peter Lightowler tilts the chair backwards to get up the step to the hall.

'You need a ramp here. And another to the garden.'

'Wait till I'm gone, can't you?' A small, despairing whisper.

'What's that, old man?' Lightowler leans down towards the thin shoulders. 'What point would there be in ramps if you weren't here? This is for you.'

They are passing the door to Elizabeth's room when Elizabeth herself catches up with them. 'It's all right, Peter. I'll take over now. Mags is still in the dining room.' She takes the handles and his hands brush hers. In silence she pushes the chair across the hall and down the corridor to the study, Downie's bedroom. Lightowler follows.

She turns to face him at the door. She's standing within the frame he has claimed. Its four points encompass her. 'Thank you for everything,' she says quietly. 'I don't know what we'd do without you.'

He moves towards her, saying nothing, staring at her seriously. He knows what his eyes are telling her, knows exactly how he appears. He touches his hand to her face, a slow stroke down her cheek. Her eyes are suddenly glazed, frosted over. He moves his right hand to cover her face, blotting out her narrow and delicate features. Then he touches his hands to the points of her breasts. His left hand moves downwards and traces the soft crease between her legs.

Then he turns and walks away.

He waits for her in the orchard. There are only a few leaves, only a few withered fruit left on the trees. The long grasses are beginning to die back. But the evening is not cold. There is no wind.

At one in the morning, he hears the west door to the manor open. The crow takes off immediately, flinging itself up into the black sky.

He stands at the gate to the orchard, looking towards the house. The moon is waning, but there are plenty of stars. He can see a figure moving quietly across the lawn and through the rose garden.

Her habitual path, taken every night before she goes to rest. He has watched her do this a hundred times. He sees it in his mind as analogous to his own progress round the house, touching every part of it. What she's doing now is marking the gardens as her own.

She doesn't know that he's been there first, laying his claim as any dog might.

The grass moves beside her.

'Peter?' She's looking for him. It's worked even better than he dared hope. 'Peter, where are you?'

'Hello, Elizabeth.' He stands there, his arms open, slightly raised, palms towards her. He's watching the movement in the grass and it halts there, waiting. It acknowledges his power. At his feet the beetle scuttles into a fold of leaves.

In triumph he draws her forward. His breath surrounds her, and her eyes look only at him.

'I don't understand . . .' she manages to say.

'Love is the strangest thing of all,' he says, half smiling, watching the shades of expression in her eyes, understanding and not-understanding.

'Is this love?'

He raises his left hand and runs it down the other side of her face. 'Oh yes, this is what men call love.' Her eyes are almost closed, deep in the dream.

And the time is right. He says her name once more, and it seems that her strength is dissipating. He holds her in his avid embrace, taking all her weight. She is his, clinging to him, her mouth moving against his face, her breath sweet and perfumed. Her voice murmurs words he doesn't try to understand.

And suddenly he's gripped, moved by violent desire. He pushes her clothes away from her breasts, tearing the fastenings. He's wild to take her breasts in his hands, to own them in reality. They are cool to the touch, smooth and soft. He bends his head and takes a nipple between his teeth. She's moaning now, and her hands are tearing at his trousers, impatient at the fly, ripping the buttons . . .

On the grass he enters her without preliminaries. She has been opened before, after all . . . He moves quickly, with urgency, not giving her a chance to think or realize what is happening. He spills himself inside her with a great, shuddering gasp, his back arching, his face uplifted to the stars, grimacing in triumph.

She lies there as if dazed. He pulls himself away from her and stands up. Her eyes are wide and unseeing. Her hands drift vaguely to touch her breasts, to touch her body as if it's strange and unknown to her. To reassure herself that it still exists as she has always known it to exist.

Too late. It is done. He dresses himself quickly while she lies there, eternally passive, spread before his gaze, her hands still drifting to touch her skin with that feathery vagueness.

Then he helps her rise, helps her dress, and pushes her gently back towards the house. She hardly looks at him, her eyes blank and unseeing. 'I love you,' he says, whispering into this half-dazed consciousness, 'and you love me.'

He sees her stumble across the lawn, sees her manage to open the door. She leaves it a little ajar but he doesn't think it matters.

Tom thought, how could he *do* it? What about the guardians, the ivy thing . . . *Leafer*, said his heart. What about the Dogfrog? Where were they? Why didn't they stop it?

Lightowler goes through the orchard until he comes to the beech hedge. He does not see the wave in the grass beside him, although the crow is fluttering a warning at him. It perches on one of the oak trees, crying harshly, and he mistakes it for victory, for glory . . .

He lays his hands on the pale entwined branches of the hedge and at once they spring apart, wrench apart with revulsion. It disdains his touch. He wants to laugh at this inadequate guardian, this barrier which is useless against him.

But as he walks through the gap a thorn catches against his jacket, holding it fast. And as he delays there, trying to free the fabric, something takes him. It springs from the hedge itself, too fast, too oblique for sight or sound. Something lashes at his face and fastens in the flesh, tearing, ripping through the soft tissue from eye to mouth.

His hands try to grasp it, to pull it away, and at the same time he's falling forward through the hedge.

And then the Leafer is gone. He staggers slightly, his face ablaze with pain. He raises his hand to his face and sees it, sticky with blood in the moonlight. He's trembling with shock. As he runs down the October lanes to the village, he feels blood drip on to his shirt.

More red stains. Red on red, blood and wine mixed. That old metaphor, written in reality on linen. It is no blasphemy for Peter Lightowler.

It doesn't matter at all.

Tom thought, and so Peter Lightowler raped Elizabeth . . . But was rape the right word? There was a certain degree of acquiescence, of course, but surely it was rape, made possible by the use of enchantment, that strange rite of marking the house.

Here Tom paused, tapping his pencil against his teeth. Was he seriously suggesting that *magic* was being used here? Here in Essex, in the twentieth century, in this middle-class, privileged environment? Hypnotism, he thought. Hypnotism was possible.

Think of those games shows, those weird tricks when people make fools of themselves at cabarets, in theatres . . . It must have been a kind of hypnotism.

And yet, in his soul, he knew that other forces were at work in the manor. The last three nights were vivid in his memory. He remembered the visions and hallucinations that had pushed him out of the house, the force of the rejection. It was the manor, he thought. Lightowler was conceived on its boundaries, on the island in the lake. The island belonged both to the forest and to the manor. He is connected to the place, he belongs to it just as the Leafer and Dogfrog do.

The words slotted into his mind without effort.

Simon knows, he thought. Simon understands more of this than the women. It's why he drinks, it's why he's so difficult. I have to talk to Simon, I have to get to know him. (He's Lightowler's son, went his mind, he's part of it too.)

He picked up the pencil again, trying to concentrate. Lightowler rapes his father's sister, his aunt . . . He went over it again. It could almost sound ludicrous, put like that, and yet think what their ages were. This took place after the war: say, in 1928. Elizabeth would be twenty-eight, conveniently the same age as the century. Peter was ten or eleven years younger than she, seventeen or eighteen when he hid overnight in the manor and became friends with the Downies.

Peter Lightowler is eighty-four now. It *would* fit, it *was* possible . . .

Was it true? He didn't know, and didn't care. This was how this story went, this was what happened. He sharpened the pencil, and went on writing.

Chapter 23

Byrne found Ruth in the kitchen. She was putting the phone down, and jumped as he came in. He saw that she had been crying.

'What is it?' Immediately his arms were round her, with no more thought than one gives to comforting a child. She leant against his shoulder, dabbing at her eyes with a handkerchief.

'I'm so sorry, what must you think?' But she did not draw away from him.

'What's wrong, Ruth?'

'It's – I keep getting these anonymous phone calls. They say *horrible* things, horrible lies, unmentionable things.'

'Have you any idea who it is?'

She shook her head.

'What about the police? They can put a tap on lines, and trace the call.'

'Oh, no! I couldn't tell anyone else about this!'

'Why not, Ruth?' He spoke gently.

'They'd ask me – they'd want to know . . .'

'What?'

'What the calls are about.' She wouldn't look at him. She'd moved a little way from him. 'I can't—' She stopped.

'What are they about, Ruth?'

He knew what she was going to say. He knew what the obsession was, where the evil lay. Tom was uncovering it in his book, Ruth was driven by the guilt of it, and Simon – well, he was trying to drink himself into oblivion, because of the obsession which gripped them all, Tom as well.

And then she said it, gave it voice.

'The family. It's always about my mother, about my grand-mother. Whoever it is keeps saying that it's incest, that I was conceived in incest, that I commit incest *now*.'

She shuddered. She was very pale. 'It's not true, of course. Quite ridiculous. Just because Simon's my cousin. He's not even a first cousin! But you don't want stories like that getting out, the gossip round here is terrible.' Her words ran out in a futile torrent of self-justification.

He took her hands. 'Ruth, tell me one thing.'

She broke off, staring at him.

'Ruth, who is your father?'

The blankness in her face was appalling.

'I don't know,' she whispered. 'I have absolutely no idea.'

She was lying. He saw it in the way her eyes wouldn't meet his, in the clenching of her hand, in the filmy sweat on her upper lip.

He turned away from her and found Simon standing in the doorway.

'Dear me, have I interrupted something? Don't mind me.' He walked carefully across the kitchen to the fridge and took the ice tray from it.

'It was another of those calls, Simon.'

'And our good, kind, dependable gardener here offered a handy shoulder to weep on?'

'She was upset,' said Byrne. 'Would you rather I'd walked out?'

Simon ignored him. 'Why didn't you come to *me*? Why won't you tell me these things?'

'I can't!'

'It's about me, isn't it? Someone's telling you filthy things about me.' Simon suddenly turned to Byrne. 'No, don't go. Do stay. It's better than a soap opera, this, and all we need now is the hook at the end of the episode. How about the return of the prodigal son? That's always a winner, that'd make you turn on again.'

'What are you talking about?' Ruth was mystified. 'Sometimes I really don't understand a word you say. Look, I'm sorry I was upset. I'm just so tired.'

'And who wouldn't be? I tell you, Ruth, you've taken on too much. You're wearing yourself out.'

Byrne heard the familiar squabble resume. He'd had enough. He slipped out of the door and no one noticed.

Byrne walked back to the cottage slowly. Get out, he told himself. There are complications in this family that will draw you in, do you no good. Simon is already jealous, and Ruth –

Ruth. There lay the problem. He could not leave her, not in the middle of this mess. It was beyond compassion now. He saw that her battle with Simon was nearly at its end. Whatever bound them together was no longer love. That did not invalidate the relationship, of course. There are powerful bonds that completely sidestep that particular passion. But he thought Ruth was free, that she had welcomed his arms, had wanted him to stay. She was moving beyond Simon towards himself.

It was madness to stay at the manor. He looked back at it, basking in the afternoon sun, the field of grass waving softly around it. The roof was gleaming in the light, through the trees. The brightness of it almost repelled his gaze. He still found the manor unsettling, disconcerting, fascinating. It teased at his mind. He had in no way become used to it. He was not surprised that Tom had been unable to live there and was equally unable to leave.

So was he. He could no more walk away now than cut his hand off.

The great beeches by the lake were shivering in a breeze he could barely detect. It was very hot again. He thought what central London would be like and knew he didn't want to be there, either. Caught between the devil and the deep blue sea, the manor or the city. He sighed. Perhaps one more week, just one, to clear the weeds from the side of the drive. It would clarify things for Ruth, it would make her feel better if the approach to the manor were neat and tidy.

He knew, deep down, that he would stay to the end. That he would see it through, whatever it was.

Chapter 24

There was a bottle of whisky on the table in the cottage, a fine single malt. There was no one there. He was amused, nothing more, at the blatant bribe. No, a distraction: a bottle of whisky was hardly going to be enough to move him out of the manor. Distraction from what?

Suddenly anxious, he went to the door and looked up the drive towards the manor as if it might tell him something. As he stood there he heard a car approach and turn into the drive.

A new Peugeot stopped by the cottage. A woman with cropped grey hair opened the door and got out. She looked over the car roof at Byrne.

'Who are you?' she asked. Her voice was arrogant. 'What do you think you're doing here?'

'I'm helping with the garden,' he said patiently. The woman seemed familiar to him, and he wondered if perhaps he'd seen her on television or in the papers. She was wearing a coffee-coloured linen suit with a black shirt, beautifully cut. She was supremely self-assured, but even so, he was surprised when she marched past him and into the cottage.

Her sharp eyes, missing nothing, fixed immediately on the bottle of whisky.

'So it's you, is it, who takes the drink to the manor?' She spoke with utter disdain. 'How much does he pay you for it?'

'Wait a minute. What's this to do with you?'

She stared at him as if he were something nasty found under the doormat. He saw that she was older than he had at first realized: her skin was covered by a pattern of fine lines and her hands were swollen at the knuckles with arthritis.

Then she moved suddenly and swiftly and knocked the bottle of whisky from the table with a sweep of her hand. It shattered on the stone floor. The smoky scent of the alcohol filled the cottage.

'Do you make a habit of this kind of thing, or is today special?'

'You are beneath contempt.' She turned on her heel and left the cottage, slamming the door shut behind her.

He was frowning as he cleared up the mess. And then he paused, brush poised over the dustpan.

He hadn't met her before. But her face was familiar to him, as familiar as an old friend. She looked like Simon.

And more than that. The expression in her eyes reminded him vividly and inescapably of Tom Crabtree.

He was clearing some of the nettle patches from beside the drive over an hour later when Ruth came to find him.

She was rather flushed, either with heat or approaching tears. 'Byrne, I'm so sorry! Alicia told me what she did, and I knew at once it was the most dreadful mistake.'

'*Alicia?* That was Simon's mother?' He stripped off his gloves and wiped his forehead. That would explain it, part of it anyway.

'She gets frantic about his drinking, you see.' Her head was tilted as she looked at him.

'Ruth, it's not me. I've never brought alcohol into the manor, for Simon or anyone else. I don't know where that bottle of whisky came from, it was nothing to do with me.'

'Oh, I know, but . . . you can see it was an honest mistake on Alicia's part.'

'Sure.' He paused, studying her. She seemed harassed and unhappy and he wanted more than anything to take her away, to find some quiet, lonely place with no responsibilities or ties. 'Is Alicia going to be staying at the manor?'

'No, she's got rooms in Epping. She hates the manor, swore she'd never stay here again once I was old enough to take charge of it. She's come to talk about this fête. She has strong views on what should happen here.'

'Although she hates it?'

'I think she's worried about Simon.' Sighing, Ruth subsided on to the grass.

He sat down next to her. 'Is it much worse?' he asked.

She was silent for a while. He had no desire to hurry her.

'It's getting really difficult. I – I don't know how much longer I can stand it. He won't leave the house, but I think it does him no good to be cooped up day after day, brooding. Dr Reynolds leaves various pills, but Simon won't take them. He's almost –

despairing. And how he gets all this drink beats me. There must be someone in the village sneaking it in . . .'

'Do you really believe that? How would Simon pay for it?'

'Simon gets an allowance. It's not much, but enough for that. And besides what else could it be? You haven't seen anyone hanging around, have you?'

Only Peter Lightowler, he thought. He provided money, he had his servants leave messages. Byrne had been on the receiving end of both.

Somehow he knew better than to mention Lightowler to her. 'I'll keep an eye out,' he promised, 'but the grounds are hardly secure. That hedge is full of gaps and anyone can come through by the lake. It wouldn't be hard. They'd just need to pick a time when you and Kate were out.'

'I can't be everywhere at once!' she cried as if he'd suggested it was her fault. 'Sometimes I think I should give up work, but we need the money, such as it is. And it's not fair to ask Kate to spy on Simon, it's not fair on either of them!'

'Poor Ruth. I wish I could help.'

Her head dropped against his shoulder. It felt very natural. 'At least you listen. And you're doing wonders in the garden. And you're always here, when I need you.'

This was no good, there was no future in this. Simon was between them as vividly as a physical presence. Gently Byrne disengaged.

She went on talking, as if nothing had happened. 'I've been thinking. There might be a way to pay you some kind of a wage, get a further mortgage perhaps—'

The temptation of it, to belong somewhere, to be *here*, with Ruth. What was he *doing*, how could he be thinking this? So soon?

'Ruth, there are things I have to do, things I need to straighten out.'

'What? I thought we'd decided, once you'd sorted it out with the army, you could come back here.'

He pulled at a blade of grass, running it through his fingers. 'It's not only the army. There was a – confusion about the way Kristen died. It wasn't straightforward thuggery, that ordinary, stupid violence.'

'I thought it was a terrorist bomb.'

'That was the story. But it wasn't true.'

'Not true? But who would plant a bomb otherwise?'

David, he nearly said. My best friend. Instead he merely shrugged. 'I don't know,' he lied.

A pause as she looked directly at him. He had the unnerving impression that she understood much more than he was prepared to admit. He saw for the first time the intelligence in her face, the keenness of her gaze. He wanted never to lie to her again.

'Give it time, Byrne. Put some space between it and you. Stay here,' she said. Her hand nearly touched his. He knew her touch would be delicate, light as a butterfly. She went on speaking. 'There's no need to stir it up, not for a while. It'll keep. A few more weeks won't make any difference. Stay until after the fête.'

He had already decided on this. He told her so, and was rather appalled by the relief in her expression.

'And then it'll be the summer holidays, and I'll have time to persuade Simon to see a proper doctor, a psychiatrist. He's much easier when I'm not out at work all the time.'

'He must love you very much.'

Another one of those weighty pauses. Was she going to lie now? 'I think he does, underneath. We were so close as children, it was as if the rest of the world didn't exist. He's three years older than I am. I thought he was wonderful. We lived here with Alicia, and it was almost perfect, a dream of a childhood.'

'What went wrong, Ruth?'

She frowned. 'Oh, it was so long ago. We went to different universities, and Alicia closed the manor during term time. She always hated living here on her own. She went back to teaching. But the manor was never the same after that. It always felt temporary, not properly looked after, like a station waiting room or something. I don't blame Alicia, of course I don't, but it's been an uphill struggle ever since trying to get it back in shape. I suppose we were too young to care then, too full of ambitions and energy to want to bother with the old place.'

'What did Simon feel about it?'

'He never showed particular signs of wanting the manor when we were children. We always knew it was going to be mine one day. But after he went to Oxford, he became . . . very unpredictable. He started drinking, got in with a rather wild set. He was the star of various student productions, much admired. I suppose it didn't do him any good, really. It was so unbalanced.

He had a couple of affairs, one that went badly wrong, but nothing stuck. He seemed different when we got back here in the holidays; bitter and self-destructive.'

'And you've been picking up the pieces ever since.'

'He says that's what you do.' She glanced at him sideways. 'Two of a kind, that's what we are.' She laughed lightly. 'Come to dinner tonight, Byrne, and let Alicia make amends. Come and be part of the family again.'

'Is that wise? What about Simon?'

'Oh, don't worry about Simon! He'll be fussing around his mother, you wait and see. He'll hardly notice you're there.'

He watched her walk up the drive to the house, and wondered if she felt, like him, treacherous. Talking about Simon behind his back, gossiping, whatever it was, seemed disloyal.

And yet if they hadn't spoken, they would have touched again. Beyond the words, the explanations and history lay another world, dangerous, unknown, disruptive.

He didn't know how much longer words would keep them apart.

Chapter 25

'So, you've started writing.'

Alicia was leaning against the doorway of the library, a glass of fruit punch in her hand.

Tom swung round. 'Alicia! I didn't realize you were here!'

He stood up and crossed the floor to kiss her on both cheeks. This was a greeting she had taught him herself, before he went to Cambridge. But she was the only person he ever embraced like that.

'Are you staying here?' he asked.

She shook her head. 'No. At the Bell Inn. I never stay here these days.' She put her glass down on a shelf and turned back to him.

'What's been going on, Tom?' she asked. 'You look dreadful.'

He was disarmed by the concern in her voice. He had always been flattered by her interest in him. 'I – I haven't been sleeping well. It's something to do with the house.'

'Don't tell me you've fallen for the three-night trick as well!' She shrugged, as if the whole subject were ridiculous. 'Of all people!'

He swallowed, embarrassed. 'It – it wasn't up to me to decide. It just happened like that.'

A small silence as she stared at him. 'And now you're in the gardener's cottage with the hired help,' she said at last.

He smiled, relieved that the subject had moved on. 'Byrne's not paid for what he does here.'

'But you've managed to avoid Ruth's work-sheets.' She was drifting across the floor towards the desk as she spoke. She stopped there, her hand on the sheaf of manuscript. But she made no attempt to read it: instead, she said,

'And the writing, Tom? How's it going?'

He coloured. How could he tell her about this? Certain vivid scenes sprang into his mind. This was her family too, her ex-*husband*! 'It's taking shape,' he said lamely. 'It's a sort of – family saga.'

'Aiming at the women's market, are you? How very unlikely.'

Her sharp eyes had never left his face. He had the uneasy suspicion that she could read his mind. Why did she always keep him on edge? What pleasure did it give her to disconcert and confuse him?

'Ruth said you'd been asking about the Bannieres. Have you found it a fruitful line of enquiry? Are you trying to base it on real events, as I suggested?'

'Good Lord, no!' He needed to deny this. 'Well, not entirely. I have been using the chronology of the family as a framework, an outline. You know, about Roderick and Elizabeth growing up together here, making up something about why he was disinherited—'

'Oh, *that* old story. I wouldn't have thought it lurid enough for fictional purposes. A squalid little incident, blown up out of all proportion.'

What did she think happened? 'Tell me about it,' he invited. 'Whatever you know.'

She settled in one of the leather armchairs on the other side of the desk. 'No. Let's hear your version first. Fiction hot from the source.'

'Do you want to read it?' He shuffled through the pile on the desk, and separated it into two. There was no mention of Peter Lightowler in the earlier sections. He needn't face that problem yet.

'Thanks.' She took cigarettes from her jacket pocket and lit one.

Tom left the library, knowing he would be unable to write while she was there reading. She'd read his work before, of course; he could trust her to be fair. He'd always written to her as a child, and then she had been his tutor.

But really he wanted to talk to Kate, to make his peace with her.

He couldn't find her. She was nowhere in the house, and he could see her from none of the windows. In the end he asked Ruth. She was on the terrace, pulling weeds from between the soft grey stones.

'Kate? She's gone into Theydon. She said she was going to see a friend. Didn't she tell you?' Her voice was kind. 'She's going to stay for supper.'

He felt as if a bucket of cold water had been thrown over

178

him. Was Kate going to persist in this? Did she really not understand why he had refused to stay in the manor any longer? 'Where does her friend live? Do you know who it is?'

'I'm afraid not, Tom. It could be anyone. She grew up here, she knows people in the village. She took her bike. You could look out for that.'

'Thanks.' He turned away from her and crossed the courtyard to the stable block where the bikes were kept. He didn't see the frown on Ruth's face as she watched him go.

He didn't need to roam the village. He knew where she'd be. Sure enough, he found her sturdy mountain bike leaning against the wall of the Georgian house on the green.

He knocked at the door.

It swung open. 'Hello?' he called, taking one step inside. 'Hello? Kate? Mr Lightowler?'

There was no one there. The house echoed coldly around him. He shivered.

He pushed open the drawing room door. No one, nothing. Just the ranks of books covering the walls. The other rooms on the ground floor were also empty.

They must have gone out together, he thought and his skin began to crawl at the mere idea of Kate being alone with Peter Lightowler. He turned back to the front door, but before he could leave the house he heard something, a faint rustling sound from somewhere above.

'Hello!' he called again. 'Is there anyone there?'

The rustle again, the sound of wind through leaves. He didn't know what it was – a cat? That weird woman Byrne told him about, the cook's daughter? It sounded like the sweeping of twigs or branches against bare floorboards.

He frowned. And then anxiety gripped him and he was suddenly terrified. He ran up the stairs, pushing open door after door, shouting Kate's name, letting it fill the house.

Nothing. No answer, no further sound.

At the end of the landing he found another flight of stairs, narrow and cramped. And then that rustle again . . .

The attic was empty. Hanging from the catch of the open skylight Kate's shoulder bag spun in the warm air. He caught it in his hands, furious and frantic.

An eye stared at him. The lens from a large telescope pointed directly at him, dazzling with sunlight.

And then he saw them.

They must have been standing there all the time, quietly waiting for him, listening to him shout, listening to him run through the house, watching him cross the attic.

He'd seen them before in the forest when he'd arrived at the manor for the first time. A mess, he'd called them then, and he saw no reason to change his estimate now.

'Who are you?' he said, and his voice sounded thickly in the attic. The woman on the left detached herself from the group. She was terribly thin, almost skeletal, her bones as pointed and sharp as starvation. Her eyes were tiny pinholes of black, ringed by black mascara. He saw rims of red under her nails, gleams of shiny redness through the black rags she was wearing.

She came closer and he stepped back instinctively. Ideas of flight ran through his mind. But the other two had moved without his noticing and were standing between him and the door. He didn't want even to look at them, let alone try to force his way through. The skylight offered a more attractive avenue of escape.

'Where's Kate? What have you done with her?'

'She's with your grandfather,' said the woman closest to him, her voice harsh, louder than he'd expected. She was within arm's reach and he could smell the sour stink of her, hardly disguised by the musky scent she wore.

'Not my grandfather,' he said automatically. 'Where have they gone?'

'Out,' she said calmly. 'You needn't worry. They'll be back before it gets dark.'

'Where did they go?'

'The forest. That's where they always go.' The man pushed himself away from the wall, and began to shamble across the bare boards towards Tom. 'Why don't you join them? I'm sure Mr Lightowler would be delighted to see you.'

Tom frowned. 'Who *are* you?' he asked again. 'How do you know so much about Kate?'

'Don't you know yet?' The man's mouth twisted. 'There are all sorts of clues for you, bright little college boy. I'll give you one, free, gratis and for nothing. Three's company, four's a crowd . . .'

Tom felt suddenly angry, furious at these games, these mysteries. 'For Christ's sake, why won't you tell me who you are?'

Still he could not look at the third of them, in the corner of the door. She waited there, and shadows obscured her face.

The man was smiling and with sick certainty Tom recognized a parody of Peter Lightowler's own features, the same scar between eye and mouth, the same flat expression in the eyes. But when this man smiled, Tom saw that his lips stretched to expose yellowy-green teeth.

He stepped back and stumbled against a chair. He found himself sitting there.

The man bent down towards him. He spoke as confidentially as an old friend, in a clipped, out-dated, upper-class accent. 'I'll give you a hint, then, old lad. Oh, we're so *kind* to you, it's like milk to a baby. Flesh of my flesh, listen to this. It's in the northern skies, the great ringed castle. There's your answer, the reason for it all.'

And then the man reached out one hand and stroked the hair away from Tom's flinching face. Softly, dry lips brushed the skin at his temple. 'Remember,' said the man. 'Three's company, four's a crowd. And watch the stars, watch the northern skies.'

And then they were gone, the three of them, and he was slumped forward, clinging to the barrel of a telescope which he only realized later was pointing, ready and waiting, at the northern stars.

He ran from the house and cycled back to the manor, his fury overwhelming reason. He didn't notice the two figures standing beside the road in the shade of the trees, the elderly man and the pretty girl in her scarlet dress.

She was holding on to his arm, as if guiding him. Or was he using her as a support? They watched Tom angrily pedalling down the lane through the forest, and he never even turned his head to see them there. The sunlight stabbed through the leaves to highlight the man's colourless hair and drained skin.

Tom was white-lipped with hurt pride. They were playing tricks on him, using him. Alicia, Kate, that horrible trio, all of them. It was like some ghastly game, puppets and masques, cat and mouse, role-playing without a script.

Sadistic games.

*

'Is Kate here?' He slammed into the kitchen.

Simon and Alicia were sitting at the table, peacefully de-stringing runner beans.

Simon stared at him. 'Whatever's the matter?'

'She's gone out with that bastard Lightowler.'

'An accurate description in every respect, but you're not making much sense, Tom.' Alicia put down her knife.

'Those bloody things, that man with the two hags—' He dragged a chair out from the table and threw himself into it. 'They said Kate's gone for a walk with Lightowler in the forest, and I could find her there. I don't like it, I don't like it at all. Those three – drop-outs, whoever they are – are up to no good at all—'

He half expected disbelief from them, but not contempt.

'If you're so worried, why *didn't* you go and find her?' Alicia put down her knife and stood up, rubbing her hands on a tea-towel. 'And I really think you're rather old to be upset by a bit of cheap make-up, a theatrical trick or two.'

'What? There's nothing theatrical about them, they're just filthy, a mess—'

'And you've been nagging me for being drunk,' Simon said to his mother, ignoring what Tom was saying.

Alicia was taking down her jacket from the hook by the door. She was looking down her nose at him, as if he'd made a faux pas, used the wrong cutlery or something.

'I'm not drunk!' shouted Tom. He crashed his fist down on the table. 'I just want to find Kate!'

'How touching!' said Simon. 'How very devoted of you!'

'Tell me, Tom. Just what do you know? Why shouldn't she be with her grandfather?' said Alicia.

'Her *grandfather*? No, he's not, you've got it all wrong, he's *your* side of the family, your ex-husband, nothing to do with Kate or Ruth.'

'Is that what you think?' Simon was razor-sharp with him.

'Shut up, Simon!' He could read nothing at all in Alicia's face, but her voice was all at once furious. 'Why don't you get on with your book, Tom?' She stood by the door, her hand on the handle. 'The best possible thing you can do to protect Kate is to write your book. There are answers there, if you're patient. The structure needs some realignment, I feel. Have you thought much about John Downie, Elizabeth's husband?'

'What are you talking about? I don't want literary criticism, I need to find Kate!'

'Then I suggest you do as my father's servants, his tame little troupe of playactors, recommend,' said Simon. 'Go for a walk in the forest. It seems an excellent plan to me. Then you can come back and get on with your writing or something, and we'll be the three of us again, just like it always used to be.'

'Three's company and four's a crowd?' He was still shouting. He swung round to Alicia. 'Where are you going?'

'Epping. I need to unpack,' Alicia said. She opened the door. 'Sorry, Simon. It looks like it's only going to be you and Ruth.'

'There's always the gardener,' said Simon bitterly. 'Good old Phizackerley Byrne. Oh, but he never stays in the house, he doesn't fit. No, you'll have to stay, Tom, at least until Kate gets back. Get on with the magnum opus. That's what we're all waiting for.'

'When *will* she be back?' He was bewildered and upset.

'Don't worry about Kate. She's quite capable of taking care of herself.' The door was closing behind Alicia. 'Better not tell Ruth, though,' she added thoughtfully.

Tom turned back to the drunken man at the table. 'What do you know about this?' He was trying to be a little calmer. 'What's this about your father being Kate's grandfather?'

'It's all circles, you know. Round and round we go, a celestial Angel Delight of sin and sex.'

'Why won't you answer me straight? What are you hiding?'

'Look.' Simon pointed to the corner of the room. The Dogfrog was there, hunched in the shadows, and for a moment a trick of the light made it appear much larger, tinged with the red of the sunset.

'Simon, tell me. I don't understand any of this!' He felt like smashing something.

'Do you watch the stars? Know anything about astronomy?'

'Oh God, not you too. *They* said, the three, they told me to watch the northern sky.'

'The Corona Borealis. Arianrhod's spinning castle, round and round we go, and who knows how to stop it . . .' Simon's words were increasingly slurred and Tom realized how very drunk he was.

'It spins and it spins and the sins of the fathers shall be visited unto the third generation, only I make it the fourth, something's out of true, it's whether he's a grandfather or a great-grandfather . . . Should only be three, of course, three generations, three people, three women like all good goddesses, except if you count the hand of five—'

'Shut up! What good is this?'

Simon reached across the table towards him, staring blearily into his face. 'It's in the books,' he said. 'And whatever you're writing. Words all the way, the inspiration of poets . . .' He stood up, waving his hands widely at the open paperback on the window sill over the sink, at the small pile near the telephone, the cookery books on the shelf by the fridge, the magazines and newspapers in a heap by the door.

'I want to see Kate. I need to talk to her. Why has she gone off with that man?'

'A bit out of date, aren't you? This possessiveness strikes me as near Neanderthal. Why shouldn't she visit her grandfather?'

'He's not her grandfather!'

'Well, clever little Tom, if he isn't, who is? Ask yourself that. I think,' he said slowly, 'that you'd better start trying to disentangle the family tree. Your book's not going to make any sense if you don't get it right . . .'

Chapter 26

Alicia drove to Epping through the forest, her hands clenched on the wheel.

God, what have I done? What have I started, what will become of us now? What will Kate do?

Nothing, she answered herself. Kate was rejecting it, just as Ruth repressed it and Ella rejected it. And then came a sudden, sharp pang of regret for her old friend, that Ella was no longer there to laugh at this most serious of situations.

Ella had always laughed, always mocked everything that Peter had said and done. It had not helped her in the end, but Alicia could not regret those fine jokes, that wicked essence of mockery. Pete, she'd called him behind his back. Old Petey's got himself in a twitch, better keep out of the way . . .

But she hadn't kept out of the way, not enough. How could it have been otherwise? How could she have known? Brought up at the manor by those two secret, bitter women, Elizabeth and Margaret, she had been sheltered and protected and kept in ignorance. Ella grew up in a state of innocence that was in fact no protection whatsoever.

They sent Ella to the convent in Epping and that was where Alicia had met her. The two girls had soon become friends, although the nuns discouraged intimacy. The nuns were easy targets, with their trivial and ridiculous rules.

Alicia remembered what had first brought them together. She had worn patent leather shoes one day, at the age of nine. Sister Anne had been affronted. 'Such footwear is a temptation,' she said, her mouth down-turned in the ample folds of flesh. 'Others may see reflected – what should be held secret. Such shoes are indiscreet, an invitation to the weak-willed and lascivious.'

Alicia had giggled and exchanged glances with Ella.

They shared glances then, and they went on to share secrets, and everything else. They wore each other's clothes and read each other's diaries. Sometimes Ella stayed the night with Alicia in Epping. This was always with Elizabeth's approval. She trusted Alicia's father, Dr Shaw. He was an old friend. Alicia's mother often went to tea at the manor. Elizabeth relied on the Shaws, if no one else.

She was prepared to trust Alicia and her family to take care of Ella beyond the grounds of the manor.

But James and Doris Shaw were busy people, caught up in an exceedingly active social life. They were members of the church, they played golf and sang in the local choir. They were not often around. Practically speaking, there was no one to oversee what happened to Ella outside the manor, except Alicia. For Jamie Wetherall didn't arrive until later, much later, and there was no one else.

Alicia and Ella met Peter Lightowler at the tennis club and he had exerted himself to be charming to them. He'd been such fun. It was difficult to admit it now, after so much time, but Alicia could still remember the way he moved, that lightning elegance and grace. He could mimic, he could crease them up with his satires and jokes, and under the wash of illicit alcohol and nicotine which always flowed so freely wherever he was, they loved it. They loved Peter Lightowler, too.

'He's reliving his youth,' Ella said wisely, 'but why shouldn't we get what we can out of it? It's rather fun, don't you think?'

And it had been fun. In spite of Ella's words, Peter was still young, when they first met him. He'd moved into the Red House that spring, and they often visited him there. He showed them his art collection, he gave them cocktails.

Alicia sighed. Peter had always worn well, kept his hair, kept the same lithe, trim figure. And apart from that scar (which only made him look rakish, said Ella), his skin was supple and unlined. He understood that they were bored, out on the edge of Epping Forest. They wanted to go to nightclubs, dancing . . . He had a record player (gramophone, they called it), and they danced to Ellington and Ted Heath and Count Basie. And Alicia had married him.

And although Alicia hated and mistrusted the way Kate was getting involved with her ex-husband, at least that was no longer a worry. For although Peter was still slim, still with that straight fall of hair, he was in his mid-eighties and his face was leather with lines. There would be no dancing at the Red House now. The idea was absurd.

The other skills would remain, of course. Charm, wit . . . And Kate had never known a father.

Oh, what had she done? Would Kate start trying to champion Peter's cause, would she feel he had been hard done by, that Alicia and Ruth were in some kind of feminist conspiracy against an old and frail man?

And then there was Tom's book. That at least was going as Alicia had planned. As the Peugeot roared through the forest, she mulled over the strange phenomenon of Tom's writing.

It was nothing new. Alicia had experienced it herself. That's what had given her the idea. Long ago, after Ella's death, when Alicia had found herself guardian to Ella's baby daughter Ruth and mistress of the manor, she had tried to write in the library there. It had been difficult. She'd had very little help with the children, Margaret having died soon after Ruth's birth. Peter wasn't living with her then. She avoided him as far as possible although sometimes she'd been driven to leave the children at the Red House (and what a mistake that had been).

She had tried to work for her thesis in the library.

She had chosen a wild, unfashionable theme: the figure of Cerridwen/Arianrhod/Blodewydd in Welsh bardic verse. Some years later Robert Graves had done a much better job than she could ever have cobbled together. Her frame of reference hadn't been anywhere near wide enough, she had not thought to compare Arianrhod with those other manifestations of the Goddess. But even so her thesis had had a life of its own. She had found herself gripped by streams of words referring to Arianrhod as a vengeful, terrifying force. She had picked up the references to the circle of stars, had even looked at astrological charts to find a candidate for the mysterious spinning castle. Corona Borealis, she had decided. Alicia had got that far.

It was only recently, long after Ella's death, that she had discovered amongst the media hype that the northern ring of stars had contained a cataclysmic variable, a variable which had last flared in 1905, during the spring when the manor was being built. At first it struck her as no more than a curious coincidence. She was no enthusiast for horoscopes and fortune-telling. She had filed the information away at the back of her mind, knowing that someday it would come into its own.

Now, this summer at the far end of the century, towards the end of the millennium, Alicia knew the time was right. The flaring star was brightening the northern skies through the brief hours of darkness, unsettling and distracting. She had faith, a curious conviction that owed nothing to reason or logic, that something would happen at the manor. She chose to think of it as a manifestation of the spinning castle, but this was her private fantasy, something she was unwilling to articulate or share with anyone else. She was excited and on edge, but she had no sense of dread.

She had always been on the outside. Even when she lived in the manor, she had felt herself an interloper, an alien. She had loved Ella, they had been best friends, and it had seemed natural after the accident that Alicia should have been left to bring up Ella's daughter, Ruth, but she had never felt truly at ease in the manor.

Never mind that her own relationship with Peter was already dead. Ella's will, the will she had drawn up when she first discovered she was pregnant, had directed that Alicia should be her child's guardian if anything should happen to Jamie or herself. She had made no mention of Peter Lightowler.

Looking back now, it seemed perhaps Ella had foreseen that Alicia and Peter's marriage was unlikely to endure. Certainly, Ella's friendship with Peter had come to an end pretty swiftly once Jamie Wetherall had appeared on the scene.

But now, forty years later, Alicia decided to act. She had discovered that Kate was becoming friendly with her ex-husband. And besides there was very little time left before the ownership of the manor would be passed on.

She had not known what to do at first. She had been waiting for a sign or some event to trigger the pattern once more. She had almost given up when Tom Crabtree announced that he wanted to be a writer.

It was almost too good to be true.

Alicia had wasted no time. She moved, carefully and decisively. Kate was invited for lunch and casually introduced to Tom.

Alicia held her breath and watched them eye each other, tentatively trying the have-you-read? conversation, the do-you-like-the-Cocteau-Twins? line. There were enough similarities, enough differences for interest.

Alicia's luck was holding. She had expected Tom to like Kate, but they had swiftly fallen into something deeper than mere liking. It was another confirmation that the time was right, that now she should act.

'You're a novelist,' she told him a few weeks later, when he and Kate were established together. 'Your mind works on the right scale, sees the complications and connections.'

She watched him absorb it, saw him fit into the role 'writer' and suffered a pang. This was unprincipled. Perhaps he was a writer, although she'd seen no particular signs of it beyond a competent academic skill. Perhaps one day he would indeed write something remarkable, but that wasn't really the point. She just wanted him to go to the library in the manor and write whatever occurred to him. She was sure something would happen, something of significance. This was manipulation, god-games, intrigue, Alicia's favourite hobby.

At Cambridge she saw his eyes scan each room as he entered it, watchful for the little things, the little betrayals that delineate character and mood. She knew he carried notebooks around, that he gave his mild taste for eccentricity free rein. He learned to cook Japanese, but listened only to French music.

(How it emerges she'd thought, fascinated, one afternoon when he'd played her a tape of melodies by Fauré and she'd almost said, what about Duparc, what about those twelve songs? But it had been too early, it would have given too much away.)

It was so difficult to decide how far to go. What to direct, what to leave to chance. In the end, the only risk had been whether he and Kate would make a go of it, but even that had fallen into place.

Kate had suggested that Tom went to the Blue Manor with no prompting whatsoever from Alicia. It was *meant*, she knew it. And the book was turning out just right, just how it had to be . . .

Alicia turned into the Bell Inn and parked the car, enjoying the anonymity of mass-market hospitality.

In the bar she ordered a packet of peanuts and a large whisky for herself. She felt strangely invigorated, as if sparks might fly from the ends of her fingers or her hair start from her head. She crunched her still-strong, still-white teeth on the salty nuts and smiled.

She had no sense of dread.

Chapter 27

Get it right. The family tree, and what *happened*. And Alicia's afterthought, pointing out John Downie to him. Should he trust her? Should he believe Alicia when she was being so bloody maddening, so superior?

Tom was sitting at the desk in the library, fretting over his conversation with Alicia and Simon. He could hear Simon in the kitchen across the hall, getting the supper ready. Ruth was out in the garden, as usual.

He looked through the French windows at the leaves fluttering in the light breeze and wondered why he had been so worried about Kate. He had been ludicrously over-impressed by that ghastly trio: what had got into him? Alicia and Simon had made Kate's absence seem quite normal. They hadn't even bothered to tell Ruth about it.

They had made him feel a fool. He resented that. And he wanted Kate back, he felt unfairly abandoned by her. He regretted, he terribly regretted, even coming . . . and yet did he? He had his book, this first few strange chapters telling a story he had not planned.

He didn't want to give it up. He was going to *use* this summer, use the family, he was going to finish his book.

John Downie, the crippled war veteran.

What did he feel about his wife's affair with the ubiquitous Peter Lightowler? Downie was such a vulnerable character, so pathetic . . . And yet was that all there was to him? He was crippled, imprisoned in a wheelchair. The effects of mustard gas. That was what it was. The stink of ammonia.

Sitting at the desk, waiting for the writer's mantle to descend, calmly poised in the Rennie Mackintosh chair, he felt suddenly cold. The pencil dropped from his fingers.

Ammonia stinking through that long corridor, driving the breath from his body.

He couldn't handle this, it was going to kill him.

And yet the blank paper waited there, the pencil poised so

carefully, as if an artist had arranged it where it had fallen, the tip pointing to the top of the page.

He picked it up once more, slowly, reluctantly. He needed something else, one more thing. Holding his breath, as if waiting for the surgeon's knife, he went over to the piano.

Duparc melodies, open on the keyboard.

> To open one's arms out and, tired of waiting,
> To close them on the void!
> But yet, always to hold them out to her,
> Always to love her . . .

His pencil was in his hand, poised and ready. He went back to the desk and began to write.

His arms feel tired even when he brushes his hair. Tying shoelaces takes several minutes, with a number of pauses for breath between each stage. It will never get any better, they told him. There's not enough healthy tissue in his lungs to give him breath for anything beyond the least movement.

There had been desperate days, when John Downie had first begun to realize the limits. Every area of life is affected. The obvious things, never running, never playing cricket or riding a horse are trivial compared to the real humiliations. Opening a window when it's too hot. Putting a jacket on when it's cold. Standing up when a woman enters the room.

Out of bounds, forbidden.

'You must resign yourself to the life of an observer,' one of the doctors said, sensibly enough. 'Action is no longer an option for you. Books, music . . . a little culture goes a long way. Card games, chess. I don't have to tell you.' The doctor leaned back in his chair, his hands behind his head. He was old, balding, his clothes untidy. Just after the war it was. Ten years ago. He'd been there in the Retreat for ten years. The doctor's eyes were sympathetic, his voice kind. 'Were you a 'varsity man?'

'A year at Cambridge before the balloon went up,' he whispered in the frail voice which was all that remained to him.

The doctor nodded. 'Reading, then. But don't spend a lot of time alone. Don't think too much, it won't help.'

He'd been right there. Thinking is the problem. John Downie did his best to fill his days, wheeling himself round the Retreat, talking to the other inmates, getting to know them, those other poor wrecks with nowhere else to go.

It could be worse. He could be in pain, or physically repulsive like Georgie Graves, who'd lost half his face in a mortar attack.

Most of them considered that he had been let off lightly, and he knew they were right. It was easier to take at the Retreat somehow, where everyone was wounded in body or spirit. He knew then he'd been lucky, watching them wrestling with artificial limbs, with the terror of daylight nightmares, with the isolation of deafness or pain or madness or deformity.

He'd been lucky, too, that Elizabeth had come to visit young Jimmy Chivvers. That she'd taken the trouble to get to know Jimmy's friend, that he'd made her laugh on that first visit.

He wakes in the nights sweating sometimes, thinking what a close run thing it was. She'd visited Jimmy twice before and he'd not known. It was pure luck that they'd been playing chess the third time.

It was luck that she seemed to want no more than friendliness from him. He could contemplate marriage with her, knowing she would not demand more. Their quiet, gentle companionship had worked so well, until they married and moved into the manor.

Living there, he realizes that there is more to Elizabeth Banniere than he has assumed. The tranquil surfaces of her daily life hide depths he cannot comprehend. There is something essentially solitary about her, a lingering sadness. He has not skill enough to draw out the secrets of her past, he has no key to the puzzle. He sees it as a flaw in himself.

His days at the Blue Manor are filled with space. He has few distractions, apart from the books. There are rare visitors, few social events. Margaret and Elizabeth have always lived retired from local society, and although Elizabeth is prepared to make an effort to introduce him to the neighbours, he knows she is not really at ease away from the manor.

Boredom doesn't come into it. He thinks all the time, despite the doctor's well-intentioned advice.

He cannot understand his wife, and thinks he knows why. He is a shell, a dried-out, depressive, cynical husk. A hollow man. He expects little. His marriage to Elizabeth Banniere seems to him almost an aberration in the pattern of loss and pain which make up all human life. He has never thought that the marriage would last for ever, but it doesn't matter. He assumes he will die quite soon, that his labouring heart will be exhausted by the unequal struggle to find breath. He hopes, yearningly, that the marriage will endure long enough to see him out but he does not expect it.

Living in the manor, things become clear. He realizes that Elizabeth needs more than he can give. Her vital centre has not been blasted away in the muds of France. He begins to think that if he does not know her, she also does not know herself.

He watches her carefully that summer. He sees her move with energy, with unusual verve. Is it just that she is comfortable within the manor, at home there? There is a springiness in her walk, as if she might break into a run at any moment. Her hair bounces with health, her cheeks are rosy, her eyes clear and shining.

He works out that the change has come after their marriage. It is partly to do with the tennis, he judges. He remembers the adrenalin thrill that comes from hard, fast exercise, and is at first genuinely glad that she has found someone to match her skill.

But he cannot like Lightowler. The least selfish of men, Downie is perceptive enough to recognize the strong thread of self-interest in the younger man. He knows Lightowler desires Elizabeth; indeed, it would have surprised him to have discovered that Lightowler is indifferent. Everyone who sees her must love her, he thinks. How can they not? She is sweet as spring, soft and gentle. Graceful as the deer they sometimes see in the forest.

He sees her come to life that summer in Lightowler's company. He cannot deny it. His depression as autumn approaches is a result of this knowledge.

Why should she live in chastity? This is the centre of it, he's sure. She deserves passion and warmth and the delight of physicality, not the inadequate friendship which is all Downie has to offer.

The least selfish of men, expecting nothing more from marriage than companionship, he has invited Lightowler into their home.

He wants to make it easy for Elizabeth to stay his wife.

'Supper!'

Tom heard Ruth's voice calling and sat up. His back was aching, his hand stiff with the tension of writing. He was beginning to see elements of nobility in John Downie's character, of generosity. Elizabeth had married him, had truly loved him. It made Lightowler's actions all the more horrific.

Kate was with Peter Lightowler. Tom took a deep breath. Lightowler was old, old and frail. Nothing would happen to Kate, she was young and strong and quite capable of taking care of herself.

I'll never be able to meet that man again, thought Tom with certainty. Because although this is fiction, although I'm making it up, I *know* that there is truth in it somewhere. Incidents, events, may be quite imaginary, but the emotional character of this story rings quite true.

He pushed his chair away from the desk and arched his back. He wondered if Kate was home yet and wandered through to the kitchen. It was crowded, too full of people.

Ruth, Simon, Alicia and Kate . . . Kate was there sitting at the table, tilting her chair dangerously against the stone flags.

'Oh, hi, Tom. How's the Muse, how's it going?'

She was sparkling with vitality, happy and relaxed.

He was irritated. He'd been worried. 'Where were you?' he grumbled. 'I went looking for you.'

'Out for a walk.' She shrugged. 'I thought you wanted to get on with the book.'

The door opened and Byrne walked in. He was wearing a yellow shirt, one none of them had seen before.

'Well, we *are* a jolly party tonight!' Simon's eyes were flashing with malevolence. 'Excuse me while I go and put on a tie. Was it bring a bottle? How remiss of me, I don't seem to have anything to hand.'

'Be quiet, Simon.' Ruth was grinning. She opened the fridge. 'There's fruit punch or non-alcoholic beer. Byrne, can I get you something?'

'I wouldn't touch the beer,' said Simon in a loud stage whisper. 'Cats' pee. Filthy stuff. You'd do better with tap water.'

'I'd like punch,' said Byrne.

'I have an apology to make,' said Alicia stiffly. 'I'm sorry about – barging into the cottage this afternoon. I'm sorry about the whisky. It was a natural mistake, but I was hasty.'

'That's all right. It doesn't matter.' Byrne sat down at the table next to Tom. 'How's the book coming on?' he asked. 'Did you get much done?'

'Quite a bit.' Tom hated questions about it.

'You got more out of him than I did.' Kate was irritated now. 'Tom never tells *me* anything.'

'Well, you're never here!' Tom said. 'I was worried, I didn't know where you were.'

'I didn't know you required a timetable of my movements. I didn't know that was what you wanted.'

'I would have liked to come too. I like walking.'

'Oh, *sorry*! I thought the book came first. I thought you were too involved in writing to want to interrupt the flow with a little thing like going for a walk.'

'That's not fair!' A full-scale row was in the offing. Simultaneously, Ruth and Byrne spoke:

'Where did you go?'

'Were you alone?'

'This is not an inquisition!' Kate leaped out of her chair. 'What is it to *you* or *you* or *you* where I go?' She pointed in turn to Tom, to Byrne and Ruth.

Alicia stood up. 'What a ridiculous fuss. It's nothing to do with anyone where you went, Kate. Nothing at all.'

'I went with Uncle Peter!' She was defiant. 'Yes, I went for a walk in the forest with the dreadful, wicked Mr Peter Lightowler, and I don't see what on earth it's got to do with any of you!'

In the silence that followed these words, Tom realized that everyone was looking at Ruth. Her mouth opened as if to say something, but it was only a small moan. As they watched, she slid sideways off her chair and crumpled to the floor in a dead faint.

Her head struck glancingly against the Aga. A thin streak of blood ran into her hair as Byrne knelt beside her and turned her over. The others stood and watched, seemingly paralysed as he examined the wound. 'No, it's only a scratch.' He took the handkerchief drenched in iced water that Alicia gave him and gently wiped Ruth's face.

Her eyelids fluttered, opened. 'Kate . . . ?'

'I'm here, Mum.' Kate was even whiter than her mother. 'I'm sorry, I'm so sorry. I didn't realize – '

Simon was standing by the doorway to the hall. He said nothing, not one thing.

Alicia hissed to Kate, 'Are you out of your mind? What on

earth are you trying to do? Don't you know anything at all about *Uncle* Peter?'

'What do you mean?' Kate looked up. She had pushed Byrne out of the way and was helping Ruth into a chair.

'*No*, Alicia! Don't!' Ruth's voice was weak but passionate.

'She ought to know, Ruth. She's grown up. It's time she understood what's been going on!'

'I'm off,' Simon said suddenly. 'I don't want to hear this.' He looked at Alicia. 'He's my *father*,' he said. 'You're talking about my father!'

'She has to know.'

'I utterly forbid it!' Ruth had revived. She stood up. 'Byrne, will you stay here, please? Until Mrs Lightowler leaves?'

'Don't be a fool, Ruth! Kate should know! She has a right to know!' Alicia was furious.

' I completely disagree. This is the past, it's obscure, indistinct, and no one knows what really happened. It should be allowed to die. I'm going up now, Alicia, and if you say one word to Kate about what happened between Peter and me, one word about something you do not understand, I will never speak to you again.'

Ruth and Simon left the room together.

Byrne saw Alicia, Kate and Tom look at each other, a complicated mix of doubt, blame, guilt.

The food was forgotten, cooling on the side.

Alicia said, 'Well, I can at least tell you my own story. It might amuse you, Mr Byrne. And, Tom, if you're so interested in the family past, this might be relevant.'

'Why did you divorce?' Tom asked. Byrne saw that he had his notebook out, his pencil at the ready like some pernicious, old-fashioned journalist.

It was disgusting. Byrne wanted more than anything to leave. He hated this gossipy dwelling on the past, this raking up of old scores.

Ruth had asked him to stay.

Not fair, he thought. What is this to do with me? It was an intolerable position, to be stationed there like some unwilling chaperon. An outsider, an observer, so the family's dirty linen couldn't be washed in public.

'Oh, there were things.' Alicia lit a cigarette. She was being uncharacteristically vague. Perhaps she couldn't face it either, not when it came down to it. Her own life was private, too. It was nothing to do with him. 'He had affairs, dozens of affairs. I could never trust him. I just – had enough.'

'Why won't Mum tell me things?' Kate cried. Her hands were held tight, but her face was naked with distress. 'Does she think I'm still a child?'

'You should make every allowance for your mother,' Alicia said. She sighed. 'I only wanted to – clear things up, but Ruth still cares too much, I suppose. Perhaps I misjudged it. I can't push it. I can't betray her trust. She has too much to worry about, too much on her plate. She's exhausted.'

'What can you tell us?' Tom persisted.

Her slow, unfathomable gaze settled on him. She said, 'Peter was part of our lives for years, even after we divorced. I lived at the manor, with Simon and Ruth, and Peter was at the Red House in Theydon. He called sometimes, he interested himself in the children. It went on until Ruth went to university. But while she was there he visited her and – well, that's out of bounds.' Her sharp eyes darted between Byrne and Tom. Kate she ignored. 'Ruth claims that she can't remember, that it's all a blank.' Alicia's words were cold, dropping between them like blocks of ice. 'But since then she has never been able to bear the company of Peter Lightowler. His name is never spoken in her company, he is never mentioned, what he does, what he is—'

'And what *is* he?' Tom's words blurted out. His pencil was avidly poised above the notebook.

That cold look again, that considering gaze. 'A bastard, a man wrenched from his social sphere.'

'What century is this?' Tom shouted. 'I can't believe you're saying this! It's not a sin to be illegitimate, it's not a sin to step outside one's *class*.' There was vicious scorn in his voice.

'Of course, you would feel like that.'

Byrne thought it calculated and outrageous. Alicia's eyes were fastened on Tom's face. 'I'm sorry, Tom, but I know this man, I know what it meant to him. It's how *he* viewed it. It explains Peter Lightowler's resentment, his ambition. Just think about it. His past. He lived alone with his mother in one of the cottages by the green in Theydon. He ran around barefoot, his mother . . . was a prostitute. He told me about it. I suppose he wanted sympathy. His childhood was one of shame and degradation. He was a loser, destined to a loser's life . . .

'But then Roderick Banniere re-emerged into the picture. Are you listening? Have you got that?' She was looking only at Tom. 'Roderick. Elizabeth's banished brother. He took his son, he adopted the little Peter. And we're back in the realm of fairy tales, back in the world of archetypes. The child is whisked away to live in luxury, adopted by an evil father – not a godfather, a devil-father – and educated . . . God alone knows how he was educated. Roderick was a man obsessed by only one idea, that of ownership of the Blue Manor and domination over the women who guard it.'

'How do you know this?' Byrne spoke softly. He couldn't work out what Alicia was up to. There was nothing straightforward about her, nothing up front. This seemed to him like a smokescreen. He didn't trust her one bit.

'Peter Lightowler was my husband,' she said. 'And I learned to watch, to observe everything about him. It was a matter of self-preservation. I have watched this story unfold, I have seen the parallels. I saw Ruth change from a joyful girl into the weary woman you see now. I remember Ella, and that's something else . . . And now I think we need to publish it, to find out about Peter Lightowler, this man who was always there at the crucial times. And we'll have to use what's to hand, Tom's book especially, before it's too late.' She stopped suddenly, this cold outpouring of words. She even smiled a little as she looked at Kate.

Kate's head was dropped against her arms, her face hidden.

'And you think it's all right, you think it's not significant that you go walking with Peter Lightowler, that he's insinuated himself into your life?'

Watching, Byrne heard difficult silence between the words, gaps in understanding, chasms of comprehension, and he knew that Alicia was behind these failures. Her explanations only begged more questions.

Kate looked up. 'If you hate him so much, why don't you publicize it? Why do you go along with the secrets?'

'Who would believe me? I am the only person who could not possibly do this: the estranged wife, the bitter, lonely aging woman. Divorce was not so common, then. There was a stigma attached. And then Simon is my son, you see.' Alicia's voice was even, unemotional. 'My son with Peter. If I am only half right about Lightowler's designs on this house and the women who live here, then probably Simon is part of it too. I did my best, I took him away from Peter as soon as I realized what he was, but it may not have been enough.'

'Because he drinks and cannot leave here?' Byrne again, still soft.

'I had no choice,' she said, almost angrily. 'Ruth was *here* and she loves him. At least, she says so. And besides, whatever it is, whatever this *curse* is, it has to work itself out here. This is a place of significance. This is the crux, the fulcrum, the catalyst for it all.'

'Rubbish, nonsense, evil nonsense. You're a hysterical old woman with no more sense than a baby!' At last Kate was on her feet, flaring. Her face was blotchy with tears and fury.

'Is it? Why did your mother faint, why did she never marry? Why does she hate men, Kate?' Alicia was icy cold again. 'Didn't you ever think to ask?'

'She doesn't hate men. You're wrong, you've got it wrong! You said it yourself, she loves Simon.'

'Whether she loves Simon or not is actually beside the point. I see very few signs of it, myself. She's bound to him by duty and guilt. And think who Simon is. He's part of this too. Concentrate, Kate. Simon is Peter's son. Just as Peter Lightowler is Roderick Banniere's son. It follows through, it's an inherited curse.'

'He's your son! How can you say things like that?' Kate's hands were twisting together.

'Why do you think he drinks? He's trying to escape his heritage, to blot out the past.'

'But if this is true, why didn't you say anything? Why didn't you stop it?'

Another silence. Alicia was staring at her hands.

'You don't know, do you?' Byrne said slowly. 'You don't know if you're right.'

She looked at him and he saw the truth. She spoke.

'Ruth hates Peter Lightowler. And Tom's book shows another rape, a previous violation. And Tom himself . . .' She was outwardly composed, still cool and elegant, and only Byrne, sitting next to her, saw the minute tremor in her hands.

'Tom's book is fiction! He made it up!' Kate again, passionately.

'No, I didn't make it up. The house did.'

And into the silence this time they heard voices, the sound of people talking in the distance.

The voices started to shout, but the words were indistinct. Far away in the bedroom Ruth shared with Simon, they heard shouting.

And then the telephone rang.

'Why didn't you stay? Didn't you want to drag it up again, the story of my infamous father?'

'No. I never want to even think about it again. It's over.' Ruth seemed desperate, almost grey with exhaustion. Her fingers fumbled as she undressed.

'It's our guests I feel sorry for,' said Simon. 'The young Lothario (or did we agree on Lochinvar?), all wrapped up in his book. You'd think no one had ever written a book before. You realize he's going to use it, don't you? The murky past is going to come oozing through our Tom's lustrous prose. Rapes, incest and all out into the public domain to frolic and frisk beneath the world's scrutiny. If he ever gets it published, of course.'

'It's *fiction*, he's making it up!'

'How do you know? Have you read it?'

She shook her head impatiently. 'I don't need to. How could it be true? No one has told him anything. There are no records, no diaries. It's just hearsay.'

'And embedded in the bricks of this house, breathing down its corridors and through each of the rooms . . . don't tell me you still can't feel it.'

'No. I don't know what you're talking about. I don't believe any of it.'

'And even if no one's told Tom anything so far, what do you think my esteemed mother is up to at this very moment?'

'She doesn't know everything.' Ruth frowned as she tugged a hairbrush through her hair.

He put his hands on her shoulders as she sat at the dressing table. 'Ruth, dear, think. Alicia will be stirring it up like the witch she is, making sure that not one ounce of sin or evil or regret is ever lost, forgotten or forgiven.'

'Do you hate her so much?'

'Hate her? No. At least I don't think so. But she's damn dangerous, for all that.'

'She wants to find the truth of it.'

'Don't tell me you think it will all come right, once every greasy wrinkle of this is out in the open? What could possibly be improved by knowing?'

'Well, what else can we do? How else can we proceed?'

'And then there's our good friend Phizackerley Byrne, lurking out there in the cottage waiting his chance.'

'What do you mean?' At last she looked at him.

'He's after you, Ruth. Haven't you noticed?'

'Don't talk rubbish.'

'Any normal man would have moved on days ago. Something's keeping him here and I hardly think it's the pleasure of my company.'

'Oh, he *likes* me, I'll give you that. He's one of those protective men who wants to feel needed. And I *do* need him, you know I do.'

'He wants to fuck you.'

She stood up and moved over to the bed, her face turned away from him. 'Doesn't matter if he does,' she said. 'I'm too tired.'

He laughed at that, getting into bed beside her. 'I wish he'd go, though,' he said. 'I don't trust him, that maddening slow voice, those deliberate movements.'

'He gets things done.'

'So long as he doesn't do you.' As usual he turned over, his back to her. 'You wouldn't let him, would you?'

'It's called being a dog in a manger.'

'Jesus, Ruth! You said it yourself, you're always too tired.'

'And you're too drunk or too hungover or too depressed.'

'Is that what you'd class as an erotic invitation?'

'Well, it's not doing us any good, is it? I feel very far away from you at the moment.'

'I suggest you give Phizackerley Byrne his cards. Get rid of him.'

'For goodness' sake, Simon, he's the one thing that's gone right round here for years. Why should I get rid of him?'

He was silent for too long. Then, 'So that's the way the wind blows. I should have known better than to trust you. You and my mother . . . bloody women!' He flung back the bedclothes and reached for his dressing gown.

'Where are you going?'

'To get drunk.'

'Simon, don't be ridiculous, this is nonsense!'

But the door had already closed behind him.

Kate picked up the phone. 'Hello? Oh, yes, no trouble. No, it was fine. Tomorrow? All right. Good night, Unc.'

She put the phone down and gazed consideringly at Alicia, Tom and Byrne. 'I'm going for lunch with Uncle Peter,' she said. 'Because I don't believe any of this. I don't believe there's any great mystery. I'm sorry, Aunty Alicia, I just can't take any of it seriously.'

'Your mother fainted. Does that mean nothing to you?'

'You said yourself she's never admitted anything. That she can't remember what happened.' Kate tilted her head back, defiant all the way. 'It might have been – a bad trip or something. He's an old man, he's lonely. He wants to make amends. I think you're being horrible, all this man-hating stuff.'

'You're very like your grandmother,' said Alicia. 'She was my best friend. We were at school together. She said much the same, once.'

'Why must you keep going on about the past? Why does it have to be dragged up the whole time?'

'Because it informs the present,' said Alicia gently. 'It is why we are as we are.'

'I can't take this. It's nonsense. I'm going to bed.' And without a further glance at any of them, Kate left the kitchen, slamming the door behind her.

Tom, Alicia and Byrne were left.

'Tell me about Kate's grandmother,' Tom said.

Byrne watched him curiously. Tom seemed unmoved by Kate's absence, unmoved by the highly charged atmosphere in the house. His face was eager with enthusiasm, lit by desire, the desire for knowledge. The pencil was poised once more over a page already filled with neat notes.

He was like one possessed, obsessed by the story. Nothing else existed for him, not Kate, not anything. He was so deep into it that nothing else mattered.

Alicia showed no surprise. 'Yes, you'll need to know about that, of course. The first mystery, the only mystery, I suppose, is that Ella was Elizabeth's child. And John Downie was crippled, without any strength. There are conclusions to be drawn.'

'I can write it . . .'

'Go on, then. Write it tonight. Find out about Ella, who her father was. See what the house tells you. I dare you.' A ludicrous, overblown childish phrase, but oddly appropriate, Byrne thought, for this is a matter for courage, for screwing up the nerve.

Tom swallowed. 'I can't stay in the manor again, not overnight.'

'I'll stay with you,' Byrne said. 'I'll do the Cinderella bit and get you to the cottage before midnight.'

Tom glanced at him. 'How very unexpected. Why?'

'Why not?'

'It's caught you too, hasn't it? You want to see for yourself. You want to know if I'm making up this haunted business.'

'I am – interested. Yes.' It was true.

'Let him stay,' said Alicia abruptly. 'He'll see you right.'

Tom looked from one to the other. 'I don't really understand what's going on. I don't understand any of this. But' – he grinned quickly at Byrne – 'I would be glad of company.'

'Right, that's settled then.' Alicia stood up. 'I'll see you both in the morning. There's dinner on the side there, if you're hungry.'

They stuck the pot on the Aga again and ladled the goulash out into soup bowls. Neither of them said much. Byrne could see that Tom's mind was refocusing, turning away from the present to the fiction he was creating.

Byrne started washing up, and when he turned to find the tea-towel the kitchen was empty. Tom had returned to the library.

Chapter 28

He tries not to watch them. He keeps out of the way as far as possible, determined to think of other things. He spends long hours every day in his sitting room, cataloguing the library, reading anything and everything that catches his attention.

It rarely works for long. When the dreadful thoughts start again, John Downie begins to roam the house. The ramps help. By dusk each day he has begun his peregrinations. He wheels himself from room to room, everywhere on the ground floor, unable to settle, unable to relax. He finds himself leaving books everywhere, in the hope that one of them might divert him, rescue his thoughts from the inevitable circles.

Elizabeth and Peter Lightowler. Walking, playing, talking together. And more than that. He sees it in her eyes, the new sensuality of her gaze. He knows what is happening.

And the flesh stirs. Traitor to his will, traitor to his health, still he feels the throb of desire, the hardening between his legs. Ten years ago, the doctor at the Retreat had been quite clear about it, graphic, almost. Death lies that way.

He tries to exhaust himself, wandering the house, although he knows that is madness, too. He begins to view his own existence as an intolerable burden, to himself and everyone else.

It's two weeks since Lightowler moved in. Margaret has gone to the States on an extended visit to an old friend, and Elizabeth is glad of the additional company.

She finds her husband out on the terrace, a rug over his knees. He's restlessly turning the pages of a book. He lays it down on the wall as she approaches.

'What are you doing here, love? Isn't it time for your afternoon rest?'

This has been his invariable habit since arriving at the manor. She sees the small crease between his brows that usually fore-shadows exhaustion.

'I'm not tired,' he says wearily. 'Well, I am, I suppose, but I don't feel like sleeping.'

She sits on the low wall beside his chair and takes his hand. 'You mustn't worry, John. There's nothing to worry about, nothing.'

'It's going all right with Lightowler, is it? He's settled in?'

She is not a stupid woman, she knows what is keeping Downie from his afternoon rest. 'He seems happy enough,' she says slowly. 'But I'm not sure if he really fits in here. I mean, I know he's here to help me run the house, but he doesn't begin to replace Mags. Not that he ever could, of course. But he has no real idea what's required here, no idea of what the house and garden need.'

'What do you mean?'

'Well, that the house should be . . .' Honoured, her mind says. 'Tended,' her voice says. 'It needs attention, constant small tasks, replenishing the flowers, drawing the curtains, the post taking to the gate, the books replacing on the shelves.'

'That's me, I'm afraid. I never have what I want to read to hand and it's a bore always having to go back to the library. It's easier if I leave a few volumes in each room . . . You don't mind, do you?' A touch of anxiety in his voice.

She smiles. 'Of course not, dear. This is your house, too. The books are fine, of course they are. But there are other things . . .'

'He's not the ideal guest, then?'

'It's nothing I can put my finger on. He just is not at home here.' She looks him directly in the eyes. 'He's not here now. He's gone up to town for the day. You know what, John, I don't think he'll be here for long.'

She sees his expression lighten, the frown disappear.

'Come on,' he says impulsively, taking her hand. 'A nice cuddle, a comfortable lie down . . . don't you think?'

She owes him this, at the very least.

'Oh yes! What could be nicer?'

It goes too far. Dangerously, stupidly, too far. He keeps telling her that it's all right, that he feels fine, much better really, and she believes him. And at first, it really does seem that no harm can come of it. They move together kindly, considerately, and only imperceptibly move into something else.

(Anyway, says a voice within him, what better end?)

But he goes all the way and he's left gasping like a stranded fish, his heart pounding as if it's going to burst his ribs, the blood thundering in his ears, a red mist before his eyes.

The shame of it is that Elizabeth is so frightened. She is crying as she hauls out the heavy oxygen cylinder which lies beneath the bed, as she fumbles with the dial. The hands holding the mask to his mouth and nose shake pitifully.

It seems to take for ever for the pounding to stop, for the gulping gasps to subside. He lies in a stupor of deadly exhaustion, barely conscious.

There are movements in the room, small sounds. Gradually he surfaces. He becomes aware that she is dressed, that the light outside has darkened.

'John?' She's kneeling at his bedside, holding his hand. 'I'm going to leave you, just for a few moments, to telephone the doctor.'

Speech is impossible. He shakes his head minutely.

'I have to, John, I need to have you checked over.'

He pushes the mask aside impatiently. Barely a sound, less than a whisper, less than a thread of vitality . . . 'Don't – don't tell anyone – '

'Only the doctor. Only Shaw, I promise.'

He has no right to stop her. He lies there fretting, hating it, hating what he has become, what he has done to her. I've made a whore of my wife, he thinks. I've bought her body and the price is guilt. He sees her white face and hands that still shake with fear for him.

The shame of it.

That night, lying there somewhere uncomfortably between sleep and waking, his heart stops.

He becomes aware of a pain in his arm and chest, a sudden cramping that jerks him from the uneasy half-dream state. He finds himself gasping, but his ruined lungs have given up. There's no air to breathe anywhere.

A pulse hammers through his body, exploding all at once in massive, crushing shock. He cannot move, rigid beneath the onslaught. The pain is everything, everywhere, and there's no possibility of breath ever moving again.

Black closes in, deadly black, worse than any pain, worse than any shock.

The breath of spirit fails against the black nothingness. All lost, all gone.

*

On a calm, high plateau of nothingness, belonging to no time or place, a creature enters. There is no sound of breathing or movement. There's just an impression of activity, of something wilful and direct.

The door does not open, nothing has changed, but there is something there now, a palpable presence crossing the carpet towards the dull flesh on the bed. There is nothing to fear, nothing to worry about. There are no more emotions to experience, no more pains to suffer.

The night-light on the table shines.

The body is lying on its back, propped on pillows. The grimacing face, the tendons stretched taut and cruel ... blue-grey skin, empty, staring eyes. All observed, noted, and forgotten.

Is the quilt depressed under its tread? Certainly, there is no one there to see. Perhaps the pattern on the carpet wavers, slightly distorted under its passing.

It moves suddenly, and the house shudders. A convulsion of energy and force leaping on the body, knocking it sideways off the bed and on to the floor. The chest is compressed, released in the fall and the weight of that leaping energy. There's a clatter of sound as the bedside table topples, the light slanting crazily.

The air in the house shifts. Down the long corridors a disturbance shivers. A light wind streams under doors and through curtains, whisking over the tables, ruffling the pages of books. Elizabeth's dark hair lifts and stirs while she sleeps.

The wind forces itself into the room, into those useless lungs, inflating the chest once more. It is expelled through the gaping mouth, drawn in again, pushed out, pulsing through the body, pulsing through the house as if the bricks and tiles and wooden beams are themselves breathing on the man's behalf.

The creature waits, red eyes gleaming, until the chest begins to move of its own accord. It sighs, and the unnatural circulation of air begins to calm.

Just before dawn it leaves the room. The house is very quiet now, apart from the sound of breathing.

Elizabeth finds her husband collapsed on the floor next morning, and calls the doctor again.

Shaw recommends a strict regime, months in bed, diet, pills and potions. 'You've been lucky,' he says, and Downie cannot reply.

Downstairs, a door bangs.
Peter Lightowler is back.

He knows at once that something has changed. As soon as he moves through the green-gold light of the porch into the hall, he feels an alteration in the house. Elizabeth's white face, coming from the dining room, merely confirms it.

'What is it?' he says, stepping forward quickly, taking her hands.

'Oh, Peter, John's so ill!' Tired, overwrought tears spill down her cheeks. She struggles for control, while he draws her close. She lets him hold her, but he notes that she does not relax, no, not at all. He's alert to this, and other things in the house. Over her head he sees the corridors yawning away into blackness. What has happened?

'He – he had the most dreadful attack yesterday. I thought he was dying, but the oxygen helped and Shaw said he ought to be all right. But then in the night his heart stopped, and I didn't find him till the morning. When Shaw came, he said it was a miracle. It's touch and go now, but we don't know how he managed even to get through the night.'

His eyes are scanning the hall and the mouths of the corridors, sensing that something waits there. For a moment he thinks he sees what it is: far away in the shadows something is watching him. An animal, perhaps, powerful, lithe ... The scar on his cheek throbs.

He ignores it. 'What happened exactly?'

'It was a massive attack, Shaw said. He should have died. But he fell out of bed and somehow his heart was shocked into beating again. I don't understand, and I don't think Shaw does, really.'

'But he's all right now?'

'For a while ...' She moves away from him. 'I didn't realize how much ... This is difficult for me to say, but you have to understand. I love John, and can't – won't – hurt him. He nearly had to die to make me realize it.'

'Shh, little one.' He lays his finger on her lips. Words are always dangerous, particularly in the manor where nothing that happens is insignificant. She has to be stopped. 'Don't say anything now, this has been a great shock. You mustn't worry, there's nothing to worry about. Shouldn't you go and lie down yourself? You look so tired.'

He wraps her round with his own words and her voice trails to a stop. He watches as she goes to her own room.

He turns to look down the corridor leading to Downie's room. If he's alone there, Lightowler will have a chance to finish what the poison gas has started. He takes two steps towards the room and then hears movement within. A nurse, he thinks. Downie would not be left alone for long.

He carries his case upstairs to his attic and unpacks, methodically, thoughtfully. Then he goes to the banisters and stands there, waiting. He has always been good at waiting, at assembling the twin forces of will and power and holding them steady. He meditates on the Blue Manor, on his presence there. He thinks of his father, his father's claim to the manor.

He identifies totally with Roderick Banniere. He shares Banniere's feelings of stunned outrage that the rightful heir should be disinherited. That he and his son should be deprived of status by the women in their own family.

The ownership of the manor is a point of honour to both of them, something to be contested with all the imagination and energy and skill he and his father can muster.

And yet, as it stands, even John Downie has more legal right to the manor than they. That pale, feeble cripple is at home here in a way Lightowler can only envy. Miracles save his life, the doctor comes running, Elizabeth Banniere weeps for him.

Even Lightowler's seduction of Elizabeth is being pushed aside because of Downie. Well, he'll have to see about that.

At length the door to Downie's room opens. Light slants across the corridor. A woman in a starched apron and headdress comes out, making for the kitchen wing. She is carrying a jug. The nurse, making a drink perhaps, changing the water . . .

This is his chance. He runs lightly down the stairs and crosses the hall. He puts his hand on the door to the library. It swings open under his touch, and he finds himself staring into John Downie's eyes.

Dark pools of black watch his approach, black, gleaming holes in the waxy pallor. Lightowler feels a sudden urge to run, to get out of the house and away from what he sees in Downie's eyes.

This is ridiculous. He looks away from the motionless figure on the bed. The window is slightly open and a cold breeze lifts through the curtain. He sees five-pointed leaves of ivy waving like hands over the window sill. He walks quickly across the room and shuts the window with a bang, conscious all the time of being watched.

'How are you, old man?' He has to keep the words coming, or the silences of the house might start dragging at the truth. 'You've had a rough time, haven't you? Sorry I wasn't here, it must have been hard on Elizabeth.'

He sees the grey lips moving and bends closer to the bed. 'What was that, old man?' He's listening for the return of the nurse. His hands move to the edge of the pillow beneath Downie's head.

'Promise.' A wisp of sound from the sick man. The grey skin of his face is faintly flushed with effort. 'Promise, don't hurt Elizabeth. Promise.'

Downie's strengthless hand brushes his own. He could be swatted out of existence like a fly. There's nothing significant holding this man to life. It is almost too easy . . .

And Lightowler's arrogant tongue leads him on. He leans even closer over the bed. 'I'll not hurt Elizabeth,' he says. 'Why should I? She carries my child.'

Smiling, he watches for the effect of his words. He wants to see tears, perhaps, hear a groan, a moan of anguish. It comes to him then that it might be enjoyable to delay this man's death. Murder is too easy, too quick. He stares into the black pits which are John Downie's eyes, waiting for a response.

Slowly the papery lids close, denying further contact. The slight colour in the sick man's cheeks drains away. Lightowler stares at the death-like mask of Downie's face and gradually edges away from the bed.

Downie has heard everything Lightowler has said. It would sour his every waking breath, it would poison every moment Downie spends with Elizabeth. Lightowler's child growing in her womb, while Downie's gold ring encircles her finger.

He walks out of the room gloating with the triumph of it, not realizing that he has conceded so much.

A promise has been made, a promise given.

He cannot now hurt Elizabeth Banniere.

Chapter 29

The door to the library swung open. 'Time to go, Tom,' said Byrne quietly. 'Don't you think so?'

Tom put the pencil down. Reluctantly. 'Just a bit longer,' he said. He could hardly see Byrne. It was completely dark, and the only light in the library came from the standard lamp by the desk. It caught unevenly on the deep lines and planes of Byrne's face.

'I think it's time to go *now*,' said Byrne with emphasis. He gestured at the ceiling. 'Listen. Can't you hear it?'

The faint rushing sound of wheels running down the long corridor upstairs, bowling into the landing, skidding round the corner.

Tom's mouth was pinched, white round the edges.

'I don't understand—' And then he heard the clang of the lift gates, the sound of the pulleys. 'Who's that?' Still he had not framed the thought, still the name of John Downie did not occur.

'Come on!' Byrne had him by the arm and was yanking him towards the French windows.

They heard the lift pulleys jerk and clang to a stop and the sliding of the hall gates.

'Wait a minute . . . I don't understand. There's someone there.'

'The door's locked!' Byrne was wrestling with the catch.

'It can't be, it's never locked.'

'The key's on the other side.'

Tom saw it too, jutting from the external lock. There was a hint of something strange in the air around them, something chemical and pungent. And then he remembered, and knew what the sound was. A feeling of pure panic gripped him, of raw terror as the wheels left the hall and bowled slowly towards the library.

'Jesus! He's coming for us!'

Byrne's fist crashed through the glass, wrenched at the key and it turned. The door opened as the stink of ammonia stung in their noses, jumped in the sinuses.

They fell out on to the terrace but that wasn't far enough, not nearly far enough. The night air was warm and still and the ammonia drifted out into the garden.

There was a crash behind them and light crazily slanted for a second, showing their faces strained and white. Without looking back they knew that the lamp had gone. *He* – whoever he was – must have got to the French doors. And there were ramps all round the terrace, leading from level to level . . .

They stumbled down the steps to the grass and ducked between the low branches of the trees, making for the drive. It was a relief to feel the uneven crunch of gravel beneath their feet. They skidded over the small stones, their hearts pounding, thudding in their ears as they ran.

The trees were quiet around them, steady and observant.

They did not stop until the cottage was reached. The door slammed shut behind them. Tom heard Byrne half breathe a curse as he fumbled for the light switch.

'Christ, what *was* that?' Byrne looked very pale in the electric glare, Tom noted. He supposed he was much the same. Byrne held his hand under the kitchen tap and then wound a handkerchief round it. Bright crimson immediately spotted through the cotton.

Tom stared at the spreading red. His lips were dry. He ran his tongue over them, to little noticeable effect. 'I think . . . I think that was the shade of John Downie. If you believe in such things.'

'And do you?'

'I have no choices in this.' It sounded dreary. 'This is not up to me. Someone else is directing this one.' He saw that the cloth on Byrne's hand was streaked with red. 'Should we get your hand seen to?'

'It'll be all right.' Byrne was fiddling with the cloth. He said, and the coolness of his voice made it seem impossible, 'So you think – that was a ghost, something supernatural?'

'What else?' Tom faced him squarely. 'Think about it. Would you go back to the manor now? Take a chance that we mistook the noise, the smell of it? Perhaps we were just dreaming.' He walked to the window and stared up the drive towards the web of trees surrounding the manor. 'Shall we go back?'

'No,' said Byrne. 'Not for anything.'

'Christ, what an evening! What I'd give for a beer!' Tom said feelingly.

'Pubs will be closed by the time we get there,' said Byrne. 'You'll have to make do with coffee. Or do you want tea?'

'Coffee.' Tom sighed. 'Strong and black.'

Byrne took a jar down and filled the kettle. 'I – liberated some from the manor,' he said.

Tom remained where he was. 'You've made yourself quite at home, haven't you?'

'It was part of the deal,' Byrne said mildly. 'Board and lodging. Much the same as you.'

'I'm sorry. I didn't mean to imply any criticism.' He sounded like a fool. He turned back to the room and sat at the table, making an effort. Neither of them wanted to talk about the manor, not with it so close, so present. Just at the end of the drive. But what else was there? The conversation was stilted and uneasy. Neutral subjects – politics, music, education – floundered. And yet neither of them could contemplate going to bed and trying to sleep.

'Have you any brothers or sisters?' Byrne asked after a while.

'No, I'm an only child. My mother . . . I never knew my father. They broke up before I was born.'

'Do you know who he is?'

'Someone Mum met at university. A one-night stand, she said, nothing significant. Not enough to build a life together—'

'But enough to initiate your life . . .'

'True.' Tom drained his coffee. 'What about you? Where do you come from?'

'I was born in London although I lived in Yorkshire until recently.'

'So what are you doing here?'

Byrne leaned back against the hard kitchen chair.

'Passing time, taking a break . . .'

'Hardly a rest cure, I'd say, gardening at the manor.'

'Look who's talking. It was going to be your role, you know. Kate asked me to stay, to let you off the hook.'

'God, and now I spend all my time in that bloody library . . . I don't really understand what's happening.' Tom ran his fingers through his hair. He did not look at ease in the cottage. As if it were too shabby, too dilapidated. 'I mean, anyone can try

213

writing books, almost everyone I know does, hundreds . . . and you think you're making it up, that it's all invented, but you don't *know*, you don't know for sure—'

Byrne looked at the strain on Tom's face, at the frown in his eyes. 'What else could you be doing?'

'It's like . . . the connections, the coincidences are piling up. I feel like I'm tapping into an alternative arrangement of events, something that's more than linear. A holistic approach to the past . . .'

'A contradiction in terms. Time *is* linear, or at least our experience of it is. We are born, we live, we die. Whatever you do, you can't escape it. But this is all rather – New Age, isn't it? I never reckoned you one for crystals and horoscopes.'

But Tom said nothing, never even smiled at the mild teasing.

Byrne tried again: 'Why don't you leave the manor? What's keeping you there?'

'The trouble is, it's working.' For a moment, Tom's eyes closed. 'The words flow, the story takes shape. There's something real there, something worth revealing—'

'So it's not Kate?'

'Kate?' For a moment, Tom looked distracted. 'I – I don't know. She's all wrapped up in it somehow and I can't disentangle her from it yet—'

'And Peter Lightowler?'

'A can of worms, ancient and rotting but still crawling, wriggling with life . . .'

Byrne said, 'What are you going to do about it, Tom? Is writing it out going to settle anything?'

'Christ, I don't know. I hope so, but I wonder . . . I worry that it won't be enough, not on its own. That somehow I'm implicated in this in a more direct way.'

'How could that be possible?'

'I don't know. I guess I'm not making much sense.' He sighed. At last the exhaustion of the past three nights had caught up with him. 'I don't know about you, but I've had enough for one day,' he said.

'Fair enough.' Byrne indicated the sofa. 'Will you be warm enough?'

'Oh yes,' he said, lying full length. His eyes closed immediately. In seconds he was asleep.

*

Tom thought he would find it hard to return to the manor the next day, but in fact the opposite was true. He ate breakfast in a rush, nodded goodbye to Byrne and almost ran towards the house.

A hurried greeting to Kate and Ruth and then the library again, the desk waiting patiently, his pencils lined up against the paper. Someone had cleared away the broken glass and reassembled the lamp, although no repairs had been exacted. They'll get Byrne to do it, he thought abstractedly. It was his fault, after all . . .

There was no lingering smell of ammonia, no sign that anything was amiss, apart from the broken window. Had the others heard it? he wondered. Had the shade of John Downie touched anyone else?

But already he was sitting at the desk, the pencil gripped in his hand and the sheet of paper laid calm and empty before him.

He began.

Chapter 30

He sees them. Every day, every hour of the day. Across the lawn, through the bare trees, he sees them twined together like climbing plants. John Downie uses the binoculars his wife has given him and squints through them until she has passed out of sight, leaning affectionately on Lightowler's arm.

It may be quite innocent. He acknowledges it. He has even thrown them together at one stage, he has encouraged their friendship. Go and play tennis, he has said, you could do with the exercise.

(He invited Lightowler into the manor, the small voice goes, he invited this affair . . .)

He remembers the words Peter Lightowler whispered in his ear. There's a child on the way and it makes all the difference. Lightowler's child. Someone to inherit the manor, someone to roam its passages and gardens and forests as if he or she belongs there.

He is furious with jealousy, mad with it. How can she have done it, how can Elizabeth have lain with that – boy, that pup? He does not for one moment doubt what Lightowler has said.

As he broods, confined to the couch in the library, feeble as a doll, useless in every way, the dreadful thoughts spawn and elaborate. Did she lie about that childhood rape too? Was it a ploy to disinherit her brother, was she deceitful and greedy even then?

No, no, says a part of him. Not Elizabeth, she's not like that, she would never do a thing like that.

Is she avid and licentious? In these dark mid-winter afternoons, his mind travels through vicious circles. She took him into her bed that one time, and he nearly died. She had known it to be dangerous. Sweet Jesus, had she known what would happen? Did she hope for it, to get rid of him?

He sees in her obsessive attention to his health and comfort evidence only of guilt. In the distortions of weakness and exhaustion, he refuses to acknowledge the sadness in her eyes.

He's glad when she begins to find reasons to stay away.

He knows what she's doing, and it gives him a curious satisfaction to have his suspicions confirmed. He keeps his binoculars to hand, and waits with increasing impatience. When he recovers and returns to his chair, he'll begin to use the manor.

He'll roam everywhere through it, watching them from all the windows. The lift she's installed would be invaluable, he admits. From the upper rooms he'll see them wherever they go, all winter long until the leaves of the trees cradle the manor in shade once more.

She'll not be able to disguise it then. The child will be showing, and she'll have to explain, and then he'll know. He'll know for sure.

Pregnancy is like dreaming, she thinks. She presses her fingers against the swelling at her waist. Your body becomes strange and unfamiliar and you know that a miracle is taking place. You think how big is he or she now? Have the hands formed, are the eyes open?

The rest of the world is irrelevant. It seems like a pale shadowland, like the vaguest of memories. Colours lose their vividness, people their interest. The odd lapses in her memory are insignificant. All that matters to her is the miracle, the growing person within.

Elizabeth is not the first woman to retreat from the difficult world into the dream of pregnancy.

She has only the haziest idea what's happening. There is no older woman she can ask, with Mags visiting old friends in America, no books or magazines that ever refer to pregnancy and birth except in the most generalized terms. She doesn't really mind not knowing. She trusts that it will be all right. It's perfectly natural, there's nothing more natural in the world. She submerges what little curiosity she feels into love. With no thought to the future, Elizabeth allows herself to love her unborn child, whole-heartedly and passionately.

There's no one else, after all.

John is better, physically. He spends each day in the wheelchair, rambling all over the house, his binoculars in his lap. She expects, like Shaw, the increasing mobility to lessen his depression, but it hasn't happened yet.

She's told him about the child but it's made no difference. He doesn't seem very interested.

He's in the library, examining the shotgun that arrived that morning. To frighten off the rooks, he claims. He's tired of their noise, that constant unpleasant cawing.

He looks up from the gun, an eyebrow raised in irony.

'A child . . . ? Well, Elizabeth, you have been busy.'

She doesn't understand him. 'It's a miracle, don't you think?' she says hopefully. She sits at the table opposite him, riffling through the pages of the book that lies there. Gunmanship it's called. 'The Gentleman's Way'.

Perhaps she hasn't prepared the ground enough. Is she rushing this, mishandling it, gauche and insensitive as usual? She's looking for signs of joy from him, for delight. 'To think that that one time, that only time . . . God has been very good to us.'

'Is that what you believe?' His voice is so sharp. 'That God has performed some kind of miracle?'

She frowns. 'Well, we never thought to have children, did we?'

'And what name will you give this one? Are you going to follow in the family tradition?'

'I – I haven't really thought. I thought you'd be so pleased . . .'

'There is no God, Lizzie.' His voice is empty of emotion. 'You should know that. No God and no miracles.'

And then he wheels the chair around, skidding over the parquet floor towards the lift, retreating once more to the upper floors of the manor.

Chapter 31

'Did you hear anything last night?' Byrne was speaking to Ruth at the side of the drive. She had stopped her car on the way to school.

'What kind of thing? There was an owl, I remember. I slept pretty heavily; I didn't hear anything else . . . What do you mean?' This was no pretence. Her warm brown eyes were mildly puzzled.

'Tom thinks it was the shade of John Downie. I heard wheels and smelled ammonia. There was definitely something there. We had to smash a pane of glass to get out of the library.' He could see that she wasn't really listening, that her attention was somewhere else.

'An overactive imagination, that's Tom's trouble.'

'Ruth, I heard it too.' He held out his hand to her, still swathed in the bloody handkerchief. 'How do you think I got this?'

She stared at it and he thought she lost colour. However, her voice was composed. 'Oh, do you want a lift into Epping? Perhaps you should show that to a doctor?'

'Ruth! Listen to what I'm saying!'

'I – I can't, Byrne. I can't afford to. Not now.' Her hands were clutching the steering wheel. He could see the shine of her knuckles. 'I will talk to you, I promise. But I'm late already. I'm sorry.' She glanced quickly at him, and it seemed to Byrne that her body was betraying her. The tension in her hands, the panic in her eyes were giving it away.

She leaned forward, turning on the ignition. 'I've got this idea. Instead of a fête we'll have a plant sale, invite the local nurseries to take stalls.'

He wasn't going to let it go. 'The Blue Manor is haunted, Ruth!'

'No, Byrne.' She spoke briskly. 'You've been listening to Simon. It's not like that at all. I really must go. Bye, see you later – ' She put her foot down and the car drew away.

Frowning, he watched her leave. This was wilful, an almost

neurotic resistance to knowledge. She couldn't bear the past to be revealed, and she couldn't handle the present either. He wondered when it would crack, this rigid denial of the circumstances. When would she realize the truth: that the manor was haunted and that her family was caught up in it?

And his own role there. Why was she so adamant that he should stay, why did Alicia insist on involving him? Why did he want to stay himself? He'd volunteered to get Tom out last night, he'd done it with no prompting.

The manor meant something to him, too. This was also his story.

He turned round slowly, looking up the driveway to where the manor waited, holding its breath.

He walked towards it reluctantly. It loomed too high above him, as if it might topple over and engulf him. Through the French windows he could see Tom, scribbling away at the desk in the library. For a moment he envied him that easy escape, that welcome retreat from reality. He didn't relish what he had to do next.

He opened the back door and the house settled its iron grip around him. It wasn't usually like that in the kitchen. Usually, the sense of constriction attacked only in the hall and beyond. But the door grated slightly as he pushed it open and the sunlight streaming through the window seemed harsh with pressure.

He found Simon in the kitchen, scrubbing potatoes, and said abruptly, without preamble, 'This house is haunted. What do you know about it?'

Simon's back was to him. He stopped scrubbing and leaned forward, his head drooping.

'Simon? Talk to me!'

Slowly the older man turned. His skin was waxy yellow in the difficult light and Byrne was appalled to see tears streaking down his cheeks. But Simon's voice, when he at last spoke, was curiously flat.

'I only know about the Dogfrog, really. It's the only manifestation which gets to me.' He pointed to the corner of the room, where an old coat had fallen to the floor.

Except it wasn't an old coat. Neither, by any stretch of the imagination, was it a mongrel.

A great hound sat there, its red eyes gleaming. Coarse, grey-white fur covered bulging, bunched muscles. Its ears were tipped with red, its claws were stained with blood. Its mouth, hanging open, panted faintly, lined with red.

As Byrne looked at it, it rose out of the corner, swelling until it was waist-high, a vast creature padding across the floor towards him.

Involuntarily, he stepped back, colliding with the dresser. The china rattled, and Simon laughed. 'Don't worry,' he said. 'It likes you.'

'How can you tell?' He was breathless with apprehension.

Its furious, mad red eyes held him steady.

'You can see it and you're not dead. *Greatly* favoured. Like me. Besides, you work in the garden.'

'What's that got to do with it?'

The Dogfrog had turned away from him and was pacing over the tiles towards Simon. It stopped at his side and sat down, one paw lying, not casually, over Simon's feet.

'The Leafer controls the garden. Haven't you noticed it? Anyone it doesn't like gets hurt ... You've met my father, haven't you? That scar down his face, that was the Leafer.'

'Is that why you won't go out?'

'Christ, at last! Someone understands!' The words were a mockery, but his eyes said something different. 'I'd like to celebrate, offer alcohol, but my supplies haven't arrived.'

'Tell me about the Leafer.' All the time, Byrne was staring at the incredible creature at Simon's feet. Its eyes were closed and it seemed smaller, not nearly so threatening. He glanced at Simon, and when he looked back the Dogfrog was gone.

Just a memory of fur, of red-tinged tips of teeth or ears remained.

'Where *is* it? Where's it gone?'

'It's here,' said Simon calmly. 'There – or there – '

He pointed around the room and everywhere Byrne saw suggestions, not glimpses, of flashing eyes and bunched muscles and sharp, ripping claws.

'Jesus! How do you *stand* it?'

'The booze helps. And this helps, you seeing it too. I'm not as loony as they think. Either that or it's contagious, and you've got it too.'

'No. This is really happening. We're not mad, either of us.' Byrne turned his eyes away from the Dogfrog's presence and sat down at the table. 'Tell me. Talk to me.'

'You asked about the Leafer. It's *lots* of fun. It lives in green things, anything that grows. You can run your hands along the hedge and nothing will be there one moment and then you try it again and the thing is living, inhabited, conscious and waiting for you. You must have noticed it, you must have seen it in the trees or the roses or the damn cabbages. You are the gardener, after all. An extra quality of liveliness, responding, acting . . . It quite likes being grass. And especially anything thorny, anything it can wound with.'

'Does no one else see it? Or have any knowledge of it?'

'Well, it's part of the house's mythology. The women *know* it's there, like the Dogfrog. But they think the Dogfrog's a cross collie, for God's sake, and that the Leafer is . . . nothing much, an odd, harmless wood spirit or something. They very rarely think about either of them *at all*! It's as if their minds – refuse to admit them.'

'Even Alicia?'

'My dear mother. Yes, you have the right of it. She's the odd one out. Not of the blood, of course, not of the Banniere blood line. She's never seen the Dogfrog or the Leafer, but I think she knows they exist. Apparently Elizabeth Banniere, Ruth's grandmother, had an imaginary friend or a toy dog or something called the Dogfrog and she used to pretend there was a guardian in the garden. Hey, that's good, isn't it? A guardian in the garden, garden guardian—'

'Stop it, Simon, this is serious!'

'It's so fucking serious that I would do anything, *anything* to get away from this place.'

'Come on, then.' Byrne held open the back door. 'I'll take you into Epping.'

'You're rather forgetting something.' Eloquent hands opened and Simon's way to the door was blocked by the Dogfrog, red tips glowing and avid and vital.

Had it been there all the time, its mouth hanging open, panting? Byrne experienced a frisson of terror as it moved towards him, seeming to grow out of all proportion as he watched it. He stepped back. Perspectives were horribly mismatched. It was surging through the air, wildly filling all the space in the room. The kitchen shrank around it, Simon became like a doll, the furniture was made only of matches.

It filled the kitchen, taller than Byrne, its great head hanging over him, hot blood dripping on to his shoulders.

'Get out of here!' Simon's voice, thin and wispy as a reed, from far away, dimensions away.

The shock evaporated. Byrne bolted.

Chapter 32

He stumbled across the terrace towards the garden. *It quite likes being grass*, he remembered and just stopped himself from running heedlessly over the lawn.

Was the terrace safe? Was *anywhere* safe? What bizarre madness had gripped him, that he could talk quite ordinarily to a man in the presence of something he even now could not accept existed?

Had it been real? Already his mind was refusing it, that surging presence, hot animal breath, the open maw hanging over his head. He shuddered, looking back to the kitchen.

Nothing. The door opened on to the empty tiled floor. Through the window he saw Simon bent over the potatoes as if nothing had happened.

What had happened?

Was he mad, dreaming? But he knew it was no dream, no hallucination. His hand still throbbed from the glass he'd broken trying to get out of the house the night before. He didn't know if he'd ever dare enter it again. The house didn't want him, didn't need him . . .

What was he thinking? The house wasn't alive, it had no will. It was nothing but a collection of stone and bricks and mortar, a rather gloomy piece of Edwardian grandiosity. Why should he persist in thinking it alive and conscious?

He walked down the steps from the terrace and stepped on to the lawn. It was all right. The grass was smooth, flat, green, unliving beyond its ragged vegetable growth. The leaves above were hardly moving. Through them he saw the sky seamlessly brilliant, a hot burning canopy of blue.

And then there was Kate, nicely dressed in vivid scarlet cotton, swinging a shoulder bag by its long strap. She was coming down the steps towards him. 'Hi, Byrne.' She beamed at him. 'What's the matter, cat got your tongue?'

He stared at her. 'Tell me about the Dogfrog,' he said. It was becoming like a test, a password. Something to use to find out if people were really sane, as he was. The garlic test, the vampire mirror scene. Do you see it too?

She's going to shrug it off, he thought. She'll tell me I'm imagining it, that it's nothing special –

'No time now,' she said happily. 'Going for coffee with the honoured unc, so you can tell them that.' She looked sideways at him, lifting her chin, as if daring him to stop her. 'See you later, Byrne. Don't work too hard, it's going to be a scorcher.'

He watched her wheel a bike from the garage and spin off down the drive to the village. She'd read him accurately: part of him did indeed want to shout after her, to stop her leaving the manor.

How could he? It was nothing to do with him, not his role. He couldn't possibly interfere.

But he could cut the grass. He kicked at the overlong leaves and decided then and there to mow the lawn. Physical action, that was what he needed. Honest work out in the open, with no strange shadows, no complications about it. It would please Ruth too, make the place look better. Cutting the grass would transform the appearance of the whole manor, embedding it in neat, tidy emerald green. It might defuse some of its glowering shabbiness. It might even – he almost laughed – make it look suburban.

In the garage he found an ancient petrol mower. There was plenty of fuel. After several attempts it spluttered into smelly life.

He pushed it round to the front of the house, deciding to start there, where Ruth would see it as she drove home, and began to mow.

It quite likes being grass, he thought again. Well, let's see how it likes being cut.

The grass fell from the blades in green cascades.

Alicia arrived later that morning. She drove towards the manor and saw Byrne cutting the grass, although she didn't stop or make any acknowledgement. Her face was set hard.

She parked in the garage yard and went to the back door.

Once inside the kitchen she stood still for a moment, as if listening to the quietness of the house. Her eyes scanned the corners of the room, paying particular attention to the coat that had fallen by the door. Then she nodded, and moved through to the hall.

Alicia went straight to the library and peered round the door. Tom was there, crouched over the desk, frantically scribbling. He was deep in the grip of the story. She smiled to herself, well satisfied.

There was still that look of determination on her face as she quietly shut the door. She was taking pains not to disturb her protégé.

This was why she had come, this was what it was all about. Tom and his story. And the house.

She found her son in the television room. It was a dark, cramped hole, the curtains drawn against the bright sunlight. She wrinkled her nose at the stale smell of cigarettes and alcohol.

Simon was slumped in an armchair, his back to her, zapping through the channels. She watched him for a moment in silence. Like Tom, he had no idea she was there.

Without a word, she walked past him to the only window in the room and pulled back the curtains. 'Morning, dear,' she said. 'A little gloomy in here, don't you think?'

He put the remote control down and sighed. 'The sun dazzles the screen, Mother, as well you know. Not that there's much worth watching.'

'Well, you can talk to me instead.' She sat down opposite him, her sharp eyes scanning the room. There was no bottle or glass in sight. Only one of the kitchen mugs balancing on the tweedy arm of Simon's chair.

Simon was looking dreadful, years older than he actually was, worn out and depressed like old shoes. She made no comment. 'Where's Kate?' she asked.

'Gone to see the old man, I expect.'

'After what we told her?' Alicia frowned.

'What did you expect? Don't you remember what it's like to be twenty? When did you ever do what your elders and sometimes betters recommended?' His voice was bitter. 'In fact, Mother dear, you have probably pushed our Kate into Dad's arms.'

Alicia shook her head. 'She's not such a fool.'

'But lover boy spends his time locked in the library and she's no hand at gardening. What else do you expect her to do here? Watch the telly with me?'

'She could do worse. Why don't you get a video?'

'Ruth doesn't approve. And I can't be bothered.'

Alicia was leafing through the *Radio Times*. 'On Four there's *Some Like It Hot*.'

His dark, fathomless eyes flashed at her. 'Seen it. Often. But it's always worth another go, wouldn't you say?'

She smiled. 'OK.' She drew the curtains again.

The house enclosed them.

The day wore on. To Byrne, sweating, baking in the monotony of pacing every foot of the lawn, it seemed interminable. The mower was unreliable and he spent too much time on his knees fiddling with the mucky thing, getting oil on his hands and clothes. His injured hand ached. The grass box was too small and he wasted time emptying it until he decided to let the grass lie. Someone else could rake it up. He wouldn't be here for long. Not long at all.

Who are you kidding? the small voice at the back of his mind mocked. You've been thinking that ever since you got here. You're not going to leave Ruth, not today, not tomorrow (not ever?).

It was the problem of the past. It ran through the lives of everyone who lived at the manor, it ran through his own life in shades of desperation.

He nearly stopped then: nearly just turned and walked away. He could leave the mower standing there, in the centre of the lawn, walk down the drive to the cottage, collect his jacket, his wallet . . .

The money. Well, he could take it back to Peter Lightowler, drop it off in Theydon Bois on the way –

He shook his head impatiently. It was too hot, he wasn't thinking straight. He was longing for a cool beer. There was no escaping this, no way out. And all the time it ran round the back of his mind: what about your own past? What about the way you're running, not facing it, not taking on board the fact that your wife, your beloved, darling, pregnant wife, was having an affair with your best friend?

He felt almost sick. His pace slowed, almost halted. The front of the house was finished, but he wasn't going to stop here. He didn't want to stop and think. Wilfully, blanking out his mind, he trundled the mower across the terrace to the side where Tom was working at the French windows.

Would the noise bother him? Byrne shrugged as he started the machine up again. Tom was quite capable of telling him to shut up.

Through the open windows he saw Tom scribbling frantically, as if his sanity depended on it. He paid no attention to the noise from the mower.

Byrne walked on.

His hand was aching. Tom let the pencil fall on to the desk and stood up, running his fingers through his hair. He began to pace the library. Someone had brought him sandwiches, had put them on the table by the door and he'd never even noticed. Absently, he picked one up and began to chew.

He was aware of a faint headache somewhere behind his eyes. Too much concentration, he thought, or was it that infernal noise from the lawn mower? But he was not seriously irritated.

Against all the odds, he had grown to like Phizackerley Byrne, even if he was making such a din. He was nothing like the meathead Simon had implied. Tom recognized a watchfulness in the older man, a patient quality of awareness he had thought peculiar to writers.

Writers, the work of making stories. He picked up the sheaf of papers from the desk and scanned through it as he prowled restlessly around the library. There was a hole in it, he decided, in this story of the Blue Manor, although he was not displeased with it so far. Still, there was a gaping void where one of the central figures should be.

Roderick Banniere. Elizabeth's brother, Peter Lightowler's father. What had happened to him, where was he while Peter was insinuating himself into the lives of Elizabeth and John Downie?

It had been Roderick who had started the whole thing off. He had raped his sister, he had raped Jessie Lightowler on the island and fathered Peter. He was at the centre of this particular web, but it was a concealed centre as yet, something off-stage.

Roderick would have wanted to stay in touch with his son. But how? How did father and son contact each other, how did it go? Tom found himself at the desk once more, staring down at the pages of neat writing. Almost without conscious volition, his fingers picked up the pencil.

They wrote to each other, of course. They were writers too.

Dear Father,
    I trust that life on Ithaca continues to amuse. Certainly, I am not without diversion here in Essex. As you ordained, so is it done. Does that satisfy, does that enliven your hours of sunshine and ease? I strive only to please you. It is accomplished. The seed sown. It came as no hardship, for your sister is beautiful still. Shall I steal her for you, shall I spirit her away to your island home? I often think of what she must have been like, all those years ago. Now she is full-breasted, mature in every way, elegant, witty. A little wary, somewhat diffident, and of course a little confused now, but this only adds to her charm. Her hair is shingled, a shining black cap . . . Shall I draw her for you, would you like that?
    Downie presents no problem, of necessity preoccupied by the wreck of his body. An ant, a fly might prove more significant than he. I have marked the house, as you suggested . . .

Roderick Banniere puts down the letter, frowning slightly. He does not always approve of his son's passion for literary elaboration. The formal, flowery words are an irritation to him. Still, Peter is very young. There's time for him to learn.

He stands at the window of the plain whitewashed room, watching a bird dipping low over the deep-coloured sea. A gull, or something. His eyes narrow against the sun.

Peter has done well, there is no doubt about it. He's moving quickly, and that is all to the good. Too much time has been wasted already.

A picture of Elizabeth? For a moment he allows his mind to wander, remembering his sister. She was always so naive, so curiously innocent. She had no artifice, no defences. Would maturity have changed her?

He doubts it. There are women who sleep their way through life, who drift with no clear aim or ambition, who are untouched by will. Content as cattle, essentially vulnerable to manipulation and exploitation.

He feels contempt, but it is tempered by something more

dangerous. He is cold now. Passionless, empty of feeling. It has been a long process, a sequence of events begun in childhood.

His mother shut him out. She was always tired, resting or practising. She never had any time for him. So he roamed the London streets, although he was quite young, only six, and his dog had been with him. But the dog had gone missing, and he'd cried that night. And his father had beaten him for making a noise, for being a softy, for losing the dog. They'd sent him to school to toughen him up, and the birth of his sister had taken place not long after. It is always associated in his mind with rejection and exile.

He has always hated her. And yet he cannot forget her, that black-haired girl who trusted him with her secrets, who pretended that the trees were her friends, that her imaginary dog was real. These are comfortable, easy memories, pictures of her that will never leave him. He needs no sketches from Peter, no words to remind him what she's like.

He reads quickly to the end of his son's letter and then crumples it up and throws it away.

Outside the villa the two women have settled just beyond the baking rocks, careless of the heat. Their black clothes are dull with sand and dust. They are crouching on the shoreline where the barely moving tide pulls at the damp rags of their clothes. They are playing with something, pulling it apart between them, red blood and feathers messy over their mouths.

The bird he had seen earlier. He remembers its wings, slow and sluggish in the hot thermals. They must have called it to the shore. They liked to play.

Roderick Banniere pauses for a moment. Then he rings the bell on his desk.

They are there then, instantaneously. Both of them with blood and feathers on their white faces, dribbling down the front of their clothes.

He smiles thinly. 'We're going home,' he says. 'It's time to take part.'

There is an unusual stillness about them.

'No.' It's the small one who speaks, the one who always watches him so closely. Her black and greasy hair is curiously twined into peaks on either side of her head. Her eyes are entirely alien, inimical. Roderick Banniere does not trust her, or the *other. He suspects that they want something from him. 'No,' she repeats. 'You can never go back to the manor.'*

Banniere frowns. 'Who are you to tell me such things? I'm in charge here!'

But actually he knows the futility of the words. He has no real control over these two.

This is not the first time they have disobeyed him.

Standing in that whitewashed room in the house on the beach, the smaller one's colourless eyes stare at Banniere. 'No. Living, you will never return to the manor.'

'Don't talk rubbish!'

'When have we ever been wrong?' The other woman, who knows no name, no family or history, this strange woman with her dark, rats'-tail hair and trailing black rags, comes towards Roderick Banniere.

'It's enough,' she says. 'We've waited long enough. It's time for you to start paying.'

'What do you mean?' He has no idea what she is talking about, but he feels his flesh shrivel with fear.

'You need to be more – flexible. In every way.'

The woman moves towards Roderick Banniere, while the other one lurks further back, her blank eyes focused nowhere. She is smiling, her painted mouth upturned in mockery.

'What do you mean?' he whispers again. He steps back, but the woman is as close as ever.

'Living, you will never return,' she repeats.

'I don't understand!' he yells.

'I am not alive,' says the woman, and Roderick Banniere realizes the truth of something he has always denied. The two of them are not living, not flesh and blood in any ordinary sense of the words. Insectoid shades, avian delusions . . . They shift between horn and wing. They belong to the manor, they are part of its strange destiny. He clenches his fists and she speaks again.

She? Why did he use these terms?

'I am not alive, and now it is time for you to know what we really are.'

Her hand rises and clutches Roderick Banniere's neck. 'Your turn to live within the three, within the pattern.'

And as the blood drums in his ears, as the vessels in his eyes burst and stain everything with red, as he realizes that there is no more air in the world anywhere for him, he knows a certain truth.

Living, you will not return to the Blue Manor.

Dead, you might try.

Chapter 33

'Where's Kate?' Ruth stormed into the kitchen. Alicia and Simon were there, pouring tea. 'Her bike's not in the garage. Where is she?'

For a while no one said anything.

'Simon! Tell me!' She was unsteady with anger, thin-lipped. She slammed her bag on the table and papers spilled out over it.

Simon said, 'Ruth, pull yourself together. She's gone out for the day. To meet a friend.'

'She's gone to see that man! How could you *let* her, how could you let her go?'

'How could I stop her? What did you want me to do? Let down the tyres of her bike, lie across the road, knock her over the head and pull her away by her hair? For goodness' sake, Ruth, she's of age, she's old enough to make her own decisions.' He sounded bored.

'Not in this case.' She slumped suddenly at the table and propped her head against her hands.

Alicia watched this, saying nothing. She placed a mug of tea by Ruth's elbow. 'Come on, Ruth, this isn't like you. Has anything happened to upset you?'

'Only my daughter, making friends with a man who . . . who . . . I loathe him! How could you let her do it?'

'It's not up to us,' said Simon.

'Nothing ever is. You take no responsibility, you duck out of it. It's as if you had no idea, no real comprehension of what this is about.'

'Oh, give over, Ruth! What does it matter? He's an old man, he's feeble and useless and lonely.'

'And he's taking my daughter away from me!'

'This is ridiculous. You must know that.'

'I know nothing but what I see! I see you in league against me, plotting to get that man back into the house, to take it away from me—'

'Ruth, this sounds quite mad, quite paranoid,' said Alicia, determinedly reasonable.

'There were three phone calls today.' She said it quietly, and they almost missed it.

'At work?' Simon asked. 'You had anonymous phone calls at school?'

'Twice in lessons and one at lunch.'

'Oh, my dear!' Alicia sat beside her, her arm round Ruth's shoulders. 'How horrible for you. No wonder you're upset.'

'They're from him, you see. From him or his creatures.' Her voice was intense. She stood up, pushing Alicia away. She went to the sink and picked up one of the wine glasses on the draining board. Quite deliberately, and with great force, she smashed it on the tiled floor. 'I'd like to kill him. I'd like to—' She stopped. 'Those creatures who go everywhere with him, they're at the back of it. They ring me up and tell me what he's doing with Kate. They say such terrible things, I can't forget . . .'

'Why don't you put the phone down?' Simon, unsympathetically. 'You don't have to listen. It's not like your pet lambs at the Samaritans, you could just cut them off.'

'I listen because I keep thinking I'll find out *why*, why he's doing this! What does he want, what's he getting at?'

'You said it yourself.' Alicia spoke quietly. 'He wants the house. He wants you out. That's what this is about.'

'Well, I'm *never* going to let him, never, no matter what he does!'

A sound in the doorway from the hall. They looked up to see Tom staring at the smashed glass on the floor. He was holding a sheaf of papers in his hand.

'I – I'm sorry, I couldn't help hearing.' He cleared his throat. 'I thought I'd have a walk, get some fresh air. I shan't want any supper. If you see Phizackerley Byrne, could you ask him to come and get me from the library later – at about ten o'clock?' He spoke with unnatural formality, and hesitated briefly. No one said anything. 'Please give him this.' He put the papers on the table. 'I'd like him to read it.' He glanced at their faces. 'I'm sorry,' he said as he left the room, shutting the door behind him.

'That damn book of his!' cried Ruth. 'If only he had paid more attention to Kate.'

'It would make no difference,' said Alicia. 'This has to be worked out in its own way.'

'I know what you're doing.' Ruth looked at Alicia with

resentment. 'You want to force the issue, don't you? To precipitate things. It's part of your own little feud. You sent Tom here because you knew he'd write this bloody story, you knew your ex-husband was ready to make a last-ditch attempt to get his horrible crawly hands on my house. You're behind this, aren't you?'

'What nonsense you do talk, dear.' Gently Alicia took her arm. 'Why don't you go and have a lie down . . . a nice bath or a shower before dinner? Simon and I will get it ready—'

'Don't patronize me, Alicia! Don't you *dare* patronize me. I will not be manipulated by you too!' Her hair was standing out wildly from her face, her eyes flashing with fury. And then she turned and almost ran from the room. They heard her footsteps cross the hall and go into the library. The sound of wood, reverberating, as the piano lid slammed back.

Those repeated, urgent notes, and then her voice, the strong, unpolished beauty of it, filling the house . . .

> *De sa dent soudaine et vorace,*
> *Comme un chien l'amour m'a mordu . . .*

'I hate that song,' said Simon. 'Of those few, exquisite things Duparc made, it's the only one I don't like.'

Alicia's hand moved suddenly, sharply, quietening him.

'When did you last hear Ruth sing?' she asked softly. 'Why now, why now?'

They stared at each other as the song drew to its mysterious close.

'Why don't you ever come to see John these days?'

Lightowler looks up from the sketch on the pad. They are drawing the west elevation of the manor and he can see the light flashing from something within the library.

Binoculars, he thinks. Downie is watching us.

'I thought he wasn't receiving visitors yet,' he says mildly.

'You're more like family,' Elizabeth says. 'I'm sure he'd love a change from my company. He's very isolated, you know.'

'How could any man want a change from you?' He stands up, putting the pad down. He has come to a decision. He has had enough of lurking around in the grounds. He wants to be established in the manor before Margaret returns from the USA. It is time to get rid of Downie.

Elizabeth is near to term. His eyes fasten on hers for a while, so that she becomes confused by his familiar enchantments, past habits.

His finger under her chin tilts her face up to him. His lips lock on her mouth roughly, and her glazed eyes hardly register anything at all.

The bulk of her swollen belly is between them. He doesn't mind, he finds it exciting. He pushes her round, hauling at her skirts with one hand while with the other he releases the top of his trousers.

As he plunges into her, he looks over her acquiescent head to the library, where the light still flashes. His mouth stretches wide in delight.

When he has finished, he gives her no time to order her clothing or straighten her hair. He pulls her face to his once more and chews at her mouth, biting her lip so that blood begins to trickle, holding her eyes trapped by his own, making sure that the trance is still upon her.

Then he seizes her hand, dragging her across the lawn, through the rose garden and across the terrace to the French doors to the library.

He flings them wide and crashes into the room. Books fall from their shelves with the force, splaying open on the floor. China smashes, flowers overspill.

He finds himself facing the barrel of a shotgun.

'Let go of her.' Downie's whispered words are nearly inaudible. He's holding the rifle up to his shoulder and Lightowler knows he will not be able to maintain that position for long. Already his breath is wrenched and shuddering. His eyes are black pits.

'Did you enjoy the show? Did it give you a thrill?'

Lightowler is alight with excitement. He pulls Elizabeth closer, so she is standing in front of him, shielding him from the gun. His hand cups her left breast, the fingers digging in. In the mirror behind Downie's head he sees that her eyes are blank, that the blood still runs from her mouth.

He'll never use that gun, not while I'm holding Elizabeth, Lightowler thinks.

Downie fires. The blast shatters into the wall to one side of Lightowler's head, causing him to leap sideways so he is half behind the desk, breathless with surprise. The force of the recoil *moves the wheelchair back to the wall, and the barrel of the gun droops in Downie's grasp. The crippled man is gasping, white with the shock of it. Around them there is a tumbling of books, pages bent and crumpled.*

Lightowler keeps his hands on Elizabeth, pulling her with him. Who'd have thought the old man would have dared?

'Have you gone mad?' he shouts, adrenalin surging, exhilarated to find that he is going to have a fight on his hands. 'Do you want to kill your wife? Your child?'

'It's your child. Your fucking whore.' The tiny voice penetrates like the hissing of a snake.

The door to the passage is open. Lightowler twists his head round, instantly alerted by what has come in.

Infinitely more dangerous than Downie, more dangerous than the woman who is even now keening, wailing, breaking through his enchantment, invisible to either Elizabeth or Downie, he sees the Dogfrog in its true shape.

Tom glanced up and shivered. There it was, sitting by the door as he knew it would be. He held his breath, conscious that the newly healed wounds on his back were throbbing. It sat there, just looking at him, and his pencil crawled across the page, writing down every detail, every appalling unnatural image, while his mind balked at the fact of its existence.

Its forked tongue flickers, the white fur growing straight from bone, it seems, flakes of white and grey ruffling about its attenuated silhouette. Wild energy lives in its eyes, ready to fix and immobilize its prey. Its muscles bunch together, ready to spring.

It takes a step towards Lightowler. Its breath is foul in the house, its teeth are sharper than razors. Great claws, tinged with red, spring from the wide-splayed paws. Its ears are pointed with scarlet and fly away into the air beyond, leaving streaks of red dribbling, splashing on the floor and furniture.

Elizabeth falls from Lightowler's grasp, and he is only distantly aware of the sound of her crying. Downie is out of the reckoning, still labouring with the shotgun.

The guardian comes further into the room and he braces himself, summoning all his prepared tricks and subterfuges.

This is no longer a game. He knows that somewhere Downie

is preparing to fire again, that Elizabeth has come to her senses, is moving towards him –

He doesn't care. Time has stopped.

'Get out.' Elizabeth is standing at the table and Lightowler sees her hands clench on a heavy glass paperweight. Beside her, the Dogfrog growls.

Lightowler steps towards Elizabeth, taking an enormous, lunatic chance. He doesn't consider Downie, struggling with the rifle. Only he and Elizabeth matter, only they can deal with each other. The other is a phantom, something unreal, something from another dimension.

Downie fires and the shot goes wide, shattering through the glass in the French windows. He slumps in the chair, the gun crashing to the floor. Without looking, Lightowler knows that he is dead.

He tries to remember what he has learned, what he knows. He tries to concentrate, to imprison Elizabeth's eyes once more, to divert her mind from the heavy lump of glass in her hand, but the floor starts to shiver beneath his feet.

He can't work it out, doesn't understand.

It isn't Elizabeth, nothing to do with her, but something is fighting him. The hound thing is part of it. The floor is sliding away from them, tilting and shifting. He snarls and reaches out his hands.

And still the manor resists him. He feels rather than sees that the room is moving around him. Books are falling, furniture crashing, her husband is dead but Elizabeth stands there with that damned hound, and her words repeat again: Get out, get out. This is not yours, it never will be yours.

The glass paperweight catches him behind the ear. Another shift, the floor rearing up before him. Caught wildly off balance, he reaches for Elizabeth, but she is not there.

His head is filled with the sound of her words and pain, and his limbs are losing their grip. With furious despair he knows he is falling, falling at great speed, his head caught in a dizzying vortex.

The house spins round him, vomiting him out into the park.

And Elizabeth falls to her knees beside the body of her husband and braces herself for a different ordeal.

Chapter 34

'They've always hated men.' There was no rancour in the voice of the old man who sat next to Kate on the sofa. They were looking together at a scrapbook of old photographs and mementos. 'There has always been something so – self-possessed, so invulnerable, about the women who live in the manor. Of course, Rosamund was a sad thing, an unhappy woman . . . your great-great-grandmother, dear, the originator of it. She was beautiful. All the Banniere women have been beautiful.' He pointed to a concert programme with its sepia background and pale pink and green colouring. *Fleur jetée* said the ornate lettering. *La belle chanteuse sings again.* 'I did not know her personally, and in fact my father Roderick's memories are a little unclear. She was never there, he told me once. She was off performing, travelling the world, La Scala, the Paris Opera, the New York Met. She was never home when they lived in London. My father ran wild then.'

'But you knew Elizabeth, didn't you?'

This was not the first time Kate had questioned Peter Lightowler about the past. There had been other lunch parties, afternoon teas, gentle strolls through the forest during the past year or so.

At first, Kate was simply curious. Her mother and Alicia had forbidden any contact so naturally the young Kate, aged only nineteen, had visited Lightowler, had gone out of her way to hear his side of the story.

It was not just perverse. There was so much mystery around it. Ruth and Alicia had always skirted round the issue, had always changed the subject or prevaricated. It maddened Kate, particularly now. She wanted to understand, she needed to know.

But Kate was neither reckless nor stupid: she experienced not one moment of physical fear or hesitation, because Peter Lightowler was appallingly, dreadfully old. His skin was frail as paper, his white hair thin and wispy. Whenever she touched his hand or arm she could feel the bones beneath the skin. There was no warm sheathing of flesh and fat and muscle. His hands were always cold. She felt a deep pity for him, and it gave her the confidence to go on meeting him.

It was not that she wanted to exonerate him, she just needed to know. She was longing to find out what he'd done, what had so terrified Ruth and Alicia.

'I was there, you see,' Peter Lightowler said. 'When John Downie died. He'd got some idea that I was having an affair with his wife, the beautiful Elizabeth. He had worked himself up into a terrible passion, poor man. He tried to shoot me, but fortunately he missed. The net result was that he lost his life and Elizabeth went into premature labour. Your grandmother Ella was born that night.'

'Were you having an affair with Elizabeth?'

He took back the scrapbook and closed it gently. For a moment he said nothing and she wondered whether he was going to lie.

'I wanted to,' he said quietly. 'I tried everything I could. I insinuated myself into their lives, I played bridge and tennis, I talked politics with John. I tried to make myself indispensable to them. I tried to get Elizabeth to confide in me. I knew she must be lonely. John had such black fits of depression – he was terribly crippled, you see. I even lived here to keep her company when Margaret was away at one stage. But, in answer to your question, no, I never had an affair with Elizabeth. Ella Banniere was her daughter by John Downie.'

'But I thought he couldn't have children!'

'Who told you that?' Pale eyes watched her carefully.

'Alicia said—'

'Alicia. My dear one and only wife.' Peter Lightowler settled back against the sofa cushions. 'Well, there you have it,' he said. 'Whose word are you going to trust? It always comes down to that. Who is telling the truth? Is there any hard and fast answer to any of it?'

'There are tests, these days. Blood tests, genetic fingerprinting.'

Peter Lightowler shrugged. 'But Ella died long ago. So did John Downie. They will have rotted into the earth (do bones carry memories?) if they weren't cremated.'

'Don't you know?' Kate leaned forward, clasping her hands together.

'They wouldn't let me anywhere near. Not for Downie's funeral, not when Ella died. They're neither of them in any of the local cemeteries or graveyards. I know, because I looked. But no one ever told me, no one ever told me anything. I was always . . . persona non grata.' She saw that a slight tremor had gripped his hands.

'I'll find out,' she said. 'It should be cleared up, don't you think?'

'After all this time?' He laid his old, cold, liver-spotted hands on the scrapbook. 'If you can, sweet Kate, if you can. It might be nice to die with my name cleared, but I think it will prove too much, my dear, even for you. There's too great a weight of years on this, and besides there's something else—'

'What?'

'The house. You must never forget the manor itself.'

'How could I?' she said. 'I was born there.'

'So was I,' he said. 'Conceived, at least. Shall I tell you about it?'

'It's not true!' The door was flung open. Kate shook her mother's shoulders. 'Come on, admit it, you're wrong!' She was shouting, her face pale, the bones vividly pronounced in the thin light from the corridor. Her fingers were digging into Ruth's flesh.

'What . . . ?' Blearily Ruth pushed her daughter's hands away. For a moment the tranquillizer she had taken dulled her responses. Beside her Simon had turned over, pulling the covers up to his ears.

Ruth hauled herself on to her elbow, fumbled at the bedside light. 'Kate, where have you *been*?' she said, beginning to remember. 'Why are you so late?'

'It's not late, only eleven o'clock. You know very well where I've been . . . and I want some answers, *now*!'

'For goodness' sake, Kate, can't it wait till morning?'

'No, it can't wait! Come on, Mum, tell me! So you were raped, were you? By Uncle Peter? You should hear what *he* has to say about it!'

'Oh, what does it matter? He only *lies*, you must know that!' She pushed back the fall of hair over her eyes.

'Why do you hate him so much? Why do you keep on with this feud?'

'I don't keep on with it, it's him! He's the one who won't let go.' Ruth had got out of bed and was looking around vaguely for her slippers.

And still the blankets were pulled high, hiding Simon's face from them, as if he were not there at all.

'Tell me!'

'It will do no good.'

'You think he's my father, don't you?' Her voice was terrible in the half-light, terrible, ringing through the empty doorway and down the corridors. 'Why won't you tell me?'

'Oh, go to bed!' Simon at last, flinging back the bedclothes. Kate took a step back as he got out of bed.

'What do you think you're doing, Kate Banniere? What do you mean by this? Do you imagine this to be some kind of public circus, some lurid twopenny melodrama?' He was shouting at her, standing there, ridiculous in striped pyjamas.

She said, 'Are we sister and brother, then? Tell me that, *Uncle* Simon? Do we share a father?'

'For God's sake, *leave* it, Kate.' Ruth pushed past her out on to the landing. 'There's no good in dragging it up. You don't know what you're doing. You don't understand anything.' Her brown hair was dishevelled. 'Does anyone want tea, now that we're all awake?'

Kate followed her out into the corridor. The chasm of the stairwell echoed their words, but otherwise the house was quiet. A deft movement and she slid forward, barring her mother's way to the stairs. 'Just one word,' she said. 'That's all. It's not so very much. Tell me one thing: is Peter Lightowler my father?'

Ruth leaned her two hands on the banisters, her face turned away from her daughter, her eyes hidden. 'No, I don't think so,' she said quietly. 'I'd tell you if I knew for sure, but I don't. There was a confusion about the dates.'

Kate whirled her round. 'I don't believe you! How can you *confuse* something like that? You were there!'

'It was a long time ago, Kate. We were smoking things, there were pills, there were parties. I used to drink a bit . . . I simply don't remember!'

Kate stared at her mother. 'So you were some kind of whore, were you? Were there many candidates, many men you couldn't remember in the haze of drink and drugs? It seems a bit excessive to hate Uncle Peter so much, if that was how you were behaving.'

'Be careful, Kate.' Simon was now standing between them. 'You must remember that my dear mama has much to answer for.'

'Not as much as your father.' Ruth's voice was still low.

'And what do you mean by that, light of my love?'

'Well, look at you!'

'Yes?' A dangerous electricity in the air between them. Kate watched them, unaware that beneath a door had opened on to the hallway.

The shadows at the centre of the house were split by light. Below, Phizackerley Byrne looked up.

'Come on, my wise and good Samaritan counsellor. Let's have it straight. What dreadful inheritance has my father landed me with?'

'All right, then. All right. You asked for this, and you know what I'm going to say anyway. None of it's new.' Ruth's voice was ragged and unsteady. 'You're a drunk, a feeble and inadequate bundle of neuroses and insecurities and resentments—'

'And you feel sorry for me, don't you?'

'And it's your bloody father's fault,' she went on as if he hadn't spoken. 'He started you drinking, he abandoned you and your mother—'

'She threw him out!'

'She had to! To survive!'

'Crap! It hurt her pride that he found other women attractive.'

'Well, at least I can't accuse you of that!'

'You're a fine one to talk. You've found consolation elsewhere quickly enough.'

'What do you mean?'

'Byrne's after you. I've seen you in the garden together, I've seen you close, so close—'

'You're mad! There's nothing in it!'

'Don't lie to me, Ruth! I'm not stupid.'

'You're being ridiculous. This is a paranoid fantasy.'

'Bitch! You—' He couldn't even get the words out. He took a step forward and hit her. Not hard, just a sharp slap on the cheek.

But the carpet was rucked up beneath her feet and her slippers

243

caught there and she stumbled backwards, overbalancing heavily against the banister.

It cracked, splintering into shards, giving way under her shoulder, and she fell.

It wasn't far, only one storey, but the hall floor was stone. She fell head-first, her white nightgown trailing around her, and Kate screamed. The figure below moved out from the door, but too late, far too late.

A sickening, thudding sound, another crack somewhere in it, a different crack of bone and stone, and then breath expelled, fading. It was a sound amplified by the house, running down its corridors, through its rooms and attics and halls and cellars.

Then silence. Nothing. No one moved, no one could think of moving. Shock sliced through their lives.

It was Byrne who reached her first. He was on his knees beside her, his hands expertly tracing the pulse at her neck. Her eyes were closed, her head twisted to one side. A trickle of blood ran from her mouth. He bent low, to listen to her heart.

'Call an ambulance. Quickly!'

For a second no one moved. And then Kate clattered down the stairs and across the hall, stumbling and sliding on the rugs. They heard her voice, breathless with fear, giving the address.

Byrne looked up at Simon.

He had fallen to his knees, hands clutching at the remains of the banisters. He was quite colourless, his mouth hanging slackly.

'She's alive,' said Byrne. 'She's hit her head and I think her collar-bone's gone, but she's alive . . .'

And then the door to the library opened and Tom was there too, drawn by the commotion. He stood bewildered at the door, his hands half-lifted.

Byrne said to him, 'Get a blanket, a duvet.'

But it was Kate who ran for the stairs, as if action might make a difference.

Tom took her place at the telephone. He dialled another number and spoke quietly. When he'd finished he turned towards Byrne. Somehow they were all acknowledging that Byrne was in charge.

'I've rung Alicia,' said Tom. 'She's on her way.'

*

Kate went in the ambulance, Tom and Alicia followed in the car.

They asked Simon if he wanted to go too, but he shook his head numbly. 'I can't leave. You know that.'

'Even now?' Tom was severe.

Simon ignored him. He caught Alicia's arm as she was going out of the door. 'Phone,' he said. 'When you get there, when there's anything . . .'

'Yes, of course.' Alicia spoke briskly. She put her arm round Kate's shoulders. 'Come on, dear. This way.'

Chapter 35

Byrne watched the lights disappear down the drive. Simon was not there. As soon as the ambulance had left, he had gone straight to the dossery and turned on the television. After the briefest of glances at him, Byrne had fetched the brandy Alicia had brought and poured Simon (and himself) a generous quantity.

Simon didn't touch it. He sat in the grey flickering light, his face entirely expressionless, his eyes unmoving. The sound was turned down and the orchestral track to the Hindu epic sounded tinny and cheap. Byrne sat on the sofa and watched it, and the American comedy that followed.

After half an hour there was a call from the hospital, from Tom, to say that Ruth was in a critical condition with a suspected fracture of the skull. They were waiting for the results of the X-ray.

The television droned on. Byrne made coffee and poured himself more brandy. Simon had drunk nothing. There was a horror B-movie and another comedy. All the time they were conscious of the phone, sitting silent in the kitchen.

Ceaseless worry, seizing every passing thought and grinding it to dust. Does she live, does she die? Byrne stared blankly at the television screen.

Live. Live. Keep going, and live. His thoughts hammered so loudly that he knew Simon must hear them. He felt an urgent need to keep remembering, to keep willing her to live. If mere thought could do it, if prayer had any possibility of working, this was the way.

'I don't know why they should all have gone to the hospital!' Simon flared suddenly. 'What did Tom need to go for, what was the point of it?'

'Don't worry. He'll be back soon.'

'Yes, of course you're right. He'll be back. Him, or Kate or my mother. There have to be three, you see. And we, in case you've lost count, are only two.'

'What does it matter?' He had no stomach for these games.

And at that point, appropriately enough, they heard the sound of a car. The front door opened. With no consciousness of movement they found themselves in the hall. Tom was standing there, his hand on the knob. He was looking like an old man, too tired to move. No one said anything. They heard the taxi draw away. The noise from the television jangled in the background.

They saw it in his face, in the strict lines around his mouth.

'Simon,' Tom said at last, softly. 'I have to tell you that Ruth is in a coma. The injury to the brain . . . there's a blood clot. She will not recover, they say. There's nothing they can do.'

Simon said nothing. His face did not change. He turned his back on them and shut the door of the dossery behind him. The noise from the television went on.

And yet dawn did not come. Darkness gripped the Blue Manor. The house was very still, the blackness at its centre sucking at the light. Upstairs, outside the room Ruth had shared with Simon, a creature scratched at the floorboards, turning round and round as if looking for a resting place. Every now and then it lifted its head and a soft howling noise echoed down the long corridor. But there was no one up there to hear it, no one to see the maddened glare of red, desperate eyes.

Downstairs the walls were heavy. The pressure of books with their old stories seemed to push the walls inwards, to crush and weight the three men into immobility. They were trapped there, with the knowledge of this imminent death held like an axe over them, waiting to fall.

In the garden a ripple ran through the trees. It ran beyond the garden to the forest, where small animals whimpered and the birds suddenly took to the wind, rising high above the dark, shivering trees to wheel in ever-widening circles.

The great spinning dance was under way. Machinery, bright and brittle, hurtled round the ring of roads, lights sparkling in the endless stream.

And the earth turned on its axis, a tiny speck in the whirling dance of the spiral galaxies.

To the north a ring of stars flickered and blazed.

In the Blue Manor, at the centre of it all, nothing changed.

It seemed hours before anyone moved. Then Byrne crossed the hall from the kitchen, his face shuttered. He opened the door of the dossery and looked at Simon, who was standing there, between the chairs, his back to the window. He had opened the curtains.

The sky was beginning to lighten. Outside there would be daylight soon. Simon was silhouetted against the grey window, his shoulders high and hunched. Byrne turned on the light.

Simon was motionless, blinking in the brightness.

Byrne said, 'I saw it. It wasn't your fault. You are guiltless.'

'No one is guiltless.' Hollow words, melodramatic words. His eyes gazed at Byrne. 'You are not guiltless. You loved her, didn't you?' There was no inflection to his voice, it was almost academic and arid.

Byrne could find nothing to say. He took half a step towards the other man. 'It was not your fault,' he repeated at last. He laid his hand on Simon's shoulder.

He shuddered, a light tremor. Byrne felt his bones through the pyjamas, as fragile as glass. 'The sins of the father shall be visited—' Simon kept his eyes on Byrne. 'Why weren't you there? That was your role, didn't you know? The gardener always saves the day. Why didn't you save *her*? Where were you, why did you miss your cue?' His voice was beginning to skitter. 'And where was the Dogfrog, why wasn't it there, why didn't it do its stuff?' He began shouting. 'God, all those bloody guardians, the Leafer, the creature, the gardener and none of you, not one of you, could stop it!'

Byrne stood there, helpless. He could see that Simon was shivering. Through the open door, he could just make out Tom sitting motionless at the kitchen table.

Somehow the time had to pass. Somehow it had to be filled with actions and words.

'You're cold,' Byrne said. 'Go and put some clothes on. I'll make a pot of tea.' And it was true that they were all cold, that the air in the Manor was icy.

Outside the sun was burning up the dew.

Later in the kitchen, over yet another pot of tea, Simon and Tom started talking. Byrne had found it impossible to keep to one place. He was in the hall, aimlessly wandering, picking up magazines and books and replacing them.

He had seen Simon do the same. Shifting, wandering through the relentless house.

Early sunlight slanted in across the scrubbed kitchen table. It was littered with mugs and glasses. No one had slept, unsurprisingly, although Tom was by now yawning.

Simon tipped his chair back, his hands cradling a half-full mug. 'So. Now we're here. Three of us. It's worked again.' He spoke a little wildly, his voice tinged with unreason.

'The manor? Is that what you mean?' Tom said wearily.

'We're all present and correct, just as the manor likes. You must have noticed, you're the observer, the recorder.'

'I don't know what you mean.'

'Think! Always, always, three people live here. You were pushed out after three nights, weren't you?' A heavy-lidded glance at the younger man. 'It was because you made a fourth. Four people are not required, are not central to the manor's function. It likes three, mother, father, child. Mother, son and cousin; woman, husband, lover.' His voice shook suddenly and dropped into silence. Then, very quietly, 'You know how it works. God, I hate this place. I hate all these rules.'

'Has it always been like this?' Tom found himself looking round for a piece of paper, a pencil, so he could take it down. If he couldn't sleep, he might as well make some use of it. It was material for his book.

And then he caught himself up short, loathing himself for thinking like this, this horrible, selfish, obsession while Ruth lay there, dying.

But Kate had gone with Alicia to her hotel and the story was calling to him. He needed it. There was a kind of revelation in this. The story gave him his reason for being there at the manor, it gave value to his existence.

Simon did not seem to mind. If Tom needed to write, he needed to talk. He picked up a tumbler of brandy and emptied a good third of it. 'OK. I suppose we have to get through the hours somehow. That's the worst thing about death. Imminent death. Getting through the time until it happens. Until you get used to it, God forbid. And then there's afterwards. Years, it takes. So they tell me ... It was Ruth who told me, actually. Back in the days when we used to chat. Those poor bastards who rang up, some of them were in grief. Have you considered, my little fledgling writer, that being in grief is directly comparable to being in love? Really very similar? Sleeplessness, not eating, dislocation, distortion, all of those. The slow moving of time.'

He stopped, his eyes flickering over Tom's face. 'Yes, well, we all know about that, don't we? Let's find a more neutral subject, something dry and academic. How about a history lesson, so you can fill in some gaps? Have you got something to write with?' He fished amongst the pile of newspapers on the side. 'Here you are.' He was holding out the biro and pad Ruth sometimes used for shopping lists. His hand trembled.

'Ready? We could pretend you're the interviewer and I'm the celebrity . . . "Mr Lightowler, when did you first realize that this house was out of the ordinary?" That's what you should say. Then I say, "I just love this house, I adored coming here as a child, I want to stay here for ever."' The extreme artificiality of his tone dropped. 'And now it looks as though I will.' He paused for a moment, taking another long swig at the brandy. 'Don't you want some of this stuff? It's good for shock, they say . . . I suppose it started when I got back here in the sixties. I'd been a bad boy at Oxford. It was Ruth's fault – although it seems tasteless to say so now, not the kind of thing to find in a nice family interview. Anyway, she wouldn't have me. Said she was too young or some such rot. I was fed up. And there were other things, a girl I knew at university got pregnant—' He frowned. 'Ruth didn't like that either. I thought Laura had got rid of it. Mum said she had, but perhaps she didn't . . . She wouldn't take any money from me. It was stressful, failing at Oxford, as a lover. Knowing Laura felt I'd let her down.'

He looked at Tom. 'I was only twenty. Not much older than Kate. I wanted to succeed academically and I wanted Ruth. But she wouldn't have me and this other girl filled a gap.'

'She was called Laura?'

Simon noticed nothing. He shrugged. 'Yes . . . It was such a bloody mistake, the first in a long, long series. A black hole in the conscience, a reason to lie awake. A blot on the karma, if you like. I think I've been paying for it ever since, that and the other things . . .'

'Where did you meet her?'

'I can't remember. At Oxford. It doesn't matter . . . Anyway, I got back here, to the manor. And Dad was here.' He picked up the tumbler and took another gulp of brandy. 'The great villain Peter Lightowler. He'd moved into the village, into the Red House, and I was glad to see him, glad to have some – defence . . .'

'Defence?' But Tom's mind was not on it; it was racing instead along quite unprepared tracks. The biro hung loose from his fingers. He'd stopped writing.

'This *house!*' Simon hissed. 'This bloody, blood-stained house! It's blue with blood, like a bloody steak, all red and raw and bleeding. A mix of things not cooked properly, not *done*, not ready. With its Dogfrog and Leafer and strange wheels turning in the night – oh, have you heard them too? I suppose on your third night. All the artillery was out.' He paused. 'And what did Tom, our little juve lead, make of it?'

Tom ignored the malice. He wasn't even conscious of it. He said urgently, 'What was Laura's surname?'

'Why does it matter? What's it to you?' Something in Tom's tone caught him. 'What do you *mean?*'

'What was Laura's surname?' he repeated, shouting.

'Jeffrey. Why?

'Christ, Jesus Christ! I can't—' He stopped, wiping back the hair from his forehead, his face working. He said, 'My name is Tom Jeffrey Crabtree. My mother's name was Laura Jeffrey before she changed it. I never knew who my father was.' The words were falling over each other, rushed, too loud, unthinkable.

For a moment they stared at each other. They could hear the pacing of Byrne's feet, up and down the hall.

'You do now,' said Simon. The words dropped into stillness.

'It can't be! The coincidence, the chances—'

'Oh there's no chance in it.' His lips were drawn back in the travesty of a smile, a travesty of ironic awareness. 'No coincidence, none whatsoever. Think. How did you meet Kate? Why did you come here?'

'Alicia – Christ, your *mother!*'

'Yes. My wonderful mother. She was so *kind*, I thought, so helpful when I told her I'd got this girl, I'd got Laura into trouble. She'd look after it, she said.'

'Well,' Tom almost laughed, close to hysteria. 'Well, she did.'

Byrne was standing at the door to the kitchen. He'd been drawn by their voices.

'It seems,' said Simon slowly, 'that Tom and I – are related.'

And as they explained, it seemed to Byrne that this was like some ghastly joke, some music-hall turn. Who was that man I saw you with last night? That's no man, that's my father . . .

'Now you know,' said Simon to Tom. 'Now you know what

it feels like.' There was a smile playing over his mouth. It was not reflected in his eyes. 'You've inherited the very devil of a family tree. But there's one consolation. At least you've not inherited the house. It'll be Kate's soon. The Blue Manor will never be yours, like it will never be mine. So you needn't worry.'

His voice fell into silence.

The house was still waiting.

Chapter 36

Phizackerley Byrne left the house soon after that, saying he was going to the cottage for a wash and change. In reality, he wanted to get out of the place. The claustrophobia of that history, of all those strained relationships, meant little to him. He didn't much care whether Peter Lightowler was a villain or not. It didn't really matter, not in the face of what had happened.

Ruth. He was vividly reminded of Kristen's death. Caught in the crossfire, just like Ruth. A crossfire of misunderstanding and confusion. It had been a bomb in Middleham, a bomb meant for himself, but here it was all words. Ruth was going to die because of stories, lies and accusations about the past. He thought of Tom's scribbled sheets, he thought of that library, lined with books. The damage that words do.

The cottage squatted at the gates like some leprous toad. He didn't want to go in. He could keep going until he got to the A11. He could cut through the forest and join it on the way to Woodford . . . Epping Forest led straight into London, into the East End, on the way to the city. He could keep walking or start hitching again. He could put it behind him, everything that had happened, everything it had meant.

He walked on, past the cottage.

Ruth was going to die. Should he be there? At her side for those last few hours, for however long it took?

He knew about hospitals, what they were like. He thought of sitting by Kristen's burned body in the hospital while they fought for her life. He remembered looking at her foot jutting from the silvery blanket and thinking, this is not her. That foot is nothing to do with the person I love. She is not there, in this burned husk. Whatever she is, exists elsewhere.

He had sat there, in the waiting room outside intensive care, thumbing through magazines. Opposite him a young man read Proust, waiting for his girlfriend to die. There'd been a train crash, they thought she was going to make it, but it had gone wrong . . .

Byrne had sat there, waiting, for two weeks. And never once

did he think that the body lying there, taped, tubed and bandaged, had anything to do with his wife Kristen.

Death takes place before the body stops breathing, before the brain fails to register electrical activity. Kristen had died when the car exploded.

Ruth had died when her head hit the floor.

He did not want to watch the end of it, the final, formal dissolution of body and soul.

There was not the slightest reason in the world for him to stay at the manor now. The police would be involved soon. They would have to investigate what had happened, what had led to Ruth's death. He knew he should stay and give a statement but it was quite out of the question. His description would have been circulated through both military and civil police. The questions would be interminable. It was all so suspicious: the deserter Phizackerley Byrne, present at yet another scene of death.

But he was not the only witness, Kate had seen it happen. They wouldn't need him.

He went over it again in his mind. The row, the disagreement at the top of the stairs. The stumble against the rucked-up carpet, the rotten banisters shattering, breaking under the weight of the woman who fell –

Ruth, who was going to die.

That dead silence in the house, the angles closing in around them. He hated the Blue Manor, he hated the way it had demanded Ruth's energy in life, the way it had splintered and broken and caused her death.

It demanded too much. It went too far.

In the distance he could hear the road. There was already a constant stream of traffic. Dawn comes early in midsummer, but commuters to London always try to beat the rush. It would get more and more frantic as the day went on, a futile race to get there ahead of gridlock. It was another world, a different set of priorities. Did he want it yet?

Tom and Simon would be expecting him. The thought crept through the mass of confusions and grief. Yes, it was grief. He had been part of the way to loving Ruth. He might have—

There was no point to this. There never had been. She lived with Simon, she was wedded to the manor. And then, as he walked, he remembered Simon's intemperate words.

Why weren't you there? That was your role, didn't you know?
The gardener always saves the day. Why didn't you save her?
Where were you, why did you miss your cue?

The words sounded loud and clear in his mind. My role? My
cue? What had Simon been talking about? He knew that the
manor was alive with horrors, he knew that it operated within
parameters he did not understand. He had been chased from the
house by a creature which could not possibly exist.

Simon understood it, Simon had been held hostage there for
months. Ruth's accident had to be seen in the context of the
manor and its history, and Simon thought that he, Byrne, should
have done something to stop it.

It was unfair, he knew it was unfair. But it hung in the air
around him, battered its way into his mind. He could not leave.
Simon, at least, would see it as running away, opting out of
responsibility. And, strangely enough, it mattered to him what
Simon thought.

Was it guilt, because he and Ruth had become so close?
Whatever the cause, Byrne did not want to abandon Simon
Lightowler to the Blue Manor now. Even though it meant
returning there, living there. He would have to see this through,
he would need to know if he had indeed missed his cue.

Anyway, Ruth was still alive. He swallowed. Return to the
manor, live there within its walls. Simon and Tom were there
already, the two of them. He would have to return, there was
no alternative. They would need a third.

He turned and began walking back. In the early morning light
the manor looked tranquil, just as it always did. Sunlight caught
across the watery tiles and turned them blue and silver, glinting
through the forest of green leaves. It was too early for the light
to catch on the windows, but as he got closer they seemed to
take on the aspect of dark chasms, deep tunnels leading into the
past.

It was fanciful, but he understood now that the manor's
secrets lay in its history. He supposed he would have to read
Tom's book. He would have to question Simon and get it into
perspective. His footsteps slowed. He remembered that first
arrival the morning after he'd met the bitter trio.

He'd been watching the house, but his focus changed. They
were there now. As he turned the corner by the cottage into the

drive the three of them were there, waiting for him, the two women in black and that man, the man who looked so like Peter Lightowler.

For a moment his understanding deepened, widened. The man in the centre *was* Peter Lightowler. He had seen the two of them merge together on the ridge in the forest. The dark man was an aspect of Lightowler, a dark half, an evil genius, inspiring his actions and movements.

And at the same time he understood that the trio were not truly alive. The man had not really died, it had been an act, a deceit expressly designed to warn him away from the manor.

They were standing across the drive, barring his way.

He could smell stale incense and sweat. He wrinkled his nose instinctively, and turned his head away. He refused to look at them directly. He would pay no attention to their next performance, whatever it was. He walked straight on and they gave way, letting him through. They stood aside and out of the corner of his eye he saw them bow, ironically, courteously. The stink of them wafted through the summer air. They were ushering him into the manor, home where he belonged.

He did not like that idea. He did not like the sense of compulsion about this, he did not want to surrender to it. But Simon was waiting for him, together with Tom. He had lived with the shadows of guilt before, after his wife's death. He wasn't going to let that happen again.

He was almost at the kitchen door before he turned round.

He didn't know what made him turn. He'd heard nothing, no sound, no rustle. He had no suspicion that anything unusual was happening.

Behind him the forest had closed in. Thick undergrowth straddled the drive, spreading over the lawn to encircle the terrace. Ferns were springing from the places he had trodden. There were trees where there had been flowerbeds, soaring beech trees, and the ground beneath their branches was crowded with low-growing hollies and alders. Ivies and vines embroidered the swelling trunks. Black and white thorns made an impassable barrier. It grew more dense as he stood there, open-mouthed. He saw nothing move, no trailing vines or creepers snaking across the grass, but as he watched the hedge of trees became more solid, more crowded with leaves and branches. Closer.

Leafer, his mind went. Leafer, closing in, isolating the manor for the final battle.

He opened the door.

'Ah, there you are.' Simon was standing at the sink, filling the kettle. 'I thought I'd make breakfast, but there's not much in. Would coffee suit you, or do you prefer tea?'

He looked dreadful. Byrne had been expecting this, but not the calmness of Simon's words.

'Coffee will be fine,' he said carefully, pulling up a chair. There was no sign of the Dogfrog. 'Anything from the hospital?'

'No change. Do you take sugar or milk?' It was as if he couldn't bear to talk about Ruth, as if Byrne was definitely out of order in mentioning the accident.

Byrne didn't know how to take the news. It could have been worse, much worse. But the terrible nagging pressure was maintained.

He remembered something else. 'Have you rung her school to tell them?'

'You do it.' Simon pushed the telephone book at him.

While the kettle boiled, Byrne made the call. Then he asked where Tom was.

'Where do you think? We're all here, you needn't worry, all three of us nicely in place. Tom's in the library, where he belongs.' He pointed to the manuscript on the table in front of Byrne. 'That's where he's got to. Why don't you read it? He said he wanted you to.'

Byrne picked up the papers and leafed through them. Pages of it, highly dramatic and emotional. He caught words, *touch*, *house*, *lake* . . . With an effort he tried to pay attention to it. Part of him kept expecting to see Ruth, tired from working in the garden, her soft brown hair unkempt and falling across her forehead . . . He put the papers down. 'Was there anything in it you didn't expect?'

'Not expect?' Simon ran his fingers through his hair so that it stood up. He looked frantic and slightly wild. '*All of it!* It's – impossible, ridiculous—'

'Why are you so upset, then? If he's got it wrong?'

'Oh, shit.' A difficult pause. 'What is it about you? Why is it people always tell you things? Have you gone through life like this, with everyone baring the heartstrings for your inspection?

Are you some kind of guru, a therapist, counsellor, something like that? Do you really want to know?' He swept on before Byrne could answer. 'I'm – upset, as you call it, because I don't think Tom has got it wrong. I think it's there, it's what really happened. He's not wrong at all.' The hand that poured water into the three mugs on the side trembled badly. 'My father . . . my father is a monster, that's what it says. Some kind of horrible trickster, a hypnotist, I suppose, with terrible, vile power. A black magician, if you like.'

'It would fit,' said Byrne sombrely.

'Well, you read it and see. I've been at it since daybreak. I'll take this to Tom.' He moved towards the hall door. 'Oh, and Byrne, don't go upstairs, will you?'

'Why not?' Although he could think of no good reason why he should.

'It's out of bounds.'

'Who says?'

'The house. And the Dogfrog. It's up there now. It doesn't want company.'

'OK,' Byrne said equably. 'I understand.'

'Perhaps you do . . .' A fading murmur as Simon left the kitchen.

He read it all, that dreamlike sequence of invasion and possession. The melodrama of it. The paranoia. Taken straight, it was impossible. But within the territory of the manor, where the Dogfrog ran free, where the sound of a wheelchair echoed at night, the ordinary appearances of events were suspended. He was prepared to admit that Peter Lightowler and his father could well have been monsters, black magicians, just as Simon had said.

Reading Tom's story must have taken longer than he realized. The light was fading and he had to squint to read the last few pages. And yet this was high summer, it could not be dark –

He stood up and turned round. The window was almost covered with leaves. The hedge of trees had overgrown the terrace, was crawling up the house.

He could not get through. The barrier of leaves gave slightly, and a branch of thorns whipped through the doorway to tear at his hand. Swearing, he jammed the door shut and bolted it. He crossed the kitchen to the hallway.

It swam in green light, as if drowned. The furniture drifted in a thick fog. The front door was blocked too. The house was stuffy and airless. He shouted, 'Simon! Tom! Where are you?'

No reply. The house caught his words and held them. They made no impression, they were not answered.

For a moment he almost panicked, envisaging them strangled, suffocated down one of the empty corridors ... And then he remembered the library. They would be there, of course. He skirted the shadowy table in the centre of the dim green hall and pushed open the doors.

The room was brilliant with clear light. Simon and Tom were both there, backs to him, staring out into the garden.

'Didn't you hear me call – ?' And then Byrne saw Simon violently wave his hand for silence. He didn't look round. Simon and Tom were on either side of the desk in front of the French windows, which were open, flung wide.

Daylight flooded through. The sunlight was unimpeded by trees. The hedge had drawn back, forming a wide avenue through the manor's grounds.

A man was coming towards them, across the mown grass. An old man, Peter Lightowler. He walked calmly, unhesitatingly, comfortable within the manor's grounds as if he owned it already. There was a huge black bird flying behind him.

'Don't let him in!' In Byrne's mind the figure of a younger Peter Lightowler stood in this very room, facing John Downie's gun. 'Shut the doors, keep him out!' he said urgently.

And Tom moved. It was Tom who pulled the windows closed and began to push at the heavy writing desk. Simon did nothing, his face blank, frozen with shock.

'Come on, move!' Byrne thrust him aside.

'Where? Where to? This is *his* house – ' His voice was agonized.

'It's Ruth's house. Still. No one else's. And she wouldn't want him here, you have to keep him out.'

'You're wrong there. It's Kate's now, as good as, and Kate *likes* him, she even gave him an invitation.'

'How do you know?'

'It's what I would have done.' His face was streaked with tears. 'He's my father. It's all lies, Tom writes only lies.'

Tom had turned to face him. 'I don't think so,' he said gently. 'I can't – risk it, in any event.'

Peter Lightowler had reached the terrace.

And Tom suddenly broke. 'What are we going to *do*?' Unsteadily.

'He's just a man,' said Byrne coldly. 'An old man. He's flesh and blood, like you are.'

'*Is* he?'

And Byrne couldn't answer, couldn't say anything.

Peter Lightowler had reached the other side of the French doors.

'Go away! You can't come in!' Tom yelled.

A voice, brittle as ice, cut through the shattered pane. 'I have been invited. As you know. And invitations must always be accepted.'

The shadow behind him, the heavy flying creature, cawed once, harshly. It was surging towards the glass doors. They saw its eyes, gleaming, its beak slightly parted as it hurled itself at the window.

The glass had not been repaired. The frail barrier imploded and the force of the crow's impact sent the desk skidding back across the room. It slammed into Tom's thighs and he crashed backwards into the wall of books. They tumbled around him, splayed open, their pages crushed and bent as the spines were broken.

And glass and feathers everywhere, flying through the air, striking skin and clothes and surface.

'Are you all right?' Byrne shouldered the desk out of the way and tried to haul Tom to his feet. There was something wrong with the boy's ankle, it would not take his weight. He subsided on to the floor once more.

Byrne saw Peter Lightowler's hand snake through the shattered window and turn the key in the door, opening it.

A large black beetle scuttled into the library, jerkily picking its way through the debris. The crow was lolloping above it, apparently unhurt by the crash.

Tom's face was ashen. 'Jesus, get it out of here, get it away—'

Peter Lightowler looked down at him. 'You know it's lies, don't you?' he said gently. His voice was dry and passionless. His clothes were beautiful, pale grey, elegantly cut. Nothing about him was disturbed, nothing showed that he had just forced an entry into the Blue Manor.

'What do you mean?' Tom's hands were fastened to his ankle, scrabbling to untie the laces of his shoe.

'Lies. Everything Alicia told you. What you've written here. None of it is true, not one sentence, not one idea.' He leaned down to his grandson. 'Tom, get out of here, you'll need to leave the manor. Go somewhere calm and quiet, somewhere you can think clearly and take it slowly. What's possible, and what isn't.'

'Prove it!'

'Let me tell you something. Let me explain—'

'No!' Now it was Simon shouting. 'Ruth is dying! It's too late for explanations! She fell through the banister and she crushed her skull. We'd been arguing, we were going over and over it, trying to explain, trying to make sense—'

'Listen.' Peter Lightowler barely glanced at his son. 'I'm sorry about Ruth. I never wanted to hurt her. I always rang off when she answered, I knew how it upset her. But don't you know? Haven't you realized what this place is?' He looked at Tom for an answer.

'It's Ruth's house! Ruth and Kate and Elizabeth and Ella—' Tom was stammering, suddenly unsure. This man was no monster, no evil rapist, no enchanter. He stood there in the bright summer light and Tom could trace every line on his face. He could see that this was an old man, a man who had suffered . . . Peter Lightowler's hands were shaking. They were trembling with age or fear or something. It was pathetic the way his hands shook.

'Tom,' said Peter Lightowler. 'Listen. This house is haunted. But not by me.'

'And something else,' said Peter Lightowler, sitting down at the long table in the hall as if he belonged there. In the greenish light he seemed as white as ivory. Tom's manuscript lay gleaming on the table in front of him. Byrne wondered how it had got there. 'This house may soon belong legally to Kate, but someone else has always been in charge. Not me, not Ruth or poor Ella, or even Elizabeth. No, a witch runs the manor, and I use that word quite deliberately. A witch who is responsible for all these hauntings, who has engineered the whole of this regrettable situation. None other than my dear wife.'

He leant forward across the table and stared intently into Simon's eyes.

Simon shuddered. 'Why must you always *lie*? We know differently.'

Peter Lightowler shook his head. He stood up again and moved slowly across the hall and down the passage into the kitchen. They heard the chink of china and glass and the opening and shutting of cupboards. 'Mr Byrne?' Lightowler's voice called politely. 'Would you mind?'

Phizackerley Byrne went into the kitchen and found that a tray had been laid out with fruit and bread and cold meats. Two bottles of frosted golden wine, a crystal jug of water, cutlery, china and glasses. 'There. You see I still know my way about the place,' said Lightowler cheerfully. 'And I knew there'd be nothing here to drink. I bet none of you has had breakfast, either.'

Byrne carried the heavy tray into the hall.

Simon said coldly, 'And what's this? A bribe? Have you poisoned the wine? If we eat six pips from the satsuma, will we have to stay here for six months of the year?'

'Surely that would be an improvement for you,' said Lightowler slyly. 'My poor neurotic offspring. Six months free of the place, free to roam where you want.' He sighed. 'No, no such exotica. I've lived here before, I know how it works. And besides, I assume that we're going to be here for some time.' His pale eyes flickered at the front door, where tendrils of ivy were beginning to droop from the keyhole.

And then he was courteously pouring them wine, mixing his own with water. 'Can't take it these days,' he said sadly. 'Digestion's not what it was.'

Then everyone seemed to remember where they were sitting. Ruth had lain only feet from the table. With revulsion, Byrne pushed his chair back and it scraped against the floor.

The sound echoed down the corridors. It was very clear to them that the house was deserted, that no mistress kept its rooms and passages.

Upstairs there was a crash, as if a chair had fallen over, and a distant howling sound, something bleak and lonely. They all knew there was no one there. Undisturbed, Peter Lightowler helped himself to a full plate. After a little hesitation, Tom did the same. There was something reckless in his movements, as if tomorrow didn't matter.

His eyes caught Simon's in appeal, in puzzlement.

Minutely, Simon shook his head. It was not so much a negative as an abandonment. This is up to you, make your own decisions.

'You see, Tom,' said Lightowler, quite calmly, 'I know that you are my grandson.'

'How long have you known?' Simon was on his feet, angry again.

'For some time. You must understand that I have always . . . taken an interest in my wife's affairs. I recognized long ago what she was up to.'

'What do you mean?' Simon shouted.

'Manipulation. She schemes, dears. Alicia pulls the strings and you, Simon, and your son Tom, have jerked and bobbed and gone through the motions just as she ordained.'

'Prove it.' Simon was watching his father carefully. 'You know the allegations against you, you know what they've been saying for years. Prove that it was different, that none of this ever happened.' He gestured to the manuscript.

'It's not difficult,' said Peter Lightowler. He picked up the pile of papers. 'Forget about this for the moment. Think of the most recent betrayal. I understand that Alicia never told you, Tom, who your father was, although she has always known. She never explained that she was your grandmother. She left you to grow up in ignorance, in poverty. You don't have to tell me that Laura Jeffrey didn't find it a struggle. Of course she did. But let's leave the past out of this for the moment. Alicia sent you here four days ago and left you to flounder, with no idea of what the stakes were. She pushed you and your father together and still said *nothing!*'

Tom was silent. This was undeniable. Alicia had concealed so much, had complicated so much by introducing him to Kate and the Blue Manor.

'But why?' he whispered. 'Why did she do it?'

'She wanted you here to write the house's story. That's what you've been doing, isn't it?'

'Yes.'

'Well, Tom. My grandson Tom. Let me tell you one, crucial, thing. Then you must make up your own mind.

'The Blue Manor is haunted, as you know. No man who has lived here has ever been in the slightest doubt of it. It is haunted because it was created and built and inhabited by women who have scores to settle. Women who hate men. You might call them witches. That is what you must remember. The house reflects only that. It reflects Rosamund's loathing for her husband, the abominable Alfred. And he *was* abominable, I have no doubt of that. Violent, hypocritical, jealous of his wife's success. She was right to leave him, no one blames her for that. But it didn't end there.

'The manor is a monument to Rosamund's hatred, to her fear of men. And it extends to all of us, all of us who sit round this table now, in the centre of this – testing ground which is the Blue Manor.' He gestured with the manuscript. 'I don't have to read what this says, I know what it contains. But I ask you to remember this. These women may have had reason to complain about men, I'll not deny it. Most women have reason, at some time or another in their lives. Neither Alfred nor Roderick nor I behaved particularly well. I've even, to my shame, made anonymous phonecalls to this house, trying to contact Kate.' He raised his chin as if daring them to accuse him further. 'And I'll not deny that my friends, my servants, may have tormented Ruth in a similar manner . . .

'But we did not do *this*!' He flung the sheaf of papers across the table. 'This is an entirely different matter. The house is a magnifier, a distorting mirror to events and emotions! Surely you have felt it too!'

He looked round the table. Tom, the youngest, had his head hidden in his hands, his elbows leaning on the table. Simon was staring at him with a curious mixture of hatred and hope. And Phizackerley Byrne, who had been turning the pages of a volume of poetry, put it down. He was unimpressed. He remembered those phonecalls and Ruth's distress only too clearly.

Lightowler's gaze rested on him. 'And you, the gardener, the outsider. You've been drawn in too, haven't you, although none of this cursed blood runs in your veins.'

'You're forgetting something.' Byrne met his eyes. 'Ruth is dying. Rosamund and Elizabeth and Ella are all dead. This is your word against people who are no longer here to defend themselves.'

'You don't know everything. You are crucially wrong about

at least one part of your statement. The *house* is proof of what I say!' Lightowler's voice rose for the first time. 'Look at the evidence! It's all around you!' For a moment he was silent and they found themselves concentrating on the presence of the Blue Manor.

It was quite dark. The windows and doors were blocked by green, ever-growing things. The surrounding forest seemed even to keep the air within the manor static. The house smelt musty, of old, decaying things. The corridors on the ground floor were darkened by shadows deeper than night. They wound away to the other wings of the house like so many black tunnels, burrowing into the heart of a living organism.

Upstairs was unthinkable. The jagged, broken banister cast sharp, pointed shadows against the ceiling. There was a draught coming from the long corridor up there, like the breath of some huge animal, sour, stinking, carrion breath wafting through the house.

There was nothing fresh or wholesome anywhere. The patches of repairs, the painted door to the dossery, the polished side-board in the hall, the ornate carvings were clouded with dust, the wood splintering and pitted with worm.

'Think of the other version. How it appeared to me.' Peter Lightowler recalled their attention to the table, to the papers filled with words and stories and rumours and gossip. 'No doubt this shows Roderick appallingly maltreating his sister. Doesn't it?'

He glared at Tom. The boy nodded, pale and unhappy.

Lightowler continued, his eyes never leaving Tom's face. 'Rape, I suppose. That was always the device, the hidden crime, the accusation no one could prove ... Right. Well, Elizabeth was quite probably jealous of her brother Roderick, the hand-some, popular and wealthy Roderick. Ten years difference between them. How could they have been friends, especially with the rigid differences in education and style in those days? He would have teased her, he was quite possibly unkind and contemptuous of his little sister. She would have been a nuisance to him, unfairly taking his mother's attention ... And Elizabeth was an imaginative child, no doubt. Does your story contain the genesis of the Dogfrog and the Leafer? The Leafer which surrounds us even now?'

The ivy which fell from the keyhole in the front door had reached the floor. For a moment Lightowler regarded it.

'Perhaps I do not have very much time. A little more, maybe . . . And then Elizabeth's marriage to Downie, that embittered, depressive cripple. No wonder Ella was such a mixed-up girl, indulged by Elizabeth, isolated here, frustrated by her mother's obsessions. Ella was forbidden to talk to men, did you know? She was deliberately deprived by Elizabeth . . . As for Alicia – well, Alicia had her reasons, too. I was not faithful.' He smiled to himself, amused by the memories. 'I could never resist them, you see, any of them. Those delicious girls, those flappers and then the land girls, the women in the fifties with their waspy waists and full skirts. So enchanting, so lovely . . . Few wives would have put up with it and Alicia has never been renowned for her patience. I never blamed her for wanting the divorce. I was glad to be free of her . . .

'Do you see what I'm getting at? Do you understand it? There were legitimate reasons for the Banniere women to dislike men: they didn't need to manufacture excuses. But this, this story that the house has written through Tom is a pack of lies. None of it could possibly be true . . . Tell me, Tom,' he said. 'Did you find diaries, did you interview anyone concerned in it?'

'No.' Softly.

'I am the only person in this tale still alive as far as you know. I was there, this directly concerns me. You can interview me, if you like. I'm more than prepared to tell you what really happened.'

Tom looked at his grandfather and saw sincerity in those old, wise eyes. He saw that Simon's hands were clenched together, that he was looking at Peter Lightowler with painful concentration, with dawning hope.

They wanted to believe him. They needed to. They were locked in unhappiness and doubt, and Peter Lightowler was offering a way out, a solution to it.

Tom stood up, took the manuscript from his grandfather and carried it to the fireplace. There was a box of matches on the mantelpiece and he lit one, setting fire to the first page.

Gradually, one by one, he burned every page of his first book. The story of Elizabeth Banniere went up in smoke.

Chapter 37

'What the hell do you think you're doing?' A vicious edge to her voice, familiar to them all. Alicia stood in the doorway from the library. A twig was caught in her hair, there were grass stains on her jacket and a rip in her skirt. Her tights were laddered. She was wearing no make-up, her hands were empty. She looked like some half-witted bag-lady, barely recognizable.

She saw what Tom was doing immediately, and gasped as if mortally wounded. But still she avoided Peter Lightowler, as she rushed across the hall to Tom. She seized the last charred piece of paper from his hand and hissed, 'How *could* you?'

'Alicia. How's Ruth?' His voice was remarkably steady.

She stopped dead, blinking. 'The same. Hanging on. But—'

'What about Kate?' he interrupted.

'I left her at the hotel. She was exhausted and there seemed little point in her staying at the hospital. But Tom, what in God's name have you been doing?'

'What, this?' He let the last corner of paper fall on to the pile of ashes. 'I don't know that it was true,' he said baldly. 'And if it isn't, it's pernicious and dangerous rubbish.'

'Oh, Tom! You idiot, you fool! Why do you think I sent you here?' Her hands were clenched.

'You used me. You told me nothing, even though you knew who I was. For all those years, you kept it secret.'

'Your mother asked me to.'

'What?' His head jerked up. 'Mum – ?'

'Was proud,' she said more moderately. She had calmed a little. Byrne felt a kind of respect for her. Tom's book may have been destroyed, but Alicia wasn't going to waste time in regrets. 'Your mother didn't want you to know, she thought it would only make things worse for you.'

'I have the right to know who my father is!'

'As we have the right to know what happened in this house,' said Alicia, her voice measured. 'You should never have burned that manuscript. It was our only proof.'

Peter Lightowler brought his fist down, suddenly and force-fully, on the table. 'Proof? You call that farrago, that web of lies, proof?'

'Oh, yes. That, and what I know of you.' She met his eyes.

'Why can't you just let it *go*?' This was Simon, angrily. 'This stuff is years old, it's behind us, let's forget it!'

'But Ruth is dying,' said Byrne.

It seemed quite clear to him. What happened between Eliza-beth and John Downie and Peter Lightowler was so remote. He was thinking obsessively about Ruth, hanging on. He knew that if he allowed her to slip from his mind, even for a moment, then that feeble grasp on life would slacken.

'The past doesn't matter,' he said. 'There is only what we have here, now. *This* is what matters.'

'Very good sense,' said Peter Lightowler. He stood up slowly as if it were a considerable effort. He had not for one moment taken his eyes off Alicia. 'How did you get in?' he asked courteously. 'Did you climb the hedge or cut it down?'

'You left your path open,' she said. 'By the lake. It was always your way, wasn't it? There was no need for violence.' She glanced around the table, taking in the remains of the meal, the half-empty wine bottles. 'A little early for the funeral feast, I would have thought. She's not dead yet.'

Brutal words. Simon stared at her. 'Why shouldn't we eat? Does it help Ruth if we starve?'

'Nothing can help Ruth. They say there's no chance.' There were dark bags beneath her eyes and her mouth was caught in a thin cage of vertical lines. 'But you'd probably be better employed at her bedside than waiting here, listening to whatever nonsense my ex-husband is saying.

'Let me guess.' Her words were sharp and emphatic. 'I bet he's been telling you about a fine conspiracy of women. Conspiracy theories are always such fun, aren't they? All those women, ganging up to keep the men out.' She saw from their faces the truth of it. 'Has he told you that I'm a witch? That I can control both Leafer and Dogfrog?' She held up her hands to them and they saw that the skin was lacerated and torn by thorns. 'Fine control. See? It wouldn't let me through either. I had to walk round the perimeter until I came to the lake. Peter's favourite place. Ask yourselves: which of us has the greater power?'

This is like some absurd courtroom drama, thought Byrne. They'll both start talking again in a moment and we'll get other bits of evidence, other rumours and rivalries and justifications and lies.

He said, 'There seems to be a fog of conflicting stories round this. Even Tom's not sure whether he's been writing a novel or a history. None of it can be proved. But there are a number of more contemporary issues here.' He tried to concentrate, tried to keep his mind on what this was about. 'The first is why you' – he looked at Alicia – 'did not tell Tom who his father was. Even if you promised Tom's mother, she died some time ago, didn't she? And why didn't you tell Simon that Laura had had his son? It seems wilfully mischievous, to say the least.'

'I wanted to keep Tom away from the manor. I wanted him to grow up free from its taint. I wanted no more men here, confusing the issue. And Simon would have invited him here years ago and he'd have met his grandfather and the corruption would have started—'

Byrne held up his hand. 'All right. What made you change your mind? Why did you introduce Tom to Kate?'

'It was time. The pattern was going to start again. I could see Kate becoming interested in the old man, I could see him getting his claws out.'

Peter Lightowler was leaning on the back of his chair, a faint smile on his lips. He said nothing.

'Something of a risk, wasn't it?' Byrne said. 'If you believe in this inherited curse, surely Tom would be the last one to help Kate.'

'It's been building up,' she said quietly and he saw her shiver. A quick glance up the stairs towards the long corridor. A tinge of red there, just a touch. The poisonous, dark air shifted.

'I didn't want to come back here,' she said. 'I wanted just – to take Kate, get away and keep away.'

'Well, why didn't you?' asked Simon.

'Because of you.' She turned towards him. 'You're my son, aren't you? Why should I leave you here to be destroyed by this bloody place?'

'Too late for those kind of qualms, I should have thought. Years too late.' Simon was pouring more wine, concentrating hard on the flow of liquid into the glass.

For a while Alicia halted. She watched her son take a sip and then drink steadily until the glass was empty.

'We haven't got long,' she commented, almost idly.

'Why did you leave Ruth? Why did you take Kate away? Who's with her now?' Byrne asked.

All the time, while this was going on, he pictured Ruth wrapped in bandages on one of those high, narrow beds, wired up to machines and drips. If he thought it would help, he'd be there. But there was a responsibility towards the people Ruth loved. Simon, and Kate. She'd want him to be here, there was nothing he could do at the hospital . . .

He didn't even know if he could get away from the manor anyway. Would the Leafer let him through?

'There was nothing I could do,' said Alicia. 'And Kate was exhausted. Ruth's unconscious. They say she won't wake up. What was the point of staying?'

There was no answer. But Byrne knew that he would have stayed, whatever *they* said, whatever logic and reason said.

'Why is it doing this?' Tom peered fearfully at the ivy strand trailing across the floor towards them. No one had seen it move, but it was now halfway across the stone floor. Another strip of green was just visible beneath the closed door.

Sooner or later, Byrne supposed, the door would give, forced from its hinges by the weight of greenery. 'Why does the Leafer want to get in so much?' he said.

Alicia barely glanced at it. 'The manor is coming to the end of its time on earth,' she said matter of factly. 'By the end of the year, none of this will remain. The Leafer will pull it apart.' She met her ex-husband's derisory glance. 'And all your plotting, all this fine scheming won't matter a jot then, Peter. The Leafer, the Dogfrog, the great witch herself, they'll have moved on and there will be only rubble.'

'You do talk twaddle, dear. You always did.' Peter Lightowler sipped delicately at his wine.

'Think for yourself,' she said, shrugging. 'Remember the stars? Do you still keep a telescope trained to the north at home, Peter? You feel it too, don't you? Corona Borealis . . . Starlight runs through this house, it even reflects in your horrible slimy lake. The manor is sick with stars, northern stars that belong to someone else, not you, not Kate or anyone else . . .'

For a moment her unfathomable gaze rested on Tom.

'Remember Graves's *The White Goddess*? That circle of stars at the back of the north wind was always Arianrhod's home, in legend. The place where poets were held in thrall until they found inspiration.'

'So romantic! Lost in the clouds,' said Peter Lightowler.

She ignored him, speaking only to Tom. 'Well, think of the words that have been read here, think of that library, bursting with words! They even hang words on the walls instead of pictures.' She pointed to the French poem framed over the door. 'And then there are the imprisoning aspects of the place, the way Simon can't leave, the way there's always a gardener here, the way Tom can't leave, even though the house is attacking him!'

A silence then, and far above them, from the long corridor, came a scraping sound, something heavy with thorns dragging across the floor.

'And the Leafer . . .' She seemed exhausted. 'Why can't you see it? The Goddess always lives with trees, she hangs her son and lover on a tree. She is always accompanied by a great hound . . . The Leafer and the Dogfrog. What else could they be?'

'So where is she? The Goddess herself, I mean.' Peter Lightowler raised one eyebrow. 'What about this deity in all her grimy splendour? Are you offering yourself as a candidate for divinity, dear? Surely this is carrying megalomania a little far, even for you.'

She was undisturbed. 'The house itself,' said Alicia. 'Its fabric, its design, its being. This is a living organism, and our actions are its heartbeat, are its raison d'être.'

'Oh, very neat, Alicia, nicely sewn up. You always did have an eye for connections. I always wondered why you never wrote fiction yourself, such an omnipotent view on events as you have.' Lightowler's ancient eyes gleamed at her.

Byrne found himself distracted. The exchange between Lightowler and Alicia seemed to thrill and sparkle in the gloominess of the hall. He was very aware of the weight of the house, of its overbalancing gables and arches suspended like dead-weights over their heads. He thought, if we don't get out soon, we'll never make it –

Simon was drinking steadily, concentrating on the glass in his hands, refusing to look at either of his parents. Byrne wondered if he'd heard it all before.

Lightowler was still speaking. 'So why the rush? Why this imminent sense of doom, the end of the manor, these vivid and poetic constructions? I would be delighted to know what theories you've constructed from this piece of fin-de-siècle mawkishness.'

'There's an eclipse due soon, but it may not be that. There's the millennium on the doorstep, but that only affects Christians. We're at the summer solstice now. Everyone's out at Stonehenge and Glastonbury and the media are having a ball. There's excitement in the air –

'But this is private. This is about you and me, Peter. And you're so old. You're at the end of it. And if the spinning circle of stars enters another phase and this place, Arianrhod's castle or whatever you want to call it, with its purgatorial functions alights somewhere else, what will it matter to you? Because this is your story, and your fate, and that's why the timing of this is significant.

'You're going to die, Peter Lightowler. Take that as read. But it doesn't mean you'll escape.'

'But what about Ruth? What about what's happened here?' Simon had hardly been listening. His eyes lifted to the broken banisters above them. 'Why does she have to *die*?' he cried suddenly. 'You two can sit there, arguing and battling and playing nasty little games with old dead stories, but *Ruth* is dying, might even be dead as we sit here, and you don't seem very upset about it.'

His father looked at him. 'I never really knew her,' he said slowly. 'Although she was possibly my daughter, I never really knew her.'

'Your *daughter*?' Simon was speaking from some isolated wasteland, but it seemed that his intelligence was sharpened, heightened. 'Oh, no. One twist too far, one knife in the back that doesn't hit the spot. I don't believe you, Father.'

'Ruth was Ella's child. I seduced Ella approximately nine months before Ruth was born.' He shrugged, seemingly oblivious to the horror on his son's face. A theatrical pause.

It was then that Byrne decided, without any shadow of doubt, that Peter Lightowler was evil. It was nothing to do with the questionable evidence of Tom's book, or Alicia's wild theories. He just saw Peter Lightowler waiting there, stringing out the moment, enjoying his son's dismay.

'Or at least that is what your mother would like to suggest. That's what this is about. That kind of accusation. That kind of – smear. Do you wonder that I get angry? My old age muddied up with all this chatter, all these old wives' tales. It's just scandal and rumour! And all because your mother can't live with the fact that her marriage fell apart and her son's a drunk!'

He leaned across the table towards Simon. 'Not that I blame you,' he said more gently. 'She's put you under intolerable pressure.'

Simon swung round to where Alicia was standing. 'Is that what you think happened? That I've been living here, sharing a bed, making love to my *sister*? You let it go *on*?'

Alicia spoke with difficulty. 'I – didn't know. For sure. I don't know about any of it. The evidence lies in the strangeness of the house, in the strange deaths that have taken place here.'

'What deaths? Who died here? Only John Downie, as far as I know,' Peter Lightowler pointed out.

'Ruth,' said Byrne quietly.

'Not yet. She's not dead yet,' Lightowler said.

'What happened to Elizabeth?' asked Tom. 'To Ella?'

'Elizabeth's still alive.' It was Alicia who said it.

'What?' Tom was on his feet, staring at her. A crash as Simon's glass dropped to the floor.

'Oh, yes. She's ninety-five. In a nursing home in Woodford. But it's no use, she can't tell you anything.' Alicia shook her head. 'She had a stroke – oh, forty years ago – and has never spoken since. I go and see her every now and then at the Briars, but it's always the same.'

'But she – she would know whether my book was true!'

'What does it matter now, Tom? You've burned it, you've denied the house its voice. And anyway, Elizabeth would understand not one word you might say to her,' said Alicia calmly. 'She understands nothing, communicates nothing.'

'But . . . where are the car keys? I have to go and see – what's the name of the place?'

'*Tom*.' Peter Lightowler spoke with emphasis. 'Don't be ridiculous. It's no good, it's like talking to a block of wood.'

'I have to try it! Don't you see? I have to try!' And then he had gone, grabbing car keys from the bowl in the hall. He limped through the darkened French windows out into the thick undergrowth.

Chapter 38

Simon was looking at him, a complicated, ironic look and Byrne could feel the pressure of it. Stay, it meant. Don't leave me here with them. Byrne knew he had to get out. There was only one place he wanted to be. He shouted after Tom, 'Wait for me!' and followed him into the garden.

The foliage wasn't as dense as it looked and Byrne soon caught up with Tom. The hedge of trees held back from them both. They walked in dappled shade through a vaulted tunnel of greenery which encircled the manor. The band of trees and bushes was narrow, and sunlight cut through in bright shafts. Beyond the foliage they could see that the grounds lay quiet and undisturbed in the midday sun. They made for the garage.

'This gives a whole new meaning to the term green belt,' said Tom, in an effort at lightness. 'I wonder if it will let a car through?'

Byrne didn't answer. He had no doubt that if the Leafer had let them leave the house, it would also allow them to leave the grounds.

'Are you coming with me to get Elizabeth?' Tom asked.

'No, I'm going into Epping. To the hospital.'

Tom sighed. 'It's a waste of time. There's no point, Byrne. Ruth's out of it. There's nothing you can do. You'd do better to stay here, stop them getting at each other.'

'I think that's beyond me, or you,' he said. 'And someone should be with Ruth.'

'She won't know you're there, you realize.'

'It doesn't matter.'

'OK.' Tom opened the door to the Escort and got in. Byrne waited for him to reverse out of the garage. Then Tom leaned over and opened the passenger door. 'Get in,' he said. 'I'll drop you off at the hospital.'

Byrne shook his head. He needed to be out of doors, clearing his head under the clear skies. 'This time of day it's probably quicker to walk. Epping High Street will be packed.'

'Are you sure?'

'Good luck with Elizabeth.'

'You'll come back?' Tom sounded anxious. 'When . . . Come back to the manor?'

Byrne paused. When Ruth is dead. Return to the manor. Both were unthinkable. 'I suppose so. Perhaps.'

As Tom swung the car round, Byrne saw the Leafer move again. There was a gap in the hedge now large enough to take Ruth's Escort. Byrne watched as the car disappeared down the drive. He hoped it was going to be that easy for him to escape the manor.

Byrne went on, past the garage towards the lake. The leaves folded back ahead of him, so that he trod on the grass he'd mown the day before.

The gate in the hedge lay north of the lake. He felt a great relief to be out of the manor, and even without the evidence of the Leafer, he knew that he was doing the right thing, going to see Ruth. Whether she still existed, still endured in that body in intensive care or not, her passing should not be unattended.

He wondered why none of the others felt it, but the answer was not hard to find. They were too obsessed with the past, locked in it, just as they were locked, imprisoned, in the manor.

He would say goodbye to Ruth for them.

Through the leaves he sees the pale silvery gleam of the lake. He'd wanted to skirt around its edge, but the path through the hedge takes him directly to it.

There's someone there, someone he knows. He feels flooded with joy, relief, delight . . . Without reasoning, without waiting, he blurts out, 'Ruth? Ruth? What are you doing here?'

But then the figure turns and he sees with crashing disappointment that it isn't Ruth. Someone much younger, with Ruth's soft eyes and Ruth's curving light brown hair. But this girl is younger, much younger, and there's no shyness, no hesitation about her.

'Hello,' she says, coming towards him. 'Lost your way?'

No, he almost says, I want to get through the forest to Epping, but somehow the words come out wrong. 'I – I was looking for Mrs Banniere,' he hears himself say, but it's not his voice, not his voice at all. He doesn't understand this. His voice sounds lighter, with a slight accent, a lift and a lilt . . . Welsh? He is so distracted by the thought of speaking with a Welsh accent that he hardly notices what he's actually said to her. 'I heard she was looking for a gardener.'

'Oh, you're after the job, then?' The girl comes towards him, her short hair bouncing around her face. She's wearing a full-skirted dress patterned with poppies, held at the waist by a narrow leather belt. It swings over her bare brown legs and he realizes that her feet are wet, slightly muddy.

She stops, following his gaze. 'Well, it's a hot day,' she says, smiling. 'Wouldn't you like to go paddling too?'

She looks so young and attractive and he's suddenly aware how hot he feels. The sun is reflecting off the lake and dazzles through his mind.

And he loses his grasp on reality. She's gorgeous, and her feet are slightly muddy and the three-piece tweed suit his father has given him is unbearably scratchy.

The collar is too tight and his shoes pinch. 'I think I ought to go and find Mrs Banniere,' he says, hardly able to tear himself away from her. She looks neat and fresh and innocent as a daisy and yet her eyes are full of mischief, ready to spark and glint and snap him up –

He knows already that he has to get this job.

'Oh, Mummy's gone into town. She'll be back in an hour or so. You do look hot. Why don't you take that jacket off and roll up your trousers and come for a paddle?'

With unsteady hands he bends down and undoes the laces of his brogues. 'My name is James Wetherall,' he says. 'You are – ?'

'Ella.' She wrinkles her nose. 'Actually it's Helen, but nobody uses that. Ella Banniere. Your prospective employer is my mother.'

'I was told that if Mrs Banniere took me on I could move into the cottage at the gate,' he says, wading out through the rushes. The water is delightfully, wonderfully cool.

She's sitting on the bank, watching him. 'So you might be staying here? Where's your stuff?'

'At the Bull. There's not much.'

'It's not luxurious accommodation, you know. I hope you haven't been misled. Poor old Shadwell made rather a pigsty of it.'

'Shadwell?'

'The last gardener. He was ancient. He went to live with his sister in Chingford.' She's looking at him speculatively. 'What about your family? Where do you come from?'

'I'm from Swansea,' he says, laying on the accent. She giggles. 'My parents are still there.'

'Why did you take up gardening?'

'We had an allotment in the war. I rather liked helping my dad there. They saved up and sent me to college, horticultural college. If I'm taken on, this will be my first permanent position.'

'Why do you want to come here?'

'It's the trees,' he says, gazing up at the high beeches around them. He can hear the leaves rustle very faintly, although there's no suggestion of a breeze by the lake. 'I'm a tree man. This is a garden full of remarkable trees. I'd love to work here.'

'And the forest is pretty special, of course.'

He nods. 'It's the hornbeams I'm particularly interested in. And the legacy of the pollarding. Do you realize that if we don't start pollarding again soon, the undergrowth will die away because the shade will be too dense?'

She's smiling at him, slightly mocking, and he grins sheepishly. 'I'm sorry,' he says. 'It's my very own obsession.' He wades out of the water and sits down on the bank beside her, reaching for his shoes.

Somewhere in the rhododendron bushes beyond the lake he hears a twig snap, as if someone has trodden on it. There's a man coming through the gap in the hedge behind the lake, a middle-aged man with fair hair, cool, pale clothes.

At a distance, Jamie thinks that the man is angry, but when he comes closer he sees only a courteous smile.

'Hello, Ella,' he says. 'Aren't you going to introduce me to your friend?'

'Petey! Wherever did you spring from? I thought you were abroad. Did the frogs throw you out?' She's jumped to her feet, has run to his side, tiptoing to kiss his cheek. The older man's hand steals around her waist.

Jamie stands up. The sun has gone in.

She's still chattering. 'This is James Wetherall, he's going to be the new gardener.'

'Really? I thought your mother and Margaret were managing very well.' The man's eyes are considering Jamie, and his nose wrinkles as if he doesn't like what he's found.

'Oh, what would you know about it?' She's laughing. 'Mr Wetherall, this is my cousin Peter, the black sheep of the family. But he doesn't bite, he's really quite harmless.'

'How do you do?' says Jamie, stepping forward, his hand held out.

Cousin Peter is looking only at Ella and somehow doesn't see his hand. 'Well, Ella-bella, I was wondering if you'd like a drive out to the Gypsy Tea Rooms with me? You seem to be in gypsyish style today.' He stares pointedly at her bare feet. 'And it's such a fine day ... Or you could tidy yourself up like a good girl and I'll take you to see Greenstead Church. What do you think?'

'Gypsy Tea Rooms,' she says firmly. She slips her feet into sandals and is about to go off into the forest with him when she remembers Jamie. 'Mr Wetherall, if you go to the house you'll find my Aunt Margaret around somewhere. She'll look after you till Mummy gets back.'

She whisks herself away from the pale man and holds out her hand to him. Her skin is soft and cool. 'I do hope you get the job,' she says and their eyes meet.

'So do I,' he says under his breath, watching them go.

He bends down and picks up his jacket from the bank, and when he looks up they are gone.

Between him and the lake a thick hedge stood, barring his way forward. Part of him was still caught up in the scene, thinking, well I'd better go and find Mrs Banniere and why does she like him, why does she want to spend time with that horrible man?

But then the thought faded like a waking dream. He almost couldn't remember what he was doing there, without his jacket in the middle of the day.

Then it hit him. He was on his way to be with Ruth, to the hospital in Epping ... Phizackerley Byrne took a step forward, and the hedge seemed to fill with leaves and thorns beneath his eyes.

It didn't want to let him through.

He sighed and it was almost like a shudder. He put out his hand and took hold of a branch, wrenching it out of place. It bent under his fingers, but the growth was new and strong and would not break. He thought, right, I'll climb over, and started to do just that, but somehow branches which had seemed strong when he touched them with his hands bent and broke beneath his feet so that he slipped to the ground. The wound in his hand had opened up again. Blood sprinkled on the leaves. He threw himself at the hedge, and twigs sprang at his face, narrowly missing his eyes.

He ran then, along the perimeter of the hedge, and saw that it went on, all the way round the manor. The tunnel Tom had driven through had disappeared.

He couldn't get out.

Behind him, the manor winked in the sunlight through its mantle of green creepers. He walked back to it with reluctance, his steps dragging.

What had happened by the lake? He still experienced lingering remnants of the daze. Memories of the incident were confused in his mind with the time when he had first met Ruth, asking for work.

He was outraged. His identity had been hijacked, stolen by the young Welsh gardener. But James Wetherall had not known it was happening, he had been as much a victim as Byrne. It was as if time had fallen into a whirling vortex, and events and people and emotions had been flung together, compressed by the force of it.

Or perhaps it was a closed loop, something that repeated over and over again. There were enough similarities for it to work – he *was* the gardener, he did love Ruth –

Oh, Ruth. On her own, with no one to watch over the last of it. It was unbearably poignant. Thinking of Ruth, he did not notice the mantle of green draw back from the front door.

He was back inside the hall before he realized it.

There was no one there.

Chapter 39

Byrne shouted, 'Simon? Where are you?' and the dead silences of the house swallowed up his words. For a while he stood there, listening hard.

The Leafer scratched faintly at the window behind him. There was some movement upstairs, a door banging softly, rhythmically, caught in a stray breath of wind. But no distant pawing or howling. He couldn't tell where the Dogfrog was and it was unsettling, disturbing, to think it might be there waiting.

There were more books out, stacked on the sideboards in uneven piles, but there was no sign of anyone having read them.

He wondered where everyone was. The table was littered with the remains of the meal. Absently, he picked up a glass and drank a little of the wine.

And again he heard it. The door banging upstairs, a faint whisper of conversation. Was that where they were?

He took a cricket bat from the umbrella stand and went upstairs. Christ, he thought. A cricket bat? What was he *doing*?

The doors on the landing were all closed. He shouted again, 'Hello? Simon? Are you there?' and there was still no reply. He wandered round the landing, avoiding the lift cage, knocking on each door. There was no response.

The long corridor waited for him. His footsteps sounded hollowly on the bare boards. Far down its length he saw a door swing against the jamb in a breeze he couldn't detect, a repetitive dull thud. He was glad of the cricket bat. Again he knocked on each of the closed doors as he went past them. He very much didn't want to open any of them.

The door that was banging was right at the end. He took hold of it and held it open. There were stairs inside, leading to an attic.

Lighted candles in sconces illuminated his way. At the top, in a room full of junk and rubbish, he found Simon sitting on a velvet chaise-longue, smoking peacefully.

There was a toy dog beside him, ancient, worn, threadbare. Its red eyes were made of glass.

'It's ages since I've been up here,' Simon said calmly as soon as he saw Byrne. 'I never liked it, really. There's damp everywhere. And cheap, gaudy tricks.'

Byrne felt ridiculous with the bat in his hand. He could see Simon staring at it with something near amusement. He put it down.

'Where are the others?' he asked.

'My beloved parents? Downstairs. Somewhere. Wrangling in the kitchen, wrestling in the library, who knows, who cares? I came here to get out of the way. And where have you been? Why this sudden reappearance?'

'I tried to get out. I—' How could he tell Simon where he'd wanted to be? 'The Leafer wouldn't let me through, although Tom made it.'

'So I see. You are rather a mess.' Simon stood up and stubbed his cigarette out on a saucer on one of the tables. With elaborate care he picked a leaf from Byrne's lapel. 'Have you been here before?'

'No. I've never been upstairs.'

'It's the worst bit,' said Simon softly. 'It's where the worst of it happens. The lift connects it all. It even comes up here, did you know?' He pointed to the cage made of iron in one corner of the attic. 'The Dogfrog always comes from here.'

Byrne looked again at the toy dog on the chaise-longue but it hadn't moved, there was nothing odd about it.

'And there's the wheelchair,' said Simon.

He walked to the end of the attic, where the curtain hung, and pulled it back.

The wheelchair with its figure of hanger wire sat there, draped with cobwebs as if it had been there for years and years.

They were both silent for a moment, regarding it.

And then Byrne realized that it was daylight, that the skylight was no longer blocked by leaves. 'What's happening? Is the Leafer in retreat?'

'You should know, you've just done battle with it.' Simon had moved to stand beside him. He pointed over the edge of the skylight. 'No, it's still there.' And Byrne saw the fingers of ivy like a fringe bordering the cracked paint.

Byrne could smell the alcohol on his breath. He turned towards him. 'Simon, what do you want of me?'

'Nothing. Nothing, now. You missed your chance.'

'I didn't stop Ruth falling.'

'That's right. That's where you wanted to go, isn't it? To be with her?'

'I don't like the idea of her dying alone.'

'In time I suppose she might even have come to love you.' Simon sounded unemotional. He refused to meet Byrne's eyes and was minutely examining his nails.

Byrne shook his head. What was the point in dwelling on what might have been? 'I don't think so. Ruth is married to the house, first and foremost. And you are an essential part of it for her.'

'The house is responsible for her death.'

'We don't even know if she is dead.'

'They all die. All the women who own the manor.'

'But Elizabeth is alive. And Kate,' Byrne said. 'It's not always dreadful. How much weight do you put on these stories, your mother's theories, Tom's book, your father's justifications?'

'It's a fog. A fog thrown up by the house to conceal what it really is.'

'What do you think it is?'

'Oh, it's a mischief-maker, a magnifier and a distorter. It plays with people and ideas and the past and makes them destroy each other.'

'Why?'

'Oh, come on! Do you want me to advance yet another set of theories about the place? Perhaps there's something in all of them, perhaps it is a place of purgatory or judgement. Perhaps the Dogfrog and the Leafer do belong to some cracked version of the Great Mother, or perhaps they really are leftovers from old Elizabeth's childhood. All I know is that they exist, that they live here with us and they hurt and scar and destroy and imprison and murder!'

'We'll get out,' said Byrne. 'I won't leave you here.'

'Good of you.' Simon's eyes were mocking and for a moment he looked disconcertingly like his father. 'Any idea how?'

'Just a moment.' Byrne paused, wondering how to say it. 'How much does it matter to you? The truth of these stories about your father? How far do you identify with him, how important *is* it?'

'Setting up as counsellor now, are you? Working in the garden of the soul, planting out health in body and spirit, weeding out the murky bits—'

'Christ, Simon, if you could only hear yourself! All these words, messing up everything.'

'And you're the strong, silent type, of course, and quite above any such frivolity as actually expressing an opinion. It's easy not to talk, it's a way of dodging the issue.'

Kristen had said as much, once. It's not a weakness to talk, she'd said. Why won't you ever tell me things?

He put this aside. 'No, listen. The house is imprisoning you here for some reason, and it seems to me that it's *shouting* at us the whole time that the past needs to be set right, somehow. It used Tom's book, these ghostly effects, everything, to remind us that the past needs understanding. The manor won't let you go until it's done.'

'And never mind who gets fucked up in the process?'

'What could be worse than what's happened in the last twenty-four hours? What could be worse than Ruth, dying?' He knew his voice was sounding ragged but he didn't care. 'Let's retrieve *something* from it, for God's sake!'

'I suppose Tom's got the right idea,' Simon said slowly. 'Back to the source, to the start of it.'

Elizabeth.

The house had changed. They went together down the stairs from the attic and hardly recognized where they were.

It was very cold. The doors along the corridor had swung open and a sense of chill emanated from each room. But the coldness brought with it a faint sound, something so subtle that Byrne thought he must be imagining it.

The very quietest of laughs, and then a snatch of speech, the words too low to be understood. A couple of bars of a popular song. What was it? Cole Porter? Jerome Kern? And then slowly, as if the volume was being turned up, the sound grew.

The corridor became noisy with people speaking and laughing and chattering. That first snatch of music grew into a symphony of diverse sounds. Piano music, ragtime, Frank Sinatra, opera, reeled in uneasy snatches through the air like a badly tuned radio. Glasses clinked together, women giggled, cigar smoke puffed at them in icy clouds.

But only darkness drifted from the open rooms. There was

no one there. In the half-light, they looked at each other in doubt. Simon shrugged, a sick smile on his face. 'Got your cricket bat?' he asked.

Byrne shook his head. The chilled atmosphere was draining energy from them. Byrne realized that they were both shivering.

Between where they stood and the landing four doors stood open.

They moved slowly towards the first. And then a woman's voice calls out, 'Jamie! At last!', and Byrne finds himself enfolded in a warm embrace, a whisper of hair drifting across his cheek, the swish of cotton and petticoats against his legs.

'Where have you been?' He speaks, but it isn't his own voice. It's lighter, a different texture altogether, that Welsh lilt to it again. He dreads it, he wants to hold on to his identity but she's laughing at him and he just wants to hold her fast, hold her safe.

'Oh, you're always so cross!' The woman in his arms leans against him, breathing sweet warmth into his face, and pulls him into one of the rooms and into daylight. Midday sun shines through the window, a lark singing somewhere over a garden he does not recognize. Over her head, over the soft brown hair she shares with Ruth, he looks through the window.

The manor's front garden, but tidy with bedding plants, alyssum and lobelia. The edges have been cut, the grass mown into neat stripes. A wheelbarrow stands on the grass verge, hoes and forks and watering cans scattered here and there.

There's a car standing in the drive, an ancient Ford Popular. But it seems new, in good condition – and there's something old-fashioned about the bright garden and the room he's standing in and the scent of the woman in his arms.

He's in a bedroom with pretty striped wallpaper scattered with roses. A patchwork counterpane is on the bed, a bowl of pot-pourri on the dressing table.

'Have you been to see him again?' he finds the strange voice in his head saying. 'I waited for you but couldn't you be bothered? Couldn't you even leave a message for me or something? Was it too much trouble?'

'Shh, don't be silly.' She's standing by the window now and he catches his breath as the breeze lifts through her hair, so familiar, so dear . . .

The brightness of the light makes him shut his eyes. He

knows who this is. The girl by the lake. *Ella*, says his mind. 'Ella,' says his strange voice. 'He means no good, you know. He – he's not a good man.'

'Oh, you're so stuffy, so ridiculous! No wonder my mother adores you!'

She takes his hand and pulls him down on to the bed. He feels her soft mouth against his own, her tongue pushing between the lips. Arms tighten around him, and his own arms hold her fast. With his shut eyes he knows that she's there, really against him, her hand feeling between his legs and then pushing at his belt buckle.

His own hands cupping her breasts, his mouth on hers.

His thoughts are someone else's. *Why* does she go to him, what's Lightowler's hold over her? And then she's speaking.

'I chucked him, you know,' she says softly in his ear.

'What?'

'Cousin Peter. He tried it on a little too strongly. Wandering hands – ugh! I didn't need it, didn't want it. I told him to find someone his own age.'

He pulls back from her, delight and relief flooding. 'Ella, you monkey! How did you dare?'

'Well!' She's laughing, teasing him, wriggling beneath his touch. 'He's just the aged cous, that's all.'

'Not that much older than you.'

'Twenty years. Positively ancient. Anyway, I don't like that creepy trio who go everywhere with him. Alicia's welcome. Let's change the subject, I've had enough of this. Come on, Jamie dear, come to me . . .'

And the gardener, James Wetherall/Phizackerley Byrne, makes love to the shade of Ella Banniere and it is not the first time . . . No, he knows it is not the first time. They are accustomed to each other's flesh, to the sighs and movements and secrets of their act.

Ella had been in love with Jamie and had never lain with Peter Lightowler. Her child, Ruth, had been James Wetherall's daughter.

Chapter 40

Out in the corridor, Byrne found Simon. He was smiling. 'There,' he said softly. 'It's all right, it's going to be all right, isn't it? Ruth's no close relation of mine, her dad was that boyo from the valleys.'

'What did you see?' Byrne couldn't comprehend how Simon had worked this out. He hadn't been there.

Simon was leaning negligently against the door jamb. 'I went next door. I saw Aunty Ella confess to her mama that she was pregnant,' he said mildly. 'And she promised to *marry* Jamie Wetherall, promised that she loved him, and he loved her and it makes it *all right*!'

'But they didn't get married, did they?' Byrne said.

'There's no *record*, of course.' Simon pushed himself away from the wall, his brow creased. 'And Aunty Ella kept the Banniere surname, like all the women in the family, but I bet they were married. Ruth was – Ruth is – legitimate, the gardener's daughter.'

The problem was that Byrne could remember everything about it. The scent of Ella's hair, the soft flesh of her thighs, the small sounds as they moved together.

But at a deeper level he knew he'd made love to Ruth, not Ella. Time is eclipsed here, he thought. And we're caught up in it with no way out. It's a witch's cauldron, everything confused, everything muddled.

He said, 'This bloody house. Let's get out of it.'

Simon was still smiling. 'But that's only one of the problems,' he said. 'There's more to it than that.'

He gestured to the next door along the corridor. 'Forget all that stuff about Arianrhod's spinning castle. We're in the hands of Bluebeard now. And what will the next chamber hold for us? The headless bodies of women? Shall I go first, or do you want to?'

'I want out of here!'

'No, no, that's my line, not yours.' Incredibly, Simon was

laughing. It was as if the revelation about Ruth's parentage had released him, had lifted the burden.

'Come on,' he said lightly. 'I dare you . . .'

He was about to enter the next room when they heard footsteps.

Slowly the old man climbed the stairs. He was hanging on to the banisters with no regard for their fragility. He was rather insubstantial himself, Byrne thought. As if the years had worn through all the liveliness and energy, leaving a pale, dry, husk. He watched Peter Lightowler's approach with apprehension.

'Well, well,' Lightowler said, puffing slightly at the top of the stairs. 'So here you both are. We were beginning to wonder.'

Simon said, 'Why have you come up here? There was no need.'

'And what have you learned, Mr Byrne?' Peter Lightowler paid no attention to his son. 'Has the house revealed any other interesting – secrets?'

'You could say that.' Byrne debated with himself whether to say it. 'It seems that Jamie Wetherall was Ruth's father.'

It sounded absurdly bald even as he said it. He watched Peter Lightowler's eyes flickering along the corridor behind them. A sour smell of sweat reeked from his clothes. Was he frightened, or was it anger?

But the old man's thin lips were curling themselves into a smile. 'It was one of these rooms, was it? You went into one of the bedrooms and slipped into some other world? Oh, I love this place, don't you? So full of surprises!'

'Well, it let you off the hook, anyway,' said Simon.

'What did I tell you?' Lightowler asked his son. 'Did you really think I was some kind of monster?' The washed-out eyes keenly searched his son's face, and Byrne knew that he was still on edge, not in the least relaxed or relieved.

'God, no!' Simon put his hands on the old man's shoulders. Byrne could see that he was within an inch of hugging him. 'Women!' he said. 'Heads in the clouds!'

'And feet in the slime.'

'But what happened to them?' Byrne said. 'Ella and Jamie?'

'They died,' said Lightowler slowly. 'Shortly before the marriage. There was a pile-up on the High Road and they were both killed. As luck would have it, Ella survived long enough to give birth. The baby was just viable. That was Ruth's nativity.'

Ruth. The name hung over them, and Simon lost all his vivacity, all the superficial relief.

'She hates you,' he said.

'She was brought up by my darling wife.' Peter Lightowler shrugged. 'You know what it was like.'

'*Why?* Why did Alicia bring up Ella's child?'

'Let's ask her ourselves.' Byrne moved towards the top of the stairs.

'No need for that,' said Peter Lightowler easily. 'They were best friends. They went to the same school. They promised to be each other's bridesmaids, although it never came to that.'

The cold at the top of the stairs was growing. 'I'd like to hear Alicia's version,' said Byrne stubbornly.

'I think she's gone outside. For a walk.'

'A *walk*?' There was a jungle out there, a forest of leaves and thorns.

A door banged, further along the corridor. It had been open, but suddenly it swung to, walloping through the air, hitting the jamb with such force that they heard splintering.

They turned towards the third room.

And there was the sound of chattering, of voices once more, sliding through the air, sliding into their minds with malevolence. The door was swinging only a little now, a faint, delicate motion. Byrne saw Simon take a step towards it.

The cold was like knives. It cut into Byrne's breath, cut into his lungs, made him want to run. Against the odds, he found himself turning.

He looked at the old man standing there at the head of the stairs.

He was not alone.

Three of them. Two women and a man, a man who seemed familiar, like one of the family.

'What are they doing here?' he asked, but then the door behind him slammed again and he spun round to see Simon enter the third room.

Hating it, hating what lurked at the top of the stairs more, Phizackerley Byrne plunged after him.

*

At first he thought that the Leafer had broken through. There were leaves everywhere, great branches hanging down in front of his face. Thorns tore at his jeans. It was night-time and the moon shone dimly through the canopy of trees and in its uncertain light he saw Simon edging his way through the trees towards the source of another kind of light.

And suddenly he knows where they are. This is the road. The great monster road that encircles the manor, traffic screeching along it at an obscene rate. He sees Simon plunging through the undergrowth, shouting something.

He can't hear over the noise of the traffic what it is. Simon is shouting and the traffic is roaring and the damn leaves keep brushing against his face, confusing his view, blotting out the scene.

The sense of cold endures. He sees that the grass underfoot is stiff with frost, that ice gleams on a puddle at the side of the road.

And still the cars roar by, their noise blocking out his thoughts. He shouts for Simon but his voice is lost in the din.

Then he sees it. Sees Simon run out into the road and a car swerve, slew suddenly on something. (Black ice, his mind says. The driver puts his foot down and the tyres lock on black ice . . .)

The car careers across the road to smash wildly into one of the trees.

The noise of it, the tearing scream of tyres and glass and crunching, crumpled metal. Simon is still running, although cars are blaring their horns all around him, their lights glaring as they slow to avoid the wreck.

Others are steadfast on their way to town, mounting the pavement at the side of the road to get past, continuing as if nothing has happened, nothing matters.

The car is crunched against the trunk of the tree, its front wheels right off the ground. The windscreen has shattered and someone, someone has come right through, collapsed across the bonnet, blood everywhere –

No seat belts, thinks Byrne. Why aren't they wearing—? And then he realizes what the car is. A Zephyr. Fifties, dated. Bulbous, strange fins. Black with red upholstery . . .

Simon is tearing at the door.

Not Simon! This is not the sallow-faced, depressed man Byrne knows. Someone with yellow hair, short cut, carefully neat. Long limbs braced against the jammed door, pulling it from its hinges.

She falls out into his arms.

Elizabeth/Ella/Ruth/Kate. Trapped in the arms of Roddy/Peter/Simon/Tom.

Byrne can hardly think. He no longer has any clear idea of past or future. He can no longer find his way through the shifting scenarios.

He can feel it slipping, getting away from him again and leaves fall across his face . . . The figure slumps across the bonnet and the man coloured red with blood stirs.

Byrne knows the flare of agony, recognizes the stickiness blocking his eyes, clogging his nose and mouth. Sharp points of pain screams through his face and chest and torso. He moves indistinctly against the shattered black paint. His arms are pinned to his thighs by glass. He is held in extremis, beyond freedom.

He thinks, and so it goes. Shadwell/Wetherall/me. And where will this end? Where, this time?

He wants to yank at Lightowler's shoulders, to pull him away from the woman, but he is wedged in glass, gripped by vicious claws.

He is screaming, 'No! Don't! Get away from her!' and it makes not the slightest difference. Is it even audible? His senses are distorted in the pain. He sees the yellow-haired man take something from his pocket, something narrow and pointed. (A knife? his senses shriek. Was it a knife?) His hand moves suddenly, decisively, against the woman's abdomen.

His scream bubbles into silence. The man stands up, looking over towards him.

Those cold, passionless eyes!

'No . . .'

He is coming closer, peering at him. 'Ah, Jamie, what a mess you are. No, no, don't try to get up.'

A violent hand seizes his chin, wrenching his head round so that they are staring into each other's eyes.

'I think I can safely leave nature to take its course in your case.' He smiles. 'I can't say it's been an unalloyed pleasure knowing you, but it doesn't matter in the end, does it?'

The hand beneath his chin withdraws and his head rolls as heavy as stone as the gouts of blood from his neck spurt.

The light flicked on.

Simon stood there, his hand raised as if it had just fallen away from Byrne's neck. His face was greasy grey, his mouth opening in shock. Without thinking, Byrne stumbled backwards until his shoulders crashed into the wall.

It was crawling with black damp, smearing over his back like blood.

Peter Lightowler was in the doorway.

'You killed Ella!' Byrne shouted. 'That was what you did!'

Simon was turning slowly to face his father. 'It's murder that's wrong, isn't it? That's why you're shunned, anathema, reviled – '

'But the house is quite capable of lying.' Peter Lightowler spoke calmly, his eyes watchful. 'Why should you think this last little display is anything other than another example of its meddling? Or the previous one, come to that? Because you prefer to believe one thing rather than another . . . It suits you to think that Jamie was Ruth's father. It upsets you to think I killed Ella. How can you believe anything that happens here?'

'It's true!' Simon's mouth was working. 'I was there, I did it too, that stabbing! You use knives, I use words! What difference is there between us? I killed Ruth . . . ah, don't look at me like that!'

This to Byrne. He was still against the wall, watching this, appalled. It was difficult to disentangle the images, to put from his mind remembered pain, the memory of murder. He tried to concentrate on Simon and what he had said. It was important to get it right.

'No!' he said. 'Not you, Simon. What happened to Ruth wasn't your fault, it was no one's fault.'

'But it happened here in the manor,' said Peter Lightowler reasonably. 'This is an evil house, it draws evil from each of us.'

'You killed Ella,' said Byrne with certainty. 'At that car crash, you were there.'

'Yes, I was there.' He moved further into the room. 'And I suppose you were right. I did kill Ella. How do you think the baby was saved? Poor Jamie was out of it, and Ella bleeding to death. I took a chance, risked it all. I gave her an emergency

Caesarian. That was what you saw, that was why it seemed so bad.' His eyes never left his son's face. 'Both of them would have died otherwise. Can't you understand?'

'Don't believe him.' Byrne stood next to Simon. He knew this for a lie, he had felt those thin hands under his chin, wrenching his face round. He searched for words. 'What were you doing there, anyway? In the forest at that time of night?'

The old man appeared embarrassed. 'I was coming back from the village. I'd been out visiting a friend.'

'You made the car crash,' said Byrne. 'You ran into the road.'

'At night? On an unlit road? How could I have known their car?'

'It's what you did, nevertheless.' Byrne had had enough. He could see Simon coming apart in front of him, see the guilt and confusion eating into his sanity. He took Simon's arm and pulled him towards the door, past the old man.

The landing was deserted, the sense of chill all-pervasive in the dreary half-light. Byrne pushed Simon to the top of the stairs.

There was the sound of traffic.

Chapter 41

There was no relief. They stood on the landing, that circular platform overhanging the hall, and heard cars and lorries and vans approaching at great speed.

For a moment, wildly, Byrne thought that the police had arrived, fire engines, ambulances. He envisaged them streaming down the driveway to the manor, ready to hack away at the Leafer and release them.

But he knew it could not be so. This was the sound of fast traffic, cars going in both directions, and he recognized it. It was the same sound that had accompanied that flashback in the third room.

And as he realized what it was, the walls pulled back, wrenching away from them. Suddenly and completely they were lost in emptiness. Wide spaces yawned around them. The ceiling, the roof, any knowledge that they were within a house were gone. Deep blackness in every direction and the feeling of travelling, of going round and round, encircling a central conflagration.

All the time, the roar of traffic.

'What's happening?' Simon, somehow still at his side. 'I don't understand. Where's the house, what's *happening*?'

The perspectives kept changing, flickering here and there. Light flaring up to the north as stars shot through the skies. Constellations soared around them, galaxies streamed beneath their feet. Suns flared, moons glowed.

They were standing on stars and the heavens were turning, reeling round and round in a great rumbling roar.

What price the Blue Danube now? thought Byrne madly. The music of the spheres, the waltzing measure of light and time?

An embroidery of sound and light stitched reality into order.

'It's the road!' he said. 'We're in the forest, it's the road again.'

All at once they realized that the streaming stars were headlights flickering between the trees, that the cold they felt was reflected in the icy puddles and crisp frost underfoot.

The trees were stripped of leaves, outlined in ice. Dead brambles caught at their ankles and dragged at their clothes, but there was nothing unusual about them. No sign of the Leafer, no sign of the Dogfrog or anyone else.

Only the monotonous drone of cars encircling the forest in a ring of light.

'It's the crash again.' He felt sick. He could see it gleaming through the trees, caught every now and then in the light from the streaming traffic.

'Oh God, what next?' Simon sounded despairing.

'I imagine we're going to get another re-run,' Byrne said bleakly. 'I hope we don't get the leading roles this time.'

Simon starts to walk through the forest, his feet crunching on the frosty leaves. Or is it Simon? He feels disorientated, as if the flaring lights from the road have disconnected him, freed him from reality.

Lightowler is frowning, not sure what to do next. He carries a tiny bundle in his arms. He is careful, but not particularly gentle. The bundle stirs, waving tiny, pudgy fists streaked with blood. A mewling sound, like seagulls.

Lights approach along the High Road. He leaves the shelter of the trees and walks to the side of the road. He squints against the brightness, but he doesn't need to trust eyesight. He recognizes the tone of the Morris and decides to chance it.

Clutching the bundle to his chest, he steps out into the road, into the path of a car. It swerves dangerously to one side, narrowly missing a Rover coming from the other direction.

She doesn't bother to park, doesn't even bother to get it off the road. He sees her struggle with the door catch and lurch out into the road, leaving the door swinging. She runs to him.

'What are you doing? What's that? Where's Ella?'

Elizabeth is shouting at him.

Peter Lightowler holds himself steady. 'My dear—'

'I'm not your dear! Where's my daughter? *What have you got there?*' She comes closer, trying to peer at what he holds.

'Elizabeth, there's been an accident. I'm so sorry. I don't want to be the one to tell you this.'

'What do you mean?' She is still shouting, still impassioned. He sees that her chest is rising and falling, that her lips are white.

He pauses. It might be dangerous to tell her here, out in the wild with no one to offer hot tea and consolation.

So he says, 'Ella's dead. There's been an accident. She was thrown out of the car and hit her head against a tree. She's dead, Elizabeth.'

He sees her sway, sees her stumble a little. 'Elizabeth, she's dead and so is Jamie. He went through the windscreen. I'll show you if you like—'

'No! No, no, ah . . .' Her hands are over her mouth.

He grasps her arm, pulling her further along the road. In the crook of his elbow the baby shifts once more, mewling its feeble song.

Elizabeth stops. 'A baby?' Her voice is all over the place, loud and soft in uneven bursts. 'You've got a baby there?'

He says nothing, concentrating on keeping her moving. The dark trees are standing between them and the road now. She's hanging heavily on his arm, but he doesn't care.

'Look, Elizabeth,' he says softly. 'Look. This is what happened.' The car crashed against the tree. The man's figure, masked almost entirely in blood, jutting from the windscreen. And on the ground, messed with mud and leaves and brambles, the broken body of her daughter, the belly ripped open, voided. Her throat is thrown back against the leaves, her eyes closed.

He sees Elizabeth's mouth open, soundlessly moving. He watches her collapse against her daughter's body, fall on to the leaf mould and then move no more. For a moment he kneels there beside her.

He puts the baby on the ground and feels for a pulse. Elizabeth lives, but he doesn't give her long. Some kind of stroke, he estimates.

He stands up again, tucking the baby under his arm.

Let someone else call the doctor. He's going home.

To the Blue Manor.

Alicia opens the door.

'Peter! Good God, what are you doing here? What's happened?'

'Well, Alicia, what a charming surprise!' But his eyes are wary. He didn't reckon on his ex-wife's presence at the Blue Manor. 'I might very well ask the same of you.'

'I came to keep Margaret company. Ella's gone to hospital

with Jamie, and Elizabeth was going to follow. What *have* you got there?'

She tries to see what he is holding, but he brushes past her into the hall.

'You're not welcome here, Peter. Get out.' But she's not really paying attention to him. Alicia's attention is focused beyond him, out along the driveway. 'Did you pass a car on the way here? Elizabeth—' And then her eyes catch on what he holds and for a moment she stands very still, completely unmoving. 'My God, Peter, what have you done?'

He holds the baby, knowing she won't do anything drastic while he's got it. 'There was an accident,' he says. 'Ella and Jamie are dead. This is Ella's child.'

'What? What? Ella is dead?' She has lost all colour, all vivacity. Her mouth hangs open.

'Yes, Alicia,' he repeats patiently. 'Ella and Jamie are dead and this is Ella's baby.'

At once she jerks into action. She lunges forward to seize the baby, but again he whirls aside. 'Oh no, my dear. Not again.'

'They're dead? Peter, what are you thinking of? Call the police, call for an ambulance. The child should go to a hospital.'

He shakes his head. 'Too late for ambulances, my dear. It would be a lot of fuss for nothing. There's nothing wrong with the child, either. Don't look so distraught, Alicia. We have here a companion for Simon, a little childhood friend. And as for what I'm doing here, where else should Ella's child be taken? Surely this is where she belongs . . . And that reminds me. Have you got my delightful son here with you? Of course you have! Such a devoted mother as you are, Alicia, *so* conscientious! Why don't you go and get Simon so he can meet his new – now, what is she? Let me think. Elizabeth's granddaughter. Simon's cousin? Sister?'

'It's a girl?' Alicia's eyes are sharp, although there are tears on her cheeks. 'Ella's child is a daughter?'

'Ella's and my child.'

She steps back from him. 'Oh, no. Not this time, Peter. I'm not swallowing that one. You never made it with Ella. She told me about you, of course she did! She's – she was my best friend. We had no secrets. I know about those confidential little tea parties. She and Jamie used to joke about it.'

'Much good it's done them. Oh, I forgot. Something else.

296

Elizabeth's not well. Perhaps an ambulance might be a good idea after all.'

'Elizabeth? Where is she? What's happened to her?'

He goes over to the phone and dials carefully, the baby still tucked in the crook of his arm. 'I want to report an accident,' he says. 'Along the Epping High Road, south of the Wake Arms roundabout. Yes, that's right, yes . . .' He puts the receiver down, crosses to the table and pulls out a chair. He sits down.

'Now, wifey,' he says. 'How about a drink for the father of your child?'

'I'm not your wife! Not any longer, thank God. And what gives you the right to make yourself at home here?' She's furious, as usual. And then her eyes catch on the small figure on the landing, the black-haired toddler standing at the banisters, clutching them with tiny hands. Through the bars his face is pinched and anxious.

'Simey, what are you doing out of bed?'

He says nothing, just gazes with those big dark eyes.

Alicia goes to the bottom of the stairs. 'What is it, lad? What are you doing up?'

'Mummy, why are you shouting?' The childish treble is very slightly wavery.

She sighs. 'It's nothing. Go to bed, Simon, it's long past your bedtime.'

'There's a nasty smell in my room.' His lower lip is trembling. 'I don't like the noise. It woke me up.'

'I'm sorry. I'll stop shouting.'

'No, the wheels,' he whispers. 'It's the wheels.'

'You've been dreaming.' She mounts the stairs and picks him up, looking back down to Peter Lightowler and Ella's baby. 'You know you can't stay here,' she says calmly.

'I have an entrée, now. Think about it, Alicia. I've saved the life of Ella's baby. I've brought her home. I have a role in her life. I'm her saviour, her protector, and if she stays here, so do I.'

'Oh, no you don't. You'd better give the baby to Margaret and go.'

Margaret, wizened, with sharp, agile movements, her head questing, emerging from the kitchen.

'He's got Ella's baby there,' says Alicia loudly. 'I'll explain later. But take the baby from him.'

297

Margaret doesn't hesitate. She has always loathed Peter Light-owler. She steps forward and he stands up. Like a bird he will crush her one day, take that wry wrinkled neck and twist it and wring it out like an old damp rag.

She reaches out her hands to take the baby, but he pushes her aside, casually as if she hardly existed.

She says, 'Peter, you cannot keep the baby, it will need cleaning, feeding.'

'She'll last a little longer yet.' But the child is crying in earnest, the regular lah, lah noise of the newborn.

She says, 'Peter Lightowler, that is not your child! Give her to me!' And her voice is stronger than it has any right to be.

'It's not yours, either. No fruit of your womb, no life from your loins, eh, Margaret? What do you think fits you, dried-up paps and all, to take a baby on?'

But he stands up, aware of a change in the atmosphere. Alicia is still at the top of the stairs, Simon in her arms.

Margaret, advancing towards him, is accompanied by some-thing he cannot quite understand. Hot, stinking breath flares over his face and he sees a faint colouring of red skimming through the air. He steps backwards. Upstairs a door slams, and there is the sound of wheels whisking down that long corridor. Simon is crying now, adding his strong lament to the baby's wails.

Alicia shouts, 'Get out, Peter! While you can!'

The redness that lurks in the air around Margaret suddenly lunges towards him.

His sleeve is ripped! Torn through as if by teeth, and he knows that next time it will draw blood . . .

The lift doors clang and the smell of ammonia fills the air, clouding in yellow fogs about him, filling his lungs and nose and mouth.

It's too much. He cannot handle all this at once. He backs towards the door, still carrying the child, and then Margaret is rushing at him – or is it that fanged thing? – and the baby is wrested from his arms, her cries reaching a fearful pitch of intensity.

He falls through the door out into the cold, black night.

In the distance, he hears sirens.

Chapter 42

The young man frowned as he followed the assistant down the corridor towards the end room. He was limping slightly, and his face was very white. The assistant's shoes were clattering on the polished floor ahead of him.

She paused at the door and turned to him. 'We wrote to Mrs Banniere's nephew, of course, months ago, he was the only living relative, but he never came. No one has been to see the old lady for years, but she seems happy enough.'

'Didn't Alicia Lightowler come?'

'Who? Oh, Mr Lightowler's wife . . . No, not for a long time. I don't suppose she knows that Mrs Banniere is so much better now. We always assumed that Mrs Banniere's nephew would tell the rest of the family. But no one came. No one.'

She waited for him to answer but his eyes were blank. He looked very tired, this young man, almost as if he hadn't slept that night. Her lips tightened momentarily. She wondered again what he was doing there, asking to see an old lady who'd been neglected for years.

She waited while he knocked on the door.

No reply.

'Go right in,' she said. 'She often drifts off and doesn't hear. It may take a while for her to remember who you are.'

He nodded briefly and pushed the door open.

The room was bright with sunshine, briefly dazzling. White walls, white bedspread. Then Tom saw the figure sitting in the chair by the window and stopped dead. For a moment he could not move, could not go any further.

This was Elizabeth Banniere.

The care assistant cleared her throat, recalling him. 'I'll be in the office, in case you want anything.'

'Thank you.' His mind was somewhere quite different.

Some of it must have showed in his face because she stepped back, turned quickly and walked briskly away down the corridor.

Elizabeth Banniere has never even met me, he was thinking. She will have no idea who I am. And how can I tell her this news? The impossibility of what he had to say struck him afresh. She was no blood relation, she had no reason to trust him, no reason to believe what he was going to say.

Would she even know who Ruth was?

He was looking all the time across the room to the old woman sitting at the window. She was silhouetted against the light, thin with a bird-like frailty, very bent, her head hunched deep within her shoulders. He moved forward. Her face was colourless, the skin almost transparent, like tissue. He could see the thick knots of veins in her forearms and wrists.

'Mrs Banniere . . . ?' Words, breaking the bleached silence. He watched the papery eyelids flicker, the head wavering, wry like a tortoise, the uneven rise and fall of her breast.

'Elizabeth, how are you?' Her hands were no longer loose in her lap. He saw the knobbly joints flex, saw the slight trembling.

There was no other sign that she had heard him.

'Elizabeth, I've some news for you, from Alicia. You remember Alicia?'

She was looking at him now, a painful crease between her washed-out eyes. Her voice was crackly like an old record, swallowed up and almost inaudible.

'Who are you? I don't know you.' Her gaze passed indifferently over him. 'Is it teatime again? Already?'

He wanted to keep saying her name, Elizabeth Banniere, over and over again, to prove to himself that she did exist, that against the odds the Blue Manor's owner was living.

He went over to her chair and squatted down in front of her. Her white face was fractured by wrinkles. Later he would remember that once she had been beautiful, that her eyes were still wide-spaced, still faintly echoing that famous blue. But now he had something to tell her, something to ask.

'Elizabeth, Alicia told me where you are. She said to ask you to come home. She wants you to come back to the Blue Manor.'

It was a lie, but he could think of no other way to get her there.

The old woman said nothing anyway, and her hands fell apart, relaxed and empty. She seemed to pay no attention whatsoever.

He could not say the worst of it. He could not tell her about

Ruth, not yet. He tried again. 'Do you understand, Elizabeth? The manor is waiting for you. I'm going back there later and I want to take you with me. You can come home again.'

The pale eyes washed over him again. 'Go away. I'm not Elizabeth, you've got this wrong. It's nothing to do with me, I don't understand what you're saying.' She paused, exhausted by all those words. 'I'd like a cup of tea. Is it teatime yet?'

This was not unexpected. He wanted to take her hands, to reassure her. He'd try again in a bit. He stood up and bent over, kissing the top of the old woman's head, not caring. 'I'll get you some tea,' he said. 'It won't be long.'

Her slow eyes followed him to the door.

The boy had gone. She knew he'd come back, that there was resolution in his voice, obstinacy. He'd not give up, not that one. Her little lie would change nothing, he knew who she was. He was young and it was always easy for the young to feel purposeful. They lived with hope, with the promise of change and progress.

Although he hadn't looked like that. She had seen something heavy in his face, something very dark. He had come from the manor, of course. That was it.

She sighed. She had thought she was safe here. Those terrible visits from Alicia had stopped long ago. She hoped, as she approached the end, that what happened at the manor would no longer weigh so heavily.

But it did. It was potent still. It showed in his face, sounded in his voice. It mattered more than anything. All that remained in her world, or in any other, was the manor. Bricks and mortar endure in ways unknown to their inhabitants.

It's waiting, the boy had said.

His information was superfluous. It was always there, waiting.

There was little to think of in this anonymous place, no events of real significance to mark these last, wasteland days. The old woman who was indeed Elizabeth Banniere, although she tried to deny it, sat alone throughout the rest of that white-light afternoon, staring through the window at the empty sky.

Time was out of control for her, a mess of memories and knowledge lacking sequence and order. The present was only tedium, a waiting place. The future, because she was ninety-five years old, was both unthinkable and undeniable.

But the past . . . That was the enigma. She couldn't remember what she wore yesterday, what she ate for lunch and anyway it didn't matter. That kind of thing never did. Time was a difficult and flawed anchor for her now, set adrift, hard to grasp and always beyond control.

The generations were confused in her mind, even the people she loved were confused. She'd lived too long. There was a boy, once, not Roddy, someone else . . .

But still the manor waited, as he said. This boy reminded her what it was like. She wouldn't be able to think about anything else now. A door had opened.

She leant back in her chair, sighing. Very well, she thought. Here I am. A hand reaching out, pushing it further.

It is home. Her memories slot into the manor calmly and naturally, although she has not been there for forty years. For forty years, she has lived elsewhere. Empty years, she thinks. I remember so little about them . . . He wanted to take her home, the boy with death in his voice, back to the Blue Manor.

Where she belonged.

Chapter 43

Two hours later, Elizabeth was waiting for Tom in the hall. The care assistant had packed a bag for her, just a few things. They thought she'd soon be back.

Elizabeth blinked at the assistant uncertainly. She knew they wouldn't meet again and wondered if there was anything she ought to say. But then the woman bustled off and it was too late. Elizabeth sighed. She was sitting in a high-winged armchair, her hands placidly folded on her lap, her bag on the parquet floor at her side.

It hadn't taken her long to decide. By the time Tom had returned with the tea, she had made up her mind to go with him. She would see the manor one last time before she died.

She had discovered that her fear had evaporated. Due to age, she supposed. What use is fear, when death is so close? What could possibly hurt her *now*? All her emotion had been burned away years ago, made smooth and faceless in that long sleep. There was no one left to love, no one to mourn.

The door opened. The boy, the young man, walked quickly across the hall towards her. She couldn't remember his name, although the care assistant had repeated it to her several times.

He looked so tired, poor boy, so serious.

'Is this all you need?' he asked. 'Should I tell anyone that we're leaving?'

The hall was deserted. The tea would be doing its rounds. Somewhere she heard the murmur of a trolley, a distant door banging.

'No. Let's go.' Now it had come, she couldn't wait to leave the place, the quiet deadliness of waiting.

He held out his arm and she stood up, glad of the support. He handed her the twin sticks she used and went ahead to open the door, scooping up her bag as he went.

There was such tense energy in him. It went deeper than the exuberance of youth: this boy had left exuberance behind long ago. But his step was sprung with power, something tight-coiled and dynamic.

He helped her into a strange, low-slung car. She sat in the front next to him and allowed him to belt her in. She felt curiously passive, content merely to let him direct and initiate.

She had spoken only a few sentences to him. She glanced sideways and saw his profile, grim-mouthed, frowning.

'The manor has changed since you were last there,' he said, breaking the silence. 'It's rather run-down. It needs a lot of work.'

The car was moving more quickly, although the traffic was heavy around them. She didn't recognize the road, vast, multi-laned, snaking over bridges and through tunnels. She had assumed they would be going through Woodford, down the High Road to Loughton and on to the Wake Arms roundabout with the forest all about them, but it seemed they were taking a different route.

'This isn't the way,' she said, unsettled by the relentlessly urban landscape.

'This stretch of motorway was opened years ago. It goes to Cambridge. We turn off at Harlow ... It's been a long time since you came this way, I suppose.'

'Yes. A very long time.' Since before you were born, she nearly said, but something held her back. She didn't want to start remembering, not yet.

'Are you warm enough? I could put the heater on.'

She was briefly amused. It was high summer, the road stinking in the heat. She was wearing a slip, a cotton dress and a cardigan and she could see that he was sweating. It came to her then that he was nervous of her, definitely frightened or in awe.

What had happened? What did he know to find her presence so upsetting, so disquieting?

'Who lives at the manor now?' she asked, her hands no longer casual in her lap.

He paused before answering and she felt her breath catch. 'Your great-granddaughter Kate lives there. And Simon, who is Alicia's son.'

'Yes. I remember Simon. He was a lovely baby. Who else? You?'

He shook his head, his eyes fixed on the road. 'I'm staying in the gardener's cottage.'

'I don't want to be the third,' she complained tiredly. 'Can't I stay in the cottage?'

'There's a gardener as well as me.'

'A gardener?' Immediately, she felt different. Reassured, confident. 'Shadwell? Is Shadwell there?' And then she stopped because, of course, Shadwell could no longer be alive.

'He's called Phizackerley Byrne. He's not been there much longer than me, but Ruth—'

'Ruth? Who is Ruth?'

She saw him check, his hands on the wheel clenching.

'Your – granddaughter,' he said slowly, unhappily. 'I – I'm so sorry to have to tell you this. She's very ill. Dying, they think. It was an accident, at the manor. She fell—' And then he glanced at her face.

'But there was a gardener there! Why didn't he—?' But the gardener had never really prevented anything, he had always been too late. That was part of the pattern, too.

Ruth. Ella's child: the child, she, Elizabeth, had never known. 'I never knew her,' she said sadly. 'I became – ill, when I first heard that Ella had died.'

'I want to know what happened.' He suddenly swerved the car over to the side of the road, on to the hard shoulder. The engine died. 'Elizabeth, there's a story in the manor and it keeps dominating everything. It takes over. I tried to write something, but I had no control and I have no way of knowing if it's true. What the story said. No one knows.

'It's about you.'

'Me?' She was genuinely disconcerted.

'About your brother. And Peter Lightowler.'

She fumbled at the door handle. How did it work, why couldn't she—?

And then the door fell open and the roar of cars and lorries hit her like a blow and she was gasping for breath, constriction round her heart, sickness in her mouth.

Oh, that white room! Those bleached silences, the blessed quietness of waiting!

She should never have left, never agreed to this! And she wasn't even there yet. The manor was yet to come.

'Elizabeth!' The boy's hands on her arm were firm and cool. 'I'm so sorry! So stupid of me, I should never—'

'Is he alive?' Her voice, hissing like a snake.

'Roderick?'

'*Not* Roderick! Peter Lightowler. His son, Roderick's son. Does he live?'

'Yes, he's alive. As a matter of fact—'

She pulled the door shut again, interrupting him. 'Why have we stopped? What are we waiting for? I want to be there now, at the manor!' She was shouting. She hadn't shouted for years.

Without a word he started the car once more and they were off, sliding out into the traffic and she kept her eyes sternly fixed forward, and all the time it burned in her mind, burned through the bleached white years of waiting, the dead silent wastes of time since she was ill.

He was there, in the manor, waiting for her.

'I'm glad he's alive,' she said softly.

It took for ever to get through Epping. Elizabeth emerged from the torrent of memory and saw angrily that the trees had gone. It used to be so pretty, Epping. Quiet shops, great trees, a market. And now there was only a squalid mess of badly dressed people and ugly cars.

She considered the boy at her side. 'Why did you let yourself get involved in this?'

'It's my family too,' he said simply. 'I'm involved in the manor, just like my father and grandfather.'

'Your father? Forgive me, I don't understand.'

'Simon Lightowler is my father. I want to understand what happened.' Determination was written all over his face.

'So Peter is your grandfather. Are you sure you want to be part of this?' Elizabeth asked carefully. She could see faint echoes of Peter in his neat blond hair, the graceful way he moved. He looked more like Peter than Simon ever would.

'It can't be allowed to linger on, souring everyone's life. It has to be resolved, it has to be ended.'

He was very young, she thought, but he was right. It was time Peter Lightowler met with judgement.

He pulled up at the hotel on Bell Common and left her sitting in the car while he went to get Kate.

She sat in the afternoon sun, considering the trees waving in the distance over towards Theydon Bois. At least they still existed. The forest was in place, the manor hidden, as ever, from public view.

Tom came out almost immediately and got in the car.

'She's back at the hospital,' he said. 'Ruth's holding on.' He reversed the car out of the car park with a crunch.

Through Epping again, those frustrating crowds and then right towards St Margaret's Hospital.

Another period of waiting, longer this time. Almost an hour before they joined her, and Elizabeth was glad of the respite. The girl with Tom kissed her shyly before getting into the back of the car. Elizabeth received a potent impression of neat prettiness and great tension. Poor girl, she thought. My great-granddaughter. Her mother is dying. What did the boy say? She fell?

'Did Ruth fall because of Peter? Was he there?' she said suddenly.

'He wasn't there. But there was an argument, a row about him.'

'Don't!' Kate said. 'Please don't, not now!'

'Go on.' Elizabeth ignored her.

'I didn't see it happen.'

'It was an accident!' said Kate. 'The banister broke, it was no one's fault!'

'Who else was there apart from the gardener?'

'Simon. Simon, Mum and me.'

'And Simon is Peter's son . . .' Elizabeth was watching the boy and knowledge fell into place. 'And you are Simon's son,' she said, repeating it like a mantra.

'I only recently discovered it.'

'Were you kept in ignorance too? Who was that, Alicia?'

'How did you know?' He was so surprised that the car swerved slightly.

'She was always like that, manipulative, secret.' She nodded, pleased with herself. 'I used to like Alicia. I thought she was tough, a winner.'

The others remained silent this time. They had nothing to say, nothing to add. She sighed. As they sped through the forest, she shivered. Nearly there.

'So, you live at the manor now,' she said politely to Kate. 'With Simon Lightowler. And the gardener and Tom are in the cottage.' She had to keep coming back to it, to work out the presences and absences. 'Who will stay there tonight?'

'You, I hope,' she said. 'It's your home.'

'There's something I should tell you,' said Tom as they swung into the drive. 'Alicia is also at the manor.'

Elizabeth could not later decide what had been the greater shock. That the trees had grown so tall or that Alicia should be there.

Chapter 44

Simon's arms were empty. His eyes were upturned, the whites glinting.

'Wake up!' Byrne slapped his face. They were on the landing at the Blue Manor, and Peter Lightowler was below them on the stairs. Behind him, seated round the table, were two women and a man.

Simon was still wrapped in the vision. 'I dreamed, I—'

'No. It wasn't you. It wasn't a dream. It was what happened.' Alicia was standing further round the landing, opposite the broken banister. Her similarity to her son had never been more explicit. Thin, nervy, sallow-skinned, dark-eyed, dark-haired. 'I was there, then and now. I saw Peter Lightowler enter the manor with that little baby and stand there and tell me that my friend was dead.

'I saw him leave, too.'

Byrne could not take his eyes off her. She looked frail and exhausted, but that was not the least of it. She was clear and defined. There was no clutter about her, no wavering or prevarication.

Fascinated, he saw that the material of her skirt was swept aside by movement. Something came to rest beside her, paused there, and air shifted around the great hound so that it could almost be seen, almost understood. There were tinges of colour hanging in the air, red and white and grey, flecking the dim light. She was resting her hand on its back, and its mouth gleamed briefly, opening, and then the colours brushing through the air contained black and triangular shapes of ivory.

'I *saved* Ruth's life!' said Peter Lightowler. The scar on the side of his face seemed more livid, more violent than ever before. 'You don't understand,' he said. 'You never did. I resent being pushed to this, Alicia. You were always relentless. You fed off vulnerability. You always looked for the flaw in men, you always sought out their weaknesses and dependency.'

And Byrne saw him glance at Simon, Simon who was watching this with keen attention.

Peter Lightowler's voice, laconic, self-mocking, continued. 'It's all quite simple. I just wanted to belong. I wanted to – know my family, to be part of it.' He frowned. 'You shut me out because I was too strong for you, I was not weak or dependent.'

In the hall below them, the three puppeteers looked up.

Alicia sighed. 'Peter, give it up. You're not wanted here. Not now, not ever. Take your nasty little trio and get out. You have no role here.'

'And you have no right to say things like that. This is not your house. You can't shut me out of the Blue Manor.'

'I have friends, however.' She lifted her hand and the presence at her side moved, filling more space, red smearing wetly in the shadows. Its breath was now running through the manor, that hot stink of carrion and blood.

Alicia smiled. 'Mr Byrne will be delighted to help.' She darted a glance at him. He nodded. The memory of the crashed car, of Lightowler's hand beneath his chin, wrenching his head round, proved it. He knew very clearly where his allegiance lay.

And yet Lightowler seemed unperturbed. 'Kate Banniere asked me here. This is her house, or it will be very soon, and she wanted me to come. You cannot keep me out.' He was smiling, becoming increasingly confident. The three puppeteers had moved towards the bottom of the stairs. 'I'm going to wait for her,' he said. 'I'll be so kind when she returns. Why, I'll even give my blessing to her marriage to my grandson Tom. And then we three shall live here together.'

'I've heard enough. Get out, Peter.' The creature at Alicia's side was looming towards solidarity. They could see the bunched muscles, the bony spine.

Lightowler stared at his ex-wife and only Byrne saw the index finger on his left hand flick towards her.

It happened so quickly that there was nothing he could possibly have done. As soon as Lightowler's finger moved, there was a flash, a blurring beneath them, movement too rapid to disentangle.

Silver flew through the air from the dark man's hands.

And then Alicia shattered like glass, her arms, her hands, hair, clothes, flaring, falling apart as she toppled, the handle of a knife jutting from her breast.

At the same time the darkness was ripped into vivid liveliness as the Dogfrog pounced.

A scattering of feathers beneath them, something between a scream and a screech. One of the two women exploded into wings and beak, odd jointed limbs with claws threshing over the table and scattering glass and china like crumbs.

The other slid towards the ground, a black horned creature scuttling with dry whispers among the shards and tipped chairs.

Perspectives became confused. Byrne could not be sure what the scale was, whether the Dogfrog was filling the hall with teeth and claws, or whether the beetle was really only a few centimetres long. A wriggling, smacking mess of tearing teeth and beak and claws seethed.

The Dogfrog was growling, a deep rumbling undercurrent to the cawing of the crow and the rustling scraping of the beetle.

Teeth crunched on hollow bones, clawed paws batted the smooth carapace of the horned insect and it skidded over the floor to smash into the door to the porch.

It shattered there, spraying blood and guts and matter every-where. It seemed that the hall was filled with stinking offal, much more than could possibly have come from the wreck of one body, one woman, one creature.

The bird thing was battering against the door, a ruined wing hanging crippled.

Abruptly the door swung open. Fringes of ivy held it wide and the Dogfrog pounced once more.

The crow limped through the opening, and the Dogfrog snapped at its tail, strong teeth meeting through flesh. A trail of blood and feathers splattered over the threshold and then the noise and violence and chaos abruptly ceased.

The door swung shut.

Something moved amidst the wreckage of the hall. A dark figure stepped out of the shadows beneath the stairs.

It was the man, the central figure of the trio, the one who had thrown the knife. In his arms he held Alicia's body. Her empty eyes gazed blankly at nothing.

Simon made an indistinct sound. He took one step towards the stairs, but Peter Lightowler was still there, his arms out-stretched, blocking the way. He looked only at his son.

'I saved Ruth's life,' he repeated. 'She never understood.'

The man placed Alicia's body gently on the table. Then he

turned to face them and for a moment Byrne thought that he was bearded, that his face was covered in hair. But then he realized, sickeningly, that the lower part of the man's face was coated in blood, as were his hands.

The man stepped to one side and Byrne saw that the front of Alicia's jacket had been wrenched apart, and that, through a shattering of bone and flesh, her heart had been torn out.

'Jesus . . .' Helplessly, he stepped back from the sight, wondering if he was going to vomit.

He was aware that Simon was moving, stumbling away along the corridor. Another indistinct, muffled sound from him. Byrne saw him turn and plunge through the door on the left.

Without any hesitation, glad only to leave behind him what had happened in the hall, Byrne ran after him.

The room is dark, just as he expects. But something shines at him, something warm and vital and coming towards him.

Ruth is there. Her face is blurred with something, softer, gentler than he remembers. Younger. Oh, beautiful Ruth, he thinks, oh my dear . . .

'Hey, look who I've got here.' Her voice is slow and very slightly slurred. Beside her stands Simon, but it's not quite Simon, there's something wrong. Something blurred about him too, something indistinct. Byrne suddenly knows what Simon will look like when he's old, how the flesh will fall away, how the bones will jut and define character, the character lurking beneath the skin. Ruth looks so young, but Simon is old, and after what he has just seen Byrne is not in the least surprised.

Simon seems rather out of place in his immaculate three-piece suit and bow tie. His hair is grey in the dim light, blond or grey or both, and his eyes are hooded. She has her hand on his arm and he's smiling at Ruth and that's when Byrne realizes that this is not Simon. It's much worse than that. Byrne wants to kick the man's teeth in, the way Ruth is smiling at Peter Lightowler.

She catches Byrne's eye and grins at him. She is happy and excited. But she calls him Francis, and again he's confused, caught in a reality which slips and slides out of control. He doesn't know where he is either, or what is happening. He turns half round, trying to work it out, but the room is unfamiliar, crowded with moving shapes, young people with long hair and Afghan jackets and cheesecloth and flared jeans . . .

He recognizes nothing. Not the place with the Toulouse Lautrec posters and candles stuck in wine bottles, nothing about it. There's tinsel draped along the edges of the shelves. He's in a student room, he realizes. Books are stacked carelessly on shelves over a modern desk, the bed covered in cushions and a couple of figures are sprawled there, locked in an intense embrace.

Led Zeppelin on the music centre on the window sill, people dancing, some shouting, a little wild. A lot of noise and the sweet scent of hash and nicotine, and cloudy glasses emptied of beer and cheap Spanish plonk. Mistletoe hangs from the light fitting.

He's bemused, caught in a sense of déjà vu, although of course the place is so familiar with its breeze-block walls, the tawny colours of carpet and curtains. He's tried to smarten it up a bit, with Max Escher prints between the Lautrecs, but it's still fairly anonymous.

Ruth is talking to him and he tries to pay attention. 'Francis, this is Uncle Peter ... Well, he's not really an uncle, more a kind of cousin. Uncle Pete, this is Francis Townsend, a friend of mine.'

'How do you do, Francis?' The old man holds out a hand to him. 'I've chosen an inopportune time, haven't I? Is this your party?'

Francis finds himself automatically taking the old man's hand, although he doesn't want to. For some reason he doesn't like this man, but he doesn't know why. The old man is still talking, an irritating, faint drawl, almost lost in the noise around them.

'I was just passing by, wondering what my dear niece was getting up to in the far north.'

'How's Simon?' Ruth's voice cut through the vague chatter. 'I wrote but he didn't reply.'

'Don't worry about it, my dear. Simon'll get over it. Young love, and all that.'

'I didn't want to upset him.' She sounded anxious.

'Didn't you?' For once there was a sharpness to the words. 'Why did you write then?'

'I hated dumping him, after so long.'

'But things are different here, aren't they, Ruth? Away from the manor it's all so different.'

'Can I get you a drink?' Francis says. The old man looks at

him as if he'd crawled out of the woodwork. But he asks for wine and Francis goes over to the desk where the bottles are. It takes him a while to find one that has something in it and a cleanish glass, and when he turns back he can't see Ruth and her uncle anywhere.

The door's open, leading on to a linoed corridor with other dark chasms opening off it. Francis catches sight of Peter Lightowler, steering through the crowd towards it, holding Ruth by the hand.

He sees an old, dry hand rise and stroke Ruth's cheek.

She stumbles and Francis realizes that her breasts are pressing against the old man's arm. Lightowler shifts and she over-balances against him. She's drunk, Francis thinks, annoyed. She needs to lie down. He tries to push through the crowd towards them, but Tony had got hold of his arm, demanding that he go for more beer or something . . .

Francis can see that the old man's arms are holding Ruth steady and that his head lowers towards her. He can't make out anything else, there are too many people in the way, but he thinks, God, what if he's *kissing* her? It looks like it, but he can't be sure. He's old enough to be her grandfather, how *can* she?

'Move!' He pushes Tony aside but then there's Jill and Mary blocking his way. He swears at them, and Mary blinks. He's offended her again, but he still can't get through. It's absurd! This is his room, why are these people being so *slow*, so obstructive?

At last he's through. They're out in the corridor and Ruth is still leaning against the old man.

'Ruth? You OK?'

Against his shoulder, her head turns. 'Francis – '

'Come on.' He moves forwards and tries to hook her arm around his neck. She smells of something that's not hash, he doesn't know what it is.

'She's all right,' the old man says. He takes her weight again. 'I gave her one of my Turkish cigarettes and I think it was a bit strong. I'll take care of her.'

'No. Not you.' He's hardly looking at Lightowler. He is purely determined to get Ruth away from this man. He doesn't care what it looks like, whether he's being rude or ridiculous. He doesn't trust the man.

Lightowler says lightly, easily, 'I'm Ruth's *uncle*, Francis, you needn't worry. She seems to be in need of a lie down. Wouldn't you agree?'

This was unarguable. 'This is my room,' he says. 'Hers is in Langwith.'

'Get rid of this lot, can't you?'

For a moment Francis stares at him. Then he moves, swiftly, decisively. The lights come on, the music is turned off. Grumbling, the party-goers drift away.

The room is squalid with ash and alcohol and crumbs from the mince pies. Francis flings open the window and cold night air washes through the fug. Lightowler guides Ruth to the bed and lifts her legs on to the blanket.

'Can you make some coffee or something?' the old man throws over his shoulder. 'I'll stay with her.'

'I'm not leaving her,' Francis says. He opens a cupboard door and there is a small round stainless steel basin, a mirror. He fills a glass with water and takes it over to the bed. Without hesitation he throws the contents into Ruth's face.

She splutters, furious, visibly sobering before their eyes. 'Francis, really! There was no need for that!'

'You've had too much to drink.'

'Well, it's a party, isn't it? Christmas? Anyway, what's it got to do with you?'

'You're making a fool of yourself.'

'So are you, Francis. A guardian of public morals, are you? How self-righteous of you! I thought you were more fun than that.'

'You should take more care, you know—'

'Shut up, Francis!' She is very angry and he wonders if perhaps he has overstepped the line. Then he glances at Peter Lightowler and decides that he hasn't.

Ruth is looking at Lightowler too, and her mood changes again. She's smiling, conciliatory. 'Sorry about this, Unc. You should have told us you were coming.'

'What would you have done? Put on a party?' He's laughing at her, charming as could be.

'Offered you coffee, at least. Francis, would you . . . ?'

It's impossible. This is ordinary, the ordinary visit of an old family connection, nothing special. And Ruth is better, quite together again. Francis has been a fool, there's nothing to worry

315

about. Still unsmiling, still with that lingering doubt, he leaves the room.

Jill and Mary are in the kitchen, making some attempt at the washing up. Red-stained glasses litter the sides. They're always conscientious, what with their left politics and their good works . . . He ignores them, aware that they're watching him, that he's interrupted some intimate gossip. He puts out three mugs and spoons coffee powder into them.

'Francis—' Mary comes and stands next to him. 'Look, I don't want to barge in—'

'Well don't then.'

'But Ruth told us. About the baby.'

He can say nothing. *Why?* What's it to do with them?

And Mary, all virtuous, heavy Catholic, *bugger it*! How could Ruth accuse him of self-righteousness when she was blabbing to Mary?

Mary is embarrassed, as well she might be. He very much doesn't want to talk to her. Is she going to sound off about abortion?

The kettle is taking an age to boil.

And then he hears music, very loud music from his room, Led Zep III. Strange, he thinks. He wouldn't have thought that was the old man's cup of tea.

He makes the coffee and puts the mugs on a tray, carries it across the corridor.

The door is locked. Stupid, he must have let the latch go. He kicks it. 'Come on,' he calls. 'Open up.'

He can hear nothing over the music. 'Ruth?' He puts the tray down and tries the door again. He remembers that his key is by the bedside.

And then the panic starts. Ruth is in there with that man who calls himself her uncle, and Francis knows he should never have left them.

'Ruth!' he yells. 'Open the door!'

'What is it?' Mary, at his shoulder again. 'Can't you get in?'

'My key's in there. Why have they locked me out? Ruth!' he shouts again. 'Ruth! Are you all right?'

There is no other sound, only that heavy monotonous thump and Robert Plant screaming. He's frantic to get in, but there's nothing he can do. He hammers uselessly on the door, kicking, shouting, yelling, and no one answers him.

Mary's there again, trying her key in the lock, but of course it doesn't work. And in the end he thinks of going and getting the porter, but as he does so the door suddenly swings open.

Lightowler stands there, his skin faintly tinged with pink. Francis hardly notices him: his attention is on the bed, where Ruth lies, her face turned away from him.

And as he crosses the floor towards her, pushing past the old man, he sees her shoulders heave and she coughs, a difficult, retching cough.

Her skirt is rucked up, her hair in a mess. There's blood on her lip. He catches her shoulders, holding her fast as tears run down her face and she retches over the side of the bed on to the floor.

The smell of vomit and coffee mix together.

Byrne looked up and there was Simon standing in the door. There was no one on the bed in the empty room. No Lautrec posters or books on shelves. Only black fingers of damp crawling over the walls. This was the Blue Manor, decaying, full of dreams and memories and stories.

There was nothing to prove what had happened, nothing. Only the smell of vomit and coffee, souring the air.

Chapter 45

In the doorway, Byrne asked, 'Were you there, at that party, as—' He stopped. Just because he identified strongly with Francis, did that mean Simon had slipped, time-slipped, into Lightowler's role, too?

It was written all over his face. It always had been.

Simon said, 'She was wanton. Then and now. She was never faithful, never true.'

Byrne knew what it was to feel one's blood run cold. He said, 'Who are you talking about? What do you mean?'

'What?' For a moment Simon's eyes were glazed, as if he were still in the dream.

Byrne took a deep breath. 'Are you talking about *Ruth*? Because if you are, you must be even crazier than everyone thinks. Either that, or you never really knew her at all.'

'Like you? You really knew her, is that it? In just over a week, you think you know Ruth better than I?'

'She is not wanton. I'd stake my life on it.' It was not bravado. Ruth's integrity was one of the only remaining constants in his life. Wife, child, friend, home, job. All had gone. There was only Ruth, and the Blue Manor.

'It doesn't make any difference, anyway.' Simon spoke tiredly. 'She's going to die, isn't she? So what does it matter? She would never marry me, Kate is not my daughter, this is not my house . . . It all comes to nothing, in the end.'

'For God's sake, Simon!' Byrne stared at him. 'What's up with you? Doesn't the fact that she's so ill mean anything to you? What the hell does it matter who owns the manor?'

'Why should I tell you?' It was as if the pressure of the moment, the fading in and out of these strange scenes, had stripped Simon, as it did Alicia, of both artifice and defence. He looked at Byrne, his eyes darkened and desperate. 'You're the one she loved. It always was the gardener, or the student friend, or the war hero, wasn't it? There was never any room for me.'

'But Ruth lives with you, she wanted you here.' It was

ludicrous to have to say these things. Byrne shook his head in disbelief. What did it matter? He tried again. 'You live with her here in the Blue Manor and it's your home too. What more do you need?'

'I need a whole lot more than that. This house is not *mine*! I have no power, no money, nothing. I'm getting old, going grey, there's nothing ahead of me and *nothing is mine*!'

Me too, thought Byrne. 'So what?' he said. 'We're all landed with that one, sooner or later.' A silence. 'Let's get out of here. I hate this place.' Around them, the windows were clogged with greenery and he knew that the doors would be jammed shut. 'This bloody house,' he said. 'It should be burned to the ground.'

'What a good idea.'

A voice from below them, that slow, familiar drawl.

Peter Lightowler stepped out from between the wooden pillars supporting the landing. He held a petrol can in one hand, matches in the other. 'Great minds,' he said.

'No! Stop!' Byrne pushed past Simon, hurling himself down the stairs. It was an automatic, unreasoning response. Something to do with keeping the evidence intact, the evidence which was written in blood and words and memories throughout the manor.

But as he leaped down the stairs, three at a time, something happened, something snagged at his ankle and he fell, tumbling into confusion, turning over and over while his surroundings whirled and spun about him.

Again, he was in darkness, somewhere else, leaves beneath his fingers . . . A bramble had twined round his leg, and there were twigs beneath his back.

The forest, not far from the road from the sound of it. Byrne shuddered. He dreaded these scenes in the forest more than anything. Remembered pain appalled him. He hated it here. There was something inexorable about the progression of noise and light around the manor's boundaries. The crashing violence of the cars created an impenetrable wall around the family, cutting it off from reality, isolating its convoluted history.

But he was not part of the family. That shift again, that fatal blurring. He, Byrne, felt his grip fading once more, the inevitable dissolution of his identity. He was being used, possessed, he,

Francis, was being manipulated by Ruth's bloody, arrogant family.

Francis picks himself up off the ground and finds himself staring with incredulity at Ruth's cousin.

They've met before. On Ruth and Simon's return from the Edinburgh Festival, he'd visited the manor for a day or two. Not long afterwards, Ruth had split with Simon, returning to York for her final year. That was when he'd really got to know her.

Both Simon and Francis are wearing flared jeans. Francis is in a tie-dye T-shirt, but Simon's cotton shirt is immaculate, full-sleeved, embroidered in silk. His hair is black and glossy, falling to his shoulders. He appears darkly romantic, very handsome.

It is early evening. A fading sun softens the outline of the trees. It is damp underfoot, a little boggy. Francis hardly cares. He is consumed with outrage because Simon is blocking the way, has just pushed him to the ground.

Simon is saying, 'Give it up, Francis. I don't know what you think you can achieve here. Ruth doesn't want to see you. She told me.'

'She's about to give birth to *my* child! She wants to see me! I have *some* rights!'

'I don't agree. It was a casual affair, a student fling, as you well know. Ruth has returned here, to me, to have her baby at home.'

'I love her! I promised I would come!'

'She has never mentioned you. She doesn't need you.'

'I need her!'

'Ah, so now we have it. Fancy living in the manor, do you? Lord of the Manor, perhaps? Is that why you were sneaking round the back way? Couldn't face tackling us face to face?'

'I hitched here, and this is the quickest way in!' He is being defensive. Why does this damn man always have him on the run?

'You didn't complete your degree either, did you?' Simon is saying, as if it is important.

Francis regards Ruth's cousin with dislike. 'This is ridiculous. I just want to see Ruth. She asked me to be here, and I've heard nothing to the contrary. I've come because I promised her I would. If she wants to end it – and I don't believe for one moment that she does – then she can tell me herself.'

'It's quite unnecessary.' Simon draws an envelope from his breast pocket. 'She gave me this for you.' He hands it over.

Under the gloomy trees, Francis tears open the envelope. An air ticket falls out into his hand, and a cheque. There is also a brief note in what looks like Ruth's handwriting.

The ticket is one way to Nepal. The cheque is for one thousand pounds. The note is bizarre.

My dear Francis,

Please take these. I know how you always wanted to travel. Don't worry about me, this is for the best. I need the family around me, I need to feel at home. I don't know if you can understand this . . . View it as part of the student experience.

We'll meet again, one day. Take care till then.

Love, Ruth.

He can't believe it. In a fury he tears up the ticket, the cheque and the note, scattering the scraps on the mossy ground. 'I want to see her!' he shouts. 'I want to hear it in her own words!'

'Why subject yourself to an interview which will surely cause great distress to both of you?' Simon's voice sounds silky with concern. 'Ruth is tired at the moment. I don't want her disturbed in her condition.'

'Her condition! I don't understand this! It's *my* child! Why should I be excluded?'

'But Ruth says it's not your child.' Very quietly.

'What?'

'There was someone else. You didn't realize?'

'Oh, I know who you mean.' The words are simple, but Francis is aware that his face is sharp with loathing. 'Do you mean your father? Good old Uncle Peter?'

Simon says nothing. He bends down to pick up the torn paper.

Francis makes a grab for him. He finds himself clutching a fold of the soft cotton. Simon strikes his hands away. Francis can see that he is breathing hard.

'Is this what keeping it in the family means? You and your father, both after her? Christ, I don't understand how Ruth can contemplate it.'

'No, you don't understand. Go away, Francis. You're not required here, this is nothing to do with you.'

'Ruth's child is *my* child! That feeble attempt at rape, that sordid assault took place when she was already pregnant. She was being sick!'

'She was drunk!'

'No, she wasn't. The baby's due any day, isn't it? Work it out, count up the dates! It's my child, I should be there! And the only reason she didn't press charges against Peter Lightowler was out of a misplaced sense of loyalty to you! How does it feel to be a rapist's son?'

'I'm getting tired of this.' Simon speaks quietly. 'Just go away, there's a good chap. Even if the child is yours, Ruth doesn't want you. She's given you the push. Take it with good grace.'

'I'm not going to leave her in this bloody family! I'm going to get her out!'

'I think not.'

'Let me through!' He tries to push past the other man.

Simon stands his ground. 'Give it up, Francis. You're not wanted.'

'Out of my way!' He lunges violently at Simon's shoulder and Simon takes one step backwards.

'*Pour mieux sortie*,' he murmurs. Francis is intent on getting through. He doesn't see at first that Simon is holding a knife.

Then it glints and he is for a moment paralysed with astonishment. 'For goodness' sake! How absurd! You're behaving as though this is some revenge tragedy!' He feels like laughing, it's so ludicrous.

'I know.' Simon shrugs lightly. 'But I don't think you realize quite how determined, how certain, I am that you're not going to get into the manor.'

'Oh, grow up!' In the sudden shafting light from the sinking sun, he can see the hedge to the manor through the trees. He dodges past Simon, breaking through the undergrowth.

But there's someone else there, three people, people he doesn't recognize, doesn't like.

Instinctively, he halts. The man in the centre of the three comes towards him. There is a long scar down the side of his face, his clothes are dusty black, old-fashioned . . .

There is something decadent about him, something which makes Francis's skin crawl. It's something he cannot handle.

The two women behind the man are smiling at Francis, and there should have been something comforting about their style, their rig. Long skirts, tatty Indian print, fringed black velvet jackets, lots of cheap jewellery. But their teeth show no friendliness. They shine almost green in the dim light, sharp and pointed.

'Friends of yours?' he says to Simon.

'Go away, Francis. We don't need you here.'

And he thinks, suddenly and clearly, all right, I'll go now and sneak back later. I'll wait until Simon goes out, I'll watch at the gates, and then I'll get in ... I don't need this aggro, it won't help Ruth. I'll come back later ...

He turns away from the manor, walking away from Simon and his weirdo friends towards the road. He's walking quickly, aware that it looks like a retreat, but not caring.

He cannot face those three. He knows they're behind him, watching him. They may even be following him, but he's not going to look back. He doesn't know who or what they are, only that he has no intention of confronting them alone.

But he'll come back. There's no way that he'll abandon Ruth to that lot.

The traffic is very loud now. He stands at the side of the road and puts out his thumb. He'll let them think he's really going to London, but he'll get out after a mile or two and come back.

He sees a tanker approaching and wonders if the driver will stop for him. He's had luck before, hitching with tanker drivers.

But this one isn't slowing, the driver isn't even looking at him.

The driver is wondering whether he should have stopped for petrol in Epping. He checks the gauge again and doesn't see the man with black hair coming out of the trees. He doesn't see him give the boy by the road a push, so that he falls beneath the huge double wheels of the tanker.

He gasped as the immense pressure on his chest lifted. He took a great shuddering breath and the world fell into place, a semblance of order with time passing, events and people grounded in the present. His eyes opened; he was slumped against the table leg in the hall of the manor, and there were three men standing on the stairs above him.

Simon was at the top, leaning over the remains of the

banisters. He was ghastly pale. Below him on the stairs stood his father Peter Lightowler, petrol can and matches held at the ready.

At the bottom of the stairs the third man lounged against the wall. His face was no longer masked by blood, although dark crimson creased the lines around his mouth. He was looking at Byrne with something very like amusement. 'Pleasant dreams?' he enquired gently.

Byrne hauled himself to his feet. There was something wrong with his left arm. He must have damaged it in the fall. He could not afford to attend to it now. He looked only at Simon.

'You killed Francis,' he said softly. 'It was you. You pushed him into the road and killed Ruth's lover.'

Simon said nothing.

Byrne glanced at the table, where Alicia lay. Part of him was still locked in the experience of shock, the crushing weight of the massive machine over his limbs. But one thing was clear to him, one horrific, unalterable fact.

Like father, like son. It ran true, the strain of violence.

'*Why* did you?' he shouted. 'Why did you have to *kill* him?'

Simon moved slowly down the stairs towards him. He passed his hand over his forehead, as if he was sweating.

'I couldn't trust her, you see. I couldn't afford to let anyone else near her, because you can't bloody trust women! Can you?'

It wasn't rhetorical. This was a genuine question. Byrne said, 'You're wrong, you're all wrong. You could trust Ruth, of course you could.'

'But you can't be sure, can you?' Simon said, and he felt it start to slip again.

'Ah God . . .' It was speeding up. The illusions, the replays, the past crowding in on him and he couldn't handle it, it was too traumatic, too strange. He deliberately jolted his arm, hoping the stabbing pain would hold him steady, resisting the drag of events. He kept his eyes fastened on the staircase, hoping that if he concentrated on that he could prevent the mantle of the past enveloping him again.

It wasn't enough. He was nothing, a receptor, a toy, denied integrity or value. The staircase was blurring in front of him, changing into something else, and he had to blink to clear his eyes, and he fell under the spell once more.

This was different. Not the forest, not the house, not the distant past.

This is his own story, somewhere recently familiar only to him. He slots into it with a jolt, with a shock of appalled recognition. And although he knows he will suffer no physical hurt this time, what happens next is worse.

He sees his friend David as he picks the morning papers from the counter.

The shop is quiet and dim. The early morning sunlight makes the window look filthy, but doesn't penetrate the depths of the newsagent's. Janet is out the back. There's no one else there. 'You're up early,' Byrne says. He's rather surprised to see David here, out in the country at this time of day. And then he notices that David is wearing a tracksuit and trainers. 'Jogging? For *pleasure*?'

David doesn't answer immediately. He seems fascinated by the headlines of the *Sun*. 'Well, you know,' he says at last. 'One has to keep up certain standards.'

Byrne grins at him. 'Certain reputations, don't you mean?' It's an old joke between them, the pursuit of physical fitness, but David isn't smiling.

'What? What do you mean?' David's really slow on the uptake this morning, unusually so.

'Nothing.' Byrne raises an eyebrow. 'Blood sugar running low? Why don't you join us for breakfast?'

He wonders if something has upset David, who is untidy, even messy. He looks as if he hasn't slept. He certainly hasn't shaved.

'No, I can't stop . . . I really should be getting back.'

Byrne leaves a few coins on the counter and picks up a copy of the *Independent*. He follows David to the door.

The sunlight is briefly dazzling. Looking down the hill, Byrne sees Kristen come out of their house, making for the car. Her black hair is bouncing behind her as she walks, briskly, eagerly, characteristically making no concessions to her pregnancy.

'No!' David shouts hoarsely, bizarrely. It sounds shocking in the morning quiet. He's already running down the hill in that bright sunlight, and Phizackerley Byrne, on the shop steps, doesn't understand, doesn't know what is happening.

David is still running as Kristen opens the car door in the

distance. He's shouting, waving his arms, 'Kris! No! Wait! Don't—'

She is standing by the side of the car. She waves to him, gets in and puts the key in the ignition. The car explodes. Instantly, irrevocably. Disappears in a ball of flame and scattering metal and there is only noise and flames and black smoke.

One part of Byrne's mind thinks, *Kristen!* But there's something else, something that defuses the first shock.

His mind is gripped, obsessed by it.

He knows immediately what has happened, he sees it all, every last detail.

David has done it. Has planted the bomb, knowing that he, Byrne, was going to get in the car to drive to the garrison that morning. David was expecting *him* to start the car and trigger the detonator and disappear in an exploding cloud of metal and flames.

He turns towards him. David is slumped against a lamp post by the side of the road. He swings there, against the metal post, unsteady, treacherous, his hands hanging loose and open as if they are unconnected to him, like clothing.

People are running. Someone has even got a hose out. Mercifully, nothing can be seen through the smoke.

Byrne feels light-headed, feels like he's moving in slow motion to a different rhythm of thought and feeling.

David says, 'What was she doing? She never drives in the morning, it's your car, how could she—?'

'Her mother's birthday tomorrow. She was going to catch the post . . .' Strange: how equal, how ordinary his words sound.

'It's your car, you should have been driving.'

'For Christ's sake!' He spins David round with utmost violence. '*You* did this! You – murdered her! Why? For God's sake, *why*?'

'She wouldn't leave you. So I, so I – '

With rigid, dreadful control Byrne lets his hands drop.

'So you tried to kill me,' he says and pauses.

That pause had held him, ever since. From that moment onwards, he had stopped thinking. He had stopped his life from taking place. He had thrown it up, run and run and ignored and put aside everything, because he was held in limbo. He had repressed and ignored the next question. The question he never asked waited its time.

And now here it was, steady in his mind, immovable, rock-like. Was Kristen in it too?

Did Kristen love David? Did they discuss it together, how to get rid of him?

Whose child *was* it?

And as the Blue Manor steadied around him, as he felt the edge of the table against his thigh and smelled the sweet, metallic scent of Alicia's blood, he understood the importance of the Blue Manor.

One day, perhaps this very day, while they were locked together within its walls, it would show him the truth about David and Kristen.

It dealt in the past and it told only the truth. There were no lies here.

He covered his face with his hands and wondered if he could endure to discover what the truth was.

'But you can't be sure, can you?'

Someone was talking to him, as if that last memory had taken no time at all. And for a moment the flickering states of memory and illusion seemed to blur the man's features. Was Byrne talking to David? About Kristen, or Ruth? Was the man standing in front of him Simon or Peter Lightowler?

'You can't trust women,' said Lightowler. 'How do you know your wife was faithful? You weren't there most of the time, I bet. We leave women in their houses while we work and who knows what they get up to? How do you even know that the child she carried was yours?'

Byrne stared at him. 'How did you know?' he said at last. 'How—?'

A complicated glance passed between Lightowler and his son. 'I checked you out,' said Peter Lightowler. 'Why did you think your wallet was taken? Did you really think we would welcome some vagrant off the streets? Into the manor? Into *this* particular powerhouse? You could have been *anyone*! But you weren't. Nothing is accidental.'

'You're caught in the same trap,' said Simon, 'as we all are. Your wife and your best friend. Fun, isn't it?'

He felt their understanding reaching out to him.

And he knew them to be evil. Most intimately, he knew what they had done. And he knew one other thing. Kristen had loved him. Only him. She carried his child. He had trusted her for ten years before her death. Why should he think she had changed because David had betrayed him?

You had to trust what you knew.

He backed away from the men on the stairs across the hall towards the door.

Which opened.

Chapter 46

Elizabeth took a deep breath. Tom and Kate stood behind her and at first it seemed as if nothing had changed.

Her eyes checked everything: the position of the table, the lift doors (closed), the sweep of the stairs. It was necessary to ascertain something else, one thing more, before entering much further.

She stepped into the hall and turned round. There it was, over the door, just as she remembered.

> *Tu verras que seul et blessé*
> *J'ai parcouru ce triste monde.*
>
> *Et qu'ainsi je m'en fus mourir*
> *Bien loin, bien loin, sans découvrir*
> *Le bleu manoir de Rosamonde.*
>
> . . . I wrought my own death,
> Far, far away, without discovering
> The blue manor of Rosamund.

'Very little has changed,' she said with satisfaction, knowing that her death would not now take place anywhere else.

She became aware that she was being observed.

She sighed. Time to take in the present, to see where the strange history of the manor had left them all.

The hall was coloured with blood. That was as it should be. Only she had never seen it there before, bright and scarlet and gleaming against the old wood and ornate carvings. It had always been hidden before in the acts and thoughts and secret, internal conversations of the manor's inhabitants. It was out now, vivid and violent, splashed against the mellow coloured wood, splattering over the piles and ranks of books. She wrinkled her nose at the smell, while acknowledging that this was only a superficial manifestation of the deep wrong.

She recognized Peter immediately, at the centre of the manor, at the centre of everything that had gone wrong. Her brother had originated the curse, but it had found its fulfilment through Peter. Where Roddy was passionate and crude, Peter was cold and clever. His malice had spread down the generations.

He was halfway up the stairs, poised with a petrol can. Her steps slowed, her breathing a little uneven. He hadn't changed, not in any appreciable way. Even his clothes, those elegant, fine fabrics which hung so gracefully, were the same, pale and luxurious. His straw-coloured hair was silvery, his face lined, but the cold eyes were exactly the same.

Exactly the same as when he had dragged her through the icy forest to the roadside where her daughter Ella lay, the same as when he had charmed his way into the life she shared with John.

The force of her loathing and fear of him made Elizabeth's heart race. He was looking at her with concentration and she felt it again, the way his will shimmered over her own thoughts, confusing and dismaying. It was as if she were a young woman once more.

With an effort, she dragged her eyes away. Her palms were damp. She thought, I should never have come, I should never have risked meeting him again.

A movement above them made her look up. There was another younger man on the landing, someone she didn't know, although he too seemed familiar.

'Are you Simon?' she said. He made no movement, staring at her as if mesmerized. She wondered if he'd come down to greet her and then realized he was up there because he was connected to Peter. They were together in this. Another frisson of fear, of regret and terror. Two of them, father and son.

'And who is this?' She turned with relief to the man standing by the table, smiling graciously to cover her dismay at Peter Lightowler and his son. She was aware that this sounded as if she were a society hostess, acknowledging her guests.

Well, it was not so very far out. This was her house. She had come home, to her bloody Blue Manor, and there was evil at its centre.

The man by the table seemed to be in some kind of shock, very white. She saw that he carried his left arm awkwardly.

'Are you hurt?' she asked with concern. 'I'm sorry, I don't know who you are.'

He came towards her, holding out his right hand, making an

obvious effort. 'My name is Byrne,' he said in a slow, deep voice that she found inexpressibly moving. 'I'm the gardener.'

And so instead of taking his hand, she raised her face to him so that a kiss was his only option. 'I'm Elizabeth Banniere,' she said softly. 'I'm so glad to find you here.'

He smiled at her, and then he looked over her shoulder to where Tom and Kate were standing.

'Is there any way out? Can we get through?' he asked.

For answer, Tom held wide the front door.

An impenetrable barrier of greenery blocked the light.

'It closed in behind us,' said Tom. 'What's been *happening* here?'

'The hags have left us,' said Byrne. 'There was a fight. But Tom, Kate – Mrs Banniere, I have to tell you that Alicia is dead. A knife was thrown by that man, the dark man.'

A small cry from Kate, a clamour of questions from Tom. The gardener gestured to the table, where a woman lay, her face covered.

Alicia. 'Poor Alicia . . .' Elizabeth touched the cold hand, but she was distracted by something else. She let the others talk, let them exclaim and mourn because by this time she was aware of this third man, a shadowy figure dressed in black beneath the arcade.

Moving slowly around the table, she tried to see him more clearly. She listened with half an ear to the gardener's account and derived a little satisfaction from it, only a little.

At least the Dogfrog had prevailed. The Dogfrog had chased the hags from the manor. She knew what they were when she heard the gardener mention the crow and the beetle, although it had been so long.

The manor was a place of balances, she thought. It gave her two guardians, the Leafer and Dogfrog, but at the same time it had created their opposites. She remembered that black crow, present whenever Roddy and Peter had acted with evil. And the stag-beetle, scuttling at their feet.

Her old friend had excelled, to drive them from the manor.

The man in the shadows was no longer hanging back. He moved suddenly, slamming a book down on the table beside the shrouded body.

Tom flushed bright red, his eyes sparkling with accusation.

'But he's still here!' he shouted, pointing at the figure. 'That man, the puppeteer!'

For a moment it seemed as if Tom might make a run at him, but somehow Elizabeth managed to get in the way. She held out a hand and Tom halted.

'So,' she said. She felt breathless again, dizzy. She took a deep breath. 'So, Roddy. You came back.'

She was conscious of the others, the man on the landing, Peter on the stairs, the children behind her and the gardener, strangers now, waiting and watching her meet this man who was no stranger.

He had hardly changed, not even a sprinkling of grey, a tracery of lines. Her memories of her brother were so clear that the years fell away. His clothes were a little outlandish, ragged, rather disgraceful in fact, but everything else was just as she expected.

The clear eyes, the fine bones. The springy, short-cut dark hair, the discoloured teeth. The scar puckering the side of his face was a shock but he still held himself in that almost military fashion, stiff and angular.

'I've never been away,' he said. 'Not really. Heart and soul have always belonged here, as you know. The body may have endured elsewhere but this is my home.'

'But even the body no longer troubles you,' she finished for him, understanding why he hadn't changed or aged. 'Somehow you've managed to give death the slip, haven't you? You must let me into the secret.' Her eyes followed the lines of his face, noticed then that they were clogged by blood. 'On second thoughts, perhaps I'll pass that one up. Has it been hell, Roddy? Is that what happened to you?'

He almost smiled at her, a sick baring of yellowing teeth. 'You could put it like that. My friends – were not always kind. It is their nature. They were prepared to assist me in my desire, but they were not kind. Although I think that life has not been gentle to you, either.'

He put his hands on her shoulders. The quietest of words, the softest whisper. 'Give it to me.'

Only Byrne heard it.

'That's not how it happens,' she said steadily. 'You have to work down the pad. That is the meaning of the Blue Manor.'

His fine eyes snapped at her. 'It's been long enough.' His

hands dropped away from her shoulders. 'Oh, you're so old, so old and ugly, Lizard. It's nearly over for you.'

'And when will it be over for you?'

'You know. When the manor is mine. Then.'

Above them, someone moved. She looked up. She saw that Peter was following this with avid attention, as well he might. He took a step down towards them.

He said, 'Elizabeth, what do you want?'

She said, 'Justice. That's all.'

'Well, so do I.' He came a step nearer. 'It seems to me that it's still in your hands, Elizabeth, outrageous though that is. That someone so decrepit, so *ancient* should hold so much power! It's really beyond belief, beyond reason!' The familiar incredulity, for once out in the open, clearly expressed.

'You're just like Roderick.' She spoke with contempt not unmixed with pity. 'Does the manor matter so much to you?'

'It's not only the manor. You know that. It is the history which goes with it. That you own it, you and your daughter and granddaughter. You had your children without acknowledging their paternity.'

'Ella was John's daughter,' she said carefully. 'I always admitted it.'

'You could hardly do anything else in those days. But I know the truth of it.'

'She was John's daughter,' she repeated. 'She looked like him, her hands were the same shape.' She was utterly certain of this, although she remembered very well what had passed between Peter and herself.

He was incensed by her words. 'You took everything from us! You would not share, you would not even give up your name. I want the manor because it is mine by right, because your elder brother Roderick was my father, by every law of inheritance there has ever been, and you are not fit to live here. Of course the manor matters.' He spoke with a degree of recklessness, as if it didn't matter what he said to her. As if she was so inconsiderable that she could be discounted. She thought, he's saying this for the benefit of his own son, and the others. He's showing off like he always did.

'Come on, Peter.' She spoke very calmly. 'There's more to it than that. This is a place which will always remember what you have done.'

333

'That's because it's yours. When the manor's mine, it will show a different version of events, a different reality. It will show how I was denied, how we were all denied our rights.' He came down the stairs as he spoke, until he was standing on the level only a few feet from her.

'It's rather late for that, Peter. Look around you. The manor is full of people right now who know exactly what happened. Our lives have been out on view. Tom has told me about his book, and I expect there were other revelations. The manor was never discreet. It exists to make plain the past. It is circled by light, bathed in light, and stories breathe from its brick. There is nowhere to hide, no way of forgetting.'

'You were always vindictive.'

'You always thought you could get away with it.'

'Lizzie.' Roddy was standing behind her. She looked round quickly for the gardener, but he had moved away, towards the young girl. She found herself praying silently, oh don't, don't be too late. Not this time –

She turned to face her brother, her unprotected back to Peter, although she didn't want to do this. She saw that the blood in the lines of her brother's face was beginning to weep in scarlet tears down his cheeks. But he was not weeping. Roddy never wept. She had never seen him experience remorse.

She was prepared to put aside the injury to herself. It was so long ago. Even what happened to Ella was no longer urgent. Those things had happened in another lifetime. But there was something else to add to the tally. Roderick had killed Alicia.

With an anger inspired by this most recent death, she shouted at him, pushing her old voice to its limits, 'You are vile! You and your son are evil and deserve your individual hells. I hope there is no mercy, no let up, no end to it.'

His teeth bared. 'You'll be joining me, then,' he hissed. 'Sister mine.' He took a step nearer to her. 'Give me the manor, Elizabeth.' His eyes were burning at her, fanatical, passionate. 'You just have to say it. Let it go, and you can all leave here.'

'But you are not in control. It is not up to you who leaves and who stays. The house decides.'

'You always were a witch, Elizabeth.' This in her ear, softly, from Peter. He had come even closer, so close that she could smell the familiar scent of Turkish cigarettes.

He was the worse of the two. He was cold, where Roddy was

passionate. Peter's old hand rested on her shoulder, dry and dead like autumn leaves. She loathed his touch. She wanted to slough it off like a poisoned skin, a deadly shroud which had enveloped her life.

'Say the word, old thing,' he said quietly. 'And it's over.'

She was still looking at Roddy, still a little breathless, wondering where Byrne was, what the others were making of this, when Peter said, 'No answer, Elizabeth? No change of heart?' The pressure on her shoulder lifted. She was dimly aware of movement behind her. Then he said,

'Well, they burn witches, don't they?'

The pungent mineral smell of petrol as liquid was flung around her, and the small, sharp sound of a match striking.

Flames immediately, shooting everywhere.

Chapter 47

Byrne had seen it coming. He whisked a rug up from the floor as soon as Lightowler struck the match. He pushed Elizabeth on to the ground, rolling her over in the rough fabric, praying that she could stand it.

It seemed impossible that someone so old, so fragile, should survive such treatment. She was gasping, her ancient face strained and twisted, eyes squeezed shut.

He unwrapped the rug. Her clothes were undisturbed, the layers of cotton and wool only slightly singed at the edges. Miraculously, she seemed untouched. Her eyes, open again, were regarding him, calm and still and beautiful.

He saw Kate approach and kneel beside her.

And Lightowler held matches. There was petrol every-where, dribbling down the bookshelves, sinking into the floor. He could see Kate's footsteps marked in dark liquid on the wood.

Lightowler, standing there, holding a match in one hand and the box in another.

Byrne ran at him, but something seized him by the shoulders. He felt the stink of decay and rotting things as hands like claws dug into his skin, holding him back.

A great weight dragged him down, loading him to the floor. The puppeteer, clinging to him like some black succubus. His limbs felt as if they were made of water. He tried to twist round, but the dark man was like a limpet, a leech. He tried to shout to Simon, a warning, anything, but the creature on his back clamped its hand over his nose and mouth.

Nails, dead flesh, raking over his face, blocking his breath. It was vile, the suffocating, deadly scent of the grave, denying the free movement of air and life.

And the flame was spreading, streaking over the wood, climbing the curtains, clambering over the books. He was distantly aware that Tom had smashed a window. Even in that extremity Byrne thought, God, he's leaving! Running away!

The draught from the window fed the flames. Byrne groped

for some weapon, anything to use against the creature on his back, but he found only searing heat. The banisters had caught like dry tinder.

He levered his feet against the bottom step, pushing backwards so that he and the dark man clinging to his back fell over towards the table.

Where Elizabeth lay in Kate's arms. Where Alicia lay, stained and bloody.

And the puppeteer was plucked away. Torn backwards, and a scream split the air. Byrne was gasping, didn't see what happened, because as soon as the weight was gone, as soon as he could breathe again, he was making for the stairs, the only thought in his mind that soon Peter Lightowler would be spreading more petrol around.

There were flames everywhere, licking over the woodwork. The treads of the stairs were breaking up, riddled with flame, beneath Byrne's feet. He kept close to the wall, away from the banister, using the window ledges to haul himself away from the collapsing stairs.

He could no longer see what was happening below. And above there was a pale face, pale-coloured hair, eyes gleaming maliciously.

'Too late,' said Peter Lightowler. 'You were always too late.'

Byrne made it. He was just in time to see Simon and his father meet at the top of the stairs, see them exchange glances, secret, intimate understanding.

He looked back, and was held there, fixated and trapped by what he was seeing, something so incomprehensible that his mind refused it. It could not be so.

They were together, Elizabeth in her old lady's white cardigan and dress, Kate in her poppy-red sundress, as if impelled by the energy of the dead, black figure on the table behind them.

The fire held clear of them. They existed in an oasis of green leaves, as if there were no flames or smoke anywhere. Lightly, easily, Kate was scooping up armloads of flowers from the floor, flowers which sprouted from the wooden floor, petrol blue, five-petalled flowers Byrne recognized. Elizabeth was sitting at the table, her brother on his knees before her. She was plaiting flowers into a rope, a noose of leaves and blooms to hang round his neck.

He was nothing, a fading memory hung with a periwinkle

garland, surrounded by the three of them. Kate and Elizabeth and Alicia.

Alicia, her face covered in black cloth, black as a cauldron. Byrne realized that death had never truly prevailed within the manor, that it was a place of triple enduring powers and that whatever was left of Roderick Banniere would find no mercy here, caught between the black, the girl in red and an old woman, white with the clarity of approaching death.

Peter Lightowler moved towards the broken banisters. Byrne saw him look down, saw him absorb what was happening. His arms opened, and there was a strange smile on his face.

'I've waited for you,' he said. 'Although I never knew what you were.'

'Come then.' They drew him down into their garden of flowers.

He stepped through the gap in the banisters, quite deliberately, as if moving into a dance. His fall was without noise or stress. A blanket of leaves received his body, held him steady as they approached.

They surrounded him. They had been at the start of his life, at its powerful centre, at its end. Most crucially at its end.

They had always been there.

Lightowler had nothing to offer them. A facile cleverness, a certain physical strength, a small skill with the powers of the mind, none of it any use. He had nothing beyond his will.

He could not stand. He could not survive against them. They took branches of fire and laid them around him.

He was burned up like a wicker man, flames spouting from his mouth and eyes, flaring down the long line of his limbs, and as the smoke billowed Byrne could see nothing else. He fell back against the wall, choking, his hands over his watering eyes.

Chapter 48

Through the drifting smoke, he saw Simon.

Another murderer, Byrne thought. He's next in line. They're going to be waiting for him. I know intimately now that he is more than capable of violence, like his father and grandfather. He kills, and there's no way out of this house for him.

Beneath them, beyond the ruined stairway, he caught flashes of colour, of blue flowers and dull green leaves subduing the glint of flame. Leaves were threading through the smoke.

'Come on,' he said. 'Time we were out of here.'

'Leave me,' said Simon. He was leaning against the wall as if he wanted to fade into its substance. 'This is my fate too.'

'You've paid already. That's what you've been doing here, all these years. It's why the Dogfrog never left you alone, why you could never leave. Come with me now.'

'I – I had no choice.' Simon looked at him helplessly. 'What could I do? It was always about love . . . Ruth, she was – is – like part of me. We were brought up as brother and sister, but what did that ever matter? And then she went to university, she slipped away from me and made other friends and it went wrong. She left me! When there was so much at stake. How could she do it, how could she *leave* me?'

'And Francis got in the way. And so did I.'

'Yes. That's what that last row with Ruth was about, didn't you realize?'

'Yes. I knew,' he said. 'I was there.'

Simon seemed like a stranger. So ravaged, so worn away with guilt that there was nothing left of the weary, cynical man Byrne had almost called his friend. His mouth was tight, his eyes slanted slightly with cruelty. The alteration was complete.

Byrne remembered the expression on Peter Lightowler's face, and knew that there was very little to choose between them. It was cruelty that marked them, the cruelty in Peter Lightowler's actions and in his son's words and actions.

He said, 'And the line runs true. You and your father and

grandfather, the three of you . . .' He felt sad more than anything else.

'I tried to escape,' said Simon, a whining tone to his voice. 'But the manor wouldn't let me go and anyway I *loved* Ruth, you have to believe me that I loved her.'

Byrne could hardly bear to look at him. From far along the corridor, they heard a door slam. And whispering, quietly, almost inaudible over those other, terrible noises, the chair bowled over the bare boards towards them.

It took a split second's decision. Byrne hauled Simon to his feet. A waft of pungent ammonia abruptly caught in his sinuses.

'Ah, they're out now,' said Simon mirthlessly. 'All the special effects, all the eighteen-rated bells and smells and splattery things.' He dragged himself away from Byrne. 'Go on, then!' he shouted. 'Get out, save yourself!'

His hands had fallen open and again Byrne saw Simon looking at him with David's eyes, saw that same mute, helpless appeal. *What are you waiting for?*

'Move,' he said roughly. He glanced towards the stairwell.

It was an empty pit. The fire had died, smothered by the weight of greenery, but there was no possible way down.

And the wheelchair was getting closer. It was gathering speed, rushing down the corridor.

Byrne pushed past Simon towards the lift. The metal doors were stiff and rusty but he managed to wrench them apart. 'Get in!' He could see that Simon was hanging back, drawn with unwilling fascination towards the banisters. The wheelchair was almost invisible, clouded by yellowy vapour. But it was now at the end of the empty line of bedrooms.

'For Christ's sake!' Byrne yanked at Simon's shoulders with such force that both men tumbled on to the floor of the lift. Byrne reached for the control switch.

Nothing happened.

'The doors have to be closed,' said Simon. 'Don't you know anything?' There was something deeply unstable and reckless beneath the words.

'Shit.' Byrne wrestled with the creaky metal but his left wrist was weak and useless. 'Give me a hand here!' he snapped at Simon.

The wheelchair had reached the landing, the vapour around it dispersing so that they were both coughing. They saw the gas-mask face staring at them, the wiry-bound hands reaching out.

'I can't take this,' said Simon on a high edge of hysteria. 'I really – cannot – take this.'

The doors clanged shut. But before the lift moved, hands reached through the bars of the iron cage and grasped Simon's upper arms. He screamed. Byrne grabbed him, hanging on with desperation, and there was a sound of material ripping, of his scream flaring wildly through the stratosphere. Gas wreathed around them, so thick, so noxious that Byrne felt his grip loosening as coughing racked his lungs.

And Simon was pulled away from him, dragged through the bars, through that fine mesh of metal, and Byrne saw none of it because his eyes were squeezed shut in pain, weeping, drenched in bitter running tears. He collapsed to his knees, gasping like a stranded fish. It felt as if his lungs were being burned out, but that wasn't the worst of it. He was aware that he was panicking, huddling towards the corner of the lift, pushing with his feet against the floor, scrabbling to put some distance between himself and what was happening at the door.

The screaming swung into extremity, filling the manor. It cut through everything, through the hidden corners, the deep secrets of history and rumour, severing past and present and future one from the other.

Silence at last, blessed, empty, exhausted silence. The lift began its slow and creaky descent, the pulleys groaning, jerking unevenly until a lifetime away it reached the ground.

For a while Byrne could do nothing. He did not dare turn round. He was half crying, half gasping still, but after an indeterminate time, a time in which Simon's scream seemed to echo through the air, something changed.

He became aware that it was easier to breathe. The deadly stink was fading. Pure clear air was blowing from somewhere. He could feel it cool against his skin. He wondered whether he should take a look, but his eyes were still streaming. They felt as if they were full of needles, welded together by tears, unusable, useless, redundant.

Not knowing was worse. Cautiously he raised his hands to protect them, and blinked his eyes open.

Immediately he saw the doors to the lift he gagged. There was blood running over the bars of the cage, blood mixed with material and gobbets of flesh clogging the hinges and joints.

The doors were closed fast between him and the hall. He could not bear to touch them, could not begin to think how he would ever get out of the trap.

But even as he looked he saw movement. A twining strand of ivy wound itself around the metal. It was deliberate, sentient, sinuous as a snake. The Leafer taking a grip on the doors, pulling them apart.

He threw himself through the gap and collapsed to the ground once more, vomiting on to the stone flags.

He thought, looking up at last into a hedge of thorns, that the Leafer was running things now. It was encircling the hall, joining each of the pillars in a dense barrier of leaves. The effect was to hide from sight everything that was happening in the centre of the hall.

It was forbidden to him. He got to his feet, and as he moved further round the outer perimeter of the Leafer, he realized that he was not the only one to be excluded.

Tom was there, between the hedge and the front door, his face white, running with blood. It was impossible to mistake what had happened to him. It was the Leafer's imprint: a wound which ran from Tom's eye to his mouth. A curse which endured to a fourth generation.

Byrne wasn't going to let it happen again.

He said, 'Get out of here. Now. While you can.'

'In there . . .' Tom's eyes were staring. 'God, I – Kate and that *thing*! That old woman, I can't face—'

'Forget it. Leave here. It's not safe.'

'But – what about Simon? My . . . father?'

'You can do nothing for him.' Byrne swallowed. 'He's dead. Tom, get out, for God's sake get away from here!'

'What? And leave you here, the gardener? Leave the manor to *you*?' There was that madness in his eyes, that familiar obsession.

'Not bloody likely.' Byrne took his arm. 'I'm coming too.'

And at last Tom let himself be hustled towards the door, the open front door which led out into the garden where the white Iceberg roses nodded in the lightest of breezes.

342

They got into Ruth's Escort, and Tom drove. Neither of them looked back. As Tom trod hard on the accelerator he said, 'Where are we going?' His voice was colourless.

'Epping,' said Byrne. 'To St Margaret's. To see how Ruth is.'

Tom nodded. They said nothing to each other for the length of Epping High Street, where the traffic was virtually stationary, the long queue of cars leaving the city fed at every junction by local commuters.

It was hot and stuffy in the car. Byrne leaned back, his eyes closed, cradling his left arm which ached abysmally. Sprained, he reckoned, not broken, although he probably ought to get it X-rayed. There seemed to be no after-effects of the gas attack. Tom's face looked as if it could do with a few stitches, too. But Byrne's injury could wait. He needed to see Ruth, to be with her in cool, calm silence.

Tom parked the car and stared blankly ahead over the wheel. 'What do you think's happening at the manor?' he asked.

'I – really don't want to think about it, not now, not here. We're free of it.' He paused. Tom had not moved. 'But if you must know, I think hell is happening at the manor. Precisely that.'

For a moment their eyes met. 'I'll wait for you here,' said Tom.

'Better go and get yourself patched up,' Byrne recommended, getting out of the car. 'Have you looked in the mirror recently?'

Tom angled the wing mirror inwards and groaned. 'It goes to prove it all, doesn't it?' he said bleakly. Gently his fingers probed the extent of the laceration. He winced. 'Like father, like son.'

'The manor let you go, Tom. As far as it's concerned, you're off the hook.'

'I haven't done anything.'

'I know.' It was almost possible to feel sorry for him. 'Get yourself fixed up. I'll meet you later – ' He could not think when. 'Back here. I don't know how long I'll be.'

'Sure. And then what?'

Byrne said slowly, 'The manor again. Kate's there, and Elizabeth. I'll have to go back.'

They wouldn't let him in to see Ruth at first. A nurse with a casual Cockney accent showed him determinedly into a waiting room across the corridor from intensive care.

There were magazines on the table, tea-making facilities in one corner, but he could not settle.

He paced the room for a while and then poked his head out into the corridor. A white-coated man suddenly threw open the door opposite and marched swiftly down the corridor.

Byrne caught up with him. 'Ruth Banniere?' he asked. 'How is she?'

He was so young. He stopped in his tracks, frowning at Byrne. 'And you are – ?'

'A friend. A close friend.'

'Ah, well.' He looked down at his notes fussily. 'Well, I don't think—'

'There's no other family,' he said. 'Her daughter can't get here . . . please, just tell me.'

'She's holding her own.' The boy seemed mildly pleased with himself. 'Yes, I think I can safely say that. She's holding on.'

He felt the colour drain and then flood back into his face. 'Not – not . . . I thought, we were told it was only a matter of time.'

The doctor was embarrassed. 'Um. Yes.' He looked up with relief as an older man in a three-piece suit came out of the ward. The doors swung behind him. 'Ah, Dr Sherwin, this is – ?'

'Byrne,' he said quickly. 'Phizackerley Byrne.'

'Mr Byrne. Come to enquire about Ms Banniere.'

The older man scanned his face. 'I think I can cautiously – with reservations, you understand, it's early days yet – tell you that the prognosis is good. Ms Banniere has rallied quite remarkably.' He smiled at Byrne. 'Good news, I'm glad to say. The clot appears to have dissipated in a most unusual fashion. Perhaps you'd like to see her for a few moments?'

Byrne took a deep shuddering breath. 'Yes. I would like to see her.'

'This way then.' The older doctor returned to the doors and held them open for Byrne.

*

344

She was on one of those high-tilted beds and was wired up to machines and drips and monitors. Her hair was scraped away beneath a white bandage, her left arm caught in a sling. But her eyes turned towards him as he crossed the room to the bed and he saw a slight smile curve her lips.

'Ruth. My dear – ' He took her free hand and leaned over to kiss her brow, very gently.

She said softly, only for him to hear, 'Byrne . . . I'm so glad it's you.'

'Shh. You don't have to talk.'

'No, but I want to tell you something. I've been thinking – '

He knew he should stop her, tell her to rest, but he could see that it wouldn't work. Something was nagging at her. Her free hand plucked at the sheet. She needed to talk. He said nothing.

'You see, I've – been dreaming, I think. I never opened my eyes to what was happening at the manor. I always denied there was anything wrong, I never wanted to admit it. I was part of it, too. I lied to Kate.'

'In what way?'

'I never told her about her father, Francis. I felt so bitter when he walked out on me.'

He understood what was worrying her. 'Ruth, he didn't walk out. Didn't you know that he died? He was trying to get to the manor to see you, but there was an accident. At the road.'

'I found out later that he had died. Years later. But I didn't know he was coming to me. I was so furious and hurt when he stayed away that I never even mentioned his name to Kate.'

He saw tears in the corners of her eyes. 'All those years wasted in resentment and anger. I was wrong. It was a terrible mistake. I should have told Kate, right from the start.'

'It's not too late.'

'Where is she?' She looked past him. 'What's been happening?'

'Ruth, there's so much to tell you, I don't know where to start.'

'Kate?' she asked again.

'She's fine,' he said, hoping it was true. How could he begin to explain what had happened to Kate?

'Bring her to see me soon,' she said. The urgency was gone from her voice. She was merely exhausted. 'But stay now. Stay here with me until I go to sleep.'

So he sat at her bedside and held her hand and in only a few minutes she was fast asleep.

So was he.

A nurse woke him some time later. She was smiling. 'We didn't like to disturb you, but it doesn't look good to have the ward full of sleeping visitors.'

'Thank you,' he said gratefully. He stood up and looked at Ruth again. The faint colour in her cheeks seemed entirely healthy. Her breathing was regular and unforced. 'She's going to be all right?'

'We'll probably put her into one of the women's wards tomorrow, after the consultant has seen her.' The nurse was checking a monitor. 'But I don't think you need worry.'

He left the hospital hardly daring to believe it. It was beginning to get dark outside. He must have slept for longer than he'd thought.

Tom was waiting for him in the car park. His wound was taped together by butterfly stitches.

'You took your time,' he said shortly. Then he seemed to take in Byrne's expression. 'How is she?'

'They think she's going to be all right,' he said.

'What are you going to *tell* her?'

Byrne noticed the pronoun. 'We don't know the end of it yet, do we? Are you ready?'

'To return to the manor?' His mouth tightened. 'I'm taking your advice. I'm not going with you.'

Byrne said, 'What about Kate? Don't you care?'

'No. Not enough to face that again. That place – ' With difficulty he looked Byrne in the eyes. 'I don't trust myself in the manor. It's too powerful. I never want to go anywhere near it again, I want to forget about it. I want to pretend this past week never happened.'

'Will that be possible?'

'It's – bizarre. I've been sitting here waiting for you, trying to work out what happened. And I can't even remember the colour of Kate's eyes. Or whether the garden was in good condition . . . Tell me, were there many books in the library?'

Byrne stared at him. 'Just a few,' he said.

'Well, I can't remember! Not clearly, hardly any of it.'

'Perhaps it's as well. Do you want me to drop you in Epping, then?'

'Yes.' He sounded puzzled. 'I've got my wallet. I think I'll go up to town. I've got friends there.'

'Very well then.'

They drove quickly through the darkening town and Byrne dropped him at the station. Central Line, direct to the city.

Byrne watched him go, with his neat, graceful gait and carefully cut hair and felt no regret. He doubted that he'd ever see Tom Crabtree again.

Then out on to the forested road. There was little traffic, and he put his foot down. He was so preoccupied that he did not hear the sirens until the ambulance was almost on him.

Immediately Byrne pulled over, to let it pass by. The ambulance dashed down the centre of the road towards the Wake Arms roundabout. He thought nothing of it.

But it turned down the road towards Theydon and all at once Byrne was touched with fear. The ambulance drew up on the side of the road near the turning to the manor. There was a police car there.

He stood on the brakes. He turned off the engine and got out, slowly. Very slowly. It was Alicia's Peugeot. Slewed off the road, scrunched up against one of the beeches, the entire bonnet concertinaed to half its usual size. One of the policeman was wrestling with the door. In the headlights from the ambulance, Byrne saw that there were three people in the car.

In that briefest of moments, caught in that strange, hard light, he saw Alicia and Peter and Simon Lightowler, securely belted in, a tight family group. Their eyes were open, but they did not move.

And then the car exploded into flame.

'No survivors,' said the policeman, his face shocked.

Byrne could not tell him that they were dead already. He said only, 'I know who they were.' He gave their names.

'Addresses?' He had out a notebook.

'Peter Lightowler lived at the Red House, Theydon Bois. And Alicia Lightowler had a flat at Cambridge.' Tom would have known her address, but he was out of it. 'She was staying at the Bell Inn. Simon, their son, lived at the Blue Manor.'

'And where might that be?'

Byrne stared at him. 'Over there.' He pointed through the dark trees. 'Next turning on the left.'

'Piercing Hill, do you mean? One of those houses set back?'

'No, before you get to Piercing Hill. Just a hundred yards from here.'

'Oh, you mean Mulberry Manor. Lot of trouble there earlier this evening.'

'Mulberry Manor?'

'That big house with the lake. Ugly place. It'll be no loss.'

'What do you mean?'

'It burned down. There's hardly anything left. Fire services have only just left.'

'Was there anyone hurt?' He couldn't work this out. How long had he been away from the manor?

'One fatality. An old lady. Everyone else got out.' The policeman looked at the smouldering wreck of the car. 'Out of luck, that family. Funny how it goes like that sometimes . . .'

Byrne looked back at the Escort. He didn't need it. Without another word to the policeman he slipped away into the trees.

It was completely dark, but the sky was filled with stars. Through breaks in the thick canopy of leaves he could see the major constellations, bright amidst the Milky Way's fields of light.

Far away, the road sounded. There were soft rustles of birds and small mammals around him, a liveliness in the air. A screech owl made him jump, bats whizzed past his head. Although Byrne did not know for sure which way to go, he knew the general direction was right. He tramped on under the starlit trees.

After a while he realized that the trees were becoming more sparse. He walked through clearings touched with dew and the forest seemed gentler, more settled.

And just when he was beginning to wonder whether he'd made a mistake and come the wrong way, the trees were suddenly divided by the lane and opposite him was the beech hedge. A little further on and he came to the driveway. The cottage stood sturdy in the starlight, exactly as he had left it. He went in and took the torch from the window sill.

He turned down the drive, reluctantly. Nothing had changed.

The drive was still split by dandelions, the brambles and nettles still thrived along its length. But they were crushed in places, as if by heavy machinery.

Fire engines, he thought. Recently.

He saw the roses first, those white Icebergs gleaming softly, and thought that the manor must be unharmed, that the policeman had been mistaken.

But the manor was no longer there. As he drew nearer he saw that the black area encircled by white roses was not an unlit house. It was a ruin. Blackened spars and girders were jagged against the starry night. The top two storeys had completely gone, and the rest stood only as an empty shell filled with rubble and ashes. There was the smell of charred timber everywhere.

He mounted the steps to the front door, but it was blocked. It probably wasn't safe, but he wanted to see what had happened. He went round the house to the back door, but that too was impassable.

Only the library was possible. The French windows had buckled, and were hanging loose. He pulled them aside with some difficulty. There was a path of sorts through the rubble, presumably cleared by the fire crews. Great drifts of damp, blackened ash draped the crushed remains of furniture. He took a few steps further.

On the floor by his foot he saw something white, shiny in the starlight. He picked up the piece of paper and turned it over, flicking on his torch.

A scrap of music, a few lines of poetry he did not recognize.

> A leaf which the whirlwind claims,
> The storm will sweep me away too . . .
> But before then, so that it carries them to you
> On the black wings of remorse,
> I shall write on the dead leaf,
> The torments of my dead heart!

He tossed it away. There were other pages of music littering the piles of rubble, the wrecked furniture.

A light breeze fluttered through the empty windows and at first he thought it was a sprinkling of ash that began to fall over him.

But it wasn't ash. Not the drenched detritus of the manor's furniture and structure, but pages. From the empty beams above him, pages of magazines and newspapers and books and music tossed through the air, fluttering round him like so many pale butterflies, a dizzying whirlwind of paper settling at last in drifts on the filthy floor. Gradually the clouds of white began to sink in, gradually they disappeared into the thick, clinging layers of ash.

He saw words and phrases flaring at him in a last, potent bid for attention: cut, green, owing, beloved, dead wood, make-up, thou, tomorrow, wild, peridot, three, until they faded, dissipated in the black, forgiving ash.

Chapter 50

He left the manor. He went back through those broken doors and crossed the terrace to the field of grass.

He walked slowly towards the orchard.

And then he saw her. Sitting in the long grasses beneath one of the apple trees, her knees drawn up, regarding him.

Kate. Byrne walked through the small ancient trees until he came to her. He squatted down beside her.

'It's over, isn't it?' Her voice sounded different, older, more mature. 'The manor is destroyed. Judgement has been exacted.'

'What do you remember of it?'

'I remember it all,' she said. 'And I never want to speak of it again.' Still, she did not look at him.

'I was there. I saw it too.' Then he realized that she did not know about Ruth. 'Kate, your mother's going to be all right. She's made an extraordinary recovery. She wants to see you.'

She gasped. 'Mum's all right? She's going to be all right?'

'She's fine, I went to see her. It's OK, Kate – '

Blindly, she reached out to him. He took her in his arms, and she was just an ordinary, over-tired, over-strained young girl, weeping with relief on his shoulder, and memories of the manor faded further yet.

Some time later she looked up. He found a handkerchief in his pocket and gave it to her.

'What have you got there?' She pointed at his hand.

He was holding a piece of newspaper. He peered more closely at it and remembered the torch in his pocket. It was a blurred photograph of someone he knew and a fragment of writing:

Captain David Crompton, 38, who was found dead last week in his car. At the Coroner's Inquest today, a verdict of suicide was given.

His hand trembled very slightly and the scrap of paper fell between his fingers. Quickly, before he could get a hold on it, it had sunk into the damp earth beneath the apple tree. He scrabbled uselessly there for a moment, trying to find it again.

'What are you doing?' asked Kate.

'Oh – I thought—' And then he realized there was no reason to keep it. It was enough to know.

'Come on,' he said, standing up. 'Let's go and find Ruth.'

She accepted his hand and got to her feet. For a while they stood there looking at the wreck of the manor.

It seemed to Byrne that greenery was already swarming over the blackened timber. That the edges were being eaten away by grass. He thought, by morning nothing will be left. None of it.

He turned to Kate. 'I don't know where Tom went,' he said.

A small smile, nothing more. 'Our budding novelist. Has he taken off?'

'I'm afraid so.'

'Just as well.' She was unworried. 'I won't go back to Cambridge. I don't think I shall want to see him again.'

'It wasn't his fault.'

'I know. But I shan't want reminding of this.'

They were walking down the drive, back to the main road.

'But you'll stay with us, won't you? There will be insurance money. One thing Mum always kept up with was the insurance. And she'll be on her own now, she'll need loads of help.'

'Stay on as gardener? Well, why not?' He paused. 'It'll be just the three of us, then?'

She smiled. At her side a small dog frolicked, a terrier or something. It had come out of the forest to join them as they approached the cottage.

It licked her hand once and then rushed off between the long grasses.

They never saw it again.